AMERICAN DREAM MACHINE

Matthew Specktor

ABACUS

First published in the United States in 2013 by Tin House
First published in Great Britain in 2013 by Little, Brown
This paperback edition published in 2014 by Abacus

A CIP catalogue record for this book
is available from the British Library.

ISBN 978-0-7515-5161-7

Printed and bound in Great Britain by
Clays Ltd, St Ives plc

Papers used by Abacus are from well-managed forests
and other responsible sources.

For RSG, and in memory of Bill Spruill

THEY CLOSED DOWN the Hamlet on Sunset last night. That old plush palace, place where Dean Martin drank himself to death on Tuesdays, where my father and his friends once had lunch every weekend and the maître d' was quick to kiss my old man's hand. Like the one they called "the other Hamlet" in Beverly Hills, and "the regular other Hamlet" in Century City . . . all of these places now long gone. Hollywood is like that. Its forever institutions, so quick to disappear. The Hamburger Hamlet, the one on Sunset, was in a class by itself. Red leather upholstery, dark booths, the carpets patterned with a radical and problematic intaglio. Big windows flung in front, but farther in the interior was dim, swampy. Waitresses patrolled the tables, the recessed depths where my father's clients, men like Stacy Keach and Arthur Hill, sat away from human scrutiny. Most often their hair was mussed and they were weeping. Or they were exultant, flashing lavish smiles and gold watches, their bands' mesh grain muted by the ruinous lighting, those overhead bulbs that shone down just far enough to make the waitresses' faces look like they were melting under heat lamps. And yet the things that were consummated there: divorces, deals! I saw George Clooney puking in one of the ficuses back by the men's room, one time when I was in.

Unless it was somebody else. The one thing I've learned, growing up in Los Angeles: it's always someone else. Even if it *is* the person you thought it was the first time. I helped him up. I laid my hand on the back of George Clooney's collar. He was wearing a blue jacket with a deeper velveteen lapel, like an expensive wedding singer. This, and white bucks.

"Are you all right?"

"Yeah." He spat. "They make the Manhattans here really strong."

"Do they?"

We were near the kitchen, too, and could smell bacon, frying meat, other delicacies—like Welsh rarebit—I would describe if they still had any meaning, if they existed any longer.

"I'll buy you one and you can check it out."

I helped him back to his table. I remember his touch was feathery. He clutched my arm like a shy bride. Clooney wasn't Clooney yet, but I, unfortunately, was myself. '91? '92? The evening wound on, and on and on and on: Little Peter's, the Havoc House. Eventually, Clooney and I ended up back at someone's place in the Bird Streets, above Doheny.

"Why are you dressed like that?" I said.

"Like what?" In my mind, the smile is Clooney's exactly, but at the time all he'd said was that he was an actor named Sam or Dave or (in fact, I think he actually did say) George, but I'll never know. "Why am I dressed like what?"

"Like a fucking prom date from the retro future. Like an Italian singer who stumbled into a golf shop." I pointed. "What the hell is with those shoes?"

"Hey," he said. "Check the stitching. Hand-soled."

We were out back of this house, whosever it was, drinking tequila. Cantilevered up above the city, lolling in director's chairs. Those houses sell for a bajillion dollars nowadays, but then it was just some crappy rental where a friend of a friend was chasing a girl around a roomful of mix-and-match furniture, listening to the Afghan Whigs or the Horny Horns or the Beach Boys—my favorite band of all time, by the way—or else a bunch of people were crowded around a TV watching *Beyond the Valley of the Dolls* on videocassette. It didn't matter. Mr. Not-Quite-or-Not-Yet-Clooney and I were outside watching the sun come up, and we were either two guys who would someday be famous or two rudderless fuck-ups in our midtwenties. He was staring out at the holy panorama of Los Angeles at dawn, and I couldn't get my eyes off his shoes.

"Why am I dressed like this?" My new friend wrung his hands

together limply. I ought to sell that fact to a tabloid, to prove Clooney is gay. "I was at a function," he said.

"What kind of function? A convention of Tony Bennett fans? A mob wedding?"

I don't remember what he said next. I think he said, I was in Vegas, and I asked him how much he'd lost. I probably gave him a sloppy kiss. *I knew it was you, Fredo!* There was an empty swimming pool nearby. It must've been February. Italian cypresses rose up in inviting cones, the scalloped houses dropped off in stages beneath us, and eventually the whole hill flattened out into that ash-colored plane, that grand and gray infinity that is Los Angeles from up above: God's palm, checkered with twinkling lights and crossed with hot wind.

"I can never remember the words to this one . . . "

"What?" I said. "It's mostly moaning."

"They're all mostly moaning."

George and I went digging into the old soul music catalog, to prove our masculine bona fides. None of those Motown lite, *Big Chill*-type classics that turdscaped so many of my father's late eighties productions. We went for the nonsense numbers, the real obscurities. We sang "Um, Um, Um, Um, Um, Um," "The Whap Whap Song," "Oogum Boogum," "Lobster Betty." A couple of those might not have been real, but we did 'em anyway.

"Nice pipes."

"Thanks," he said. "I was up for *The Doors* but I never got a callback."

We spent the rest of the night drinking and singing. People blame Los Angeles for so many things, but my own view is tender, forgiving. I love LA with all of my heart. This story I have to tell doesn't have much to do with me, but it isn't about some bored actress and her existential crises, a troubled screenwriter who comes to his senses and hightails it back to Illinois. It's not about the vacuous horror of the California dream. It's something that could've happened anywhere else in the world, but instead settled, inexplicably, here. This city, with its unfortunate rap. It deserves warmer witness than dear old Joan Didion.

"Don't do that, man." My voice echoed. I clapped my friend on the shoulder. "Don't do the pleading-and-testifying thing. You'll hurt your knees!"

"I'm all right."

By the time we were done, we were deep into the duos, those freaky-deaky pairs from Texas or Mississippi: Mel & Tim; Maurice & Mac; Eddie & Ernie. Those gap-toothed couples who'd managed to eke out a single regional hit before fading back into their hard-won obscurity. My new friend seemed to know them all, and by the time we were finished I didn't know which of us was Mel and which Tim, which of us had died in a boardinghouse and which, the lucky one I presume, still gigged around Jacksonville. Him, probably. He was dressed for it.

"I should get going," he said, at last.

"Right." Not like either of us had anywhere to be at this hour, but he needed to go off and get famous and I needed to find my jacket and a mattress. A man shouldn't postpone destiny. "Later."

We embraced, and I believe he groped my groin. After that I never saw him again, not if he was not, as I am now forced to consider, George Clooney. I just watched him climb the steps out of the swimming pool, into which we'd descended in order to get the correct echo, the right degree of reverb on our voices. This was what it was like inside a vocal booth at Stax, or when the Beach Boys recorded "Good Vibrations" at Gold Star Studios on Santa Monica Boulevard. So we told one another, and perhaps we were right. For a moment I remained in this sunken hole in the ground that was like a grave slathered with toothpaste—it was that perfect bland turquoise color— and sang that song about the dark end of the street, how it's where we'll always meet. But I stopped, finally. Who wants to sing alone?

This is what I remember, when I think of the Hamlet on Sunset. This, and a few dozen afternoons with my dad and half brother, the adolescent crucible in which I felt so uncomfortable, baffled by my paternity and a thousand other things. Clooney's cuffs; the faint flare of his baby-blue trousers; the mirrored aviator shades, like a cop's, he slipped on before he left. It was ten thirty in the morning. I held a bottle of blanco by its neck and looked over at the pine needles, the brittle coniferous pieces that had gathered around the drain. Clooney's bucks had thick rubber soles and made a fricative sound as he crossed the patio, then went through the house and out. I heard the purr of his Honda Civic, its fading drone as he wound down the hill and left me behind with my thoughts.

PART ONE: A DROP IN THE BUCKET

I

"NATE, MAN! NATE!"

I'd fallen asleep. And when I woke up—has this ever happened to you?—it was a different house, a different season, a different day altogether. In fact it was, although it felt much the same. I'd fallen asleep on a chaise lounge, outside another house in the hills. Same neighborhood, even similar patio furniture.

"Hmmh?"

Different season, same hangover. But this one, of course, I remember, because it set up the most disastrous night of my young life. This particular morning, which was not the one after I met semi Clooney, was in April 1993.

"You were out there all night?" Someone was yelling to me from inside.

I rubbed my eyes, which burned with pollen. "Yeah."

My voice was hoarse, my throat was dry. It didn't seem unusual to me: falling asleep was what you did when you'd been up a certain number of hours and weren't into cocaine. Still, I'd come out last night and lain down to look at the Italian cypresses and the stars, and suddenly it was morning, and hot, with the sun hanging overhead, the sky almost white. My back was sore, as there were no pillows on the chaise, just wooden slats. I levered up and rubbed my skull.

"You want breakfast?"

I couldn't even tell who was talking. It was either my half brother, Severin, or it was our friend Williams. The three of us were so close, it almost didn't matter.

"Yeah," I yelled. "I'll be right in."

Severin, Williams, and I. We'd known each other all our lives, and until this particular morning we were just young Hollywood princes, wastrels who'd never stood anything to lose. None of us were yet twenty-five.

"Coming," I mumbled. But then I stopped and knelt down for a minute by the swimming pool. This one was full. I dipped my hand into the water. *Unheated*. What I wouldn't have given for a siphon and a skateboard. From one of the windows upstairs came the sound of people fucking. Whose place was this? Another night in the Hollywood Hills, another evening of people living both way above and beneath their slender yet infinite means: young actors between gigs, bastard children of wealthy executives like myself. I waited for the erotic clamor to pass, listened to the Santa Ana too as it battered the treetops and rattled the foliage all the way down to Sunset. I thought I heard my father, his voice buffeted around in all that crazy wind. *Nate! You skinny little shit! Why aren't you home writing? You wanna make something of yourself, you should be working, working, working!* He was always harder on me than he was on Severin, though hard enough on us both. Eventually, after the sex stopped, I got up and went inside. I collided with Williams as I strode through the sliding glass doors into the living room.

"Hey, bub." He hugged me. We pawed each other like boxers, forehead to forehead, mauling each other's ears. "Did you eat? I was calling."

"No," I said. We wouldn't let each other go. There was a barely suppressed violence to our embrace, as if at any moment one of us would throw the other to the ground. "I didn't want to interrupt anybody."

The room smelled like bad dope, cheap marijuana seeds and stems. There was a white couch, and a pair of high-top sneakers lay shucked off beside it. The place had that characterless mood of a ski condominium, everything pale and impersonal.

"Who lives here?" I let Williams go. He wasn't dressed, except for his shorts.

"Tudor." The head of his dick protruded, a little, through his fly, but he didn't seem to know or care. "He's out of town."

I didn't know who Tudor was. Williams had scumbag friends in those days, twentysomething punks who swaggered around like

Robert Altman was their best pal, who hung out at the Viper Room and Dominic's after hours, sharking the pool table and powdering their noses. Guys like that could get a freewheeler like Will into trouble.

"Cool." I forgave Williams everything, because we were like brothers, too—we'd known each other since kindergarten—and because his dad was killed when we were fifteen. What else did he have to hang on to, besides any old bit of driftwood that came his way? "I'm gonna get some chow."

How handsome he was: tan and lithe and flawed only by the little scars a lifetime of skateboarding had left him with, a chipped tooth and the crooked stride of someone who'd sprained an ankle often enough to favor the other one permanently. I was pretty good-looking myself, fortunate enough to take after my mother, one of those glossy blonde sylphs, neither actress nor agent, who haunted the corridors of power in the sixties. But almost inevitably when there were women around, they were Will's. He had a magnetism neither my brother nor I could match. This time, though, it was Severin who'd gotten lucky. I heard feminine footsteps coming down the stairs.

"Bye." The girl peeked in. She was like this place: pale, Nordic, pretty. Her face was pure, almost featureless, like sunlight on a white curtain.

"Later," Williams said. I waved. I recognized her, too. After she slipped back down the hall Williams chuckled.

"Dude, that's your dad's intern."

Sure. Emily White was her name. I heard her calling out to my brother. *Severin, have you seen my keys?* Our dad used to be business partners with Little Will's. The two men founded the most powerful agency in Hollywood. They were like mismatched halves of the same being. We grew up under their shadows, the three children of twin fathers.

"Are you cold?" I said. Because Williams was shivering a little, rubbing his biceps. He was high, but that wasn't unusual. We were teenagers, basically, who saw nothing wrong with hitting the bong at eight in the morning. His oval eyes shone, those dark apertures that only underscored his supercilious beauty, his sunstruck good looks.

He shook his head. "I gotta go find my shit."

He went upstairs. I watched him amble away and then followed the sound of banging and clattering to the kitchen.

"Hey, man." Severin was bustling between the fridge and the stove. "You want eggs?"

"Yep. Lox 'n' onions."

I looked around. The girl was already gone, having left through the patio door.

"No lox. Wait!" He opened the fridge. Even then, long before he moved back east and got famous, he had a New Yorker's haste and energy. "Yes! Lox, from Canter's." He sniffed. "I dunno how good it is."

Shorter than I was—and barely six months older; he and I had different mothers—he came over and ruffled my hair. I was the accident, the product of an affair, where he was Beau Rosenwald's legitimate son. That made all the difference.

"Sit." His headlock was a lot gentler than Will's. "I'll make you something to eat."

I flopped at the table and watched him, playing absently with a Zippo lighter while I did. He *was* our father's son, though he certainly didn't look it. He was wiry and small, with pitch-black hair and a boundless intellectual confidence.

"What's wrong?" He plunked a plate of eggs down in front of me. "You look sad, Nate."

I shrugged. "I'm nostalgic."

"Dude." He laughed, collapsed into the chair opposite mine and began to attack his breakfast with wolfish energy. He ate like our father, at least. "It's a little soon for that, isn't it?"

"Maybe." The air hung still with the smell of browned butter. Outside the day was clear and palmy. And we had nothing to fill it with except our twenty-three-year-olds' dreams. "Maybe it is."

He shrugged. He always seemed to carry his burdens a little more easily than I did. Even then he wore a certainty neither Little Will nor I could match. Long before he became a famous novelist—if that's fame, because as our father went on to joke, *If you're so famous, Severin, how come I've never heard of you?*—even before he won the National Book Critics Circle Award in '99 and a MacArthur grant after that, he seemed to have it all together. But he wasn't anything special back then, just another punk with Hollywood in his veins, another struggling screenwriter who worked all day in a video store. In his smoggy horn-rimmed glasses, shorts and horizontally striped

T-shirt, one of those thrift shop Hang Ten Muppet numbers, he looked like he'd barely made it out of junior high.

"Yo." Williams swaggered in, still shirtless, slapping his chest.

"Dude, put that thing away." Sev shoved his plate back, slurped his coffee. "I don't need to see it any more than I already have."

Will shoved his hand into his boxers and adjusted, then laughed. His gaze was a little veiny, now that he'd baked himself properly. He grabbed a carton of milk from the fridge and guzzled.

"You should talk," he gasped, finally. "You were the one making all that noise."

He mopped his mouth with his forearm, then stepped to the stove and plated up. We had no shame, it seems to me now. Or we were *all* shame, the way boys are. Humiliation was our currency. Williams sat down next to Severin. He looked at me, chewing, eggs flecking the corners of his mouth.

"What's with you?"

What *was* with me? I was the dreamy one, where they were the Hollywood heirs. Already I was full of regret. I had my mother's last name, Myer. I'd been through my entire childhood without knowing my dad at all, but Sev grew up in his house. I found I missed him. God knows why. *You really wanna be Beau's kid, Nate?* Severin used to ask me, straight up. *D'you really know what he's like?*

Perhaps I didn't, but I could imagine. I could imagine him even now, in that gruff, almost Tourettic way of his, throwing his arm around my shoulder, barking in my ear as he did all the time now that I had the mixed fortune of being acknowledged. *It's all shit, it's all bullshit, this business. Nobody knows anything.* This last phrase was William Goldman's famous folk wisdom about Hollywood. No one knows anything. Only Beau could embody that knowledge and surpass it at the same time.

"Aw shit, man." Little Will was laughing now. My two friends, brothers, whatever they were, were having an argument. "Don't start in on Richard Burton."

"Go ahead." Sev tilted his chin forward, gave Will a haughty, goading look. "Show me what you've got."

Funny that none of us were actors. Especially Williams, who had not just the looks but the tragic penumbra, the half-doomed quality, of one. Like Burton.

"*Julius Limbani is alive!*" He shook his lustrous brown hair back. It fell below his collarbone. I could smell the bong on his breath.

"Not quite." Sev snorted. "Lock your teeth, and pretend you're holding a cat turd on your tongue."

They were mimicking, quoting *The Wild Geese*, a crappy action movie from 1978. It seemed we were always quoting something, memorizing our lines from *The Long Goodbye* or *California Split*.

"Let's go watch it again," Sev said. "We'll swing by the store and grab it."

"No, no," I said. "Let's watch *The Big Sleep*."

"Again?"

This was us, before the shit hit the fan. And after all the massive losses and small gains that preceded us, long after our fathers, Beau Rosenwald and Williams Farquarsen III, had built and demolished their partnership. The elder Will was dead, under circumstances that were still a little hard to explain, and Beau had reinvented himself as a producer, again. There was no end to their story yet. Nor to ours.

"Come on. Nate'll drive." Sev yanked me up by the collar. Things were about to get crazy. "He's clean."

"Yeah, I'm clean." I whiffed Will's resinous neck. "But we might have to stuff stoner boy here in the trunk."

"I can't find my pants!"

"Where'd Emily go?"

"She left."

"Nah, she came back in and fell asleep, upstairs. She couldn't find her keys."

Back then it didn't even matter which of us spoke. We weren't completing each other's thoughts so much as having them together.

"Leave 'er." Severin said, in his best hard-boiled voice.

"Leave 'er," Williams repeated, with a shrill, mimicking laugh, the hysterical bray of a psychotic henchman in a movie. Everything is everything. That's what I'm trying to tell you. Everything is everything.

"Let's go!" We grabbed pants and socks and tennis shoes, wallets and belts and glasses. Will took his bong off the glass table in that strangely denuded living room. We left something too, because you always do, some residue of ourselves brooding over that girl, Emily White, upstairs in a stranger's bed. The room held no sense of habitation: there were no photographs or paintings or books. Just the hungover haze of our energetic debauch. Through the windows I could see the blue towers of Century City, Beverly Hills' putty-colored plazas, those places where men with millions came to waste their money, and where our fathers' story, too, began.

"Nate, dude, come on!" Sev's voice drifted from outside. "Let's bail!"

Outside, Williams's opal-green Fiat exploded to life. Its ailing engine had no muffler, and the stereo played Black Flag, grainy LA hardcore like the puny violence of bees.

"Come on, man! Vidiots opens at ten!"

I reeled into the driveway, shoved slack, stoned Will into the passenger seat, then toppled into the back. We were making a getaway, under all those laurels and cypresses, the otherwise-quiet of this house in the hills. I threw the car into gear. And we roared off, laughing, leaving this house with its doors still flung open, wafting its scents of eggs and stale fish and sex, as if from this place—this pale chamber—we had all just been born.

II

"Excuse me?" The receptionist blinked up, staring. Staring and staring. "May I help you?"

In 1962, our father walked into an office on Bedford Drive. He was so young then. He didn't even know his favorite show business joke yet, the one about the five stages of an actor's career. He knew nothing.

"Sir?" The receptionist looked at him, her black hair swept into a truncated beehive, eyelashes too long. She looked like a brunette Tippi Hedren.

"I'm Beau Rosenwald." He swung his arms, in a suit that was too warm and too tight. As any suit might've been, for a man who weighed 285 pounds. "I'm here to see Sam Smiligan."

"He's not in." A chilly smile. "Might I know what this is regarding?"

"Abe sent me."

"Abe?"

"Yes. Abe Waxmorton. From New York."

"I see." Another tight smile, which he was green enough to take for hospitality. "I'll let Mr. Smiligan know when he returns."

He must've seemed like such a rube! She would never have behaved this way otherwise. He went over to the far end of the reception area and sat down. These were the West Coast offices of what had been minted in 1897 as the American Amusement Corporation and grown into a vaudeville empire. In the teens, Abe Waxmorton's father had led the industry-wide fight against a controlling monopoly of theater barons.

"Talented Artists, how may I direct your call?" The receptionist sat with her Kewpie-blue eyes, her stiff hair and unaltering expression, the muted black-and-white check of her skirt and jacket making her subtle, like op art. In the dark marble tomb of the reception area, she was the only thing that moved on this Monday morning. Her hands flew as she routed calls through an old-fashioned switchboard. "One moment please."

Beau could hear the labored weight of his own breathing. He sat on a black leather stool beside a glass coffee table laden with newspapers and pristine ashtrays. To his left a smoke-tinted window disclosed the green and palmy panorama of a street whose stillness unnerved him.

Until this morning, he'd never been any farther west than Jersey.

"I beg your pardon?" the receptionist chirped. "We do receive mail for Mr. Peck, yes. One-two-four Bedford Drive."

Inside, the building hummed with activity, the murmurous commercial sound of a train station. At long last, Beau stood up.

"Excuse me." He approached after a thirty-minute exile. "Has Mr. Smiligan returned?"

The girl stared at her hands. "No sir."

"Do you expect him? A—Mr. Waxmorton was sure he'd see me."

He'd removed his jacket. He was five eight, and at the peak of his girth, and his powers, he would tip three hundred pounds. This morning, he was hapless in his heavy gray pants, white sleeves rolled, perspiration stains spreading under his armpits. His hair was mussed and the short brown curls, unruly even at this length, plastered his forehead. That face! The receptionist patched a plug with an agitation close to fury, punching the cord home like a dagger.

"Hi, Sarah, there's a Mr.—"

"Rosenwald." He cleared his throat.

"Rosenwald. Waiting here to see Mr. Smiligan. He says Mr. Waxmorton sent him. Yes."

She nodded back at the waiting area. "Someone will be out."

If she had looked closely, she might have noticed his shoes. They were Church's brogues—English, expensive—and anyone here who saw them would have recognized Waxmorton's hand. *A man is judged by his persistence, his substance, and his shoes*. Waxmorton had offered Beau the same lecture he did everyone who came to work for the company. *An agent must possess the first. With any luck, he possesses the second. But the third! This business forgives eccentricity...*

From here he would taper off, as if there were many things "this business" might tolerate, but poor haberdashery was not one. The job was to know where the restaurants were, to understand hotels. It involved an accumulation of secondhand knowledge, circulation of gossip that became, if repeated long enough, true. Jack Lemmon is hot. Fox is going to offer Kim Novak a three-picture deal. Agents were simply almanacs with energy, aggregations of rumor that flew into truth.

"Would you like to go to the pictures?" Beau's voice echoed across the lobby.

"Pardon?"

He was sunk into the black leather couch, by the table with its issues of *Daily Variety* and *The Hollywood Reporter*, fanned out in their respective green and red like decks of cards. A bowl of fruit—oranges, grapes, and bananas—sat in the middle. Like the receptionist, it was really just for show.

"Would you go to a picture with me?" He leaned forward and snapped off one of the bananas and peeled it. "The movies. I understand they make them out here."

He took down half the banana with one bite.

"You aren't supposed to eat those."

He sat with the fantastic solidity of a toad. You could imagine his stillness lasting for days. He wolfed the second half of the banana and snapped off another, then sauntered back over to the counter where she sat behind a lip of cold marble.

"Will you go to the pictures with me?"

"Sir, I—I don't know you."

"Yes, you do. Everybody knows me." He smiled. "At least, they never forget me."

She stared. He had a tuberous face, lips damp and pursed like a trumpeter's, one eye slightly lower than the other like a disappointed hound's.

"I'm sorry," she stammered, "but I'm engaged."

"Your fellow doesn't buy you a ring?"

He leaned over her desk. Beyond confidence, he had confidentiality. He said hello like he was telling you a great secret. He glanced out the window and then, very casually, peeled and demolished his second banana.

"What's your name?"

"Trix."

"What's your real name?"

"Carol."

"Carol what?" He set the peel down on the edge of her desk.

"Metzger." She blushed.

"Nice Jewish girl." He smiled. "How come they call you the other? Is it a stage name?"

He could never be handsome but look at anything long enough—a street lamp—and it establishes dominion, a quiddity: it becomes itself.

"It's just a nickname."

"How'd you get it?"

You didn't have to be handsome when you were the last man standing.

"Mr. Rosenwald!"

He turned. Waxy strands clung to his fingers, his lips. Sam Smiligan stood by the glass doors, dry and immaculate in his navy blue suit. He was small and walnut-colored and, from the looks of it, completely humorless. His fingers folded over to touch his palms in a gesture less hostile, more dapper than a fist. There were intimations of gold, a discreet glow along the cuffs.

"You're the one?" Sam removed his glasses. The room rang with his incredulity. "You're Abe's boy?"

Beau Rosenwald never graduated from college. His education consisted of one man, one book, one thing. The day he left high school he answered an ad in the *Herald Tribune* about a mailboy position. Told the agency only hired university graduates, he went and enrolled in Queens College, then came back after three years of academic futility, when at last he paid someone off for the degree and the transcript. Thus, every morning of July 1955 began the same way.

"I'd like to see Mr. Waxmorton."

"Mr. Waxmorton is busy, sir."

"Really?" Beau nodded. "I'm here since eight o'clock and I haven't seen him come in."

The Talented Artists Group offices in New York were different from the ones in LA. They were humid and ugly, with low ceilings, corrugated acoustic panels, parquet floors. Ficus plants swooned in the corners. The male agents were shrewd, the girls spoke Beau's language. Their accents were Jackson Heights, Astoria Boulevard. This receptionist had a nose like a flight of stairs. Beau could imagine her writhing in the back of a Bonneville, just how many times her legs might snap shut before she gave it up.

"Listen, sweetheart." He leaned over and murmured. "I'll keep coming back. You want to look at this face every day?"

Eventually, he won his audience. Abe Waxmorton was the son of the company's founder. He'd had his start, long ago, in vaudeville. He'd fought the company back from bankruptcy twice, most recently in 1934 when the studios had put the squeeze on talent in an effort to recoup the higher costs of producing talkies during the Depression. That year, in which the combined force of Roosevelt's National Industrial Recovery Act and the talent's decision to unionize had almost decimated the business, Waxmorton sent his lieutenant Sam Smiligan to open an office on the West Coast. He was old enough to remember when apartment buildings hung signs that read NO BLACKS, NO ACTORS, NO DOGS, old enough never to drink tomato juice, so-called "clients' blood," in public. To Beau, he seemed monumental.

"You have any experience?"

"No sir. I see a lot of movies."

"A lot?" Waxmorton tutted. "You should see them all."

He was fifty-five, old as the century, with the battered face—squashed nose and cut expression—of a pugilist. His silver hair was shot through with black strands, and he cupped a mandarin orange between his palms. He didn't peel it, merely rotated it between his fingertips as he leaned back in his chair.

"Education?"

"Queens College." Beau had the purchased diploma in his pocket.

"What else? What makes you special, besides your good looks?"

Outside, on Fifty-Third Street, a light snow fell. Waxmorton set the orange down and inhaled his citrus-kissed nails. Through his window the sky was a lithographic, late-afternoon gray.

"What does your father do?"

"He makes shoes."

"Shoes!" Waxmorton shook his head. "Ask him to make you a better pair."

What was it? Was it the hardness, the hatred in Beau's eyes when he spoke of his father? Herman Rosenwald was a world-class son of a bitch, to hear Beau tell it: an angry widower with a heart as tight as a clamshell. But maybe Abe Waxmorton just liked my father's energy. Maybe he just needed a buffoon.

"Come tomorrow. You'll start in the mailroom, like everybody else."

"I'll start today."

"Not in those clothes."

Not in those clothes. Abe taught him to think like an agent, act like one, dress, like an undertaker or a G-man, too, in dark, solid colors. Abe's office walls showed photographs with Greta Garbo, James Cagney, Olivia de Havilland; in the corner was a bat—*the* bat—Ted Williams had used to bring his batting average to .406 on the last day of the 1941 season. Beau worked in the mailroom, then was promoted to handle the great man's desk. Then, for slightly longer than was good for him, he became something else. Abe's driver, or his attaché. Technically, the job didn't have a name. He was Waxmorton's shadow, his advisor: he did everything short of wipe the man's ass. Walked his dogs, measured his golf handicap, squired his wife, sitting in Flora Waxmorton's kitchen in North Fork, where she made him inedible tuna sandwiches. For three years he did this. This was the education he'd had, and it was enough. One day he came in and his own office, the little nook adjacent to his master's, stood empty.

"Go."

"What?" Beau turned. Waxmorton hunched in the doorway, staring with eyes gone bulbous, accusatory.

"You need to go to Los Angeles."

"Los Angeles?" Beau was close enough now to be peevish. "What the hell for?"

Beyond tan carpets and walnut trim, the only things left in the room were books. Shelves of them, belonging to Waxmorton. Beau's boss was an enthusiastic autodidact, and many of these leathery volumes were written by people the agent actually knew. Eugene O'Neill, Tennessee Williams.

"There's nothing *in* Los Angeles. You said so yourself, it's all desert and horse piss and guys with sixth-grade educations."

Waxmorton turned his palms up. "You want to keep shuttling me out to North Fork every day?"

"You're firing me?"

"Your clients will fire you. Your friends will stab you in the back. The sooner you get used to that the better."

Beau was twenty-eight, an indifferent student all his life; he'd needed to repeat second grade. Waxmorton was all the finishing school he'd had.

"Will you back me?"

"Am I your mother?"

He'd waited for this moment all his life, and still it had the force of a betrayal. Beau's boss appeared to understand this as he shuffled over to one of the shelves and took down a leather-bound volume.

"What's this?" Beau turned it in his hands. *Coriolanus.*

"It's a play."

"I know that. Is it for a client?"

Waxmorton shook his head. Those half-moon eyes peering over the tops of his glasses.

"You read much history, Beau?"

"Not much," Beau smiled. "No."

"The story of one bloodbath can prepare you for the next."

Often enough, Beau had sat in this office and stared at the spines of Waxmorton's books. *The History of the Decline and Fall of the Roman Empire.* Who read such a thing? Edward Gibbon's name merged in his mind with an adjective he didn't know the meaning of either, *gibbous.* A pet word. *Good morning, Darlene.* He'd sway over the receptionist's desk. *You're looking gibbous today.* Odd that Severin and I turned out the way we did; Beau's own verbal gifts were strictly for patter.

"Control the talent." Waxmorton shuffled forward to shake his hand. "You want to know how to get ahead? Control the talent, you'll bring the studio to its knees."

Beau had read the play twice on the plane. Now it rattled around his otherwise empty briefcase as he chugged down the hall after Sam.

"Will I, uh—will I have an office?"

"Unless you'd prefer a stall."

In the air, on a red-eye flight, he'd scoured the bloody story of a Roman general for clues. But the play had provided no answer to what he should do now. He followed Sam Smiligan past a long row of secretaries. Pretty girls from Chatsworth and Loma Linda and Beverly Hills. Occasional among them was a man, whose white shirt and whipped expression signified a trainee.

"Here," Sam snapped.

They'd stopped before a corner room, as dark and shabby as a janitor's closet. Its blinds were drawn and its desk was dusty and there was nothing else inside it but an enormous circular Rolodex and a phone.

"You were expecting grander accommodation?" Sam lifted one eyebrow, his tone an ocean of sarcasm.

Behind them the air filled with the brittle chatter of typewriter keys and the cascading half harmony of female voices. *Edwegabenmartadigian's office?*

"Do I get a girl?"

"Do you need one?"

Sam Smiligan had unfurled his fingers but once, briefly, to shake hands. There was something about him that resembled a gingerbread cookie: an easel-like splaying of his legs, a neatness that suggested he might never eat, or shave, or defecate. He had the precision of a minor general.

"Why don't you concentrate on making the phone ring first," Sam said. "Then we'll get you someone to answer it."

Beau stared at the Rolodex. There were at least a thousand cards inside it, and every last one of them was blank.

"At least you know how to drive, Mr. Rosenwald." Another punctilious smile. "That's one thing you won't have to figure out."

The two men glared. It took my father ten minutes to make his first enemy. Here too, he was ahead of the curve. Then Beau bent down and picked up his briefcase. He disappeared into the empty room, the leather-bound volume banging audibly as he walked.

III

HIS FIRST CLIENT was an actor. Even before he met Will's dad, the man who would teach him so much about the game—how to negotiate, how to woo, how to close—it turned out Beau had a knack for it, for the long-form seduction it often took to represent someone. The trick was to find men as desperate as you were and when, like Beau, you'd been desperate since infancy, they were easy enough to recognize. He scoured episodic television, watched *Wagon Train* and *Perry Mason*, watched *Alfred Hitchcock Presents* and later *Burke's Law* and *I Spy*. He hung around outside the open calls, sweet-talked his way onto the Universal lot and into the various production offices.

"Hey, Bryce!"

"Huh?" A skinny and kinetic man, lithe as an eel, was leaving one of these when Beau cornered him. He was handsome, but not distractingly so. "Who're you?"

"Beau Rosenwald. Talented Artists Group. I've seen everything you've done and I love your work."

"Everything?" The man's eyes were a little too close together. His teeth were faintly rodentine, and his face telegraphed an anxious skepticism, like he was scanning the horizon against an imminent calamity. Still, handsome. Authentic. "You must have good vision, because I'm never up there for very long."

"That's your agent's fault." They stood on the steps of the *Wagon Train* office, in the patch of shadow thrown by one of the hangar-like soundstages.

"I don't have an agent." Bryce pushed his hand through coarse blond hair. "Mine just fired me, said I'm too difficult to cast."

Beau smiled. "You know the five stages of an actor's career? It starts out with *Who's Bryce Beller?* Then, *Get me Bryce Beller.* Eventually, *Get me a young Bryce Beller.* And then, *Get me a Beller type.* Then—"

"*Who's Bryce Beller?*" The actor snickered. "I like that joke."

Beau had done his work. Bryce was twenty-two when my father first saw him onstage doing *Sweet Bird of Youth* in New York. Now Bryce shook his head, astonished to discover a short, fat fan in the industry.

"That Hitchcock you did where you scared the old lady with the squirrel? Fantastic!"

Bryce cracked a smile that lit up half his face. "You really have seen it all, haven't you?"

This was how it started. The effort to move Beller out of bit parts and into features. The campaign to make him first a working actor, later a star. There was something unnerving about Bryce—he projected instability, discomfort on-screen—but the same could be said of Warren Oates and Harry Dean Stanton. Half the men Beau knew looked like future stars, or small-town mechanics. He signed Tim Zinnemann, a director; he signed Strother Martin, and then another actor named Walter Tepper. Beau built himself into the rank and file, expending nothing but time and nonsense and shoe leather. Around him were the foot soldiers of the motion picture department at Talented Artists. Ned Bondie, Peter Katzman. A man named Teddy Sanders, wise as an owl behind rimless glasses. New York had a lawyer named Williams Farquarsen III, a Princeton-educated sharpie everyone was afraid of for some reason. But all of them had style, each man had a rap. Told Red Buttons was too short, Fast Marty Bauman sold him by seating the actor on a stack of phone books while they had lunch with a director. When a client died in the middle of negotiations, Teddy Sanders had the skills to convince the studio to pay for his funeral—and offer the widow an annuity.

I remember those offices just as they were a few years later, a warren of rooms all beige and clubby, tucked discreetly away from the street. Desk lamps glowing, cigarettes smoldering, posters signed by Billy Wilder, by Rex Harrison. Beau Rosenwald spent hour after hour at his desk, with his leg elevated like a patient in traction and the phone crooked to his ear.

"Listen you little shit, just make the offer. My client is there for forty-eight hours. After that, get someone else to wear the fucking horse costume and shovel up Connery's leftovers!"

Even at his most profane, it was impossible not to love him. He ripped up an executive's Rolodex card and sent it to him in the mail. The man sent back flowers and an apology. Beau had one skill: negotiation. The way he fell still and listened, also, his face gone grave as a statue's as he sat there on the phone.

"Beau?" His secretary, now that he had one, peered in. "Lew Wasserman on line one?"

Smoke from a Pall Mall clustered, cirrus-like, around his head. He shifted the receiver and gave the barest of smiles.

"Better act fast, Sy. Beller's got another picture he'd like to do."

IV

"LOOK AT THAT CHICK!"

How thrilling it must've been for him! The fat kid from Queens, loosed into a world like this one. Can you blame me for wanting to crowd in before my time, for wanting to jam into a booth at Dominic's, at the Factory or the Haunted House, next to Beau and Bryce and Nicholson and Bob Skoblow, the man who'd booked the Beatles onto *Ed Sullivan*? It was Skoblow who nudged Beau now, pointing across.

"Where? Skobs, I don't see any—ooh." He spotted her. "Nice."

The girl had blonde hair peeking out from under a fur-trimmed Santa hat, a zebra-striped mini, and a top so tiny you could make out her nipples, stiff in the room's Arctic, air-conditioned freeze.

"I can see her cooze," Nicholson leered. "When she walks by, drop your cigarettes."

It was Christmas, 1965. There was fake snow all across the floor, gold and silver tinsel trimming the bar.

"Get her over here."

"You do it, Skobs." Beau said. "Tell her you know Paul McCartney."

They were all equals, then. Nicholson was doing Corman movies, and some thought Bryce had the greater chance of becoming a star. Beau sat between these two, in the middle of the booth. With his arms splayed out atop the banquette, he looked like a king. He'd learned how to dress and was carrying an umbrella. It was a conversation starter, nothing else. In the two and a half years since he'd moved here, he could count the days of rain.

Bryce snapped his fingers. "I'll go."

"You?" Nicholson snickered. "Brycie, the last woman you pulled was your mom, and she's still not over it."

Bryce sat on the booth's edge. He had a long, almost equine face, that caged intensity that still made him hard to cast. But he was coming along. He'd done a few Corman movies now too, was making that step between B movies and the mainstream. The two actors were on parallel tracks: for a moment it was possible even to confuse them.

"Just watch me, Jack."

He crossed the room on spindly legs, moving with a restless syncopation. He talked to the girl for a moment, then came back.

"She's coming over." A smile cracked his knifelike profile. He was dressed tonight like a ranch hand, in a denim jacket. "She wants to talk to the fat man."

Beau sat with his umbrella atop the table, clutching it against his belly like a bar on a roller coaster.

"We're doing Pontevecchio," Bryce added.

"Again?" Beau's face assumed a grave, faintly injured expression. The most European he could manage. "We've worked this one too many times."

Skoblow went to the bar, where he stopped and talked to a cherubic kid with a pageboy, a buckskin fringe. His own hair was dark and kinked out into short but unruly curls. His face was wry, sly, Jewish. He nodded vigorously, scratched below his black turtleneck. The girl approached and Bryce took her fingers by their tips.

"Allow me to present my friend . . . " Bryce spoke and Beau feigned total opacity, cocking his head like a bewildered dog. "Carlo Pontevecchio."

"Pontevecchio?"

"Yes," Bryce said. "The filmmaker."

Beau took her fingers and pressed them between his thumb and palm, briefly.

"I . . ." the girl hesitated. "I'm afraid I don't…"

"You've never *heard* of Carlo Pontevecchio? You don't know his work?"

She shook her head as Bryce mimed amazement. Nicholson had joined Skoblow at the bar. It was more fun to watch this trick from a distance.

"So are you, uh, making movies in America now?" The girl cleared her throat. "Will you shoot films in English?"

She wasn't as pretty up close. They never were, quite. She had one of those farm-girl complexions, a milky iridescence in the siren-red light of the bar. A band was setting up in the room's far corner.

"Where you from, honey?" Bryce cut in, while Beau held that expression of soulful idiocy. He hadn't yet breathed a syllable. "Ohio?"

"I'm from Bloomington, Indiana."

"I knew it! I'm from Illinois." Bryce leaned in confidentially. "Mr. Pontevecchio doesn't know Idaho from Iowa. But he's a very important filmmaker, and I'm going to be in his next picture."

"Really? I knew it, too! I saw you guys sitting over here and I *knew* one of you was somebody!"

Her flaws might've been invisible anywhere else. Her eyebrows were slightly crooked, forehead a little too long. Everything else was right: the cheekbones, the smile.

Bryce slid a hand around her shoulders. "Are you an actress? You look like an actress."

Her head bobbed up and down. "How did you know?"

"Strasberg thinks this man is one of the most talented filmmakers in the world. He said to me, *Bryce, the two directors you most want to work with in your lifetime are Kazan and Carlo Pontevecchio.*"

"Why haven't I heard of him?"

Across the room, the band plugged in, eliciting little burps of feedback as live cords met amps. The buckskin kid Skobs had talked to at the bar was now up there among them, dragging his cord free of his feet and coiling it behind him like a lariat.

"I don't know. His last movie, *Olio e aglio*, won the, uh, Golden Gondola at Venice last year. I'm honored just to sit at his side."

"Wow."

The girl was hooked, with Beau having said nary a word. He leaned into her now, placing his manicured hand on her leg.

"Signora," he screwed his lips into a would-be Italianate scowl, which came out closer to Hitchcock's pout. "My Angliss is not so good—"

The accent was disastrous, but who noticed? Not when there was such genuine need beneath it.

"I wonder if you might dance with me?"

"Dance?" She stared as if wondering whether Beau would be physically capable of such a thing. "I, uh, sure."

A pasty-looking kid stepped onto the stage in the corner. He brushed long hair from his face and spoke into the mic.

"Ladies and gentlemen—the Byrds!"

The band began and Beau launched into a series of preposterous arabesques with the umbrella, spinning around the room with the girl, dragging her along with his free hand.

"What were you *doing*?" At last they'd stopped, panting, on the edge of the floor, after two minutes of circus ballet that made even the band laugh. The guitarist snapped a string. "What was that?"

Beau gasped. "I'm a talent agent, honey."

"Huh?"

Onstage, Gene Clark fiddled with his Gretsch, grimacing merrily at the distraction that had just taken place. Beau led the girl around the bar, away from the rattle and the twang and the feedback, where she might more easily hear him.

"I'm not a director." He spoke with his regular accent now too, the bluff touch of Queens that had mostly been sanded off, rounding itself toward something else: the Universal Judaica of Hollywood. "I'm a talent agent."

"God." She looked off toward the stage, away from him. They were over behind the pay phones. "God."

"No, wait." He put his hand on her wrist. "I'm really sorry."

"Don't touch me."

"Wait."

He kept his hand where it was. There was ash on his cuff, a few sickly black crumbs—somehow—of her mascara. His fingernails were trimmed; he wore a Patek Philippe watch. Among his friends, he was suddenly the most elegant. His Devon cream shirt had subtle pink stripes.

"What do you want for Christmas?"

"What?" The girl stared. Her face sharpened into perfect prettiness: there is nothing like scorn to render feminine beauty. "Now you're fucking Santa Claus?"

"I could be."

She swept off her fur-trimmed hat. Strands of hair clung to skin that was flushed, damp. The exertion had enlivened her, overturned a certain doll-like quality. She was Cynthia, from Indiana. Her pulse fluttered as Beau gripped her wrist.

"Don't pull that Lana Turner at Schwab's shit," she said.

"I'm not. I'm just asking, what do you want?" He nodded. "It's a simple question."

He held the umbrella now slack, point upward. He stood like an exhausted commuter.

"I want not to be serving drinks to jerks at Ciro's." She yanked off her hat and tossed it toward the bar. "That's one thing."

"Of course. What else?"

"To go home and see my parents."

"Really? You wouldn't rather show them how beautiful it is out here?"

"You say it's beautiful. I think it's lonely."

"I think it's lonely too."

She sneered. *You should, fat man.*

"I do. Even I miss my parents, this time of year, and my dad used to beat me." He spoke plainly. There was nothing demonstrative in this admission, no bid for pity. "I'd like to go home."

"So why don't you?"

He jammed his hands now in his pockets. The way he looked at her, you'd think he'd never seen a girl this pretty. Even if he did every day, his amazement was genuine.

"This place compels me."

The floor was sticky beneath that fake snow, scattered around their feet like powdered slush; the bar's tinsel waved gaily in the air-conditioned breeze. The band's guitars sparkled and chimed as they launched into Bob Dylan's "Spanish Harlem Incident."

"I can't make myself better looking." Beau nodded. "I can't make you a star. All I can do is buy you breakfast."

She watched him. Nodding herself now, slowly. It wasn't even voluntary! "OK."

They went out through the bar. She towered over him by a good four inches. Nicholson snickered as they passed, and Beau whirled. He pressed the point of his umbrella to his friend's throat.

"Fuck off, Jack." He winked. "This one's nice."

They careened along the strip in his battered white '63 Jaguar. Beau drove like a man who'd just been introduced to the wheel. Not Greenblatt's tonight. Canter's. Egg salad and the 2:00 AM confession.

There too he kept the focus off himself, even as his fingers dented the thick-cut yellow challah and he talked with his mouth full.

"Eat," he said.

She watched him like someone coming down to earth, wondering what everyone in the room had to be asking. What was she doing there, and with him? The radio piped jazz from another decade. Tony Bennett was like a sudden restoration of sanity.

"Everybody's hungry," Beau said. "Everybody wants something."

"How did you . . . get to be this way?"

"Which way?" He burped, gently. "What are you talking about?"

She nodded up and down, but it wasn't just his body. Even the way he parked his car was spasmodic, strange, violent, and elegant. Jerking it into a space where it wouldn't quite fit and then banging his palms on the wheel. *Hah!*

"My mom," he said finally. "It's all her fault."

"Really?"

As if this wasn't, too, something he'd spent his entire life thinking about. As if this question wasn't the whole of his being!

"Sure." Still chewing, he smiled. "Ask a Jewish man, we'll always blame our mothers. Cause if we don't we'll catch hell for criticizing our fathers."

They sat in the orange booth, the candid light of the delicatessen, the pebbled floor like an obscure beach, tan and coarse. The waitresses wobbled on orthopedic shoes; the ceiling tiles' stained-glass patterns shone in the surface of their coffees.

"You know, you're not *that* ugly." She tilted her head. "You don't have to be."

"From your lips to God's ears."

"No." She took a cigarette from his red pack, with its white crest and Latin motto. "I mean it." Her hands flew, but his were quicker as he lifted his lighter across the table to spark it. "You're almost appealing."

"Thank you." He watched her. "Marry me."

"What?"

"You heard."

He couldn't possibly be serious. But he was. She burst out laughing.

"Not if you were the last person on earth." She hissed smoke. "Sorry."

"Oh." Having heard this all his life, he could scarcely even suffer hurt feelings. "Thought I'd ask."

"Keep trying."

"I will. Why don't you sleep with me?"

She laughed again. "Keep trying, elsewhere."

They faced each other. A bit of egg salad clung to his mouth. There was something *unsavory* about him, yet also something relentlessly honest. His shirttails had come untucked. He slouched against the Naugahyde.

"Why don't you?"

"Listen, I'm wise to that, your little questioning thing, so stop it."

"All right." He dug out his money clip. He peeled off a twenty and laid it on the table. "Sorry if I offended you."

"OK."

"But I'm going to ask you one more time."

"I just said no."

"I know. I don't expect you to change your mind."

"Then how come?"

He turned his palms up, slowly. And just watched. At 3:00 AM, this place was crowded with lupine hipsters, kids with pudding-bowl haircuts and the self-absorbed faces of martyrs. Their pants were tapered and their shirts brightly checked. Any one of them would have stood a better chance with this girl. But when Beau finally stood, she did too.

"Why?" In her own amazement, she asked aloud. "Why am I doing this?"

He could've told her. When you'd been denied so many times, refused those things you wanted, you took everything else. The world gave itself to you like an apology.

She followed him out to the parking lot, bowing her head as he held the car door open for her, her gold hair flashing under a street lamp, her body shivering with cold, with submission.

V

BEAU WAS STANDING on the corner outside the TAG offices in New York, scanning the horizon for a cab.

"I beg your pardon." A man sidled up to him, all silken Southern accent. "Would you have a light?"

My father tapped his pockets. He'd just left a meeting with Stanley Donen. And recognized the man, a well-dressed, wiry, ginger-haired figure he'd spotted in these very offices behind them. He drew out a lighter and the man cupped his palm, drew Beau's hand toward his mouth to light the cigarette.

"Thank you." His speech was delicate; his manner, beautiful. He didn't look like any of the other agents. He wore a pocket square and John Lobb shoes. His hair was the color of copper filament, worn long in the early spring of 1966.

"I know you," he said, finally letting go of my father's hand. "I've seen you upstairs."

"I'm Beau Rosenwald."

The man nodded. Another long moment, in which Beau felt sized up, examined: he felt *recognized*, in some way. By this dapper, aristocratic figure whose stare was piercing and green.

"I'm Williams Farquarsen," he said, finally. Even his pauses felt strategic, like he was teasing out of you an authentic need to know. "I work with the old man."

Smoke drifted from the Lucky Strike that rested, unworried, between his lips. His voice made you feel like you were swaddled in velvet pillows. They stood with their backs to the building, sheltering against a rain that was still more threatening than real, a vague and scattered mist. And with this simple introduction, its gentle nudge of apostasy ("old man" Waxmorton; the phrase as Williams spoke it balanced between respect and subtle contempt), something ignited in Beau. They stood for a moment in silence.

"I've heard of you," Beau said.

"Only good?" The way Williams smiled, the uptick at the end of the sentence, though it wasn't really a question, said everything. What Beau had heard was that he was a killer, the converted attorney who was Waxmorton's new right hand.

"They say you're the best."

This was true. He was rumored to be a hardballer, but people loved him. Skoblow in LA, Teddy Sanders, the colleagues who'd already done deals or shared clients with him. Williams grinned. And the skies opened up, leaving Beau to charge for a cab, ducking against thickening rain. He'd come to New York for one meeting, and now there'd been two. He was about to have a third: fate forked and forked again. Williams called something after him, but Beau didn't hear. He was racing for his cab when a tall, angular woman cut right in front of him.

"Lady, that's mine."

It was. His hand was on top of the roof and he was folding his big body into the backseat when she dove past him. He lurched down and slid in after her.

"No, it isn't."

The cabbie pulled away onto Fifty-Seventh Street, indifferent. She'd come from inside the same building, but unlike Williams Farquarsen III, wasn't familiar. She gave an address far uptown—151st Street and Riverside—just as Beau told the cabbie he needed to go to the West Village.

"What? No." The cab lumbered up Fifty-Seventh and then shot around Columbus Circle, north, following a feminine imperative. "I have to get downtown!"

"For what?" The woman spoke. She was cricket-like, thin enough for there to be space between her body and my father's even as he took up the bulk of the cab.

"Lunch."

"Ah." She smiled. Her eyes were wide-set, her face weird: almost reptilian in its triangularity, yet still beautiful. Her skin was the whitest he'd ever seen. "Surely you can do without that for once."

He sputtered. There in his dove-gray overcoat, with rude flecks of rain staining its brushed surface. There was a wheezing complaint of fabric, springs, and limbs as he shifted his weight to be comfortable.

"My client," he said. "I represent an actor who's doing a play. But I need to tell him I just got him a picture with Natalie Wood."

She smiled again. He'd never seen anything like it, the chill that came off this woman. Her body had an aspect of brutal erasure, like something sculpted of wire.

"Good for you."

The cab jounced along Broadway. Outside the air was gray, a cocktail of cloud cover, rain, and steam.

"It's good for *him*. He's doing *Rhinoceros* right now, but this could make him a star." He leaned back, took a good look at her, the fractured *Z* of her limbs, lap, and torso. "You work for the agency?"

She tutted. It sounded more like *yes* than *no*.

"Then you should know why this is good. Are you Abe's girl?"

"His 'girl'?" She spoke disdainfully. He'd meant assistant, or mistress, though the latter seemed improbable. "I'm an agent."

"Motion picture? Theatrical?"

"Literary. I represent writers."

"Ah." This did explain a lot, why he didn't recognize her, hadn't seen her around the offices. Hers was a different species. Her hair was red, cut sharply across her jaw. Compared with California women, her calm asperity came as a relief: it made her real. "Is that where we're going?" He nodded uptown. "To meet one of your clients up there on the moon?"

"You're not coming with me."

"Why not? I'm a good agent."

Up front, the cabbie hunched like a jockey, flannel taut across his shoulders. Beau sat like a despot, both hands resting on his umbrella's sceptrous handle.

"I represent Stanley Donen, perhaps you've heard of him. I represent Bryce Beller, who's going to be the next man to kiss Natalie Wood on-screen. For that alone, he should up my commission."

"You really are . . . quite something," she snorted. "It's just like people say."

"So you know who I am."

"Everyone at the agency knows who you are. Your reputation precedes you."

Outside the city's signage thickened—CHOCK FULL O' NUTS; MAN TO MAN SMOKE A ROI-TAN!—then dissolved as the cab banked over to Riverside. The rain was already passing, the sun streaming weakly now through feeble greenery.

"So you'll have dinner with me, after we have lunch."

"Never. I'm never going to have dinner with you."

"I've heard that before."

God, Beau. The man to whom *no* was never anything but the predecessor to *yes*, to a pure and unqualified surrender. But even he could feel this woman's resistance was different, that it stemmed from a private, perhaps even an existential, well of refusal.

"Tell me your name."

"It's Rachel." She stared straight ahead. He could feel that steel in her, a raw negation that was the exact opposite of his level, pestering joy. "Rachel Roth."

"You're Jewish."

"Yes, why?"

"You don't look Jewish." It was true, she had that lunar, *goyische* coldness that he could never seem to get away from.

"I am."

"Great." He dug into his pocket for a handkerchief, which he produced and used, rather mysteriously, to wipe his mouth. "It's what I prefer."

She gasped. "You're terrible."

She didn't mean this teasingly. She seemed to say it as if she recognized something in him that was truly awful, the real monstrosity which she, somehow, could match.

"OK," he said. "What about that?"

"Nothing about that." Her eyes were gray, like a whitecapped sea. "I don't want to speak to you."

"You got into *my* cab." He looked at her, wry, amused. She fixed her level gaze on the horizon, clutching the plastic loop above the door while he was impervious to the vehicle's lurching. "Where are we going?"

"Nowhere. You said you were going downtown, so I gave an address uptown. To get away from you."

He burst out laughing. She was so like him, in a way, this Rachel Roth: she shared his obduracy. They flashed through Harlem in a jaundice-colored fog. He watched the brown faces of the houses, their powerful solidity; watched the pink and gray street life that swirled in front of them, a weird mixture of porkpie hats—the older men—and loose-limbed cats with processes, girls in short skirts.

"I'm going back to LA tomorrow. But I'll be here again in a few weeks, and after that."

She said nothing.

"I will keep coming back."

She shifted on the seat next to him. A delicate movement, vague as a pulse. She didn't say a word.

"I'll take that as a yes to dinner."

Wind fluttered through her window, cracked open at the top. Beau'd never really been tested, but was about to be. By this woman whose strength and oddity, and whose palpable loneliness, seemed to offer a rare invitation. He watched her, watched and watched. But Rachel gave him nothing, just gazed into the distance of the afternoon.

VI

RACHEL ROTH GREW up in Brooklyn. She was from Gravesend. Beau never would meet her parents, and she scarcely spoke of them. Her dad sold sewing machines, or else was a bookie. He might have made a killing betting against the pre-diaspora Dodgers, for all he knew. But he'd never met a more austere, or less dependent, woman. She was pensive, wistful—such things as my father would've had to look up in the dictionary, had he owned one, to define. She lived alone, worked alone. At home she had no telephone, no name on the mailbox outside her fourth-floor walk-up.

"How do you get along without a phone?" Beau asked her. "Don't you get lonely?"

"I'm lonelier at work."

"How can that be?" He shook his head, and she turned to lock the door, revolving her key twice. "And how come you won't let me come up?"

She smiled. Half smiled. "A girl has to have her secrets."

A humid night in June. Bugs battered Beau's hands as he stood beneath a street lamp on Waverly Place, where he'd been waiting fifteen minutes for her to come down. Unsure if her buzzer worked, he'd remained there haplessly pitching pebbles at her window. This was the fifth time he'd seen her, and she seemed to evaporate when they were apart: to disappear from the world at large and return just so, to establish her sudden reality.

"How d'you get your Chinese food?" he muttered. "How do you survive?"

But he liked her. He liked not understanding her, the way—in her business, too—she receded from him into the purest privacy. She worked without an assistant, running the literary department from her perch at the end of a long hallway. Sometimes he called the office and her phone just rang and rang. Maybe her business in New York was conducted in strict silence, a matter of nods and whispers.

"I feel like I'm drowning," she said, but brightly. He couldn't tell what she was referring to. With him? Her work? He liked this too.

"Come on."

"Don't you ever feel that way?"

He shook his head. But of course he did, and could imagine, too, the surface of the world closing over her head, small bubbles drifting up and then—nothing.

"Let's get something to eat," he said. And led her away from where she lived, that delicious tesseract where the street intersects itself, Waverly folding into an impossible knot.

"Where are we going?"

"You'll see."

It was all there, right from the start. Later, he'd remember things she said: how exhausting her work was, how her clients were like babies. *Don't you like babies?* he'd asked. *No*, she'd said. *I'm not interested in children.* But just then he took it all as part of her elegant resistance. After five dates, she still hadn't slept with him.

He led her to Carmine Street, a tiny place like a ship's galley with four tables, red-checkered cloths. It was tucked back, with no sign. You'd have to know it existed.

"Are you trying to impress me?"

"I never try to impress women. It's sort of a lost cause." He leaned forward, blew on his spoon. "The food's good."

He ate like an Italian, long before Hollywood embraced the fashion. Clams, scungilli, *brodo di pesce*. Jewish, yes. Observant? Not in a million years. Rachel stared, watching him with an appalled fascination.

"D'you think we met for a reason?"

Empty clam shells clattered into a wooden bowl in front of him. Beau snorted. "Not so long as you're not sleeping with me."

"Would it make a difference if I did?" Her eyes filled suddenly with tears. "You're like a stray dog! You just keep coming back!"

"Persistence." He smiled. "I learned that from Abe."

"I believe things happen for a reason. There are no mistakes."

"You mean like God?"

She shook her head. His mouth, his bristly beard glistened with broth. She wore an odd smile, like her despair might blossom into hilarity. Behind them, a wizened woman slaved over a cast-iron stove in the corner, ignoring them for her smoking pan of quartered tomatoes.

"Aren't there prettier women in Los Angeles?"

"It isn't about pretty."

"Then what is it?"

There was something broken in her, he knew that. He knew that even at the beginning. There was the desperation of someone—the beautiful could have this as easily as the deformed—who'd been shunned or misunderstood.

"I don't know," he said. "I just like you."

She smiled. Perhaps, being striking, she was unused to being "liked." Perhaps she just bowed before the fat man's relentless energy at last, appreciating the humility of the sentiment.

"I like you too," she said.

The room was empty, except for the wizened woman in the corner, who gave no sign of having heard. But Beau felt like he was onstage, the moment weirdly public. He put down his fork, and his crust of bread.

"I don't want to take advantage of you."

It could've been the most sincere thing he'd ever said. But she pealed with laughter.

"What's funny?"

"Isn't that what you do for a living? Take advantage?"

"I don't know." Beau blushed. Taking her banter seriously, as he mirrored her own thoughtfulness. He pawed the table, staring back with a guarded and bearish vulnerability. "What kind of advantage could I possibly have?"

Rachel and Beau went back to his hotel. I've tried to imagine what this was like for her, too, submitting to Beau's blustery assault. Even if she loved him, and I believe she had begun to, it must've been difficult. Repulsion's not so easily overcome.

In those days, Beau stayed in a shabby place on Sixth Avenue. His room had a rickety window staring onto an air shaft, yellow pillows malodorous with sweat. He liked this place for its noise, the kitchen echoes and elevator hums that traveled up the air shaft all night. They mitigated his loneliness. It was like sleeping with one's ear to a conch shell.

She began to undress the moment they entered.

The room was dark. By the scant light of the moon and the borrowed lumina of Manhattan, Beau watched her take off her clothes. She folded them carefully, graceful as a heron while she set them on the bed. He sat on the couch and lifted his short legs to remove his shoes. He and she were the same height, although he was twice as wide and three times as thick. His breasts were fuller, more generous than hers. His watch clanked like a shackle as he removed it and set it on the wooden table, next to his money clip and billfold. The cramped room held just this couch and the low table and a bed, which pulled out of the wall. In the corner a television set poked its broken antennae skyward. They looked mangled in the semidark, the splayed *V* that signals cuckoldry in other cultures.

"Don't hurt me." She flinched the moment he touched her.

"What makes you think I would?"

He lay a gentle hand across her flank.

Up the air shaft came the hydraulic whine of the elevator, the Cuban-accented patter of the busboys. He turned her, slowly, in that space between the couch and the window. She lay her palms against the sill.

"Do you have a rubber?"

"I can't get you pregnant," he said. Using a line he thought was true, since the doctor had told him so a few months earlier, when he went to get checked out for the possibility of the clap. "I have a varicocele."

Her back was angled up, her ass plummeting sheerly down and her cheek pressed hard against the glass. It took him a moment to find the angle, to let the head of his prick find its way inside.

She moved little, pressing back rhythmically to meet him. A squeaking sound, like bedsprings, came from her. He wasn't immediately sure it was human, that she in fact was making this noise. Pain or pleasure, it sounded far away.

"Hah!"

Beau's knees buckled; he plummeted into that loneliness that, given his nature, may have been greater for him than it was even for other men. Her body slackened, swooning against the glass as he fell away behind her. His arms slipped off her hips and dropped to his sides. He fought the impulse to say *sorry*.

"Umm . . . "

In the darkness, she trembled. Perhaps she was weeping again. The event seemed unrepeatable. He was sure she'd never sleep with him twice.

"Are you all right?"

No answer. He reached to the coffee table and fumbled for his cigarettes. She stayed where she was, in the staggered, vertical posture of a drunk hugging a street lamp. Moonlight slicked her knuckles, her cheek, the small curve of her right breast. The wales of her ribs, dented like an accordion's. Finally she turned, and, without a word, began gathering up her clothes from the bed.

VII

"YOU'RE KIDDING." A few months later, Beau and Rachel were on the phone. He was in his office on a hot afternoon. He'd seen her just once since the night they slept together. Sam was really killing him about travel. "That's impossible."

"Call it a miracle."

"I'd call it a nightmare." He scratched his cheek. "Sorry."

November. The air-conditioning in his office was out. He was thinking about all the other women he'd been screwing too, trotting out the same excuse to avoid using protection. *It's all right. The doctor told me I have a leaky vein.* His new assistant, for example, had also fallen for that one. Her name was Ren Myer.

"It's not," she said. "I think it's wonderful."

His blinds were drawn and his jacket was off. His sleeves were rolled and his Patek Philippe, which chafed, sat on his desk. He mopped his face with his free hand.

"Don't go away," he said.

He got up and closed his door. He didn't want Ren to hear, but also, a new tenant had moved into the adjacent office. Williams Farquarsen had come to the coast. That Princeton-educated Southerner he'd met the same day he'd met Rachel, and whose good opinion meant the world to him. He could hardly say why. He came back to his chair and lowered his voice.

"You know I see other people," he said.

What was it about Williams that conjured this sense of honor? He never knew. This sense that he needed, and wanted, to be his better self accordingly. The two were becoming fast friends.

"I don't," Rachel said, then sighed at his confession. "I don't care. It's twins."

"Twins!" The word exploded from his mouth, Williams be damned. "What the hell are we going to do with twins?"

"Raise them."

"Raise them?" She might as well have suggested sending them to the moon. "How do you propose we do that?"

"Very carefully." She paused. "Beau . . . "

Even at this distance, he could hear the warmth, a tenderness of which he had not, till now, believed her capable. Whether it was directed at him or at their unborn children, he couldn't tell, didn't care. He brought the phone, with its long black cord, to his couch. He sat beneath a framed poster that had just arrived for Stanley Donen's next movie: Audrey Hepburn and Albert Finney in *Two for the Road*.

"You really want to have it?" he said.

"They're not an 'it.'" She was calm, behind the pneumatic crackling of their bad connection. "They're two people."

"I know." Things had been going so well, too. That poster was for *his* movie, put together with Sam's star clients. They shared Donen, though Beau was increasingly the point person there. "I'm just a little surprised. I wasn't ready."

"Man proposes, God disposes."

He was up now, pacing. *Religion, again.* By the foot of his desk was a square brass spittoon. This was Sam's prize possession, brought for him from Claridge's by Laurence Olivier himself. People were always stealing it and planting it, whisking it around the offices like a hot potato. Sam would explode whenever he discovered it missing.

"I'm not ready," Beau murmured.

But then he stared at his desk. Stared and stared, at a glass of orange juice and a bottle of vitamins; a half-eaten apple that oxidized alongside a silver Tiffany paperweight. He could hear the loose, gravel-like patter of rain, now, outside. Where did it all come from, or go? He was thirty-four years old.

"My God," he said.

"What?"

It was as if he had just rotated into the position of his own posthumousness, could see his life, for a moment, from outside. The empty desk. The spittoon, which he'd have to rush upstairs before lunch was over, set back in those tiny divots it had worn in Sam's rug. A man was superfluous, unless he was ready. Unless he was *utile*, like these things.

"Twins." He rubbed his sweaty scalp. "Fantastic."

"It is fantastic." The connection crackled. "It's wonderful."

He set the phone down. He was going to be a father! He perched there with one palm braced against the leather edge of his desk blotter.

"Rach, honey, let me call you right back."

"Yes?"

"Yes. It's all right. This is great." He hung up, stormed over to the door and flung it open. He whooped.

"You OK?" someone called from down the hall. "Beau?"

But it was Williams who came in from next door, strolled over and stuck his head inside.

"What's happening?"

"Twins! Rachel's pregnant with them."

So many things were unknown. He and Rachel weren't even on the same coast, and like she'd told him, she didn't want kids. So what was this?

"Congratulations," Williams said. He sauntered in. "Congratulations, my friend."

"So what am I going to do?"

"What d'you mean?"

Sleek, paternal Williams Farquarsen III, who was two years younger than Beau and married with a two-month-old son. He came over and sat on the edge of his friend's desk. Already he was my father's confidant.

"You're going to let it happen." He smiled. "It's the best thing that could."

Perhaps he was right about this, although it's different for every man. Williams was a closed circuit. Unlike Beau's other colleagues, he wasn't out there swinging from the rafters, partying till dawn. He and his wife, Marnie, lived quietly, rarely even entertaining at home. Oddly, this was what made Will dangerous. Every other agent in those offices was on the make. Even Sam. Will was just a foot soldier, yet he lived like he'd already won and consolidated his power. He had the controlled swagger of a natural-born king.

"I suppose." This was why Beau trusted him all the way. His other friends might betray him over some scrap. Will never would; he felt it. "It is, right?"

Williams beamed. He represented something new in those offices, too: you could see it in the longer hair, the crushed velvet jackets and the pocket squares. He may have hailed from New Orleans but he dressed like an English flower child, one of those Carnaby Street groovies who owned the acts they managed.

"It's fantastic, Beau. It's going to make you a happy man."

"I don't belong with this girl."

"Who does, though?" Williams chortled. "People are always a strange fit."

Indeed. And he clasped my father's shoulder and shook him warmly, with love.

"Whaddya think, Will? Isn't this romantic?" Bob Skoblow pressed his fingers against glass and squinted down at the shadowed canyon of a Manhattan street. A trail of antiwar demonstrators was snaking north from deep downtown. "Didja bring your shotgun to lead the happy couple to the altar?"

"Shut up." Williams smacked Bob's shoulder with his knuckle. "It's *Beau* we're talking about here."

A wind-whipped afternoon in February. The two men stood in the third-floor corridor at City Hall while Beau splashed his face with cold water in the men's room.

"You gonna kick my ass, Will?"

Williams narrowed his eyes. "Would you like me to?"

Williams weighed all of 155 pounds. His voice rarely lifted above that honeyed and persuasive murmur that was like something you heard in your dreams. But everyone was afraid of him, everyone except for my dad, who loved Will with all his heart. In an office full of streetwise, coastal Jews, this man was certainly an anomaly. He stared Skoblow down.

"I'm just kidding, man."

"Cool." Green eyes and creamy skin, smooth like a girl's. He cuffed Bob's cheek, almost hard. "Be nice."

They could hear Beau retching, violently, down the hall. A moment later he emerged.

"Did we show you too much of a time last night?"

Beau shook his head. His face was gray, one arm dead by his side.

"What's wrong?"

Beau coughed. He didn't feel right. In the bathroom he'd almost passed out, from something worse than a hangover or nerves. His tongue was a brass clapper, his skin a gelatin suit. How could he explain to Will, this deliberate and responsible man, how he'd seemed for a few moments to float outside his body, how his torso felt even now like it had no weight?

"Just nerves."

"Nerves, huh?" Williams nodded. "You'll muddle through."

Williams and his wife had been married seven years. There were so many things, really, my father admired in his new friend: the patience, the loyalty, the discipline. The Roman numeral alone suggested a pedigree that Beau, the shoemaker's son from Queens, couldn't imagine. Williams was faithful to Marnie, never flinched at the starlets who crawled across his lap. Even the night before, when they'd been out, Will drank only water.

"What if I can't stop fucking other women?"

"Can't?" Williams cocked his head. "Or won't?"

"I dunno." Beau shivered. "Is there a difference?"

Bob stalked down the hall to smoke. Beau and Will stood alone in the aqueous brilliance outside the clerk's office, the window shades drawn against a painful winter light. Lower Manhattan now seemed abandoned, on a Saturday afternoon. The brown floors were waxy; the men's patent loafers shone. Williams fiddled with Beau's boutonniere.

"It's not that hard to control yourself, partner."

"Maybe. But why would you want to?"

Perhaps it's easy to see how the two men were matched, like mad horse and pale rider. My father wasn't being specific with Will. He'd kept fucking his secretary, Ren, more feverishly than ever. Almost as if he wanted to knock her up too, as if he wanted to populate their entire world. He loved Rachel, but this had nothing to do with it.

"You'll learn," Will said. Such recklessness was something he could never understand. "What aren't you telling me?"

From the beginning, my dad was half in love with his future partner. He joked about it. *I should be more like you, Will.* They stood together now like they were dancing.

"Is that what makes a successful marriage? Self-control?"

"Nah," Williams smiled. "It's forgiveness, friend. All strong partnerships are based on forgiveness."

The elevator doors opened. Rachel stepped out alone. She dazzled in a dark gray dress—gray like smoke, like opals, like cloud cover at night—and her red hair swung free. Her beauty struck him at odd moments, but none seemed odder than this inevitable one of their own wedding. He strode down the hall and seized her shoulders.

"Are you sure?"

As if he might shake sense into her, at the last minute. The hall smelled of solvent. The tips of his loafers curled up slightly, unexpectedly elfin. He wore a signet ring he'd borrowed from Williams, but she wore no ring at all.

"How sure do you need me to be?"

She smiled up at him. Of all possible mercies, this was the kindest: that she could turn her uncertainty into a joke.

"Come on." She pivoted toward the clerk's office, monstrously pregnant yet cool as a nurse. "Let's go."

There was a moment during the ceremony Beau was never to mention. As they stumbled along, racing and tripping over the words, he looked down. Stared for a long instant at his shoes, the patent leather and linoleum.

"Do you, Beau—"

He looked back up and saw not the officiant, but his father, complete in every detail.

"Beau?"

Coldness spread through him, moving up through his calves, his haunches, his balls. For a second, he thought he'd vomit. Those furred, fearsome eyebrows converging toward the bridge of the nose, the lank, silver hair and the myopic squint. This was his father precisely.

"Beau?" Williams touched his arm, the two men side by side in their morning coats. "Beau?"

"Huuuuhhhh—"

Beau lifted his hands. Stared at those raw and swollen palms. It would never have occurred to him to invite Herman Rosenwald to this event: the two men were completely estranged. Will's voice roared in and out, the light detonated around his head. Somehow he kept a singular focus, on his hands, on the tips of his shoes, on the dark-eyed glare of the justice and of President Johnson—that matte formality of his portrait—hanging on the wall behind him. *O, Mr. President!* Beady eyes and a looming schnozz, *that sick fucking peckerwood! Can't breathe—*

Beau's legs gave out, and he pitched toward the floor. Its freckled brown surface raced up to meet him before Williams dodged beneath and broke his fall.

The next thing Beau was aware of was his friend slapping him gently.

"Hey. Hey." Williams swatted each cheek twice. He prodded my father's fleshy face with his fingertips. "Beau?"

"Huh?"

He came to, after a glass of water and some ammonium carbonate were applied. Tears sprang from his eyes, his heart palpitated. Beau found himself on the floor, and then—his friend was so much stronger than he looked—Williams helped him over to one of the benches.

"What the hell was that?"

"Dunno," Beau said. "I fainted. Am I married?"

Williams nodded. "You made it that far. What happened?"

Beau stared down. Forearms resting on his thighs. The two men were alone now, as Rachel had run to call a doctor and Bob had followed.

"Nothing." He hesitated. What he did not say was, *I thought I saw my father's ghost. I hallucinated.* "Just nerves."

"That's natural."

Williams would've turned it into a joke. He would've quoted all of *Hamlet*.

"I was just thinking . . . about my dad. My goddamn old man."

The blond featurelessness of that room, with its twin flags, the United States and New York State, slack in the corner, made Beau think of school. The officiant was long gone. He sat with his arms by his sides, chastened by these narrow little benches.

"That's natural too," Williams drawled.

Will stood up. With one arm clasping Beau's shoulder, he twist-ed around toward the door. There's a photograph of this moment, though I don't know who took it. The bright spray of Williams's white carnation, his easy smile as his bantam body turns. That congratulatory posture of an attorney who has just seen his client exonerated of all crimes.

"That's what happens when you get married." Williams slapped his friend's back. "The whole family crowds into the act."

"Now what?"

They'd planned it badly. Neither could relocate. Rachel's business meant she had to stay in New York, while Beau would go home to LA. Once the children were born they'd figure out what to do.

"What now?" In the limousine he turned to her as they rode up-town. Street lamps slid by, massive and blurry. He batted among them like a moth, but it was all in his head. "I don't feel any different."

"What made you think you would?"

"I always thought the day would come when I felt like an adult," he murmured. "You get older, but you never really age."

Typical. But it hadn't happened at Beau's bar mitzvah, or since. He lay his palm on her belly.

"They're going to depend on us," Beau said.

"Your clients depend on you."

"That's different."

Was it? In any case, Rachel was his match here too, in private ambivalence as in gathering professional power. She looked like a little girl, gazing out the window: wonder-struck, confounded. The darkening streets flashed past.

"I'm not ready for it either," she said. "When I was younger, I wanted anything but this."

"So you've said. What did you think you wanted instead?"

"Escape."

Later, he would remember this. Scan this conversation for clues. Just then he thought it was something else they had in common, as if—as if!—they had anything at all. Beau's alliance with my own mother was more likely than this. Rachel was a literary agent, representing Charles Portis and Thomas Berger. Beau had barely read a book since *Coriolanus*.

"Let's go to the Bahamas tomorrow."

In the lobby of the Plaza Hotel, he stood and windmilled his arms. She looked at him.

"We can't."

"Why not?" They hadn't even planned this, would take their honeymoon off the cuff. "Abe will let you go, and as for Sam," Beau waved his palm. "Fuck him."

"I can't fly." She smiled. "Not in this condition."

He looked at her as if even flight were something he could suddenly achieve, without machines. The two of them were alone now. They'd had dinner at Tavern on the Green and their scattering of friends had left them.

"Let's do something else. Drive to Miami."

"We'll drive?"

"I'll drive. You can climb on my back and I'll carry you."

"Really?" She stared; he sounded so serious.

"Yes. Hell yes. We'll make Will carry the luggage."

There at the Plaza, she climbed on his back, and he charged around the lobby like a bull. What could you do with a man like this, whose boorishness was inseparable thus from exuberance, and whose ugliness so shaded, almost, into charm? Even the way he squatted, like a little boy playing leapfrog, his tux-black hindquarters shiny as he bent to accommodate her. She couldn't help rattling with laughter.

"Oh God, I'm heavy, careful—"

"No—*whuf!* It's all right. Not you. The kids, the kids are heavy."

She whooped as he bore her into the air, past a bellhop, the telephone operator, some ladies taking four o'clock tea. A man, a silver-haired troglodyte with an incongruous Beatle haircut, looked up from his *New York World Journal Tribune*. Finally Beau set her down in the shadow of a potted palm.

"I can't wait to make love to a pregnant woman."

"What makes you think I'll let you?" she said.

"Isn't it my right?" Huffing and puffing, he recovered his breath.

"I wouldn't say it's your right."

"Really?" He leaned against a pilaster. "According to Jewish law?"

"Nope."

"Muslim law?"

She laughed. He closed his eyes and rested his head against the wall.

"Do that again," he said.

"What?"

"Laugh." He didn't move. "I like to hear you laugh."

He opened his eyes. His face was long, jowly. He was still young. His eyes were a dry and placid green. He gave her a heavy-lidded glance and she smiled back. She lay three spidery fingers and a thumb against his wrist.

"I like hearing someone laugh *with* me," he said. And closed his eyes again.

She held his hand, standing beneath him there on the stairs. If he'd opened his eyes, he might have seen her smile, might have seen more than just the absence of ridicule that was all he ever hoped to encounter. She brushed her hair back, and leveled her jaw up as if willing him to kiss her. But he didn't.

VIII

WHAT MUST IT have been like, raising those children alone? My father always talked about the pressure—*the pressure, the pressure*, that mania of the business even before the acceleration brought on by car phones, faxes, Blackberries—but what about the pressure on her? Rachel Roth never complained. When the kids were born, at Lennox Hill Hospital in April of '67, she was alone. Beau flew in the next morning.

"Yours," she said, dazed, out of it, as he staggered into the maternity ward feeling a little whiplashed himself, clutching some wilting tulips that were, like him, too late. Severin was born with a sister. "See?"

The little girl slept. The twin infants weren't identical, but in their squashed, pudgy frames he recognized himself. Severin had a full head of black hair even then. Kate was exquisite, named after the mother Beau himself had never known, who'd died when he was two. She had Rachel's arctic eyes, and her alabaster complexion.

"Not too much mine," he offered, as he sat on the edge of the bed and took her hand. Rachel was so slender, pregnancy had made her almost the size of a regular woman. "Thank God."

She looked back at him, her eyes half-shut. Reclining, while Severin squirmed on a pillow on her lap. The baby looked uncomfortable. Maybe *Beau* was uncomfortable.

"The things they give you," she murmured, and fell asleep. He couldn't tell if she meant the nurses, the drugs, or the children at her breast. He peeked into Kate's bassinet and then picked up Severin, who wailed and writhed in his arms. A nurse clacked past, checking on her patient, then scowled at Beau. He didn't care, staring down at his son, who was blind as a mole, his little mouth flexed awfully with hunger.

They could cleave you in two, he thought. And they did.

"What are we going to do?" Rachel asked him.

This was later, after he'd brought her home, installed the twins and a nanny in her cramped place in the West Village.

"Should I come to California?"

"Do you want to?"

She shook her head. And he felt the shame of his own uselessness, was wracked by the comparative ease with which she handled their children. Whose need for *her* was obvious.

"Pick him up."

Suddenly, he couldn't. He was afraid of these kids, of the purely instinctual way she took up maternity's burden where he had the sense of his own absolute superfluity. When Beau bent over Kate, she immediately started suckling, mistaking his nose for a nipple.

"You're going to have to get used to it," she said.

"I know."

Her apartment had been a mystery zone, and it still was: bricked in with books, smelling of sandalwood and the faint edge of something burning. Diapers, domestic smells now, too. There were three rooms, a twin bed. She could've had more but evidently didn't want it. It was as if the asceticism of her person, her body, extended into her environment. One room was painted robin's egg blue. An ironing board stood in the corner, next to an empty fridge. Yet he could feel in all this, inside the spareness that rejected a television set, or even a radio, a preparedness. For what, he wasn't sure.

"What will you do," she said, "if something happens?"

"To what? To me?"

"To me," she said. It wasn't selfishness that tipped him into thinking first about himself; a 280-pound man was at risk for all sorts of things. "You have to be ready."

"What could happen?"

She shrugged. Preoccupied with feeding Kate, too. The washed-out gray of her eyes, of a piece with the hazy sky outside, met his.

"How are you feeling?"

"Fine."

"No, I mean." She equivocated. Tilted her head just slightly.

"Oh. Nothing, lately." *Untrue.* "I'm fine."

She meant the fainting, the fits and fugues which had begun at their wedding and had troubled him ever since. These moments were rare, but there had been dizziness while shaving, one or two times in his office when he'd leaned back in his chair and felt the earth rotate with him. It wasn't physical, he checked out improbably well, but the sight of his own blood, or his red-rimmed eye in the mirror, was sometimes enough to drop him into a trance.

"I worry," she said.

But again, she never told him about what. Exactly what was the matter with Beau Rosenwald? I've always wondered, myself. But Rachel only bent now to look at suckling Kate, the sky a grimy white through the window behind her head. And it would take more than a simple visit to make him a competent husband, or father. Nothing could do that, yet.

IX

"REN—"

"Oh stop, Beau." The woman on the edge of his couch rolled her eyes, which were wet. "I don't want to hear your excuses."

"I'm married," Beau snapped. "What exactly do you want me to do about it?"

"Nothing." She sniffed, and blew her nose. "I just want you to be honest, for once."

"Honest." He sighed. "Why is it that people think being honest is the same as being faithful?"

"I don't think that."

My mother, for indeed, this was she, was naked from the waist down. She stood up and began to dress, striding over to where she'd dropped her skirt in the middle of her boss's office.

"I just wish you'd admit what you *need*."

"What do I need?"

She straightened up. This woman was fantastic, Beau thought: Ren Myer had worked for him now for six months, and they'd been sleeping together for five. He admired her strength, her ferocious patrician intelligence. Unlike his wife's: she was an autodidact. Ren Myer had been a theater major at UCLA, but she'd dropped out. She read everything, walked around the office with Edward Albee tucked in her purse, took cigarette breaks with a paperback Yeats. Beau had stolen her from Yul Brynner.

"Someone who won't put up with it."

"You think Rachel puts up with it?"

"I think she doesn't know, or care."

Cornflower blonde, willowy, serious. Was it *his* fault Beau couldn't resist her? What did she actually want, since it was unlikely to be the fat man himself? She buttoned her blouse now, looking like someone on the bridge of a ship: you could read defiance in her body language, a certain braving of the elements—the densely masculine atmosphere of those TAG offices—other secretaries couldn't handle. He watched the brittle knobs of her wrists flashing below her cuffs.

"I'm sorry," he said. "I don't know what's wrong with me."

She did, maybe. Or maybe Ren, too, was prey to the same confusion, what madness seemed to run through the halls at that point. On Beau's wall, next to the old-fangled image of Paul Scofield, Orson Welles and Robert Shaw—*A Man for All Seasons*—there were posters for *Twisted Nerve*, for *Candy*. Everything seemed to go now. What *wasn't* permitted? My mother, who was all of twenty-five when she worked for Beau, had no idea what she wanted from life. What she didn't want—ex-model, ex-actress, soon-to-be-ex-secretary at TAG—was to be pregnant with Beau's baby, herself. Having just missed her period, she feared she might be.

"*I'm* sorry," she said. "It's not my place."

"It is," he said. "I shouldn't be married."

She tugged the hem of her blouse. And almost spoke. She parted her long, silken, canyon girl's hair away from her face and fixed him with a steady look. *Beau, I forgive you, but please, straighten up and fly right. Also . . .*

"What is it?" he said.

She shook her head. Recognizing, I suppose, that to say anything would be a mistake. What good might come of telling him I existed, if indeed I did?

"Nothing." She turned on her heel and went back into the hall. Settled down at her desk, cool as could be. Beau could hear the friction of a match, and her inhalation on a cigarette, before the phone rang and she spoke.

"Beau Rosenwald's office. Hold please."

Beau had a lot to think about already. Even without his children—even without yet knowing I would exist—he had to deal with Sam, who was giving him hell.

"What have you brought in?" That punctilious old fucker was always ducking into his doorway, prodding. "What are you working on, Beau?"

"Something for Stanley."

"Stanley." Sam's hand described a circle of contempt. "Stanley doesn't need you. He made *Singin' in the Rain*."

That's why he needs me, Beau wanted to say. *No more musicals, you sad queen. He needs something stylish, like* Bedazzled *again.*

"Why don't you get a job for one of those circus geeks you represent?"

Because they don't need me, Beau wanted to say. *Because that's the way the business is turning. It's men like Stanley, your clients, who are in danger of extinction.*

"I need to go to New York," Beau said.

"Why? To slack off? See those ugly kids of yours?"

"No." *Temper, Beau. Temper.* "I'm trying to sign someone. A kid from Yale drama."

"No," Sam said. "No travel."

"I have to—"

"Do your job," Sam snapped. "Or drive a cab, I don't care. But you work for me. And putting together Corman movies ain't cutting it."

No, it wasn't. But the smug satisfaction on Sam's face, the animal disgust with which he treated Beau—he wouldn't even set foot in his underling's office, made a point of drawing back into the hall, as if the very air repelled him—was the most anguishing.

Day after day after day. How did you love, if the world forever insisted you were appalling? If even the women you slept with cringed?

"Do your job." Sam strode away, stiff-legged, military. "You worthless puddle of whale crap."

Yeah. Beau rocked back in his chair, took a deep breath, then another. His heart was hammering, his palms were wet. It took everything he had not to charge down the hall and smack Sam. But he couldn't. This job, besides being the one thing he could imagine now, the sole alternative to ignominy in Queens, also kept his kids. He sent Rachel money every week. What would he do if he couldn't?

"Why don't you come see me?" she pleaded.

"I can't."

"Your children miss you. *I* miss you."

"I know. I can't. Sam's killing me."

"Is there another reason?"

Was there? He closed his eyes, rolled his palm against his forehead. His face felt hot.

"I think you're afraid, Beau." She spoke softly, gently. Who would have known that under that cold woman he'd met in a taxi lay someone who'd understand him? "Afraid of what home might do to you."

Did she? Sometimes it seemed she really did.

"What about you?" he said. "What about *your* future?"

"It isn't the future I'm worried about."

Times like this, he felt like a different man. All around him there was the mania of Hollywood in 1968: elfin little hustlers, goatish Jews and bullies. Somewhere in the world were his children, and somewhere, in his ear and yet nowhere to be seen, there was this woman he'd married, whose very absence felt like love.

"Are you all right?" she asked, after he'd been silent awhile.

"Yeah." He *was* afraid, of her, and his children, what softness they made him feel. "I'm fine."

But there was more to it than this, of course. An open insurrection, closer each day to all-out warfare, had broken out in the motion picture department. Jeremy Vana, who occupied the corner office, popped off one afternoon to Waxmorton over the phone. *Listen old man, don't tell me how to close a deal. Your tactics might work for Bobo the Chimpanzee, but this is Peter Sellers we're talking about, here.* He was gone so fast his chair was still hot while they whitewashed his parking space in the garage. But he landed on his feet, instantly, as a producer. Ren quit and went over to Teddy Sanders's desk before she left the agency altogether. Beau didn't care. There was the wonderful license he felt, the expansiveness that was in the air. You did what you wanted, whatever the cost.

Fatherhood was part of this too, surprisingly. Severin and Kate gave him greater license, even when they were just mute little beanbags. They gave him some freedom to be himself.

"What are they eating?"

At all hours of the day, twice in one afternoon he might call Rachel to ask this innocuous question.

"Mashed bananas. Rice. Sev likes green beans."

"Really? I like green beans. Had some today, amandine." This was the best of it, somehow. He might charge around all night with his fly unzipped and his shirt unbuttoned, but at four o'clock in the afternoon, in the mellow cave of his office, his son liked green beans. "That's fantastic."

"You really do need to see them."

"I know."

"Then come."

He'd lost weight, grown almost gentle in the temporary softness of his first marriage. He stood there, a sleek 270, behind his desk with his shirt hanging loose and a cigarette burning. He drained the warm dregs of a can of Tab.

"I dunno, Rach." The can made a tinny clank as he set it down. This woman actually liked him. Incredibly, she did. Now that he'd laid his hands upon the one thing he truly wanted, he found himself in flight from it. "I'll try."

"Is it the responsibility? I understand that."

"That's part of it."

The afternoon was mild, sun burning beyond the blinds to paint the whole room peach. The plastic cubes on the telephone's console blinked mutely. His brand-new secretary came in. Her hair was long and her clothes exploded in riotous color. But it wasn't philandering, either: it was just fear. He watched as the girl bent to straighten a pile of scripts on his couch, the pastel skirt riding up to show the buttercream backs of her legs.

"I gotta go," he murmured. "I'll call you later."

Oh, there would be time for him to regret it. For him to wonder what he'd missed, how he'd misread the signals. But when Rachel called in late autumn and told him what she wanted, Beau was almost thankful.

"Let's stop this," she said. "I want a divorce."

"Really?"

"What good is a husband who's never there?"

Her voice was unexpectedly tender. Beau spun in his chair. It was a good day, work-wise—he was *this* close to making a deal for Stanley Donen—but a bad one for his mood.

"I'm sorry, Rach. I'm not cut out for this. I don't know how to be married."

"I know."

Even now there was an affection he'd miss. He'd become a more vigorous father, in fact had made several trips back to New York over the summer without Sam catching him at it, out of his own pocket. Now that the kids were more interactive, he found how deeply he cared. Their silver-framed pictures were on the edge of his desk: puttyish, six-month-old faces, so faintly resembling his own.

"I'll always be glad we did it, Rach."

"Me too."

She spoke lightly, but in the silence that followed, there was the pressure of something unsaid.

"I'll try and be a better father than I was a husband."

She murmured something indeterminate. He sat up and guzzled a glass of water, then poured another from the carafe on his desk.

"What does that mean?" he said. "'Muh.' I can still come and see them, right?"

"I think so."

"What does that mean? 'I think so'?"

He slugged water again. He thought to ask Williams's counsel—after all, his colleague had a legal background—but just then his secretary rapped his doorframe sharply with her knuckles. She strode in holding a green folder.

"We'll have to see," Rachel said.

The secretary had his attention. She raised her eyebrows and held the folder toward him. *Now, Beau.* He listened into the phone a long moment. To this day, he couldn't really imagine his soon-to-be-ex-wife's existence, didn't know what she did beyond care for their children, even though they had nearly identical jobs. This, too, was his failing.

"I'll call you back." He looked at the girl. A redhead, this one. Faint freckles like rust-tinted raindrops. "What is it?"

She handed him the folder. "It's from Sam."

Beau flipped it open and squinted. "The hell is this?"

He peered down at the deal memo, committing his client—technically, still shared with the senior agent upstairs—to do *Staircase*. Beau hated that script.

"What the fuck?" Beau had other plans for Stanley Donen. Stanley was supposed to do a hip comedy with Bryce Beller called *Mellow Yellow*, about a mountaintop guru. Instead, Sam had prevailed upon him to take this . . . feeble chamber piece.

"Are you all right?" Cloudy-browed, the girl watched him.

"Yeah." He dripped sweat, excess water. He drank another glass. "That was my wife on the phone." He gulped. "Ex-wife."

"Oh." She stood with her hand on the back of his chair. "I'm sorry."

"She wants to file." He shook his head. "It's all right."

She stood above him, smiling down with her hair swaying faintly. *Something I can do for you, Beau?* A smell of mimosa. He pushed up out of his chair, instead.

"I'm gonna go upstairs."

"Don't do that." Girls mothered him, too. It was never really about sex for Beau. His loneliness was too acute. "Maybe you should calm down a little, first?"

"I am calm!"

He wasn't. One thing calmed him, only one. *Kate.* The rest of the world, even his infant son, just drove him to different forms of distraction. His daughter at six months, though: that buttery skin scent when he buried his nose in the folds between her neck and shoulder!

"Beau, think."

"Uh-uh." He stormed across the office. "I'm gonna go give that son of a bitch what for."

He stepped into his loafers, which were parked by the couch. She just watched him. Of course he was fucking her: just because you didn't like sex didn't mean you didn't have to have it. He stalked into the hall and made his way toward the stairs.

This storm had been brewing forever. Sam had hated Beau from the moment he arrived, but in a way this collision had been set up long before he even got here. This was a tectonic moment in Hollywood.

Outside, Williams's door was closed. Roland Mardigian's lanky, cowboy frame was propped back in his chair as he listened on the phone. There were Milt Schildkraut, Teddy Sanders. These men held a bigger share of Beau's future than I ever would. He stopped at the water cooler, glancing back at the one-sheet Williams had hung in his secretary's nook, the famous image of Warren Beatty and Faye Dunaway laughing behind a pane of bullet-pierced glass. Williams knew the score. He saw where all this was going. He knew the future, perhaps, long before my father did. Beau took a cinnamon candy from an assistant's dish and then trotted upstairs, cellophane crinkling between his fingers as he breezed past Sam's male assistant.

"What the fuck is this?"

Sam looked up. He was having his nails done. His office was elevated over the rest of the motion picture department; the second story was otherwise just television and payroll. The room cantilevered away from the street, around the building's side, jutting like a humped back. Sam liked the view it gave him, with windows on three sides.

"What does it look like?"

"It looks like you double-booked our client for the spring. He's doing *Mellow Yellow*."

"He isn't." Sam stared, behind his desk. "*Staircase* is a better picture for Stanley."

Beau glared back, surrounded by the various appurtenances of Sam's power. Along with Olivier's spittoon, which sat at the foot of the horseshoe-shaped desk, there was a framed poster for *Lawrence of Arabia*, inscribed to Sam from David Lean. There was a handwritten note from Elizabeth Taylor. There was a sectioned purple couch and a white alpaca rug, drifting carelessly on the parquet floor. The manicurist's black hair shook as she buffed vigorously.

"I respectfully disagree."

"Do you? Tough."

"Stanley told me yesterday he was in."

"Yep." That scritching sound of the emery board. "I convinced him otherwise."

"Why would you do that?"

Even in these few years, this walnut-colored man had withered. Sam was sixty-three, back when that was old, and his complexion had the spotted, browning quality of oxidizing fruit.

"Because *In the Woods* or whatever it's called"—Sam couldn't even remember *Mellow Yellow*'s original title (it was *Does the Pope?*)— "isn't commercial."

"It's a lot like *The Party*. Which was very successful."

"I don't understand it," Sam barked. "I hate it."

Figured. Beau shifted his weight from one foot to the other, hands cupping his crotch. He'd been so thirsty. Now he needed to pee.

"Look." He squirmed. "Why don't we try and make him available to do both? *Mellow Yellow* doesn't have a start date. I'll see if the studio can push it." Beau omitted the fact that Abe Waxmorton's old abuser, Jeremy Vana, was the executive in this case. "Why doesn't Stanley do *Staircase* first? It's a chamber piece, it won't take that long—"

"He's not doing your bullshit movie at all."

"My bullshit movie? Stanley loves that script!"

"He needs a hit."

Scritch scritch scritch. The Asian girl didn't look up. Her face was shuttered, symmetrical: eyelids and lashes drawn down. Sam's hand hung, inanimate, platformed in the air.

"A *hit*," Beau sneered. "Stanley needs a hit."

"You look like shit."

"Thank you."

"No, seriously." Sam's abuse had intensified over the years, and Beau just stood there and took it and took it. "Even by your sad standards. What Abe saw in you, I have no idea."

Beau shifted his weight again. He cracked the hard candy between his teeth, sucked vigorously.

"I'd fire you, if I could. If Abe wouldn't raise a stink about it."

Beau cocked his head. The sound of the candy, between his teeth, was a form of insubordination.

"Get out of my sight." Sam yanked his hand back from the manicurist now. She bent and began packing up her things, but Sam said, "Not you."

Beau turned. He really did need to pee. But then he looked back over his shoulder at Sam.

"Forgot to mention, I have to go to New York next week. It's an emergency."

Sam sighed, a low whistle between those pursed, ever-consternated lips. He studied the surface of his desk, its piles of papers arrayed like pieces on a game board.

"What kind of emergency?"

Beau turned again and stepped back toward the desk. "I'm getting a divorce."

"You can do that from here."

"Why do this?" Beau said. "You don't like me, fine. I don't like me either, but I produce. I'm a good agent. So why shit on my plate?"

The manicurist had moved around to Sam's opposite side and was now working on his other hand, dipping a small towel into a basin filled with warm water.

"You go, and I'll fire your ass so fast you won't know what hit you."

Beau loomed over the desk. His toes nudged the precious spittoon. Sam wore a turquoise shirt, the color of an antacid. He looked like a mummified gangster.

"Have a heart, Sam." There was irony in this, too, in the sly ridiculousness of this appeal. Have a heart? *Aw, gee willikers.* "My kids need me in all this."

"That's your problem."

"I suppose it is. But I'd still like to see them."

"Nope. Your problem." Sam sighed again. "Though I understand how it could also be theirs."

The manicurist jumped up. She folded her kit and pocketed her clippers and left, leaving the little plastic basin and the warm towelette still on Sam's desk.

"I feel terrible for your kids," Sam said. "It must be difficult having a fat tub of shit like you for a father."

He had no idea. And yet Beau stood his ground. Cinnamon curled his tongue. Behind Sam's head, through the window, the green fans of palms swayed in the afternoon breeze; the Spanish brick roofs lay atilt in sunlight. A landscape with less tension was difficult to imagine.

"Listen, you miserable little cocksucker, just because you'll never have children doesn't mean you can take it out on me."

"Pardon?"

"You heard me. You can cornhole your secretary all you want, you can pick on *me*—I don't give a shit—but leave my kids out of it."

Sam stared. His homosexuality was an open secret. It was never, ever acknowledged. He peered through square-framed glasses that only made his expression more bilious somehow: they were like tiny twin television sets for the eyes.

"You're fired," Sam snapped. "Pack up your things and go."

"I'll call Abe."

"What do you think he's going to say? You just called me a cock-sucker. What do you think Mr. Waxmorton will make of that?"

The pressure from Beau's kidneys was killing him. But he grabbed his prick, which was suddenly half-hard—as it always was when he argued—and strode toward the older man's desk.

"You know what I think? You've had it in for me from the begin-ning, but the truth is, you disgust *me*."

"How so?"

"Because you're a fucking fraud."

Sam blinked. The look on his face, too, was ironic. "You picked a funny place to come looking for authenticity."

"Maybe. But there's room in this business for people to be them-selves. I don't expect a relic like you to understand that, but it's true."

Who spoke to Sam this way, who slung as much truth at power? He represented Billy Wilder, Fred Astaire. Sam may have been an antique, but he was the real deal.

"Get out."

"Fuck you." Beau laughed. It felt so good, didn't it, to be him? When it wasn't a living nightmare. "Go fuck yourself, Sammy."

Even to this point, he might have done something to save his job. People acted like assholes all the time, and there was nothing, even now, a little groveling couldn't have fixed. So why didn't he?

"I'm going to steal your clients, Sambo! Stanley Donen, he's com-ing with me."

"You're fucking delusional."

"Who isn't?" Beau cantered in place like a triumphant horse. "I'm gonna take all the business you've got."

I don't believe he knew what he was saying. Agents didn't poach from one another back then: there was a code. Waxmorton had lectured him about how you could steal a man's wife before you went after his clients. The former was always replaceable.

"Go on."

He felt *great*, in that moment. Even if he would be miserable in twenty minutes, his head was clear, he was so lucid when he did the thing that would follow him the rest of his career. He cupped the front of his trousers again, rubbing the brushed, custard-col-ored cotton. Then he unbuttoned his fly.

"Betcha haven't seen one of these in a while." He lifted his eyebrows. "Not without paying."

His foot nudged the spittoon. And then he aimed his penis toward the ground and let go.

He could have peed on the carpet, or on the desk. Either would have been sufficient, but of course he aimed it straight for that gift from Olivier: twelve inches by twelve inches, a rectangular box whose sloping sides were meant to catch cigarettes and gum wrappers but instead facilitated Beau's accuracy. He peed and peed and peed and peed. How many glasses of water had he had in the last hour, six? You could hear the plash of liquid on metal, the satisfying clank of that thick, heavy stream.

Finally, Beau finished. He tucked his penis back into his boxers, did up the tortoiseshell buttons of his fly. Then he walked around to Sam's side of the desk, dipped his fingertips in the manicurist's basin, and dried them carefully with the towel.

The two men looked at each other. There wasn't anything to say. Beau backed away with his hands on his hips. A drop of urine gleamed on the tip of his shoe. He wore the same Church's brogues he'd come in with four years earlier. In the hall the phones burped and purred, and Sam's posh British assistant murmured, *Sam Smiligan's office. Please hold.*

Then Beau turned and walked away, striding downstairs and out of Talented Artists Group's offices, crossing the palmy green street for the last time. By the time he reached the garage, Sam had demanded his assistant get a mop, and this story was raging through the halls. Beau Rosenwald was already a legend.

PART TWO: **THE DOG'S TAIL**

I

"HEY, WAIT," Little Will said. For the moment he was sober. "Wait, wait, wait, wait, wait." Sober-ish. "Let's . . . let's stop and get a slice."

"Yeah." I was also sober, believe it or not. In the spring of '93, as the three of us cruised down Fairfax Avenue at 10:00 PM on a weekend—or during the week, it hardly mattered—this almost represented some form of achievement. "Pull over."

Severin did. He jerked his crappy little hatchback over to the side of the road, then angled it around the corner into the lot on Rosewood. My God, he was a terrible driver! He bumped up the little hill into the lot and we abandoned the car across two spaces. It was kind of a sleepy night, I remember. We'd been out late the night before, and Fairfax was oddly depopulated for a Saturday. Up and down that little strip, the diamond merchants and kosher markets, the galleries and pawn shops all looked more shuttered than usual, bars and grates crisscrossing their darkened windows. The three of us had spent the day doing what we did back then, watching *Beyond the Valley of the Dolls* and then *The Big Sleep* before Severin went off to his video store job and I pecked at a terrible script on his IBM Selectric. Eventually I fell asleep at my brother's apartment on Franklin while Williams went out for a while. I didn't think much of it. Little Will's disappearances didn't mean anything to me yet. Everyone was back by nine o'clock, and now here we were, shambling along Fairfax toward dinner, or breakfast, whichever it was.

"Where'd you go?"

Williams shrugged. Severin wandered at a slight distance from us both. It was like—perhaps this is only hindsight—he'd decided to become someone, finally, whereas Little Will and I would have to have our individuality pummeled into us. We would.

"Out."

He wasn't feeling talkative. Neither was I. The orange beacon of Canter's was across the street, but we were headed for Damiano, that strange and dreamy little pizza joint directly opposite. Back in those days, everybody went there, dull-eyed twentysomething faces drooping over lukewarm Pacifico and scalding slices. Old Hollywood—our fathers' Hollywood, as well as Sam's—had ended, and we were left to pick through its ruins and prowl after hours at places like this one, rooms dark enough they might've belonged to any era. Warren Beatty had dated Madonna; Marlon Brando was fat and staring down the barrel of *Don Juan DeMarco*, rolling around on top of Faye Dunaway in his pajamas. We liked places that literalized our blindness, that made it possible still for us to romanticize the present as well as the past.

"I have to take a leak," Little Will said. It was packed in here: Damiano was as crowded as ever, no matter how it looked from outside. We'd jammed into a booth and now were waiting for our food.

"Don't get lost."

He rolled his eyes at Sev. "At least I know how to use the can." That story about Beau just kept on giving.

"We'll be here."

We watched Little Will insinuate his way toward the back of the restaurant, pushing through the people jammed around the edges of booths, disappearing back beyond the kitchen. Beer bottles sparkled dimly; the wayward embers of cigarettes moved in the humid darkness. Then an older man, lean and greasy and not a member of our tribe, slid into Will's spot.

"You cats wanna go to Gazzarri's?"

Severin gave him a sidelong look. "Gazzarri's?" Also, *cats*?

The guy shrugged. "You look like dudes who could use a pick-me-up."

"Maybe," Severin said, "but Gazzarri's . . . "

What he wouldn't say was that Gazzarri's was for heshers, metalheads, a different kind of Sunset Strip enthusiast entirely. But then, this guy seemed to be one, skinny and vegetal in his purple jeans. His hair was a peroxide wreck.

"What's wrong with Gazzarri's?"

"Nothing," I said. "It's . . . "

The guy just bobbed his head. "I thought you fellas were cool."

"We are," Sev deadpanned. "Just not *as* cool."

The room was so loud we had to shout. I took a long slug of lukewarm beer.

"We can't go to Gazzarri's," I said. "It's closed."

"Not tonight."

"Why not?" I looked around. Where was Williams? He'd been gone a little too long.

"Guns N' Roses secret show."

"Bullshit." Severin snickered. He leaned back in his Peckinpah T-shirt, which depicted a shoot-out from *The Wild Bunch*: a silk-screened pattern of spattered blood and viscera. "That place holds like five hundred people."

Metal Man nodded, closed his eyes. He had the serenity of a prophet, which is exactly what he was. "I know. It's a big deal."

"There'd be riots on the Strip if they tried to play that place instead of the Coliseum."

He bobbed his head. I had the feeling he could see us through closed lids.

"I'm just telling you what I know." *Kneyow*. He sounded like we did in seventh grade. "Take it or leave it."

"We'll leave it," Severin said. "No offense, guy, but we're . . . classicists."

Williams came back. He jammed his hands into his pockets and stared.

"Classicists?" the guy said.

"Yeah," Sev said. "Bob Dylan, Leonard Cohen. That kind of thing."

"Huh." The guy blinked, dazedly. "I thought Bob Dylan was dead."

"I think we should go," Williams said. He must've caught some of this on his way back from the bathroom. "I think we *have* to go."

We looked at him. *You do?* But Williams offered the guy a little soul-brother handshake, tips of the fingers hooked and thumbs crossed. "Dude."

"See? I knew there was a reason I came over to talk to you gen'lemen."

"I guess so." Besides to remind us that certain customs never ended, that stoners were an imperishable subset of the human race? "We're certainly glad you did."

"So how do we get into this little shindig?" Williams leaned down. The guy hooked him with another soul-brotherly handshake. "Just tell 'em you know Twink."

"Twink?" I said. "Your name is fucking Twink?"

The guy didn't look like a "Twink," he looked like a Gunnar or an Ebbot. I watched him jounce off, hair-fronds waving. Part Viking, part toothpick, part *Ficus benjamina*.

"Where'd you disappear to?" I asked Will.

He shrugged.

"We're not seriously thinking of going to see Guns N' Roses, are we?" I said.

"We are," Severin said. "We're thinking seriously about it."

Williams sat down. "Dudes." He kneaded his forearms a moment, languidly. Just like that, it *was* junior high again. "We gotta go. We're there."

Out in the parking lot, Williams staggered and slurred. "I'll drive."

"No," Severin gave him a once-over. "I will."

I watched Will. "You all right?"

Truthfully, he was always like that. I don't know what I thought I was seeing. He smoked a lot of dope in those days, as did Severin, but they got high in different ways. Severin was hyperkinetically lucid as he jolted from one wack "insight" to the next. He could wrap up a crackpot history of cinema in ten minutes, one hand on the wheel of his AMC Gremlin while the other sparked up another doobie, never moving the car out of second gear.

"I'm fine, man." He had beers in his pockets, one apiece in each side of his khakis, and he was wearing a ski vest and knit cap. Also a Nirvana T-shirt that read FLOWER SNIFFIN KITTY PETTIN BABY KISSIN CORPORATE ROCK WHORES.

"Don't wear the cap and ditch the vest when we get there," I said.

"Then they'll see the T-shirt and think I'm picking a fight."

We piled into Sev's car, that eggshell-yellow, dusty, and antiquated machine. Williams was in the backseat and I rode up front.

"Listen," I said. "I'm not so sure . . . "

"What?" Severin said.

We rode the swept corridor of Fairfax slowly, at cop-repelling speed. The yellow lights flashed overhead, the street was deserted. We passed the dark marquee of the Silent Movie Theatre, then a stucco nursing home with prison bars across its windows.

"I don't think we should go to this," I said. "I'm having that feeling."

"What feeling?"

Williams lounged behind us, his head flung over the seat back.

"Something bad is going to happen. Not just, we're going to get hazed by a bunch of spandex-wearing assholes. One of us is going to get hurt."

Severin snickered. "You in one of your spooky Chandler moods tonight, Nate? *Meek little wives feel the edge of the carving knife and study their husbands' necks.*" I could practically hear his eyes rolling. "You know you're the one person in this car who isn't stoned."

"I know. And I feel that way, and I'm right." I was. "Think about that."

"Leave the paranoia to the experts." He shifted gears. "We're going."

Laurel Canyon loomed in front of us, the black humps of the hills and the grayish, antemeridian sky, the inky-white blots of cloud cover and the road, the narrowing thread of Fairfax where it twisted up to meet Laurel and then lost itself among the trees. *Everything is everything.* Will's father's ghost haunted that road in a red Ferrari. There was enough terrible history in this city to justify any amount of fear. Mine had nothing to do with headbangers and less still with a Chandler obsession. It was ontological, pure. We turned left on Sunset. Around us the city unwound at speed, in flashes and fragments of neon. People clustered outside the Whisky, the Roxy, in the parking lot of Tower Records. There was no evidence this "secret show" was real. A cluster of heshers outside the Rainbow, but there was always that. And then right there, outside Gazzarri's. A crowd: a sea of peroxide white and black leather, denim and lipstick, scratch tattoos.

"Looky there." Severin swung a U-ie, scanned the street for parking. "We're in luck."

"Or out of it."

We found a spot and got out of the car. Williams last, on unsteady legs. He had his hands in his pockets, weaving like an awkward sailor, as if the ground might start bucking beneath him at any moment. He worried me most: he was more like our dad than his own, so purely at the mercy of his own appetites.

"You seen Beau lately?" I nudged Sev.

But neither of us had seen him. We were about to embark on something that would require our own answers. A hot wind kicked up around us, one of those sinus-rattling Santa Anas that meddle with the mood of the city. Above us a billboard swarmed with images of Robin Williams in drag. Before us lay destiny in the shape of men in lipstick and eyeliner, women who'd drop to their knees to do the cocaine crawl.

"Let's go," Sev said. "We're late enough as it stands."

II

BEAU ROSENWALD OPENED his eyes around noon. He clutched his head, twisted the sheet across his waist as he sat up straight on Bryce Beller's pull-out couch. *Ugh.* His temples ached, the top of his skull. His eyes were flaming, and his tongue felt like he'd dipped it in a vacuum bag.

"Belll-ERRR?" He reached out toward a dented can of yesterday's Tecate and then thought better of it.

"You up, Rosers?" Bryce's voice drifted over from the kitchen. "You want eats?"

Beau sat with his face in his hands, legs over the side of the couch. He looked like he was weeping.

"Nurse," he muttered. "Nurrrsse."

From outside the room's picture windows came the sound of surf. They were out past Zuma, where the city tapered into oblivion. Beau had an apartment along the fraying edge of Beverly Hills, on Sherbourne Drive, but he never went there. He and Bryce were trying to produce a movie: all his energy, all his time went into this. The rest of his life was a ruin.

"You makin' breakfast, Brycie?" Beau lurched up. He knotted the humid sheet around his waist and moved toward the kitchen. "Or are you makin' weird stuff?"

"Little bit of both," Beller yelled back. His voice rode over the sizzle of butter. Beau passed a set of white wicker chairs, trampled a careless assemblage of Navajo blankets and throw pillows. He entered the adjacent galley. "Egg whites."

"Egg *whites*?" Beau blinked in the kitchen's explosion of light. "What kind of person eats only the fucking whites of an egg?"

"A healthy one." Beller turned from the stove as Beau entered. He was naked. "Yolk fucks with your chakras."

"Put some pants on."

Beller shrugged. "Can't. Can't afford 'em. I used to have an agent who could book me a job."

"You used to have an agent, period. I keep telling you to go back and sign with Teddy Sanders, let Williams look after you—"

"Fuck those people. Seriously, Beau. I'm *your* client, through thick and thin."

"Thin, right now."

Bryce looked him over and shook his head. "I wouldn't say that, fat man."

Beau slid into the breakfast nook, jiggling the salt and pepper shakers, the empty bottles, the desiccated limes and dirty ashtrays. Plates were caked with red residue; his elbow rested on a yellowed copy of the *Herald Examiner*, its headlines reporting Bobby Fischer's victory over Boris Spassky, an editorial about Hanoi Jane. Weeks ago. It was late September, 1972.

"You ruined my couch," Bryce said. "It tilts toward the middle now."

"Sorry."

"No, no. You paid for it." Bryce chuckled. "You stay as long as you like."

It was true, though. Bryce owed his career to the big man behind him. Hardly so very illustrious, but the days of waiting eight hours on the lot to say a single line of dialogue, of mooching around the commissary to split a chicken wing with Harry Dean Stanton were over.

"Stay as long as you like," he repeated. He'd been a deranged piano prodigy in his last movie, a man whose hands were injured during the war. He'd just wrapped a picture in which his character shot John Wayne's. "Once we get this picture off the ground we'll both be in clover."

Ghee sizzled. Bryce's movements were loose. His back was a uniform bronze from his heels to his nape. The light in the room was dazzling, almost white as it spun up off the Pacific. They were out past Broad Beach, even, where all they could see was untracked sand and craggy rocks.

"This picture," Beau murmured. Days could pass without the two of them encountering another human. This was the closest thing he had now to a "career." Except for Will, all his colleagues had abandoned him. Most wouldn't even take his call. He kicked his feet against the sandy linoleum. Bryce's browned body moved in front of the stove. "This picture's a fucking mess."

Bryce whirled. A Smith & Wesson .45 was in his hand, a long-barreled pistol which erupted, twice. The room filled with the smell of cordite. Smoke drifted from the nozzle.

"I got you!" Bryce yelped. He folded to his knee and wheezed like a seal. "I got you motherfucker!"

Beau grabbed his rib cage and then—*what?* It took him this long to realize he hadn't really been shot: the two ear-splitting pops had been enough to make his heart stop.

"Jesus." Beau's voice was dull in his ears, blunted by the noise at close range. "What did you d—blanks? Those were blanks?"

"Yep." Bryce laughed. "I had you there."

Beau stood. His belly slopped over the twisted top of the white sheet. Bryce twirled the gun around on his finger, then handed it over to Beau.

"You know who gave me this? John Wayne hisself."

"Put some pants on. I don't like to be shot by someone in the nude, it's like being an adulterer."

"It's a nice gun." Bryce took the gun back. "I could hunt with this thing."

"Then why don't you?" Beau pointed toward the sea. "Go out there and shoot us some fish."

"Aw, don't try me, Rosers. Be a good guest."

He set the pistol on the counter and spun it. Round and round until it rested, pointing somewhere harmlessly between them. *It shoots blanks*, Beau thought. What could happen? What worse was going to come to them? Just then he couldn't get a job to save his life, and Bryce's career really hadn't followed the lines it was supposed to either. Nicholson had become the star instead. Who would've guessed that? Bryce handed him a plate of some suspicious-looking eggs: they were brownish-green, and scrambled. Beau sniffed.

"What's in these?"

"Nothin'. I made yours light."

Beau took the plate. Some weird stuff, Beller was into. Transcendental meditation, yoga, running. What sort of person deliberately ran for miles on end, without really going anywhere? Beau turned away, to stare at the Pacific and eat his eggs in peace.

What's the matter with Beau?

After the pissing episode, some people obviously began to wonder. But right now the biggest problem was a certain constriction of his options. He'd gone back to New York for a while, but that life—in his native habitat, closer to his kids even if Rachel didn't want him to see them—amounted to nothing. Was he supposed to produce plays, or drive a taxi? Here there was some hope, however faint, of resurrection. Friends had landed in medium-high places. Jeremy Vana was an executive vice president at Columbia Pictures. No one could be too helpful. Sam still wielded a lot of influence. But Beau's day might eventually come.

It was around this time I first met him. Not that either of us recognized what it meant. My mother had married Teddy Sanders, Beau's former colleague in TAG's motion picture department. Did Teddy have any inkling I was not his own child? I can't imagine he cared too much, if he did. Those were different times, and while I strongly suspect Teddy knew, my mother never told Beau. Not for a long time. Why she waited, I'll never know either. She'd left the agency not long after she started dating Teddy. He could've done the math. But Teddy and Beau had been colleagues, and so I remember him having the fat man over to dinner together with Williams, my mother cooking pepper steaks and uncorking bottle upon bottle of Margaux. Both men were indelible: my kindergarten classmate's father for his sleek and mellow elegance, and as for Beau, who could forget a person of that size? But I was too young to understand trouble, to know that the huge man roaring with laughter in the next room, keeping me awake with profane jokes, could in fact be close to suicidal.

"What do you think it is," my mother murmured when he left the table to hit the head. "What's Beau's problem?"

"You worked for him." Teddy gave her a sly glance. "Wasn't he always like this?"

"Not like this," Will drawled. "This is different."

My mother nodded. "He seems . . . desperate. I think there's something wrong."

I stood in the shadow of the sideboard in my pajamas, one of my earliest memories. I gnawed a toothpick, prosciutto and melon from Greenblatt's Delicatessen. This was in the old house on Warnall Avenue in Westwood. Walnut floorboards and crystal chandeliers.

"This is the movie business." Teddy was at the dining table, deflated in his chair. He wore his off-hours uniform of scuffed Gucci loafers and pale denim shirt. His long hair was already thinning, his blond mustache pale at the tips. "Nothing gets done without desperation."

"That's the flaw," Williams said. He studied the glass of ice water in his hands like it was a diamond. "It's what's wrong with the business, and it's our friend's tragic flaw."

Leave it to Williams to put it in Aristotelian terms. He set his water down, spotted me, and winked.

"Nathaniel, c'mere."

I walked over to him. I could hear Beau's heavy tread beginning at the far end of the long hallway that ran past my room.

"D'you like school?"

I nodded. Maybe I did, and maybe I didn't: it was too soon to know which of these men, which father, I'd come in time to resemble. The educated or the more instinctual one. Will took me in. I felt it, what Beau must have felt when they met too. The strength of his whole attention, neither gentle nor harsh, a caress without any love in it. Already, I was friends with his son. Little Will and I had been paired off by something besides being the two youngest boys in our class. Call it fate.

"Go to bed, sweetie." My mother could hear Beau coming down the hall also. "Go on."

Williams winked at me. There was alarm in my mother's voice, the way there'd been when she'd spoken up earlier. *I think there's something wrong.* It seemed to carry some balance of affection and horror. But I was far too young to interpret that. She stood in her regal turn-of-the-decade beauty, black turtleneck and flower-print skirt. Long-faced, ash-blonde, and somber. She waved her True cigarette at me. *Go.*

I love remembering my mother this way. Twenty-nine, not yet consumed by alcohol and disappointment. She took a sip of wine, her profile whittled, elegant. The convivial Hollywood wife. Williams turned away, but I could feel him still, the enigma of his strange concentration. Few men are truly fathomless, yet he seemed so.

"Who's this?"

A booming voice sounded above me as I collided with Beau in the doorway. I couldn't help it, I walked right into his elephantine leg. I looked up and saw him staring down at me.

"You're Nate," he added, and smiled. And absently stroked the back of my head and shoulder, once. It was like being pawed by a clawless dog.

I bounced off him. Without anything to say, and a little bit intimidated by his fatness, by his slothful and easy bonhomie.

"G'night, kid," he murmured, as I slithered around and off to my bedroom. I was six years old and of course didn't mark any of this out as unusual. But I remembered it all the same. My bare feet kicked across the polished brown floors; our terrier, Suzie, followed; Teddy's voice carried after me.

"Sweet dreams, Nathaniel."

Thus, I met my father, and with him the man who was his necessary concomitant, Williams Farquarsen, whose future would haunt us all. Understanding none of it, just letting their laughter blend into typical adult chatter, while I left them behind, in dream.

Now Beau sat and ate a plate of curdled, kelp-colored eggs with windows on two sides of him overlooking the sea. Thinking about the only two kids he knew he had and protecting his plate as though someone might take this, too, away from him.

Rachel, be reasonable!

Reasonable? He could still hear her sneering. *Reasonable people have jobs!*

These past few years, it had gotten worse and worse between them. She'd left Waxmorton and set up shop on her own, yet having her independence made her controlling. She'd grown secretive, paranoid.

Maybe she was crazier than he was. Maybe she was jealous. Once a month he came and visited, crawling around on the floor of her brownstone apartment like a wildebeest, exotic and particular and large. The children adored him. Severin attacked with his tummy, just charged and screamed and started smacking Beau's head with his own belly the moment his father knelt down to greet him. Was this why Rachel was pissed? Because Beau's son resembled him after all? He'd walk around the Village with one twin over each arm, both of them black-haired, green-eyed, and lovely. These were the moments the world belonged to him, and he to it. Even as a child, Sev had the purest whiff of teenage disarray, his untucked Mickey Mouse T-shirt torn and slovenly; Kate fanned out into alien beauty, her hair cut straight along her jaw like her mother's. They'd just turned four. With their father they sat in a booth and drank milkshakes, all three inclining their heads in a way that told everyone they were a family.

It's healthy for them.

Healthy? I don't want them eating sugar.

The last time he was out, he and Rachel really went at it. *You're a fitness freak now?*

That's not what I meant—

I know what you meant. Standing there in the vestibule, because more and more she didn't want him in the house. *Are you taking your drugs?*

My— he'd begun laughing inappropriately. *I haven't had anything happen in a year and a half. They're just anxiety. My . . .*

What should he call them? Episodes? Fits? But the sight of a man in his late twenties, some bearded Christ-y type who looked like a tranquilized Manson looming into view behind her only made him laugh harder. *That's your boyfriend, Rach?* Jesus, no wonder all this macrobiotic blather and stuff about her "karma," questioning whether she even wanted to sell books.

"Where do you go, Rosers?"

"Huh?"

Beau stared, as Bryce interrupted him. The look of a man whose real life, as vivid as it was, stayed trapped in the confines of his head. "I'm right here." He scratched his cheek. "Just thinking things over."

"Right. Think on this. We get a green light, this movie will change our lives."

"This movie is 183 pages long. It's written on a bunch of paper place mats, and it doesn't have an ending."

"This movie is forward-thinking. Progressive."

"Or a beginning. Now that you mention it—"

"It will win us Academy Awards."

"—this movie is a fucking boil, an open sore on the ass of humanity."

Bryce looked at him. That cliff-like stare that was never quite handsome enough, those yellowy eyes. His face was too upper-crust, too haughty, too volatile, too something. The gun sat over on the counter.

"Like that ever stopped anyone before, Rosers. Come on."

He laughed. They both did. Their lives were like this gun in a way, adjusted to harmlessness no matter how voluble.

"We gotta do something. I'm running out of fuckin' money."

"Me too," Bryce said. "I get it. Melody sweats me the same way."

Melody, his ex-wife. They'd met years ago, when Bryce did an episode of *F Troop*. Their son was the same age as the twins, himself a rare visitor.

"So what do we do?"

"We do what we've always planned to do." Bryce stood up and stretched, his concave runner's torso arching forward. "We make this fucking film."

"You gonna take a meeting like that?" Beau nodded at his naked friend's crotch. "Enough of the noble savage bullshit."

"It isn't bullshit. It isn't the savagery in people that's noble, either, it's the nobility that's savage. That's an important distinction."

Beau watched his friend's eyes widen as the actor began to get high off the hash oil that was in his eggs. "All right, fine. We still need to hire a writer."

"We don't need a writer. We can *be* the writer. We can *be* the movie if we just let it happen."

Poor Bryce, with his faith in these things. He sounded like fucking Rachel. "No one in Hollywood is crazy enough to make this."

"We are."

"Fair enough." Beau was tired of thinking about it. He got up and stalked toward the cupboard, with its yellow paint blistering off the door. "I'm gonna have some of that mary-jew-wanna, myself. I need to feel *invulnerable* again."

III

"SO WHAT AILS?" Williams leaned across the table toward my dad. "What do you need, Beau?"

"Money." It was hard for him to ask, but he did it. "I'm broke, Will."

The two men were at Duke's Coffee Shop, attached to the Tropicana Motel. "Seedy" barely began to describe it. Yet just up the street was Dan Tana's. Barely a mile separated them from TAG and the bustling places in Beverly Hills where Sam's henchmen did their business, the Bistro and La Scala.

"So?" Williams removed his sunglasses. "There's no shame in that, partner."

"Isn't there?"

"No. The business tells you that there is, but there isn't."

The air smelled of chlorine, from the motel pool. Grease. Beau ate pancakes and Will ate nothing, just sat, clean and dapper, at breakfast with his old friend.

"How's Sam?"

"Fucker." Behind Williams a man, really just a pile of hippie-beatnik mannerisms, twitched in a booth, slurping his coffee. Will snorted his contempt. "He's ancient, Beau. You can't worry about him."

"I can't work." *We can't eat in a normal restaurant, where you'd be seen in my company.* "I can't get anyone to sign on to this picture."

"For now. Beau." Will turned his palms up on the table. "How much?"

"What?" For the rest of his days, he would remember this. "What d'you mean?"

"Just tell me how much you need. You said you needed money. So?"

Beau had never before asked overtly. Once a week he drove Bryce's old Chevy into town to have breakfast and to scream at his psychiatrist. Afterward, he met his old friend, who might leave a hundred-dollar "tip" on the table that would enable Beau to meet certain obligations, but Williams had never opened up this way either.

"Five grand. Would that help, Beau?"

It would save his life, at least for a while. Beau was hardly more disciplined with money than he was with anything else. But this would allow him to see his kids, buy his medication. It would keep his little dinghy afloat a bit longer.

"I can't accept that."

"You can. You will." He'd remember this. "I'll get you a check."

"Will . . . "

The two men sat. Beau, near tears, and Will with an untouched elegance. He could walk into rooms as greasy as this one and still retain his dignity, in booths dampened by whores' pussies and junkies' necks.

"It's more than I need."

"No." It fucked with you, this town, besides. So-called "needs," luxuries. They ran together like a soft-boiled egg. "You need to see your kids, Beau. You need to stay alive until the worm turns."

"It's not gonna turn." Williams just nodded at Beau's pessimism. *Stop.* "OK, but I don't even know anymore," Beau went on, "if it does, what'll happen? This picture with Bryce, it's important or it's just a goddamn pipe dream. How do you know? When is it ever enough?"

"When you stop suffering." Will lolled, with one arm up on the back of the booth, imperious. "That's when."

Sunlight swam in the air above Santa Monica Boulevard; the door with its bell tinkled and swished behind Beau as the scenesters came and went. A gang of grubby musicians shuffled in and collapsed in a pile of buckskin in an adjacent booth. There was the click of a Zippo.

When did you stop suffering, ever?

"All right." Beau inhaled. Tobacco smoke, lighter fluid, syrup. His hands were shaking, he noticed. "Thanks, Will. Thanks."

This was a kind of heroism. Five grand was a lot of money for both of them, then. And Williams just came out and gave it to him, more than Beau would have ever thought to ask. It was something the fat man would never forget. But what really struck him wasn't the money (it was never the money, for Beau, if you can believe that). It was Williams, and his cool sense of proportion. *When you stop suffering.* It was simply that Williams knew how much was enough.

Then again, what was "enough"?

"Scream, Beau. Let it out."

"Excuse me?"

Twice a week, Beau drove into Beverly Hills to see Dr. Horowitz, who urged upon him meditation, marijuana, and who wrote him a prescription for lithium.

"Let's do something about your anger." Horowitz was a dainty little fellow with a blond horseshoe mustache and elbow patches. He wore white trousers and swanned around his office barefoot because he believed we should all be closer to the dead. "Let's take care of Beau."

It was hard not to laugh. This man was insane. But he saw all sorts of people, Roland Mardigian, Jeremy Vana. He was the go-to guy for every anxious Jew in Hollywood. He had a tiny hourglass on the edge of his desk and op art on two of his four walls.

"Come on." He insisted they do their sessions standing up, and toe-to-toe. "Scream."

"Aaaahhhhhh!"

It was like visiting the fucking zoo, with those animal stripes and spots splayed across the walls. This was supposed to help him? With what? But he went, since for a while he could afford it. And yet nothing ever seemed to change . . .

"Hey, Rosers!" Bryce hammered on the bathroom door with his fists. Now it was December, the days at the beach short and cool and bright. "Get dressed, we got somewhere to be!"

"What?" Beau spoke over the thin trickle of the shower, its hiss and steam.

"Meeting! Let's go!"

Beau twisted the rusty tap. The jade green tiles were blotted with mildew; the showerhead was oxidized brown.

"Who we meeting?"

"Davis DeLong."

"You're shittin' me."

"Nope." On the other side of the door, Bryce whooped. "Get dressed."

Beau hustled along the hall, into the downstairs bedroom where he kept his clothes. It was too dingy to sleep down here, all the furniture draped with sheets, but it would do for possessions.

"What does Davis want with us?"

"*The Dog's Tail.*" Bryce's voice drifted from upstairs. Beau heard the jangle of his keys. "He wants to do our movie, my friend!"

"Bullshit!"

Beau scrambled into agent-wear, clothes he hadn't had much occasion for lately, but they still fit if he inhaled and you were stoned. Davis DeLong had bigger fish to fry. He had to.

"What makes you think Davis would touch a picture like this?" Beau clomped up the stairs now. "We don't have anything to give him. May as well go after Steve McQueen."

"Pessimist," Bryce sneered as he emerged into the living room. Beau did a double take at the sight of his friend in a tie. "We have poetry."

"Poetry." Beau exhaled. Their lives up here on the second story of this house that was built down along a low bluff that sloped to the sand: these were poetry, too. "Davis gets seven-fifty a picture."

"Davis has a chance to work with us."

"OK." Beau smiled. "That'll tip the scales, I'm sure."

Bryce's paisley tie triangled his chest like a penguin's underbelly. He wore an untucked denim shirt and sandals. Still, a tie. The sun was beginning to go down outside, the tide rolling in all the way under the house.

"Where are we going?"

"The Luau. We're due in forty-five minutes."

"Davis'll be late. How'd you get the meeting?"

"Jack made it happen." Bryce led them toward the door. "I'll tell you, we don't even need a script if Davis wants to do it."

Lassitude. Reverie. "Poetry," Beau guessed, was another word for it, but wasn't the key to their movie tedium? *The Dog's Tail* took its name from something Nicholson had overheard at a party. It was meant as a descriptive, applicable to anything from women to vacations. *It's the dog's tail*, they might say of a bad booth at Dan Tana's, the girl who crawled under your table at last call. It wasn't always bad: the dog's tail could be what you secretly yearned for, the life lesson you needed like a small loss at roulette. The dog's tail, Beller reasoned, was existence itself, which was why this movie had to be made. The story, which Beau, Bryce, and Jack had cooked up over a 4:00 AM breakfast, about two brothers being pursued around the country by an assassin. They had everything but motive, but it didn't really matter. The movie had begun as an inside joke, one of those flashes of "inspiration" you had at that hour. Bryce, though, wouldn't let it go. He'd dug into his own pocket to hire a kid named Mitchell Gibson to write it, after everyone else had passed: Dennis Hopper, Curly Bob Rafelson, Buck Henry. Mitchell's script had "poetry," sure, it had a rugged desert beauty—even Beau could see the kid could write description, was aiming for American Antonioni—but the movie didn't make *sense*. It lacked drive. Mitchell wouldn't even confine it to a single time period.

"I hope you brought dope," Beau said. "We'll need all the persuasion we can muster."

"Davis read the script. He *likes* it."

Beau wore a navy jacket, a white shirt with cuff links. Most days, he dressed like a distressed beachcomber, lay around watching *Sesame Street* and scratching his ass. But he could still put it on when he needed to.

"All we gotta do," Bryce said, as they stepped into the courtyard that led to the garage, "is convince Davis's agent."

"His agent?" Beau's shirt was immaculate, arcing over his belly like a sail. "That's Sam."

"Sam? Shit, Rosers, he's coming to the meeting!"

"How could you miss that?"

"I told Davis over the phone we needed to talk about the script. He said he already loved it and would bring his agent. There are a thousand agents in this town."

Beau laughed. "There's only one who knows me so up close and personal."

The courtyard's fine white gravel crunched under their feet. To their left was a separate property. No house, but Bryce kept an unruly garden that stepped down to the sea. On its various terraces were recessed wooden benches, cozy fire pits, bonsais and Japanese maples. Bryce had a meditation shed there too, the little gray outbuilding where he went to clear his mind. Beau looked over as they passed. Nothing could ever go wrong in this place. So long as neither of them had anything to lose, everything that came their way was gravy.

"Maybe I should just whip it out and offer to freshen Sam's drink."

"Maybe he won't remember." Bryce turned the key in the ignition and backed out of the garage. "Teddy Sanders says the guy had his second angioplasty last month."

"Maybe he'll just drop dead." Beau studied his face in the passenger's side visor, began to trim his mustache with tiny scissors. "That'll take care of that."

Bryce drove a '68 Porsche, sluicing through an absolute absence of traffic, past Zuma and Carbon Beach, the maroon hood gleaming, their voices carried away by wind. Past GLADSTONES 4 FISH and up Santa Monica Canyon. Only when San Vicente Boulevard merged with Wilshire, and the light was gone and the air was suddenly dank, only then did their mood too darken.

"I need this movie," Bryce murmured. Fog hung over Westwood. "I haven't worked since spring."

"I know." Beau was almost tapped again, too. "I know we need it."

They parked up the block, to avoid the valet's charge. Beau cracked his knuckles behind his back as they stepped out of the car. The street was white and cool, the shop windows studded with oversize snowflakes and drab golden orbs, plastic Santas and flock-covered sleighs.

"Happy holidays."

There in the islandic depths of the Luau, all tiki darkness and volcanic flame, Sam oozed sarcasm. He looked like a shriveled head on a stick, prunier than ever as he stuck out his palm.

"Sam." Beau shook it. "Good to see you."

Davis DeLong, the real prize, reclined in the booth's deepening center, both arms extended along the top like a groggy fighter's. He was even more handsome in life. Bryce slid in beside him while Beau stayed on the edge, as far from Sam as possible.

"We've met once before," Beau said. "I don't know if you remember."

"Sure." Davis was cool. "At Vana's."

Sam kept his feet outside the booth, facing the room as if he were about to leave. There was no way he'd abandon his star client to these loons, but there was that feeling of Tinseltown cubism, like two or three separate meetings might happen at once.

"So you like the script," Bryce said.

"Love it. It's existential, you know? Deep."

"Yeah," Beau said. "Mitchell did an excellent job. He'll do a polish, but—"

"Shit," Sam said. "The script is complete shit."

"Oh?"

The room was kitschy, fifties absurd. Pineapples floated; there were big blue goblets flavored with Curaçao; bowls topped with jets of yellow-white flame circled the room like fireflies.

"My client is not doing this picture. I came here for the exquisite pleasure of letting you know, you'll make this movie in hell."

Davis lolled. He seemed almost will-less, as if loving the movie were one thing, making it quite another. He was as blonde as a ski instructor, handsome and dumb, with a cleft chin and a pedigree that included a turn at the Yale School of Drama. He brushed a long lock of hair away from his eyes.

"So?" Beau smiled. "Looks like we're at an impasse."

"We are. The client and I are leaving."

Beau threw one arm up on the back of the banquette. "Is that right?"

Sam swung his feet back into the booth, happy to join a fight. He looked at Davis. "This lardass pissed on my floor."

"I was a little overexcited."

"This"— Sam flourished his hand in small circles—"person. This human being."

"Yes. Did you get my apologetic note?"

Davis just leaned back a little farther. His green eyes were worn and dull, a forest color. "I heard about that also."

"You fucked up," Sam said. "C'mon Davis, let's—"

"Client."

"Excuse me?"

"You called him 'the client.'" Beau leaned, calmly. "Davis can't make up his own mind? Is he meat?"

Bryce sat quietly beside Davis, as if the two actors were in one world and the barking elders in another. Beau was all of thirty-eight, but he held seniority.

"Pretty nice, huh Davis?" Bryce lifted his eyebrows. "That's my guy."

"You're a fine one to lecture me," Sam snapped.

"It's not a lecture. Consider Davis's interest. Why shouldn't he do this movie?"

"Because it's uncommercial."

"You said *Mellow Yellow* was uncommercial, and Blake Edwards made a killing."

"*Mellow Yellow* was a comedy. I have no idea what this is."

"It's a poem."

"A poem!" Sam's eyes flashed contempt. "You'd be unemployed even if you were potty-trained."

Davis smiled, a curved and scornful look that was the key to his success. It gave his bland face an air of superciliousness, even danger. He'd used this look in a movie with Paul Newman, playing a young ranch hand apprenticed to a cattle rustler; with Steve McQueen, he was a rival racer; against Lee Marvin, he played a rube cop on the trail of an aging bank robber.

"A poem." He thumbed his lip. "I dig it."

"You dig it?" Sam looked at him. "Davis, the sixties are over."

"No, no. There's *love* there, between the brothers. I dig that."

"Nothing *happens*, they just drive around for ninety pages until it gets violent."

"So? That's life, isn't it?" He looked at Beau. "I really like this."

Beau couldn't believe it. The waiter came by and he ordered a pupu platter, winking sarcastically at Sam. *For you.* The older agent stood up.

"This is suicide. You know that, Davis? This could kill your career."

"It isn't suicide." The word hung over the table a moment. "I'd like to do it."

"You would, huh?" Sam's voice was phlegmy, tremulous. "How come?"

Davis just leaned back, cool as ever, and shrugged. "I think it's neat."

Neat. Now the men faced one another and ate and drank and were as civil to one another as they could muster. Davis's dopiness, his aw-shucks manner that played against the smile was the reason besides, the genius in casting him opposite Bryce.

"This picture could destroy you," Sam glowered, clutching a skewer of shrimp poke like a tiny conductor's wand. "You could never work again."

"Naw." Davis shrugged. "It'll take more than a poem to destroy me."

Poor Sam! He looked like a little buzzard, pointing his stick at Beau.

"The king of Hollywood, eh Sam?" Bryce chuckled. "That's you?"

Sam jabbed. "You think I'm old-fashioned. My time will come."

"I never said that." Beau leaned across. "But you don't understand this movie."

Sam's face was painted red by the light above the booth. There was something primitive and ugly, garish and loud and at the same time civilized about this place: the waiters in their island shirts and the affluent customers, the Mexican busboys and the six-dollar drinks served in voodoo goblets. Sam licked his lips and lifted a finger.

"Everything comes around. There are worse things in life than being antiquated."

He shook his head sternly. Beau laughed out loud.

"Come on, Sam." He crunched an egg roll. "Let's be friends." He swallowed. "Let's not let animosity get in the way of doing business."

Sam smiled. He might have been waiting the whole time just to let Beau's euphoria crest. "Oh, I won't. But there isn't any business to do."

"What do you mean?"

"This movie isn't set up," Sam said. "Davis won't commit without a guarantee."

"So?" Beau belched. "Any studio in town will make it with him."

"Maybe. But he still needs a real offer. Pay or play. Davis?"

The actor just grunted. He had returned to the lolling, indefinite posture he'd held at the beginning. "Neat" the project may have been, but love wasn't about to trump money.

"Come to us with an offer." Sam smirked at Beau and folded his hands with serene assurance. Glasses flamed around the room, a lounge piano tinkled, the perfect setting for an adding machine ritual. "Then we'll talk."

"No." Chain-smoking Jeremy Vana was a good friend, but not crazy. "I'm sorry, but no."

"Why not?" Bryce snorted. "Let's hear the studio executive's reasons."

Jeremy was beefy, blond, with a thick beard and a square jaw. He looked like an old-school politician: there was something almost nineteenth-century about his crooked, sturdy frame. He flicked a cigarette into the standing ashtray by his desk.

"Davis isn't as bankable as you think. His next picture's a turkey."

Antsy Jeremy. He might be expected dead of a heart attack before he was forty-five. Yet he was their appointed salvation, there on the Columbia Pictures lot when it was still in Burbank. His office was like a Mandarin explorer's, a room full of parchment shades and faded leather. An antique globe stood atilt by the couch where Beau and Bryce both sat. Davis's next picture, in which he played Thomas Egerton, Lord Chancellor of England, would turn out all right, but others who'd told our men the same included Ted Heller at Fox and Lewis Spruill at Universal. Paramount had passed, and they brought it back to Jeremy. Still no. MGM, no; UA, no. Dennis Hopper had agreed to direct and they'd come back to Universal. *Absolutely not.* They'd gone outside the box to Hammer Films in the UK and even met with Melvin Van Peebles. You can imagine how that went. Now here they were in Vana's office again.

"I wish I could tell you something had changed," Jeremy plunked one boot onto his desk. "But I'm going to get shit-canned if I make this movie."

"So?" Bryce sneered. "You're gonna get shit-canned anyway. That's what happens to studio executives."

Failure had made Bryce reckless. He hadn't worked at all in nearly a year. Now he lolled contemptuously, having kicked off his shoes to show bare, bunioned feet. He wore running shorts and a sweat-soaked Fighting Illini T-shirt.

"How am I supposed to help you fellas?" Jeremy laced his hands behind his head. "Seriously."

Beneath that boxy, almost Lincolnian beard lived an interesting man. His blue stare was dully attentive, the look of someone who invested too much time in the brackish, illogical process of studio filmmaking.

Beau stood up. Like an orator without an argument. "You can make this fucking movie, Jeremy."

"No can do." He'd worked with Beau before and so was equal to the usual tactics, wasn't about to be snookered by that gentle badgering that was like being cuffed, relentlessly, with damp towels.

"Why not?"

Jeremy sighed. There were so many reasons. This studio had teetered on the lip of bankruptcy a year ago, and a picture like this wasn't going to help. They'd been here before, and Jeremy was about to resort to chucking them out of his office once more.

"What's that?" Bryce leapt up. Yippy and irrational, so like his on-screen persona, he pointed and stalked toward Vana. "Whaddya got on your face, Jer?"

Jeremy had pushed up out of his chair but now froze. "Huh?"

"There." Bryce approached. "Right"—he jabbed just below Vana's left eye—"there."

Jeremy flinched. "That's just my freckle."

"No sir." Bryce shook his head. "Too big. That's a melanoma, my friend."

"A melawhich?"

"A melanoma. That Coppertone's no good for you. You need a dermatologist."

A dermatologist! Bryce was into some weird shit, but at least he now bothered to wear clothes once in a while. The mark was black as a fly, just above the cheekbone. It mightn't have been noticed by anyone who wasn't accustomed to hunting for such things.

"Tell you what. You get that checked out and it's nothing, we'll never set foot in here again."

"And if it isn't?"

"You'll push this movie," Bryce said. "Whether it shit-cans you or not."

Jeremy laid his hand on that old-fashioned globe. He spun it. On the coffee table beside it were a backgammon board and two sweating glasses of iced tea. On the walls were one-sheets for *The Way We Were, I Never Sang for My Father, 1776.* Through the window, beyond

Jeremy's desk, they could see where an elaborate castle had been built for *Lost Horizon*.

"All right." Mortality trumped common sense. "All right."

Beau had been through enough. It was late 1973, and if he didn't get this movie made soon he'd go back to New York. Or wade into the Pacific. Severin and Kate were five. He'd given up being a part of the best and most innocent years of their lives to chase these meaningless hopes and fugitive elations. He could feel the helplessness rising in his chest, the desperate knowledge that he could only, once more, be disappointed.

"Jeremy," he said, "I love you. But I hope you're fucking dying."

IV

PRODUCTION BEGAN THE following spring. *The Dog's Tail* would shoot in New Mexico and a few days in Georgia, for the modest budget of $850,000. Davis and Bryce were the two brothers, and Udo Kier, of all people, was their mute pursuer. For a brief, delirious instant John Schlesinger had agreed to direct it, but left to do *The Day of the Locust* instead. The director they had ended up with was a relative unknown, a young German named Morrison Groom. Mitchell Gibson was on the set, and Davis's girlfriend, and Beau. Everyone's expectations were low. They waded into the desert with too much script and too little story and a director whose experience amounted to a few episodes of *Laugh-In* and a documentary feature on Aboriginal songlines, with all the audience that implies. The weight of the movie, such as it was, sat on Davis's shoulders. Jeremy Vana climbed the steps of the star's Airstream trailer, the only one on the set.

"What the fuck is going on here?"

He squinted into the trailer's humid darkness. The windows were all taped up and the shades drawn. There were dim intimations of nudity, the smell of enclosed human sweat.

"Shut the door, Jer."

"Why in God's name?" It took him this long to see they were only meditating, the actors and Davis's eighteen-year-old girlfriend, who was also in the film. "Why are you just sitting here in your trailer?"

"Shhh." Bryce spoke. "Throw that cigarette away."

"Where's Morrison?" They were all shirtless. Even the girl, Li, who had a child's bony shoulders, her profile pert and pubescent-looking in the dark.

"How should we know? Cocksucker's crazy."

"He doesn't speak much English," Davis murmured.

"Your director *abandoned* you?"

"I wouldn't say abandoned. He'll be back."

"Where's Beau?" As he stooped in the doorway, Jeremy's eyes adjusted until he could see Li's face. She was Asian? Indian? In any case she was perfect, with skin so smooth it seemed like igneous rock, giving off neither heat nor moisture.

"He's with Mo," she said. "Both of them just went into town for groceries."

Mitchell squatted in the dirt outside. Supposedly "working on the script." Vana might as well have trusted a monkey with a typewriter, since all he ever seemed to do was write things up and then throw them away, barely stopping to read anything between. Fuck all these people. Jeremy turned. Li stuck out her tongue at his retreating back.

"We saved your life, Jerry! Never forget it!" Bryce called.

A spring-weight gray jacket was slung over his hand; he clutched a briefcase. He looked like a disappointed salesman. His tie dangled, fat as a parched animal's tongue. "It was fucking benign."

He left them alone after that. What was to be said? In the rocking calm, the roaring quiet of the desert, he'd let them sink their careers. And his, if need be.

"I got it!"

Beau sat up. He'd kidnapped the writer in hopes of forcing a little "inspiration," and here it was the eve of the scheduled first day of shooting. They were bunking at a wan motel in Flagstaff, Arizona—the *L* on the neon sign was out, delighting Mitchell to no end—and it was three o'clock in the morning. "What is it?"

A tap dripped. Beau's yellow bedspread was psychedelic Dacron hell. A wrecked crate of champagne, a congratulatory gift from Williams, lay underneath the writer's table. Mitchell sat by the window, gazing out at the buzzing pink sign.

"Come look." In front of him were an Olivetti and a bottle of Kahlúa. An array of index cards fanned across the table. "Just look at this."

Beau came over, in his underwear. A week was enough to grow used to Mitchell's midnight fancies. The writer was skinny and blond, with long hair and round glasses. He looked like a distaff John Lennon, feminized by twittering mannerisms.

"What if Udo steps up his pursuit at the beginning?"

"Huh?"

"We turn it around in the middle here. Look." Not gay, sexless. Mitchell was a strange cat. He pointed limply at one of the cards. "What if they meet Udo there, instead of where we had it? We'll put that other sequence up front."

"That doesn't make any sense."

"It would. It could. If. If—"

He had these incredibly long fingers, which he used now to shuffle the cards into an unfamiliar order. There were fifty-six of them, whittled down from ninety-four.

"See? See, Beau?" His voice was high and excitable. "If we do that, Udo suddenly has motive."

"Because the boys have kidnapped his sister."

"Right. Right!"

April '74. It had taken them two years to figure this out, and at 4:00 AM in this misbegotten motel opposite a Texaco station Mitchell began to type like a fiend. Beau stood beside him. He'd grown a beard, taken to smoking a pipe. He looked like a hobbit. Mitchell wore a white kurta with an embroidered neckline, bell-bottoms, and sandals. Their problems had no solutions, even if the movie cohered. Beau's hole of debt was so deep his fee could only allow him to break even. He went to the kitchenette and kissed the two pictures taped to the freezer's pebbly door.

"Ha!" Mitchell barked, keys rattling. "Fagstaff! Falstaff!"

Was it a sin to love the girl child better? Both Kate and Sev would be six in April. "You finally figured it out, huh Mitchell? Why not two years ago!"

A cockroach hurried across the floor by Beau's feet, monstrous, blurry. He'd last seen the kids three months ago, at a hearing held to reestablish his partial custody. Rachel had looked drawn and exhausted. Something was going on with her. She'd dropped a bunch of her clients, stopped returning his calls, was mute when Beau harassed her in the hall. *Why are you doing this, Rach? Why?*

Nothing would ever put things right.

"And—action!"

These words always sounded tinnier to Beau than expected, the clapper barely louder than a clipped fingernail. That they initiated his movie meant nothing. The studio paid him, as they were obligated to do upon commencement of principal photography. Beau stood with his hands in his pockets and watched. He wore an ascot and no shirt, mirrored sunglasses. Indeed, Beau Rosenwald had gotten weird. Udo Kier stood beside him, not needed for this scene in which the boys pulled up in their GTO. The first shot was a long view of the highway while the car, no bigger than a distant bird at first, arrived at last at a gas station that was the film's only "set." The brothers' names were Hector (Beller) and Hal (Davis). Li staffed the station's diner. She played the disputed sister, originally the boys' but now, according to Mitchell's rewrite, Udo's, a dusky sphinx whose silence mirrored that of the desert. The inside of the diner, which had been built in the gas station's former garage, looked like a Western saloon, its apparatuses all dating back to the end of the last century.

HECTOR
No fucking town with these here cows.

HAL
No fucking cows either.

The BOYS get out of the CAR.

HAL (CONT'D)
Let's pump ourselves some octane and split. Flagstaff's 150 miles.

Beau watched. Beside him Udo sucked in his breath. Even when he wasn't playing a vampire he resembled one, with his puffy cheeks and pouty lips. His looming presence intimidated everyone on the set.

HECTOR

I'm just gonna step in there and hit the can.

WIND. Hector takes three strides toward the diner and stops. The sign sways above him. He turns back to the GTO and pulls a machete out from under the seat.

HECTOR (CONT'D)

I might shave, too.

On it went. Mitchell's script was fathomless, yet apart from the shuddersome beginning and the end, not much happened. Morrison wanted to shoot the thing chronologically and then reshuffle the deck again—and again—in the editing room. He talked about releasing radically different cuts.

"That girl, she is ruining everything." Udo folded his arms across his chest. His *S*'s and digraphs hissed, *G*'s clinked like a true German's. "Beau—"

"Shh." The producer lifted his hand. Li walked out of the diner, dressed in her denim short shorts and gingham shirt. "We've waited for this long enough, Udo. Let's not screw it up ourselves."

Principal photography was done before Memorial Day. They shot altogether too much, as Morrison's melancholy Teutonic style met Mitchell's overlong script. The director called it an "Existential Road Western." Inside the movie's diner/saloon, people wore pocket watches and talked with rugged civility. It was Western like *Heaven's Gate* would be, not like Peckinpah. Outside, the gas station itself was a platform for violence. The two worlds didn't overlap. The rest of the material consisted of footage shot on the highway, and was mostly speed, solitude, pebble-kicking, and wind. Davis pissing against a cactus in silhouette. You could see his cock. Years later, Severin and I would watch it and find the film not transgressive but inscrutable. Too thoughtful to be awful, too drab to be anything else.

In June, Morrison Groom returned to Los Angeles and began his own process of assembling the rushes. So few people had been involved in the film's making, and fewer still had seen even a frame. From dailies, Beau could determine nearly nothing. Davis and Bryce had chemistry; there was that. The psychopath (Davis) comforted the shy brother (Bryce), which was another of Mitchell's sly reversals: that Davis played the killer instead of Bryce was a stroke of the unexpected. But what would happen was anybody's guess. The director took up residence in a post house in the Valley, a brown building on Ventura Boulevard that looked like a fifties apartment complex. It was half a mile from the Burbank gates and fully worlds away. Peter Konrad, Morrison's editor, was there too. Beau spent his afternoons on the couch, catnapping, and his evenings scrubbing his eye sockets with his fists while Morrison and Peter examined take after take after nearly identical take. Occasionally Beau would venture forth to give an ignored opinion, or would stagger across the wide, hissing stream of Ventura Boulevard to eat steak in an ancient chophouse. The two rooms were equally dark, the restaurant and the editing booth, and the one was distinguished by decrepit waitresses and shitty food while the other was lit by Udo Kier repeating, in variant Teutonic ways, the film's climactic line: *Not this head! This is the wrong fucking head!* After which the frame would appear to burn through and Morrison hoped to create a Möbius loop with sound, the word blurring with Bryce's pronouncement of the same during the first scene. Beau was tired. Sitting inside the Coach House with his martini, or in the editing booth, which was the only one occupied of the facility's three, he wasn't sure what kind of movie he'd made: good, bad, or—*and*, he supposed—indifferent, since it could've been all of these at once.

"This one."

"Zis one?" Morrison was German too, born Maurice Grumbach. "Peter, it's wrong. Udo steps on Davis's line—"

"Look where he is in the frame."

"Huh?"

Peter was Ukrainian, born in the same town, Berdychiv, as Beau's father.

"Just look. Here. It tracks better with the previous shot."

Beau lay on his back on the black velvet couch, pinned between Europeans, chest heaving with boredom. Someone had tacked a

Gunsmoke poster to the ceiling, James Arness pointing his pistol right in Beau's face. A low table held out-of-date, thumb-smudged issues of *Playboy* and *Variety* beside a Styrofoam cup of coffee that preceded their arrival. A solid skin had formed on top, furred with bluish mold.

"Huh."

"See?" Peter said. Greasy, bearded Peter, whose vegan diet some-times filled the booth with an intolerable stench. "There, right there, see how he enters from the right."

"Not this head! The wrong fucking head!"

"Christ, his reading's terrible."

"Doesn't matter. Look."

He hunched forward to indicate something, lank hair falling around his face. They worked on a Steenbeck flatbed. Morrison crowded in beside him. Cigarette smoke, too, filled the booth.

"So this one."

"Yeah," Peter said. "This one."

Morrison let out a dry cackle. Pudgy, short-armed, he wore his dark hair slicked back and round glasses just like Mitchell's; late-ly, he'd affected a Western shirt and bolo tie. He looked like a de-ranged game show host.

"I see. Yes."

Beau cleared his throat. Morrison turned.

"Does the producer haf an opinion?"

The two men hated one another by now. Looking over the tops of his glasses, Morrison was happy to play the cartoon German with Beau.

"None fit to print."

Amazing how all this went into the film too, how off-screen ten-sions were part of its texture. Udo's frozen, ravening glare filled the frame.

"I'm going home," Beau said. And the director and editor turned back to one another. The inscrutable image rested, still, between them.

The director settled on one cut, then the next. The studio had scheduled the film for release in November, yet no one there had seen a frame of it. Jeremy had turned his back in private, although he continued to enthuse about the movie to any *Variety* reporter who bothered to ask. Most didn't, and maybe Jeremy could bury this picture between successes. *Death Wish* was his, and *The Odessa File*, so who cared if the impossible German—*he'd* never make another studio movie, at least—fucked up a bit of inexpensive arthouse fluffcore? He'd written the production off from go. Beau moved back to his apartment, in a two-story building just south of Olympic. He couldn't live at Beller's forever. In the little efficiency unit, its gray carpet as mangy as a long-haired terrier's fur, he spoke on the phone with Rachel, begging, hectoring, pleading.

"Rach, please." Agent or no, this mode was his life. He leaned on the kitchenette's counter, bare arms pressing against Formica. "I just want to *see* them."

"I never said you couldn't."

"What?" Was his ex-wife losing her mind? "You said—"

"I worried about your influence." She sighed. "Come to New York."

"I can see them? What made you change your mind?"

Silence on the far end of the line. He thought of Morrison locking him out of the editing room, locking everyone out except Peter. You hostaged your treasure. Rachel knew that as well as anybody.

"I don't know. They need a father."

"Can I bring them out for a visit?"

Silence, again. This place had one bedroom and it was pristine, laid out just so. Beau slept on a mattress that drifted on the living room floor like a raft. There were piles of scripts, cartons of takeaway, voluminous white underwear drying stiff on the windowsill. A cracked piano, left by the last tenant who'd died intestate.

"All right," Rachel said at last. "For a weekend."

If he'd listened a little harder, perhaps, he'd have heard something else, a dislocation that had crept into her tone. But even when they were married and he'd felt she understood him, had she ever felt that way about him?

"Thank you." His kitchen window looked down at the courtyard's swimming pool, its surface spotted with brown leaves. Two elderly neighbors puttered crab-like around its kidney-shaped edges. "Thank you, Rach."

"How soon would you like to come get them?"

To what could he owe this volte-face? Did it matter? It was twilight, that hour when the Hasids began to walk along the avenues toward the synagogues on Fairfax, on Pico. Beau loved this time of day, the men in their wide hats dappling the street like blackbirds. His life's disorder suddenly seemed a form of joy. The bills, the un-read scripts, the letters from creditors, the greasy chopsticks jutting out of their cartons. Few people even knew he lived here. But when he came here to sleep, he plunked down on the mattress and let the room spin overhead. He'd stand out on the balcony, the nar-row terrace that circled this third floor of an eighteen-unit complex, and consider a swan dive to the concrete below, the mottled lip of the pool whose salted coping looked like pitted skin. This was his life. And in the midst of it he kept dreaming of order, imagining a way his kids would become part of it. The extra bedroom here was the only thing he looked after, twin pallets running under the two windows, the air sparkling while the rest of the place smelled like mildew and dirty socks and old food. It was a life fraught with cha-os no child could resist, and for a moment it seemed he'd already lived it, that the hours spent leaning over to watch Kate play "Tea for Two" beside him had, in fact, actually happened.

"Friday," he said, now, on the phone. "I'll come get them Friday."

V

BEAU PICKED THEM up at Rachel's apartment, standing out on the stoop while they filed past an unknown housekeeper to greet him. He hadn't had an unsupervised visit in three years. Both were so somber! A pair of serious six-year-olds who barely deigned to recognize him. Severin butted him with a shoulder, a half hug for a greeting, while Kate sat apart, staring out the cab window as they pulled away.

"Where are we going?"

"Los Angeles."

"Why?"

"Because I—I live there, remember? *Do* you remember?"

Shrugs. They rattled around in the backseat alongside him, headed for LaGuardia. Severin seemed preoccupied with a comic book he was carrying (*Fantastic Four* #45, "Among Us Hide the Inhumans!") along with a copy of *Huckleberry Finn*. Kate fiddled with her hair, dry and black as a horse's tail.

Beau looked at his son. "You're six years old and you're reading *Huckleberry Finn*?"

"Yep."

"You're your mother's."

Severin gazed at his lap. Kate leaned into Beau a little. He put his arm around her puffy parka. The twins wore identical ones, but otherwise had grown very much unalike. Severin's hair was clumpy, and he was thin like a carrot, and tufted on top. He wore horn-rimmed glasses, and sniffled as he stared down at his comic. Kate's face was wider, her large eyes a liquid green.

"You don't need those," he said. The cab raced toward the airport. "Where we're going you won't need jackets."

Severin kept his on. Underneath it was a shirt for his T-ball team, the Lions.

"You play baseball?"

He did. What position? Center field, just like Don Hahn, inexplicably his favorite player. Did Beau know Don Hahn hit the first inside-the-park home run ever at Veterans Stadium? Beau, no more a jock than he was an intellectual, just shook his head. Sev seemed to know a lot about the game, as he did about several things already at that age. Geography, for example, and dates. He was an avid consumer of almanacs. He had a strange obsession with Idi Amin.

"Did you know Amin was a boxer?"

"I—the Ugandan? Him?" Beau blinked at his son as they strode through the departure terminal, Kate having taken his hand and Severin lugging a little suitcase on rollers. "I did not know that, no."

"Yep. An athlete."

"Ah." Beau didn't know what to say. *Cool*? Was that what you said to a six-year-old lugging a cracked plastic suitcase who suddenly began talking about a military dictator? Beau knelt down.

"I'm not scary, you know."

Severin just looked at him. Again shrugged, like this wasn't the question he'd asked.

Kate thawed first. On the plane, she draped herself over his lap and fell asleep. They flew the old Pan Am. Severin peered out the window at the golden beds of clouds while Beau sat on the aisle, leaned his seat back and drank scotch while his daughter napped.

"The weather patterns are changing," Sev said.

Beau gave him a heavy-lidded, confidential stare. He had a strange son, was his thought, though God knew Sev's weirdness was beginning to grow on him. He'd have talked about Idi Amin all day if it meant he could stay sipping scotch with fifty-pound Kate dozing in his lap, while the cabin filled with afternoon light. His hand shook when he reached down to touch her cheek.

"So what do you like, besides genocidal maniacs and meteorology?"

Yet another shrug.

"Surely you must like something. Tom Sawyer. *The Inhumans*, there."

"The Beatles. I like the Beatles."

"It's a start."

"*Beatles for Sale* is my favorite."

"Really?" Another heavy, sidelong glance. "You're a weird kid, Sev."

"I like being a weird kid."

"I hated it. You want a soda?"

"Mom won't let us drink soda."

"You want some of this?"

"What is it?" Severin sniffed. "I don't think so, it smells like . . . like a doctor's office."

"You sure?" Beau pulled from the plastic cup, just plain scotch with a little ice. "It's good stuff."

"No, it's sting-y. It smells like it does when they give you a shot."

"Oh, OK." In his lap his daughter's chest rose and fell, rose and fell. "Sometimes I have bad ideas, you know? That was probably a bad idea, offering you liquor."

"It's all right." Severin cracked a smile.

"You won't tell your mother?"

"No." Smiling at him like a tiny adult, like this was what he'd wanted all along, to find the seam of his father's vulnerability.

"I never know," Beau muttered, "sometimes I just don't know. But I try, I try to do right."

He finished the rest of his scotch. Severin carefully tucked his comic book back into its glassine baggie. Beau closed his eyes and listened to it crinkling, even above the vast gasp of the plane.

It was the happiest weekend of his life. It was better even than being married, better than any dream he'd encountered. He and his children landed and he whisked them off to a derelict theater in the Marina where they were still showing *Sleeper* and *Bananas*, the same two movies over and over for nearly a year and a half. They went to Ships Coffee Shop, with its individual toaster in each booth, and built towers of cinnamon bread. On Sunday afternoon they went to Roxbury Park and played tag, then drifted around the city in a rented limousine. In his fridge were a jar of peanut butter and a gallon of milk, but it didn't matter how busted he was. They should have everything. On the red-eye back to New York they flew first class. Profligate, he watched them, their tiny bodies sprawled out, one on each side of him.

"I want to see *Freebie and the Bean*." Now they waited in the arrival terminal at LaGuardia, where Rachel was picking them up, and Severin petitioned his father to see a movie that wasn't due for several months, whose release had been pushed back.

"Nope."

"Why not?"

"Violence." Beau grunted. "I don't mind you seeing things that are over your head, but I do mind things that you shouldn't see at all."

"What about your movie?"

"Never. Not until you're an adult, Sev."

Kate sat in her purple skirt, thin for what was still winter in the city. A pair of sunglasses was propped atop her head. She was chewing Fruit Stripe gum and reading *Vogue*.

"Come on, guys, let's go meet your mother. Come on."

They didn't want to leave him. A single weekend wrought this impossible change. Severin clung to his stubby wrist, his thick paw, and Kate ambled along detached. Some plastic perfume she wore made her smell like a French courtesan.

"Daddy." She perched on the edge of the baggage carousel, arms outstretched.

"Yep?"

"Don't leave."

He kissed Severin's cheek. The early issues of *The Inhumans*, which he'd tracked down at a comic shop in Santa Monica, were tucked under his son's arm now as well.

"I'll be back," he said.

Rachel startled him. He hadn't seen her in a year and a half, and her head was shaved like a Krishna's. She was skinnier even than she'd been and looked luminously unwell. He studied the sinews on her neck, the skeletal tilt of her head.

"Have you gotten to a nunnery?"

He'd wondered for an instant if she was sick, but he could see as she drew closer across the concourse floor that her physical health was fine.

"Have you discovered women? I could've told you before we were married and saved you a lot of aggravation." He gave an ingratiating smile. He was never less charming than when he was trying for charm, never more boorish or coarse.

"Thank you for bringing them back on time."

Her voice hadn't changed, at least. It was still flat, imperious, and annoying.

"You wanna have coffee?" he said.

"I'm fasting."

So they sat in the terminal and she had hot water while he ate a Danish and the kids flocked around them both. The novelty!

"Did you guys have a good time?"

They nodded, mute in the airport's drab and timeless light. In their mother's presence, they became shy before their father again. Kate sucked her thumb.

"They had a good time. I had a good time. I really want to do it again."

"Do it twice a month if you'd like. I'll adhere to the original agreement."

Beau eyed her. "What is this?"

She sighed. There was something she wasn't telling.

"How's business?" he said.

She wore a floral-print skirt and a leather jacket, looked like some sort of acid-punk hybrid, one part downtown while the other might've been milking cows in the Berkshires.

"All right," she sighed. "But I'm sick of it."

"You're still selling health books?"

Her head swung up and down. He thought her narrow neck might snap.

"What's wrong with that?" he asked. "It's a living."

"I'm tired of selling. Don't you ever feel that way?"

Beau wondered what her clients thought of her, the ones she'd kept from the days when she was quietly ruthless, with the neutral aggression that was the one thing they'd shared, before children.

"I don't know that this is what I'm meant to be doing with my life."

"'Meant to be'? Isn't that a little fanciful?" He wanted to say, *I don't know that I'm meant to be living in a senior citizens' apartment complex, pumped full of anxiety medication and drowning in debt.* "You do what's in front of you."

"That's such a retrograde idea."

"Retrograde?" He smiled. "Isn't that another one of your planet things?"

Severin sat beside them engrossed in his *Inhumans*. Kate was walking around now with her hot chocolate, orbiting them at a medium distance. They were both such dreamy children.

"You can make fun of it all you want—"

"I'm not making fun of it, Rach."

"There's talk of the stars in Shakespeare."

"I wouldn't know."

"There is, there's plenty of superstition in Shakespeare."

"OK." He didn't want the kids to see their parents fighting. "I was just teasing. I know you meant it differently. I don't believe in fate, is all."

"Fate?" For a moment she seemed the old Rachel, ironic and sharp. "What do you think brought us together?"

She stood up. He met the pale gray difficulty of her gaze.

"Two weeks," he said. Then kissed Sev and Kate goodbye. "I'll see you."

He watched them go. This trip had pretty much decimated him. *Next stop, debtors' prison.* Except these kids belonged to him now. He would never be free, and never want to be. Now he knew, at last, what it was to be a man.

Beau borrowed some more money from Williams, who wouldn't dream of asking his friend to repay what he'd already borrowed. *They're your children, Beau. Whatever it takes.* He didn't say it, but Beau felt almost that his kids were in Will's care, too, that his friend would do anything for him, for them. He never forgot it. From Davis, he chiseled two thousand dollars; from Bryce, something similar. I believe Teddy Sanders loaned him a few bucks, too. Being an adult didn't require nobility. Being a man was an emanation of love.

Every other weekend in the autumn of '74, he flew to New York. Every fourth, he brought the kids back to Los Angeles. It cost a fortune, but so what? Soon, he would raise the idea that was gnawing at him, the notion that they should—might—come to LA to live for a bit. Maybe just for a year. Maybe Rachel would let them reverse their terms, allow Beau primary custody for a while. Things she said seemed to point in that direction. *They always come home happy after they see you. Maybe it's good for them to spend more time there.* She seemed preoccupied, more remote all the time.

"Hey Rosers, whatcha thinking?"

Beau sat with his feet in the surf, chair pulled close to the edge of the water, out at Beller's house in Malibu. A stack of scripts in his lap, a pile behind him in the sand. A soft yellow hat shaded his eyes, and sunglasses sat low on his zinc-spotted nose.

"Hey?"

"I've never seen you read like this before. What's crawled up your ass?"

Bryce stood on the wooden steps behind him, the ones that led up the terraced garden. There was that whiff of rotting seaweed, the oystery freshness of ocean air.

"We need something," Beau said. "This picture's coming out in two months—"

"So why worry?"

"I don't have anything on deck. And this Kraut cocksucker won't even show me the movie."

"You're worried." Bryce tossed a small pink Spalding up into the air and caught it. "Things work out."

"That's easy for you to say."

"It is. Because it's true."

Bryce leaned against the rickety rail that ran along the stairs. He'd been meditating in his shed. His torso was glossed with sweat while he stared off at the Pacific. That shed was like a sauna. From where he sat on the sand Beau could sometimes hear him playing music in there, cassettes he'd made of Gregorian chants or else one that he had from his nearby neighbor, Brian Wilson himself, of a song that had something to do with the child being father of the man.

"You sound like my ex-wife," Beau said.

"I am your ex-wife," Bryce snickered. "You know you've always been the only one."

He aimed his stallion body up the stairs, naked except for a pair of running shorts. "We gotta get your mind off this."

He vanished into the garden, past the ice plants and tiny cacti that grew on the bottom level. A chill wind kicked up off the water, ruffling the script in Beau's lap. Ambition was the bug that had bitten him. When he was younger there had been an impulse to do things, to spend money and impress girls. He'd wanted to lay hands on the trappings of success, because he'd imagined these would make him happy. This was different. It was a need to *become* something, to increase not just his holdings but his name.

Bryce had just done another Western, with Keith Carradine and Peter Fonda. Whereas Beau hadn't found a single thing in the months he'd spent reading and being distracted by his kids, not one solitary script. The more he read, the less he liked.

"Hey!" Bryce was coming down the stairs, carrying a small stack of Frisbees. "Wanna shoot?"

Beau stretched. "Now?"

"Why not? It's Tuesday."

"All right." Beau heaved himself out of his chair, bending backward, almost, while he gripped the aluminum rests and pushed. "It's better than this lasagna."

Bryce lobbed him the Frisbees, one by one at his feet. The script, this "lasagna," fell onto the sand. Beau picked up a Frisbee and waited while Bryce loaded his pistol, that Smith & Wesson he loved so much he all but slept with it. He kissed the barrel.

"Ready Rosers?" Beau nodded. "All right, PULL!"

Beau torqued and flung the Frisbee up and out over the ocean. Bryce shot at it and missed.

"Ah, fudgsicles."

They'd taken to cursing this way because of their children. Bryce's son was here more often too, and the few times Beau had brought Severin and Kate over he'd been careful to lecture the actor about staying clothed, cleaning the weed off the table.

"PULL!"

Bryce clipped the edge off a Frisbee this time.

"PULL!"

Bryce drilled it.

"PULL!"

They lived exactly as they wanted. Beau twisted and threw disc after disc over the ocean. They ordered Frisbees by the boxful, and by the time the cops came usually the gun was buried safely under the house. *Don't know what you're talking about, officer. We didn't hear anything.*

"PULL!"

After a pause Beau spoke again. "Brycie, we're out."

Their voices carried out over the water, above the whitening lull of the surf.

"Wait, hang on a second." Beau scurried over to his chair and returned. "OK, now this."

"What? That?"

"Yeah. It's no good anyway!"

Their laughter wheeled up and out above the waves, like gulls. Nothing would kill it, or them. He turned and flung the script up, twisting around and letting go like a discus thrower, while Bryce Beller aimed and fired low and shot a bullet straight through the plain brown regulation agency cover, right into the heart of the heart of the story.

VI

"ROSIE, WAKE UP! We gotta get to the airport!"

Beau lifted his head. Bryce was standing at the foot of the couch in the living room, while Beau was prone on his palms like a lizard. Everything ached. There was pain in his skull, a rawness in his cheek as if someone had punched it.

"What the hell time is it?"

"Three thirty."

He moved his jaw, which felt dislocated. *Fucking tequila and sleeping pills.* "When are we due at the studio?"

"Seven thirty. Your kids get in at four fifteen."

Beau rolled off the pull-out, rubbing his bristly jaw. He dragged the sheet around his waist like a toga, found himself decorated with red greasepaint of some kind. He saw it on the backs of his hands.

"The hell is this?"

He bent to pick up his socks and underwear. Once more, he couldn't go home, was being hassled there by creditors. A repo guy had tried to take his car.

"We thought it'd be fun to make you up as an Injun."

"We?" Beau coughed. He couldn't even remember who had been here last night, what wastrels—men in their early thirties at least—had cut open a pillow and doused him with fluff, little fragments of feathers that fluttered now as he brushed himself off. "Goddamn Skobs, with his chicken jokes."

He padded around the glass coffee table, trotted into the next room to brush his teeth and wash his face before—fuck it. The kids would take it for sunburn, for just another dash of normal insanity. He dried his hands and strode across the living room.

"You understand women, Brycie?"

His children were coming, for an indefinite visit this time. They were going to switch schools, starting next week, and then they'd simply see what happened. He'd have them at least through the school year. Rachel had caved!

"Do I look like a guy who understands women?" Bryce shook his head. "You're the one wearing makeup."

But here they were. Rachel's voice rang in his ears. *I suppose they could do with some more of you, Beau, and I suppose I could use a little time to myself, too.* Enigmatic as ever. Time to herself, how? Agenting wasn't for introverts. And Bryce had his own problems with his ex, anyway. No matter: in less than an hour, they were picking up Beau's kids at the airport. Then, as a group they would head to the studio, where Morrison Groom was finally willing to screen *The Dog's Tail*. The adults would watch and the kids would have a sitter and some ice cream. Beau stepped into a pair of slacks, broad as a sloughed shower curtain.

"I'm the one wearing the pants," Beau said. "I'm king of all I survey."

"Who do we blame if it's a turkey?"

Bryce laughed. "Everyone except ourselves."

"The studio. Blame fucking Vana."

They were sliding into Beau's '65 Cadillac, the enormous white boat with a ragged drop top that was the only vehicle big enough to accommodate them and the kids.

"Fucking Vana. He has a piece of this. Morrison."

"Morrison!" Beau turned the key in the ignition. "Why did we hire that guy?"

"We would've hired anyone. I think he was the only director left in the shed."

They pulled out of the garage and onto the street, the dusty access road that connected the beach to the Pacific Coast Highway above it. Beau had streaks of red across his face. His thin dark beard had golden highlights. There was no gray in his hair yet, and he looked exactly as he was: barely middle-aged and secretly prosperous, dripping with time. He still wore the expensive watch, and his laugh rang clean and untormented.

"We'll have to blame it on somebody." He drove with one hand, feeding them onto the PCH. "Not you, of course. You're blameless as a newborn, Brycie."

"Give us a kiss."

"Seriously. A movie is a system, and you have to blame someone when it breaks down. Just like a mechanic, who tells you it's the carburetor. So who do you blame?"

"Yourself?"

"Fuck it," Beau muttered. "Udo. Let's blame him."

Their speech fluttered above the highway, their laughter ending in hysteric coughing this time. *Udo!* The one person who was truly without fault here, as his performance was exactly what they'd contracted it to be—if "performance" it truly was, if he wasn't in fact simply being German. They hit every light before they reached the 405, Bryce's cassette tape of hillbilly gospel—the Stanley Brothers, the Louvins—blaring. There was no blame. Any real failure was still in front of them. The tape flipped, off a ragged track called "How Many Times Have You Bypassed Salvation?" and began playing the soundtrack to *Pat Garrett & Billy the Kid*. They found Kate and Sev standing at the terminal's curb.

"Daddy!" How Kate had flowered! She crawled over Bryce to get to him, piled into the front seat while Severin tumbled into the back. "Are we staying at your apartment?"

"Nah. In Malibu."

Sev mussed his father's hair from the backseat. Kate nestled between Beau and Bryce. He stuck the car back into gear. There were no plans, no contingencies in place. They'd merely affix to him, as part of an ongoing slumber party.

"What's happening, Sev? Face front, true believer!"

The car jerked forward. Bryce had grown a mustache, slicked his hair short in preparation to play a gentleman oil prospector. Brilliantine gleamed in twilight. His posture, too, had a nineteenth-century strangeness and charm.

"Where am I going to school?"

"You're worried about school? Take it easy, kid, and give your dad a hug first."

Sev clasped Beau's neck with his forearm. Figures this would be his first concern, before even "hello."

"Public, this fall. I'm gonna see about getting you into St. Jerome."

"What's that?"

"Private. Episcopal," Beau said. His friends' kids went there: Williams's, Teddy's. One of those funky Santa Monica enclaves where tradition met progressive ideology. "You'll love it."

"Sounds great, Dad." Even then, Beau never knew when Severin was being sarcastic.

"Hey, Sev, you know who owned this car? It belonged to Montgomery Clift, the actor."

"Who?"

The tape deck played Bob Dylan, a song that was just a sloppy, repetitive shanty. *Rock me mama, like a wagon wheel.*

"Hey Severin, you know what this car really is?" Bryce turned so he could be in on the game. "It's Rocinante, Don Quixote's nag."

"Don Quixote?" Severin was skeptical. "I don't think that's true."

"He knows Don Quixote, not Monty Clift?" Beau roared. "Severin, you are your mother's!"

But he wasn't, not then. Nor was Kate, leaning in the crook of her father's arm, hair smelling of lemongrass or wheatstraw as she gripped his body with hers, adhering. The sky was lilac, the soft-brushed color of six o'clock. By the time they reached the lot it was proper twilight, all of them stumbling out of the car in a daze of wind and travel. Down the lot's alleys, past the hangar-like sound-stages and warehouses.

"Let's go, let's go!" Bryce's voice echoed as he called for the kids to follow.

"Why?" Severin said. "It's not like we're going to be allowed to watch."

They sounded innocent, *felt* innocent, as if they were merely witnesses and not the film's perpetrators. Outside the screening room they ate chicken piccata and lobster salad off paper plates, drank Chablis from paper cups. Morrison was late, and he arrived dragging the film's second reel in a canister.

"Morrison." Jeremy stuck out his palm, and Beau was reminded why he liked Vana, the fact that he never held a grudge in a town filled with Sicilian temperament. But the director just brushed by him.

"Let's get this thing started, eh? Let's see what you people make of my fucking masterpiece."

He was drunk, maybe. Why were directors, to a man, such cowboys? Little Morrison, tottering there in his boots.

"Wanna get tight with a dictator, kid?" Beau leaned over and whispered to his son. "Mo there's your man."

He folded his paper plate and tossed the last of his lobster salad into the garbage.

"Please, Dad?" Sev said. "Can I watch?"

"No."

If only he could hold other lines as firmly as he held this one. The teenage sitter he'd hired led Severin away.

"Come on, let's get some dessert."

The rest of the cast had already filed into the screening room, except for Udo the no-show. He'd cut bait the last day of shooting. Sam was absent too, not even bothering to guard the hen house in this case, perhaps attending to some other client's catastrophe. Beau took a seat up front beside Vana. Li slid in on the studio exec's other side.

"Hey, Jer," Beau whispered. He eyed the actress, as girlishly inscrutable as ever while she worked on a red lollipop. "Why don't you ask Sue Lyon there to move into your lap?"

The executive shifted uncomfortably. Beau chortled. There were barely a dozen of them, in a room that could've sat forty. Bryce sat in the back with Davis, whose eight-year-old son, Rufus, dozed across his lap. Jeremy's boss sat by the star also. The studio chief and the star would always be buddies, never mind that the president was thirty years older and they had nothing in common. If it failed, these two men would walk away without a scratch.

The projector whirred, and light hit the screen. The studio boss, who reminded Beau of Waxmorton, moneyed and gray and doughy and intelligent, coughed. The movie unreeled in front of them.

"It isn't that bad," Beau whispered.

"It isn't about bad." Jeremy wouldn't look at him. "We can't make movies like this and survive."

Li had her hand on his leg, Beau noticed. But Jeremy had a point. This was a plotless road epic, a few years past the prime of such things in this country. Beau saw plainly: the movie wasn't *bad*. The

violence was a little gratuitous—beyond Penn and Peckinpah—but
these moments only punctuated the film's melancholy stasis. It
made sense to Beau. Life, or at least *his* life, was like this. Stillness,
torn by pornography.

"Bah," Morrison muttered. "Fucking suits." *Focking zoots*. Davis
and Bryce burst out laughing.

Beau would never make a movie like this again. He knew that.
His sensibilities were too vulgar, too crassly in line, really, with
Waxmorton and Sam and even Davis, who by the end of the decade would be playing rascally rum runners and smug Southern
cops. The film ended on Udo's howl and Li's head toppling across
the sand, the appalling shot Beau had seen a thousand times before.
The head looked real, unlike those gloppy Polynesian-seeming fak-
eries you saw in midnight horror movies. And then the lights came
up and there was a clumsy silence.

"Was that you?" Beau glanced over his shoulder finally at Davis.
"Or was it a stunt cock?"

Davis grinned sheepishly. A silhouetted glimpse of his penis
might've been the movie's best commercial hope. Bryce had already scampered from the room, while the studio head looked miserable. Glowering from the depths of his chair like a constipated
king.

"Nice work, Mo," Beau called across the room. "I mean that."

The director glared. Praise was less fun than provocation.

Beau rubbed his hands vigorously. "Just wait'll people get a look
at this!"

Light dropped from the ceiling, the aspic glow of small theaters,
where you could read the feelings on every face in the room. The
boss's despondent expression finally resolved into something sharper.

"They won't."

"What?" Beau tried to keep his tone airy. "What are you talking
about?"

"We're not releasing it."

Beau felt in his chest that terrible constriction, that feeling that
had led him, once, to do something stupid and rash. He fought it
down now, or at least his medication did.

"You can't." He moved toward the executive's chair and the man
recoiled slightly. "Please."

"Are you begging me?" He certainly enjoyed this part. "Are you begging me to release it?"

"No."

He had a silver pompadour and a blue oxford shirt, a thick red tie with a Windsor knot. The guy's face was a beveled rectangle, he looked—as Severin would've seen it—like a Jack Kirby drawing, with three distinct sides to his chin. His loafer sat on top of his knee and he jiggled it slightly.

"You do what you have to," Beau said. "I'm just saying there's an audience for this movie."

"Who?"

Beau faltered. "In Europe. On college campuses there are kids who—"

"Who what?" The look on the studio head's face said it all. "Who can't sleep?"

It wasn't the first time, nor would it be the last, that Beau had problems with this sort of authority. But now he just stalked out of the screening room. He'd learned at least a partial lesson. Severin and Kate were waiting in the lobby.

"How was the movie, Dad?"

"I liked it."

"When's it coming out?"

What would he do? Davis DeLong stood by himself, pacing in stupid circles. Vana and Li clustered by the buffet table. Jeremy drained the dregs of a bottle of zinfandel. Bryce hung back in a corner. The studio wouldn't hang the film's failure on any of their shoulders, what was such a *fakakta* idea to begin with. Who, then? Morrison? Forget about it, that guy's future was teaching film studies at Cal State San Diego, his exile was already assured. *When's it coming out?*

"Someday," Beau said.

He was fucked. His kids had been dumped in his lap, and he had nothing. He moved to the buffet table to pick at the scraps, as if to get all the free food he could before the world ended.

"Someday when?" Severin followed him.

Beau gulped a glass of water, shoveled a whole swatch of cold chicken piccata, pounded flat, into his mouth. He shivered with the need for release—vocal, esophageal, bowel—but none was forthcoming.

The studio boss darted out of the screening room and went right for him.

"You fat fuck! This is all your fault!"

"Not in front of my kids." Beau put down his plate. His hands shook.

"You bring me a piece of shit like that and you're worried about the ratings board when *I* talk?"

"Behave yourself, little man."

You. The boss didn't have to say it. Somehow, he pinned the whole failure on Beau, who had an opportunity to throw one of the others under the bus. All of them may have deserved it more than he did. But he just let his hand fall onto Sev's head. The top of his son's scalp was warm.

"Come on." Three years of his life were gone, but who cared when you had what mattered more? He looked across the lobby at Kate. "Sweetheart, let's go."

VII

"HEY NATHANIEL! NATE! Nice jump shot." Williams Farquarsen hung against the fence of our school playground, watching Little Will and me play basketball. "Good hustle."

He drew his son aside. "You all right?"

Little Will gulped air. He went all out, as he would doing other things, later. Neither of us was particularly athletic. Kickball, hand-ball, the other competitive sports that swept our elementary school playground weren't our beat. We were good students, both, bonded since kindergarten. I was into reading and language arts, whereas Little Will was more of a math geek. But he was already wild and graceful. He didn't look much like his dad—olive-skinned and blond-haired, he was more like Marnie—but he had a little of Williams's chilly fire.

"Suck it up, suck it up. No water yet. Go on."

He wanted his son tough, disciplined. He treated us hard, like little adults. The only softness I saw in my friend's father was at home, when I slept over at their place in the Marina. When I watched Williams with his wife, he was almost a different person: solicitous, tender. But after school, when he made Little Will and me play basketball—Teddy didn't think it was a bad idea for me either—I gleaned what he might've been like at work. Driven by something too cool to be ruthlessness, that lacked even that much passion.

"C'mon." He taught us spin moves, a relentless dribble, taught us to heave shots at a low-hanging hoop. He made us run laps, our bodies flopping like puppets as we skittered around the yard.

He was unexpectedly athletic himself; it turned out Williams was a surfer—had been since the mid-sixties. While Beau was reeling in the wake of his failure, drummed into a retreat from which it seemed there would be no easy comeback—it was one thing to antagonize an agent on the decline and quite another to piss off the corporate head of a studio: this was a problem even Williams Farquarsen couldn't help him with—my friend and I were gasping, wheezing, skinning our little knees and palms on the playground in back of St. Jerome. "Nate, take the charge. Will, you go after him. Hard. No man plays except to win. Come on!"

No man plays except to win. Over and over he said this. I suppose it was part of the philosophy that would guide him, with which he would later marshal his troops to greatness. We took it to heart.

"OK, OK." After an hour or so, he'd call it off. We did this a couple of times each week, until we collapsed into the backseat of his car and he drove us home, gasping, parched. It was unusual, but then Will's dedication to his family life was also that. He never did do the reckless things my father had and would. "You want some of this, Nate?"

He handed me a thermos of cold water. At the other end of the playground a clutch of older kids, sixth graders, played catch and made horizontal forays on primitive, clay-wheeled skateboards. How that world was about to change. We were in one of our own, at the far end with the kiddie hoop and its one tattered net. Williams, in a pale gray sweatshirt, cuffed my neck.

"There you go. It's good for you." He meant the water, the exercise. Those humid afternoons in the spring of '75, sunlight pushing through afternoon fog to paint the bricks around the playground yellow. Girls skipped rope; a transistor radio, belonging to one of the teachers, played Minnie Riperton's "Lovin' You," Elton John's "Philadelphia Freedom." "I'll give you a ride home, Nate, but I have to stop and pick something up first."

"OK."

We waited in the car, a Peugeot that smelled of trapped air and sweat, a sweetness of beach debris, while he stopped in front of a law office and ran inside. We had no idea what he was doing, there at Albrecht Ellis Associates—a small firm, one of those sleepy little businesses in Santa Monica that would've had no truck with people in the industry, which is exactly what Williams needed—we didn't know anything, or care. We sat there panting, fiddling with the radio dial, shoving and jostling. Little Will pointed at my leg.

"Look."

Blood ran down my calf. He wrinkled his nose and snorted. I did too. I didn't feel anything. The car door opened and Williams ducked back in. He threw a manila folder on the passenger seat.

"What are you boys up to?"

We fell into the back, and I looked down to where I'd cut my knee. Williams's eyebrows lifted a little.

"Did you hurt yourself?"

I wouldn't forget this moment. Who's to say why? A little scraped skin in a childhood full of it, the pink and pale flesh mixed with the black gum of asphalt and the bright red of my blood. Maybe it was the way it didn't hurt until someone pointed at it, or how the elder Williams's face—he had such delicate features, little buttons of sclera and bone—opened up in raw curiosity. He wasn't like other fathers. There was something missing, but also something extra.

"D'you need a bandage, Nate? Let's get you one."

Right before he ducked back out to go retrieve the first aid kit that rattled around in the trunk, Bactine and Band-Aids in a white plastic box, right before I burst into tears, I saw it. Williams's eyes flashed green, his pale lips tugged down at the corners. A wince or a grimace that was nothing like Beau, the fat man I automatically, if not yet consciously, associated with him. It was a terrible expression, small and involuntary: in it were fear and hunger, and some private pain that must've mirrored my own, else I would never have noticed it.

Traffic washed along Wilshire Boulevard, behind him. The yellow air drifted and eddied, with traces of fog and exhaust. Little Will kicked the seat, restlessly, and if either of us had been old enough to open our eyes and stir from our childhood's sleep—*What was in the folder Williams had just retrieved? If I had to guess, it was paperwork surrounding an incorporation: he must've been laying his groundwork early, for what else would he have been doing visiting a sleepy little law office like this one? He wasn't going to divorce his wife, and TAG had its own lawyers, for deals*—if we'd been able to do this, what else might we have seen?

Williams turned and circled around to the trunk. Just another
Hollywood father, too, playing hooky for an afternoon. Little Will
shoved me. *Junior shark*. We weren't too young to be turned on by
blood. Just so, I burst out screaming, the need for attention dawn-
ing in my consciousness at last.

VIII

"Huh?" The man in the black-and-white shirt looked him over as Beau inhaled. That smell of polish and plastic. "I'm sorry, you don't really look like someone who—"

"Beau Rosenwald." At his weakest, my father always fell back on his name. "I made movies. I was a talent agent."

"This is a sporting-goods store."

"You think it's easier to sell actors than shoes?"

Beau's face flamed. *Imagine* what this was like! They were in a store on Wilshire Boulevard in Santa Monica, Beau having cornered the manager over by a rack of orange skis. K2, Kneissl. This was how fast you could fall in Hollywood, no matter that you were already near the bottom to begin with. Just days ago he was toe-to-toe with a studio head. Now he was shivering, quavering before some schlub with Bozo tufts.

"I know more than you think," Beau said. "Sizing, soles. I used to work in my father's shop in Queens."

The manager was jug-eared, tiny, and balding. His name tag read IRV.

"You wanna fill out an application?"

"You think I should?"

Strange, that beneath his shame, Beau Rosenwald felt peaceful. He'd gone home from the screening last night and slept better than he had in years. In time—sure—the movie would sneak out anyway. Morrison would buy back the negatives and screen it around town, then with Vana's help they'd be able to find a distributor and show it in New York, Chicago, Montreal. They'd tone down the violence, and so the whole thing might become what it perhaps was always meant to be, a semi-interesting cult movie designed to appeal to distant obsessives. Maybe all Beau did then was submit to fate, there in the side room of Tex's Sporting Goods. As the excruciation of the moment peaked and then subsided. *Shoes.*

The manager looked him up and down. "Get a vest."

Hired on the spot, he'd go back to his roots and flog sneakers. This was a comprehensive admission of defeat. Yet it was also oddly satisfying. The fat man, hustling in middle age. He had become what everyone else wanted him to be, had fulfilled some prediction of his failure. This was what it was like, *not* to be the hero of your own story. Shuffling from stool to storeroom over and over, opening those boxes—size ten, or ten and a half—and removing the shoes from their bundles of tissue paper and lacing them up while he knelt and looked at the toes. *How's that feel?* Every box smelled new. Dripping flop sweat, his skin felt buttery as a calf's. Day in, day out, for three months, five. One afternoon a kid came in and cornered him.

"You were in that movie, weren't you? With Davis DeLong?"

He'd had one line in the picture, played a trooper Udo shot and left for dead at the roadside.

"Uh-uh."

"Yes, you were. Morrison Groom's film. They just showed it to us at AFI. He spoke to our class." Oh, for God's sake. There was an enthusiast for everything. "I never forget a face."

Beau had forgotten his own face. He said, "Nope."

The twins were in public school. Sev and Kate had lived with him at Bryce's for a while, and then Beau had moved to Santa Monica, closer to his job and his benefactor, who continued to live his off-the-track, bohemian, and domestic life in the Marina. Williams had offered to help with the twins' private school tuition if Beau wanted them to go to St. Jerome. That's how good the man was to his friend.

"Beau?" The phone rang at work, in the afternoon. He picked it up and found his voice recognized straightaway.

"Yep?"

"It's Davis."

He was standing on the floor at Tex's. Wearing his own referee's shirt and a TEXAS LONGHORNS cap, looking less like anyone who had ever been in the movie business than you can imagine. Like a fucking zebra, stranded there against the store's puffy neoprene jackets and jumpers.

"Davis!" The actor had quickly recovered from their debacle and would soon receive a nod for best supporting in a picture he'd just shot opposite Gene Hackman. While Beau was repricing all the skis and hanging out new wetsuits, accommodating the change of season in April. "How'd you find me?"

"Through Beller." There was a sound as if he were chewing tobacco, juice flowing down the line. "You're selling shoes, now?"

Beau didn't say anything. Just stood with his name tag and his whistle around his neck and rubbed his chin. The full ridiculousness of his situation had never hit him, or else it hadn't existed until an actor, a man who tried on and discarded selves like a hyperimaginative three-year-old, pointed it out.

"I want you to represent me."

"What?" Surely this was a joke, fate rubbing his nose in the wet plate of failure.

"I'm unhappy with Sam. There's a picture I'm wanting to do at Columbia and he's trying to talk me out of it."

"You don't think you should listen this time?" Beau laughed.

"No. Look, Beau, I need *your* advocacy."

"Why me?" Not for the last time, Beau asked this question. "Why d'you want me?"

"I need a new agent."

"I'm inactive. Haven't had a client since '72."

"So?"

"Conflict of interest. I'm a producer. I can't be an agent *and* a producer."

"Why not? Have you seen any money beyond your original fee?"

Beau leaned against the glass display case, next to the register. He stared down at jackknives, bandannas, pins for different ski resorts—Alta, Whistler, Mammoth—and thick tubes of Bonne Belle lip gloss. Kate loved it when he brought those home.

"Not a dime."

"So represent me. You'll sign a waiver, resign from the guild. Whatever it is you have to do."

"Why me? Davis, you could have anybody."

"Why not you?" Davis said. "You're Hollywood's last honest man."

Beau rubbed his forehead and stared down, down, down into the case. Root beer was Kate's favorite flavor, then bubble gum, cherry. He was perspiring, he suddenly realized, his face not just damp but dripping. Was it the thought of a lifetime selling shoes that frightened him, or this other life, in show biz, that scared him half to death?

"Columbia won't negotiate with me."

"Hmm?"

His boss swung by and clipped him on the shoulder. *Back to work, Rosenwald.*

"You said Columbia. They won't negotiate with me even if I offer you to them for nothing."

"Not true."

"Why not?"

"Vana's in charge now. Haven't you heard?"

Over and over, he'd play this moment in his head. For years there would be nightmares in which he found himself menaced inside Tex's yellow thicket, clutching an unloaded BB gun against the threat that had already passed. If only, if only, if only he'd said no. Would the rest of his life have been different? Would he have saved himself the greatest tragedy of all? But what he felt when he hung up the phone was a surge of ecstasy so violent he might've exploded.

"Beau, we need you—"

"Fuck you." He yanked the phone free of its rickety wall brackets and tossed it onto the floor. His jug-eared boss just stared at him in amazement. "Fuck you, Irv. Nothing personal." He flung the cap, name tag, whistle behind the register, plunked down ten bucks, and took a fistful of lip gloss. "I've got places to be."

"You're quitting?"

Of course, Irv was a screenwriter, not a very good one, and Beau had shown him the courtesy of reading his work.

"I'm gone, Irv. In fact, if anyone asks, it's safe to say I was never here."

This was all it took to transform a life. Beau drove home from the store and picked up his kids and, later that night, took them both to

Ma Maison for dinner. *Hungry, guys?* If Kate wanted to eat fresh berries and pastry cream until she was blue in the face, she could, always.

He bought a car, even before he placed a call to open negotiation. He was that confident.

"Jer, it's Rosers."

"Beau!" Jeremy sounded transformed, weightless with power, himself. "Good God, man, it's great to hear from you."

"Yeah. Listen, Davis is going to do this movie and you're going to pay him more than you've ever paid an actor in your life."

"That's an interesting gambit, Beau. You're supposed to play hard to get."

"Fuck hard to get." Through the sliding–glass window of his two-bedroom apartment in Santa Monica he could see the grass square of a park on Lincoln, his new silver Jag gleaming in the sun. It still had the tags on it. "You'll pay through the nose."

"I dunno, buddy. Davis's new movie isn't doing too well. The last one, you'll recall, wasn't even released by this studio."

"So what?" He looked out at the park, its semiderelict benches and statuary. This apartment was like the one on Sherbourne, too: humid with the sour smells of incontinence and chicken broth, the sound of hissing pipes. He'd take one of those houses on the other side of Montana soon, too.

"*So what*?" Jeremy snorted. "What else is an actor's value based upon but past performance?"

Beau leaned back in his chair. The wrecked bedroom was also his "office." "The future."

"Hey? I don't get you, buddy. You can't possibly pay an actor based on what his agent thinks he *will* be worth. That's suicide."

"How come? You think you can get him on the cheap the way you used to?"

How he loved negotiating. Hated business, but loved negotiating. It wasn't closing the deal but creating it. This was the thing he loved.

"No, no. But there's a middle ground here. You don't even have a second client."

"A million bucks."

"WHAT?"

"Yep." Beau snickered. "That's what you're going to pay, Jer."

"That's nuts."

"It's *fair*. Think of what our movie did for you."

"It nearly ended my career."

"It didn't. It kicked you upstairs. I've been selling shoes."

"Is that where you've been?"

"Yes. Your wife bought a nice pair of Rossignols there, a few weeks ago."

"Ex-wife."

"Oh, Jer, I'm sorry. When did that happen?"

"Not long. Listen, there's no way I'm giving Davis a million dollars. Melissa's breaking my balls. Don't you do it too."

"Do I have to?" Beau smiled, and as always his expansiveness surged down the line, his warmth and desperation making themselves felt as surely as if he were in the room with Jeremy. "Sounds like they're already broken."

Beau didn't have to mention how he'd once spared the executive blame before his boss. Davis DeLong would get his million dollars. In bicentennial America, this was still a fortune. Ex-wives, ski trips ("Maybe if you hadn't fucked Davis's girlfriend, you wouldn't be in this kind of mess," was Beau's next retort), these things were chump change compared to what Beau saw. You could buy a house, cold cash, with just his ten percent. Imagine what the rest of it, the gloating alone, was worth.

"You coming back to me, Brycie? You gonna be my client again instead of Teddy's?"

I remember my father, from this period. I remember tennis whites, a sort of country club affectation that fell upon him for a while. I met him again just before I met Severin, before our paths crossed at St. Jerome in the fall. He'd come around to see Teddy that spring, and he brought champagne, dressed in a V-neck pullover and shorts, like some sad aristocratic refugee from the Jazz Age. *So you're Teddy's son, huh? Nathaniel?* He certainly didn't seem to remember me. *Good-lookin' kid you got here, Ren.* I recall his hand falling, awkwardly, on my scalp. With no suspicion at all on his part. There was only that bluff, half-assed curiosity these men always showed, that amped-up enthusiasm pretending to charm. *Hey*

*Teddy, you heard I'm back in the game? What's Sam saying, now that I
stole his golden calf? I'll bet that really gets him, huh? Huh?* For a brief
while, he was intolerable to his friends. Even Bryce had difficulty.

"Are you gonna come crawling?"

"Give it a rest, Rosers."

At a party in the Malibu Hills—Richard Jordan's place, a stone
castle at the end of a long dirt trail—he'd cornered his ex-client by
the crudité table. Their kids were playing outside. They were up in
the canyon wilderness, the air silty with russet dust, drunken adults
spinning around the access roads in their host's jeep. A courtyard
filled with languid retrievers and bored chickens.

"Aw, c'mon Brycie!" Beau wheedled. Teddy had stepped in to represent Bryce out of necessity. After the fiasco with *The Dog's Tail*,
the actor had to defect. "Who am I without my first and favorite
client?"

The kids' feet slapped against stone, their shrieks rising. An open
window, without glass, was at Beau's elbow. The actress Bryce was
schtupping came over. Her pink, flat-chested body looked concave
in a bikini, its string taut across her hip bones.

"Look at this." She held a clip in her hand, torn from a magazine.
"Look."

"*Morrison Groom's* The Dog's Tail *may not be the most interesting
movie of the year, and it certainly isn't the best, but it warrants your attention anyway*." Beau read the beginning of the review, from *New
York* magazine, with stentorian pretension.

"Excellent," Bryce said. "Anything that lets that maniac make another movie."

They laughed. The kids passed out of the courtyard's gateway and
came tramping around toward the front of the house.

"But see, look, look." The actress pointed at the bottom of the
clip. "Right there."

Beau squinted. A carrot stick larded with spinach dip was in his
hand. A shaft of sunlight passed through the window by his side, lit
a bright red carpet runner on fire.

"This guy's crazier than Sarris." In the *Village Voice*, the house
critic had seen some nonexistent connection between Morrison
and Max Ophüls. "Here, my God, look—*in Li Chang's performance,
Morrison Groom locates not just emptiness but The Void, she is Bardot in*

Contempt, or—I can't go on." Beau dropped the clip. "I should sign Li, just to make Vana pay through the nose again."

He laughed. But he would soon do exactly that. This was how easy it became for him, all his failures looping back to reward him at last. Even the shoe store, where he sold one of Irv's wobbly little cop dramas to TV. *The ABC Tuesday Movie of the Week*! He couldn't lose. The kids came in, Sev with a sunburn and a peeling nose, zinc daubing his cheeks and chin. He was never a Californian, was more like a tiny lifeguard, a midget Jew from Miami.

"You OK, sport?"

"Yeah. Rufus was throwing rocks at us."

"Rocks?" Beau asked, as Severin wasn't a tattletale. "What kind of rocks?"

Kate arrived now, drinking fizzy water from a plastic cup. "Just rocks."

There was something wrong with both DeLongs, Beau thought. The axis of human feeling sat askew, and where in Davis this manifested typically as an actor's sociopathic charm, his son had the cold mask of a political consultant. Maybe he had that syndrome, whatever you called it, where you couldn't stomach touch or anything other than numbers. Rufus sulked by himself, while Severin and Kate and Bryce's son Sergei went out to wash the dirt off their feet and Davis chatted up another starlet. Rufus had his father's golden-boy looks, but on him they seemed strange, almost simian. He'd just turned nine.

"Whatcha drinking?" Beau sniffed his daughter's glass when she came back in.

"Quinine."

"Quinine? Are you afraid you're gonna catch malaria?"

"I like the taste." Kate shrugged. And with this shrug articulated his own puzzlement, the wonder he felt confronted with his children. Why does anybody like anything?

"Let's go, grab your shoes."

"Is it time?"

"Yeah." Mostly, he just liked watching her be responsible, scurrying off on little errands. How delicious it was, to watch them grow. "Time."

"Can we go to Neptune's Net, Dad?"

"You wanna see the motorcycles, Sev? All right."

Sunday afternoon, lazy weekend days in which he felt sluggish even if he hadn't had any wine, no Soave Bolla or strawberry margaritas, whatever the hell these people were drinking while James Taylor sang "Shower the People," then Lindsay Buckingham did "World Turning." Twin feelings of permissiveness and oppression seemed to compete. Davis was getting his dick sucked in an upstairs closet, while fifty feet and an unlocked door away his son played with a magnifying glass, focusing the sun's rays to see if he could burn his own knee. Beau just led his kids out to the car. Not his problem. Rachel was right to trust him. He might get another year with them, if he was lucky. He passed the courtyard gate and strapped them into the backseat of the Jag. Behind him the mother hens clucked, approvingly.

IX

Still one more party. Why would you ever stop? It was the Fourth of July weekend at Bryce's house. A sense of bicentennial dissolution, of gaudy extremity, hung in the air. Stale cigarette smoke, the stinging sweetness of blender drinks might make you weep. The crowd included many of the old faces. Bob Skoblow, Roland Mardigian, Teddy Sanders.

"Davis has gotta be with that broad," Bryce said.

"No, no." Beau was drinking cold Pacifico in his old friend's kitchen. Pale linoleum felt sticky beneath his tar-darkened soles. "Warren's here, so there'll be competition."

"Fuck. Davis or Warren? They'll take turns. Two biggest gash hounds in Hollywood."

Beau snorted. How far they'd fallen from Waxmorton, all those more courtly and better-regulated men in New York, who'd at least had the decency to conceal their indiscretions. Now, though, what was to hide? Beau missed his old boss's elegance, even if a world like this one was more his speed.

"I saw him before," Beau said. "He was chasing after Vana with that pop gun of yours."

"Was he?"

"He said it was loaded, too. He was just fucking around."

Did Davis fuck around? Was there a sense of humor in there somewhere? He was so stupid it was impossible to know. Doing deals with him was a trip since you called and laid out the terms and after a cud-chewing silence he said either *yup* or *nope*. If only Bryce were half as easy to represent, let alone work with.

"I put it back in your shed."

"Cool."

Beau'd reclaimed the gun from Davis and taken it outside. He'd snapped the safety back on—it wouldn't have been loaded, he figured: they hadn't skeeted any Frisbees for nearly a year—and tucked it back under Bryce's pillow.

"Stinks in there." *You paranoid nutball!* "You really oughtta wash those sheets."

"I have no fear of my own body's excretions."

"No wonder you don't work much."

A garden party. Kids were running around with sparklers; glow-worms blossomed on the bricks. There were nearly a hundred people there. Teddy and my mother were, though I was home with a sitter. Usually, Bryce's parties had folks puking under the house, old and new girlfriends colliding in licentious rage, some reckless, hair-pulling disaster. Today, though, Kate and Sev sat on the sand, eating hot dogs, and Sergei was playing with Wonton, his father's German shepherd, down by the water. The tide was out, and the day was hot and calm.

Beau stood near the windows of the main house, looking out at Severin and Kate where they sat side by side. Even when they were engaged in separate activities they seemed complicit. Sev was reading a mass-market paperback copy of *Dandelion Wine*. Kate was sunning herself, rubbing her legs down with Coppertone.

"We made it, eh Brycie?" A wind picked up outside, stirred Kate's hair.

"You did."

"No, we did." Words did not describe the happiness Beau felt at this moment. "Together, we did."

Words. *What is the matter, my lord?* Long ago, Bryce Beller had played the Prince of Denmark badly. Now they could both afford to be nostalgic about failure, about mornings waking up with a skinful of tequila and the breath of old cigarettes.

"I'm going to find Davis," Beau said. His palm print streaked the glass where he'd just been leaning and then faded slowly away. "I need to tell him something about the Warners' thing."

He could mention to one client an offer for another, without inciting jealousy. He could balance all his responsibilities. Even he was envious of himself, the man he had seemingly become.

"Hey, Rosers, you want a drink?"

Nicholson clasped him as he made his way out past the narrow bar, the high wooden ledge that had launched innumerable debauches.

"We just whipped up a batch of Naked Assholes." He extended the blender's mug toward Beau. It smelled like ethanol. "Won't tell you what's in 'em, but you'll be out till Tuesday."

"I'll pass."

Once upon a time, Nicholson and Beller were so close, they were occasionally mistaken for one another. They didn't even look alike. Every once in a while Hollywood did this, like with the two Bills, Paxton and Pullman, a decade and change later. It liked to remind you stars were not only replaceable, they were scarcely unique. One man could easily be another. Beau swam through the crowd, pressing against the bikini-clad people with their spritzers and rum drinks, swaying in stances of sexual aggression or surrender.

"Hey, Rosers!"

Half of them hadn't even spoken to him for years. He turned to see Bob Skoblow tilting toward him, Roland Mardigian towering by his side.

"Where you been, man?" Bob hugged him. "We were just discussing you."

"Just now?"

"Last week, or last month—where were we, Rollie, whose house was that?"

"Vana's? I don't remember."

"Yeah, Vana's. We hear good things. You're representing Davis now?"

"That's what he tells me."

"Listen." Roland lay a heavy arm on Beau's shoulder. "We have a proposal."

These men were Sam's minions, even if Sam's power was fading— he had one foot on the banana peel, perched above the grave—and still, they did his bidding. What could they want?

"A proposal, huh? You got a ring?"

"Gotta talk to Will first." Roland swayed above him. His pitted skin was an eczema red, and his hair was entirely silver. "There's a little something we're putting together."

Beau nodded. It could wait. He tapped Roland's bicep and moved on. *Soon.* He went outside to check on the kids.

"Hey, Sev, you guys OK?"

Severin didn't look up from his book. Kate was napping, her wrists crossed as she lay on her stomach atop a towel. *All's well.* He wondered for a second why he hadn't heard from Rachel. She'd been incommunicado all week. He hustled back into the house, sand scalding his toes.

For an instant, his vision flickered. His tongue curled. There was nothing like calm to set a man off. Watching his kids sleep drove Beau crazy. He needed the chaos of the movie business to match that madness inside him.

"Teddy!"

"Barrett." This was Beau's real name, strangely enough: Beau was just the nickname he'd earned when he was too little to pronounce it. "What can I do for you?"

"A little Panamanian improvement? I'm having a rough day."

"I see that." Teddy took his elbow. "Let's grab some air."

The thing about these episodes was that they also felt great. Just as he had in Sam's office, he stood within an eye of serenity. His tongue tingled and bent, as if he had just licked a battery.

"I saw you talking to some girl about poetry, Beau? Have you turned over a new leaf?"

"No." Beau inhaled. "I prefer the old leaf."

Teddy wore a linen suit, a Panama hat. He looked like a plantation owner, ruddy and bewhiskered, with straw-colored hair and a subtle, conspirative expression. He chewed his mustache.

"Good shit, huh?"

Beau nodded. "The best."

Marijuana always cooled him out. It made the world feel spacious enough to accommodate even him. They stood on the terraced garden's second level. Long shadows fell across the grass, beneath the acacias and bonsais and lemon trees. Torches smoked in the breeze.

"Has Will been in touch with you?"

"Skobs and Rollie just asked me the same thing." Beau studied him. "What's going on, Teddy?"

It was late, of a sudden. The red sun doused in the Pacific. Where did the time go, where was it ever? Seven o'clock or seven thirty. Soon they'd be starting up the fireworks, shooting them from a barge out on the water.

"You'll need to talk to Will," Teddy hissed. The tiny flame of his lighter repeated itself in the lens of his round, rimless glasses.

He held the joint out to a girl as she passed, an actress Beau almost recognized. From where he stood he could see Kate and Sev, at last standing and shaking themselves off, brushing sand from their legs in the final golden crescent of day.

"Will's not here," Beau said. True, Will never went to parties. But what could Will be up to, that he wouldn't tell his friend? Then again, even he had to be careful, now that Beau was twice Sam's enemy for stealing the golden goose. "You people are planning something."

"Maybe." Teddy's face was illegible, perfect for an agent. "Code of silence, my friend."

The two men stood without saying anything. Down on the sand, Kate streaked back to pick up what looked like a hairband and then followed Rufus DeLong into the house. Sunlight flamed over the water.

"Better?" Teddy said, after a moment.

"Yes." Beau sighed. "Theodore, you are a lifesaver."

"We all feel that way, Beau." Teddy searched him. "Whatever it is that ails you."

Neither of these men was an introvert. Teddy had been to Stanford on a full scholarship, was easily the most educated man—even beyond Williams—Beau had ever known. He was also just a poor boy from the deepest reaches of Burbank, beyond where the studio lots had ever existed to prop up the economy, where the city tapered off into shabby ranch houses, yards filled with arguing Hispanics.

"Thanks, Teddy." Beau chortled. "You scan the very reaches of my soul."

"An agent's job." Teddy's eyes gleamed, as ever, with irony. "We're the Jewish confessors."

He tucked what was left of the joint in Beau's pocket, before the latter turned and moved through the crowd. The air smelled of briquettes, lighter fluid, the hopeful scent of barbecue. The dope should have relaxed Beau finally, but it didn't. The patio thronged with his friends, people who'd known him for years. Yet who did they know? The friendly fat man, bonhomous Beau. Not the fearful fetishist, panic-stricken dreamer. His forehead felt cold, the tops of his ears. He hadn't had an episode like this since before *The Dog's Tail* was in production. He found a bench on one of the lower levels of the garden. He wanted to be alone. He dropped his face into his hands and waited. The moon was full, the sky purple. Beau sat in the posture of a man grieving. Around him the torches flickered, offering up their obscure signals of smoke and fire.

"You wanna see it?"

"What?" Kate spoke. "See what?"

"I don't want to see it, Rufus." Severin, as ever, was the voice of reason.

"No." Bullying Rufus's voice had already dropped an octave it seemed, and he was easily three inches taller than the other kids. They were out on the sand again. "That's not what I'm talking about."

Kate stood next to him. Bryce's son, weak little Sergei, was in Rufus's shadow, literally and figuratively. A sickly blond, with sunken cheeks and dolorous gray eyes.

"I don't want to see it either," Kate said, echoing her brother. "I know what one looks like."

Four children were on the sand. Alone, unnoticed.

"Have you ever held one?"

"No!" Kate's tone said, *gross*. "That's a boy thing."

If Beau had overheard this, would he have put a stop to it? Of course. *The fuck are you doing, Rufus?* He'd have swatted his client's kid as surely as his own father had once swatted him, because Davis DeLong's little pig of a boy deserved it. They were down on the damp sand where the surf lapped in, close to the shadow of the house. The waves were thunderous enough to drown their voices. From where he sat, Beau might have heard only wind-ripped pieces.

" . . . not what I'm . . . " Rufus again protested. " . . . *else*. Sergei's dad has one."

"My dad has one," Sev said.

"No, he doesn't," Kate said. "Sev, he does not!"

They'd lit a few sparklers before, and smoke bombs. The gray cadavers of glowworms littered the sand, the baked stubs of Roman candles. The adults were all upstairs, waiting for the real fireworks to begin.

" . . . come on," Rufus said to Sergei, to all of them really. "Come on . . . "

Beau stood up after a while. He felt better: sane and heavy and restored to himself. He felt hungry, and not just for food. He waded back toward the house while the first *ooh* went up from the crowd, a blue shower of sparks bursting out over the bay.

"Hey Jeremy, seen my kids?"

"No sir."

"What about that girl?" Beau stretched, his stubby arms pointing to the corners of Bryce's den. "That one that came with Davis."

"Her?" Vana scowled. "Big game, Beau. Not sure she's old enough to vote."

"I'm not looking to poll her."

The two men chuckled. Vana sank in his armchair as if despairing, blinking dully at an empty glass. Most of the others were out on the balcony, so the two were alone inside this room where Beau used to sleep. The house looked prosperous, redone and repainted. A pair of nice couches had replaced the battered pull-out.

"What's cooking?" Beau dipped down to the table and picked up a saltine, slathered it with Brie. "You look like someone pissed in your spittoon."

"Never give it all up for an actress," Jeremy said.

"That Li's a tough nut," Beau said. He represented her, so he should know. "I warned you."

"That girl with Davis is an actress."

"It's OK." Beau clapped Vana's shoulder. "I wasn't planning to sell the farm."

He moved on, into the kitchen. What was he really after, anyway? Like a lot of actresses, this girl seemed quietly sexless. The kind of girl who'd come like someone stretching in her sleep. He drank a Perrier and set the empty bottle on the counter. He belched and then prowled until he found her.

She was alone in the back bedroom. She sat on the edge of the bed, staring at her face in a compact, adjusting her lips.

"I was looking for you."

"Yeah?" She snapped the compact shut. "Do I know you?"

Beau shut the door. "I'm Davis's agent."

"Oh. I've heard of you." Her face collapsed, like a soufflé.

"What's wrong?"

"Fucking Davis." She was close to tears. "He's such an ass."

He came into the room. He moved toward the bed with his shirt untucked and a rumpled, easy manner, the comfort he'd attained in all things. Was this simple for him? Of course it was, but it wasn't like you'd think. This girl was a person, he met her in empathy. He sat down on the bed, amid the scattered purses and coats.

"What did he do?"

She shook her head. Beau knew. Davis was a bigger pig than Steve McQueen. Didn't even need to fuck a girl to enjoy dumping her. The latter was more fun.

"You want some grass, sweetheart? I've got some dynamite shit."

Beau was a man who'd suffered all his life, enough never to get his kicks from pure exploitation and was torn, thus, between conflicting impulses. This girl was pixie-ish, pale and frail: that waiflike, Mia Farrow look. Her hair was auburn, highlights red in the lamplight.

"Don't worry about Davis," he said. He didn't even want to sleep with her now, it was more important to console her. "Actors are such beasts."

Outside the fireworks boomed. The voices of the crowd rose and fell, in towers and showers of disappointment.

"I've been doing this since '65," he said, "and it's never any different. The stars think it'll never end. But the worm always turns."

If he'd listened closely he would've heard a sound, different from all the others. It was sharper, higher than those booming shells along the beach. Beau lifted his head a second.

"You don't know," the girl said. Suddenly, she was eager. "You don't know the things Davis is into."

"Sure I do," Beau said. "There's nothing in sex that doesn't come out in business."

But the girl would tell him. They were rapping about acting and politics. Suddenly his hand was on her knee. She didn't move it.

She just sat cross-legged in front of him while the lamplight spilled shadows across her face.

"Carter's a *farmer*," he was saying. "He's weak—"

But she was leaning forward to kiss him and vice versa. They were ready to meet.

"Dad!"

Severin ran across the beach. He'd come down the splintering stairs from the terraced garden and now went up the ones that led to the balcony on the other property, tracing a big *V* because he couldn't find the path that connected the garden to the house.

"Dad! Dad!"

I don't think anyone knew. He was so small, and at the same time so intrinsically self-possessed there wasn't any way to measure; he was just an eight-year-old boy scrambling to find his father.

"Have you seen my dad?" He tugged Vana's sleeve in the living room, where the adults had just finished watching the fireworks. The mood was smoky and mellow and logy and calm, with people getting ready to have coffee and brownies, including some special ones Beller had made himself. "Have you?"

He'd gashed his foot on the dull end of a nail that was sticking up from the stairs but hadn't yet noticed. Blood streaked the pale carpets, the trail of an injured animal.

"Nah. Hey, what's wrong?" Vana set down his snifter. "Is something wrong?"

Severin worked his jaw. But nothing happened.

"What is it?"

Little kids got upset when they were hungry, right? Clueless Jeremy didn't have any. But Severin opened his somber mouth and what came out was a chest-deep wail.

"I want my daddy," he said. "I WANT MY DADDY!"

As every adult in the room turned for a moment to look.

Beau balanced the girl on the bathroom sink. Some people were leaving through the vestibule right outside, and they didn't want to get caught, so he'd carried her into the next room and they were fucking with his hands under her thighs. Her head banged against the medicine mirror. She was so brittle it was like carrying a paper doll.

"Fuck me!" She wasn't at all the way he'd expected. She was one of those: a director. Clawing his back and spitting into his ear. "Fuck me!"

Ordinarily, Beau wasn't into this. He hated being told what to do. But this girl was hot. His fingertips slid against her thighs. She grabbed his hair, his ear, and yanked hard.

"Ow—fuck!" He came, he liked it. Davis had bragged this girl was a she-wolf, but Beau hadn't believed him. Everybody lied about the women they were with. "Jesus!"

He bucked up against her and the sink's cold porcelain, which felt good too, icing his balls. His knees and his legs shivered. His arms fell, and he pinned her onto the sink. There was sweat on his forehead, breath on the mirror. He closed his eyes. As she went slack too, her hands draped around his neck. His ear and the side of his head still stung.

"Wait." There was always this moment too, when the girl seemed to realize abruptly whom she was with. "Ouch." She shifted. "Get off!"

"Dad!"

Severin couldn't speak. This was the only word he'd say. Jeremy Vana led him around by the hand, room to room while they searched for his father.

"Dad!"

The tears were dry now, but his voice was tense with emotion as they circulated through rooms of oblivious adults topping off their glasses and feeding the munchies. Even Vana could tell it was serious. He'd bandaged the kid's foot with a napkin.

"What's wrong?" Jeremy said. "What's wrong?"

Severin shook his head. A reflexive little jerk.

"I want my daddy," Severin repeated. "I can only tell him."

They checked the living room, the kitchen, a quick peek downstairs. A woman's voice rose, feigning peevishness. *Where is Mitchell? Why isn't he here?*

"Beau?" Vana poked his head into a laundry closet. "Hey Beau?"

They made it to the back bedroom last. Beau was just coming out of the bathroom, with that semicomposure that says only one thing, when Jeremy opened the door.

"What's up?" Beau said. "What is it, Jer?"

"Your son." Severin stampeded into the room. Behind him that woman's voice lifted again. *Oh my goodness! Oh how awful!* "He was looking for you."

Beau knelt as Sev raced toward him. "Hey, killer. What did I miss?"

He gathered his son in his arms. Severin was still light and small enough to pick up without difficulty.

"Thanks, Jer."

But Vana was already gone. Beau felt Severin trembling and had the presence to spin around so his son wouldn't see the actress, who was just now exiting the bathroom. She stopped and hung back when she saw what was happening.

"Is something wrong? Sev?"

But he could feel it, in his son's shell-shocked vibration. *My God.* The actress just watched as Beau kissed his son's cheek and whisked him outside.

"Talk to me, Sev. Talk to me."

Beau felt his son's forehead. There was no fever. But he couldn't go outside, wouldn't. They knelt for a second at the edge of the living room.

"Will you show me?" Responsibility argued with terror and won. "Can you show me what's wrong?"

Severin shook his head, more virulently than ever. Guests drifted around them, but the party had thinned. Traffic would be bumper to bumper on the PCH. The jangling of keys as people searched for their wits and their host. A woman dressed in white passed by, swirling dregs of wine in her glass, a murky, blond, hypnotic swill.

"I can't help if I don't know what the problem is." Beau stood. "Where's Kate?" Severin was solemn as a little soldier. And Beau fought the fear, as anyone would. "Where's Katie? Severin, take me to your sister."

On these words, Severin took his father's finger and led him onto the balcony. Out toward the wooden stairs and the sand.

Beau followed his son down to the beach, then looped up the terrace garden's steps. His feet were still bare, and they slapped behind Severin's on the brick. He should've put shoes on.

"Sev?" He called up to his son, who just kept marching ahead. "Sev?"

He made his way up the steps, through the different portions of the garden—most were just scalloped platforms, planks on which there grew cacti or bonsais or iceplants—up toward where it flattened out and there was Bryce's shed and a courtyard leading onto the garage. Teddy had left his hat on one of the benches. But the garden was empty. It was cold, now. Most people had either left or gone inside.

"Hey!" He called up. Severin had stopped on the landing and looked at his father. Inscrutable now in the dark.

"You understand." Beau squatted down before his son. He clasped Sev's shoulders. "You understand . . . whatever it is . . . "

He couldn't breathe now, couldn't get the words out. He meant to say, *It's not your fault.* Without knowing what it was, without daring to imagine.

"Wait here." He held Sev by the shoulders, rooting him in place. "You wait."

It was so quiet. There was just the thunder of the surf, and wind. The fizzle of fireworks farther up the beach and the dispersive murmur—not much, now—of the guests next door. He kissed Sev's forehead and rubbed his hair. *Wait.*

He stood up. His whole body felt cold, spreading from the chest. There was moonlight on the brick, and snails glistened among the wind-pushed roses. There was steel in his spine as he approached the shed and went in alone.

Bryce's shed was five by eight. There wasn't anything in it, besides a cot and a Coleman lantern. A primitive rectangular tape-player for his chants. No magazines, no cigarettes or dope. Any other night, the kids might've ignored it, but children go where they are most forbidden. Most nights too it was locked, but someone had forgotten earlier to fasten the padlock Bryce had bought to keep out the critters.

Someone.

"Lemme see it!"

Beau would have to imagine this scene. No one else ever described it accurately. For Severin, it left a kind of blank. A caesura in the thick of his experience: he claimed never to remember it.

"No, Rufus." Beau would picture it, though, over and again. How Sergei was the only one who knew how to handle the gun safely. Bryce had shown him. "No!"

Rufus pulled it away. The safety was on, unless it was off. It was Beau who'd last handled this too, and what did he know about guns? Bryce usually kept it in the house, in a safe. Sev was the last to come in. Outside, the sky was bruise-gray. Moonlight and fireworks glowed across the water.

"Give it here, Rufus." Sergei, a Cub Scout, picked up a pack of matches.

"No." Rufus snickered. He and Sergei sat on the bed while Sev and Kate stood. "What are you supposed to do with this anyway?" Rufus said. "Is it just for playing?"

"Uh-uh. It's real."

"It's not. It's just like in the movies. You can't shoot anybody with this."

"You can. My dad says—"

"He shot John Wayne with it, and John Wayne didn't die in real life."

True. Yet surely you'd have to be an idiot to confuse life and the movies, even if you were still a kid.

"It was only loaded with blanks then," Severin said. "Those weren't real."

"It's not loaded with anything now."

"How do you know?"

How stupid did you have to be?

"My father keeps it unloaded," Sergei said.

Through all this, Kate didn't say anything. She just stood where she was in the lantern's flickering glow. It was the flame's motion that caused her shadow to jump. And this was where Rufus aimed.

"Bang!"

That was all it took. One kid's stupidity, or else just that fractal difference. The twitch of a finger, which was all that ever separated real from make-believe.

Rufus pulled the trigger. This was the sound Beau had heard in the bedroom while all the other adults had stood out on the balcony and watched the fire-spattered sky. The shot was louder, but noises were everywhere: Roman candles, firecrackers, strings of M-80s. A few people turned their heads, but most were too drunk or stoned to put it together.

The moment it happened, the instant the gun went off, the two other boys, Rufus and Sergei, took off running. They weren't going to hang around to see what they'd just done. Rufus dropped the gun and they bolted, bashing past Severin through the door.

He didn't see it either, really. His eyes were closed, and he was already running, even as he heard the shot and then the sound of something heavy, the suddenly inanimate freight of a body as it clattered against the shed's wooden wall.

Beau entered the shed. Severin remained behind him, outside. The lantern was still burning and the gun was on the floor and Kate seemed to be breathing still as the lamplight flickered around her face. The air was cold and wet. It smelled like the sea. Firelight trembled across the bare wooden planks. And Beau knelt down on the cot, beside her. He brushed her hair aside, and then he saw it. The lower half of her face was missing, her left cheek blown away to expose teeth, viscera, bone. He doubled up and vomited, one strong and pitiless stream. The smell of powder hung in the air, rotten kelp. Beau puked and when he was done, he could not move. One long moment in which his body was locked tight, bitter as a crustacean's.

"What happened, son? What happened?"

A cop jostled Severin. Someone had given him a blanket. But still, he couldn't speak. Sitting in the dirt outside Bryce Beller's shed.

"Ahhh, cock— fuck—"

This, my brother remembered. Beau's hands splintering wood. While Severin knelt and willed his mind white. A pillbug rocked on the brick in front of him.

"Mother—"

Beau Rosenwald was sobbing, a high-pitched and unfamiliar sound. Bryce came running around from the house, gazelle-like down the garden path.

"Severin! Get inside! Severin!"

Sev's mind was empty. Who remembers life before tragedy? He prodded the bug with a stick and Bryce straightened him up and handed him off to the girl he was dating.

"Come on, sweetheart." The girl, whose name was Mary Altschul, coaxed him. Behind him the lantern shattered, and Bryce ran into the shed. "Let's go in now, let's go."

Severin couldn't move. The cops were there, they were searching for the other kids. Rufus, blubbering, came up from the beach, his hand swallowed by a policeman's. Were they in trouble? Was anyone in trouble?

"Follow me, honey." Mary Altschul dragged him away. "Let's go."

"Oh, God!" Bryce's voice shot up in discovery. "Oh, Rosers, God, c'mon—"

Severin followed Mary. They gave him a tetanus shot inside, bandaged his foot. The sky over the Pacific was silver, almost white. Mary Altschul was weeping, now. Someone ran water in the kitchen sink. And Beau's voice rose away from coherence as he shrieked like an animal, some words about a head, her head, that head, the wrong, the wrong, the wrong motherfucking head!

PART THREE: **DREAM BABY DREAM**

I

MY SUSPICIONS BEGAN that fall. I had nothing to base them on, no real feeling that Teddy Sanders—sly, nebulous Teddy, who took me out to lunch every Saturday and drove me around town in the passenger seat of his Jag—wasn't my father. It was subtler than that, a drift. I was eight years old. I had some inchoate sense my parents didn't quite fit together like other people's. Not like Little Will's, who seemed like equal portions of a balanced unit, no matter how contrasting. I'd hear Teddy and my mom talking, and whenever there was an argument, my mom always took my side. But when Severin came, everything changed. The whole world threw itself open to question. Even if it would be years before it was explained to me, before I learned my father and his were the same. I knew, before anyone said anything. Isn't that always the way?

"Hey, Sev!" And as we made our way through the headbanging crowd at Gazzarri's, all those years later, I couldn't help but think back. "Remember?"

"Remember what?"

Perhaps my brother should never have been asked to remember anything, considering where he'd been. He was entitled to a whole lifetime of erasure. But as we pushed toward the stage I looked up and saw three dudes hanging over the balcony, three leather-clad heshers staring down with intent. They were smoking, glowering, scanning our sea of neon bodies and hair. Severin looked up and smiled.

"Hey, Will."

But Williams had already clocked it too, was thinking just what I'd been.

"They look like us."

They didn't, of course. The three of us were never such wastrels, such utter cartoons. But Severin had arrived late in September of third grade, had come into our class at St. Jerome just like a package delivered into my care. And the moment he and I and Williams were united, we found ourselves arrayed just like those guys. Standing outside the classroom in our Keds and our Toughskins and our pale blue short-sleeved shirts—the St. Jerome version of a uniform—while we hocked loogies over the edge of the upper grades' balcony and mocked the kiddies below.

Our schoolhouse was two-storied: administrators and lower grades downstairs, third through sixth above. Williams and I of course were already friends. We still played basketball under his dad's watchful eye; on certain Saturday mornings the elder Will would take us to Bond Street Books in Hollywood to buy comics. But Sev was the glue that cemented us, that activated our friendship for life. He came over that morning without a word. Seven fifty, on whatever September morning of 1976. We were trying to hit the God's Eyes, those woven clusters of yarn on popsicle sticks, on the tables below. A smell of rubber cement and wet papier-mâché rose up to greet us.

"Ooh," Williams said, after I let a long string of spit hang off my lips and released it down. "Bombardier!"

It was a small school, about twenty-five kids per class. Both of us had heard about the boy who was coming, the one whose sister had died and whose mother had just—this was the rumor—vanished, after that. We knew our fathers, all three of them, had worked together, but what did that signify to third graders?

"Ha!" I'd streaked some little towhead's navy sweater. "He doesn't even know it's there!"

Severin sidled up to us. You could smell the New York stink on him, this outlander. Williams and I were just beginning to piece it all together, to sprout through our boyhood into pre-pre-adolescence. Vans sneakers and OP shorts, Sims Skateboards and Independent Trucks were soon to become the new currency. Our schoolyard selves matched imprecisely with who we were at home.

Severin came over in his horizontally striped Hang Ten T with his horn-rimmed glasses. He looked like a little boy, only wiser, made serious by something—even I could see it—beyond our ken.

"Hi."

"Hi." Williams mimicked him. Sev looked, in other words, like a total feeb.

"Whatcha doing?"

"What does it look like? Valley."

"He's not a Valley," I said, only because I wasn't sure this particular cruelty was justified. "I'm pretty sure he's from somewhere else."

This was it, the dawn of meanness. God knows we'd marinated in it long enough.

"Where's he from then? Where you from, then?" Williams loved this part. "*Val.*"

"Stop it," I said, but Severin just folded his arms then and leaned forward against the metal railing.

"New York City," he said. "I'm from Jane Street."

In a few minutes we'd be called into Mrs. Ginsberg's class, the kids we were drooling on downstairs would be summoned into theirs—Mrs. Duncan, Mrs. Julian, Mrs. Schwartz—but for now we were struck by Severin's imperviousness. It wasn't cluelessness. He didn't give a shit if we teased him.

"I have a *Fantastic Four* #1," he said. "You want to see it?"

"You brought a *Fantastic Four* #1 to school with you?" Williams stared. "That's worth fifteen hundred bucks."

"Yep. It's in my backpack."

Those geeky new clothes. He didn't even know enough to wear the school's uniform! But not a word from Williams now about his backpack, its sartorial violation—just like that, a whole set of codes had begun—since he was too impressed, too impressed as well with Severin's unwillingness to impress.

"Wow." Who cared what it was worth? It was totemic, priceless. "Where did you *get* this?"

Another shrug. We didn't actually get to see it until recess. Ask any one of us and we'll tell you, however, those of us who *can* still remember—whose memories haven't been compromised by subsequent events—that we met on a balcony, standing together and leafing through a *Fantastic Four*.

"Can I hold it?"

"No, Williams, it's my turn."

Severin was generous. *My dad gave it to me*, was all he said. As our families gave us plenty of stuff, as Teddy and my mother spoiled me too, I doubt Williams and I worked out that it might have been offered recently as a salve, a bribe, a desperate plea. By lunchtime we'd decided we'd never part. Picture three boys gathered over one comic book, the Spanish-style schoolhouse dissolved in Santa Monica fog, its milk-colored interior walls covered in construction paper, time lines, dinosaur dioramas, silver foil. Long before Severin and I learned the truth, we knew. All three of us did, really. We were our own invention.

"Those fags could never be as cool as we were." We remained our own, some fifteen years later. Williams glared up at Gazzarri's balcony, drawling the word *fags* in a way that was ironic and preemptive, bending our own weakness into a gesture of self-protection.

"Yuh-huh."

This place was jammed to a point of excruciation. Faces melted, bodies scrunched up against the walls. It was Bosch-like, infernal. Capacity was barely five hundred, but there had to be twice that in here. The fire marshal would've shut down all of Hollywood if he or she had known. Only those folks up there in the VIP section—or whatever it was, exactly, perhaps they were on the outside looking in—could breathe. The rest looked like the band, the rumored band, since the stage remained empty except for Marshall stacks that could've belonged to anybody, bottles of Jack Daniel's ditto. The crowd nipped at JD & Coke, shots of schnapps and Jägermeister. The women all wore fishnets and leather. I copped not just feels but whole lifetimes of inadvertent sexual experience while I moved, writhing between pillowy tits and invisible asses. The girls couldn't have cared less about me, in their pilot caps and heels, their torn T-shirts and long-strung beads and hair that was teased up into all sorts of vari-colored contortions. Their faces were waxen, gorgeous, cold. In the morning you'd be able to read their failure but just now, under the house lights, they were goddesses. Of the men—skinny flamingo-punk junkie scumbags, dumb tunnel kids from the other side of the hill—the less said the better. *Valleys*, we would've called them back in the day, these Reseda heshers and wishfuls from out of town, dudes who had their own bands that would never fly.

"Where are we going?" I followed Sev, who was suddenly our true leader again. He was on a mission.

"We're moving up so we can see."

"You didn't want anything to do with this band a half hour ago." I had to raise my voice above the PA, which played a ballad about every rose having its thorn. They were teasing us now, baiting us with songs that suggested this "secret" show was real.

"I do now."

"Why?"

He turned to face me. His eyes gleamed. "It's an experiment."

"What kind of experiment?"

The crowd swirled, opened up a little bit to allow us our passage, or to allow it its own tint of hostility. Finally, we were noticed, just enough. A couple of dudes grumbled, snickered. *Nerds*.

"We're going back."

"What? 'Back' where?"

"I want to see if it works. To see if we can transport ourselves."

"You're serious?" I stared at him. He wasn't talking about *backstage*, he meant back, chronologically. A journey through the past. "You think this band is a fucking time machine?"

He nodded, slowly. That Peckinpah T-shirt, those glasses. He looked like a doomed scholar. The ruined Marxist, adrift in a sea of hair metal faces, squared against the late-capitalist flower that was Guns N' Roses.

"Christ, Sev. If you're gonna be this high, I should join you. Did you leave everything in the car?"

"I'm serious."

"I know you're serious. This is a fucking metal band." Someone shoved me. "This is not metaphysics."

Someone else jostled me in the groin. It was so crowded in here I couldn't see what was what or who was where, but I felt that spiky vertigo of being kneed in the nuts. I gasped, folded over.

"It's *music*," he said simply. "That's all there is."

I blinked away tears, straightened up finally. "What the fuck are you talking about?"

"Beyond music, what is there?" Sev spread his hands now, in a gesture almost Egyptian. "You're the nostalgic one, Nate. You know about all this."

I shook my head. All I knew was that my brother was most enviably wasted.

He just turned away. "It's going to work."

The lights were up at that murky, post-ambient level, that golden tone that suggests a band may be coming on soon. The few people around us who'd tuned in to our conversation just snickered. *Fuckin' pussy*, said one guy. The air smelled beachy, like suntan lotion and cigarettes, like cheap island rum.

"Hey!" I tugged Severin's sleeve as he made his way forward, ever forward to the stage. "Where's Williams?"

"He probably went to take a piss."

"You think?"

The danger here was not lost on me. This posse that surrounded us was predicated on violence: asses were there to be kicked or fucked, nothing in between.

"Look!" Sev pointed. There was Will on the opposite side of the bar. Unless it was someone else in one of those wrinkly faced Nirvana T's, receding toward the cigarette machine. "All right?"

"Sure."

The lights dropped, suddenly. The PA cut out. We were left with the red buttons of the Marshall stacks and monitors and the wash of a blue overhead. I watched my friend vanish down the hall toward the restroom in darkness. The room swelled with an anticipatory roar, a few exuberant voices twittering above it. *Guns N' fucking Rooooosssees*, someone yelled.

A skinny man came onto the stage, looking vaguely like Axl. A drummer, a guitar player—not Slash—and someone else, their cigarettes wandering through the dark. A top hat sat on the drum riser, two bottles of Jack. There were all these signifiers, suggestions of the band, and yet—

"All right, fuckin' Los Angeles!" the singer said, not Axl, as the lights came up. "Let's fuckin' get it on!"

The band blasted into a cover of Aerosmith's "Mama Kin," which was a song Guns N' Roses, too, had covered, but it was not them.

What the hell?

The rest of the crowd roiled, perplexed but into it. They were like dogs, you didn't need meat if you could just wave a bone in front of their noses. *Aerosmith*, *metal*, *right on*, went the equation. Something like this. A few boos, maybe a distinct plateauing of what had seemed ready to become a frenzy. But they were digging it.

I grabbed Severin's shoulder. "Dude, what's going on here?"

He shrugged. "I dunno."

Not that I didn't know all the words, myself, the ones about dreaming, floating downstream. It was loud, but not as loud as I wanted it to be. I missed Slash's guitar, that crunching, kinetic, teeth-rattling sound that was their essence for me. These guys were understudies, some sad relation—they had the hair, the scarves, but they weren't superstars.

"Opening band," Sev yelled.

I didn't think so. It was nearly three in the morning. Were Guns N' Roses going to go on at five, were they going to be upstaged by openers playing their own version of someone else's song the band had already appropriated? This had the feel of a complete experience, something final in itself. We watched the rest of the show, and this ticky-tack outfit turned out to be, on closer inspection, L.A. Guns. In the mid-1980s, Melrose Avenue was littered with fliers advertising the two bands, L.A. Guns and Guns N' Roses, as if they were interchangeable, which they almost were. Axl Rose was *in* L.A. Guns for a while, and then Tracii Guns was in Guns N' Roses, a perfect mess that should've confused everyone. It was the Paxton-Pullman Principle in full effect, except the one band made it and the other most definitely did not. And maybe, just maybe this wasn't even L.A. Guns, maybe it was some still more tragic set of impostors—like that guy from Florida you'd read about in *Rolling Stone* who'd pretended to be Paul Stanley of Kiss—crawling around in the shadow of a has-been glam metal band that in fact never got very far in the first place, never-weres if ever there was such a thing as a never-was, this being something of a contradiction in terms to begin with.

"Keeping track!" The singer was up there vamping now, on and on about keeping tabs on Mama Kin, not knowing where she'd been.

Still, though. Wasn't everyone in Hollywood a part of this liminal condition, chasing the apparitions of our future selves, falling out of favor with our pasts? One's yearning never ended. Even so, it almost worked. For a moment Severin and I were like dogs ourselves, pogoing in place to that Aerosmith number that described to us the sound of sixth grade.

Where's your mother been?

I scanned the crowd. Where was Will? He would've eaten this up, should've been levitating over our heads and floating toward the stage. But he was gone.

"All right, you fuckers," the singer—Tracii, I supposed—sneered after three songs, two more I didn't recognize. "Here's what you've been waiting for!"

Just like that, fuckin' Axl Rose—*fuckin' Axl*, but what else was I supposed to call him just then?—walked out of the wings, with Slash, the two of them arm-in-arm almost, like they were still the best of friends. The howl that went out from the crowd was indescribable, a primal shriek that might only occur after expectations have been dashed and then, unexpectedly, fulfilled in an instant. Slash jacked his Telecaster into the main amp and flipped on his top hat and the band railed right into "Paradise City." Holy shit!

Severin and I were swept up, carried in this great moshing wave toward the stage. Electricity jolted through our skulls. It didn't matter whether we hated this band on principle. They killed us. They played everything, all the songs we knew, including the shitty ones (ahem, "November Rain"), which we were suddenly unashamed to love. They finished up with the really big one, the *t-na-na-na-na-na-knees, KNEES* one. Sev and I were pulverized, torn apart from the very first note as the crowd spun us off in separate directions, but this didn't matter either: we were complete. I spotted him once, with the glasses knocked off his face and the sweaty, hectic expression of a swimmer fighting a riptide. Then he was gone and I was too, whirled away in my own crossfire hurricane. It wasn't that anybody was trying to hurt us. Violence was just the name of the game, the lingua franca, the American method as it came down at the end of the twentieth century. My foot, my eye, my chest, my ribs and thigh: all these parts were banged, punched, jostled. The women in the crowd might've been taking revenge for all the subversive squeezing I'd enjoyed before the set. Except I didn't see any women now, not one. It was all men, doing all this homoerotic hammering, a fistfight ballet.

"Where's Williams?" I screamed in Sev's face once I found him, once it was over and the band had left the stage. I'd yelled myself hoarse during the set and now confronted semideafness there on the edge of the throng while it clapped and pounded for an encore.

"He's here."

"No." I looked around. "He wouldn't watch from this far away. He wouldn't hang back at the bar. *He* wanted to be here in the first place."

"Yeah," Severin said, but it went up at the end like a question, like he suddenly understood my concern. At last. "Where is he?"

As disciplined as his father was, as clean, Little Will was the opposite. I grabbed Sev's elbow, and since we didn't care about seconds, about anything the band might think to do now, we raced toward the bathrooms. The crowd had thinned just enough so we were able to push our way through. My vocal cords ached; the room was so dense with cigarette smoke and marijuana it hurt just to breathe. My eyes stung with the sweat that dripped off my forehead. We raced past a couple making out and into the bathroom, Severin and I like cops on a bust. We kicked open the door but the room looked empty. Surely no one wanted to blow it and miss the encore—they might play "Patience," or "Sweet Child"—but the second stall was locked. The "stall," such as it was. You can imagine what the crapper was like in this place. One set of walls was completely demolished, leaving only a basin without a seat, while the remaining one looked like a public school broom closet.

"Yo," Severin said. The green door was crisscrossed with switchblade graffiti. To our left was a slender urinal, one tiny sink. "Anybody in there?"

No answer. *Yo* would've provoked one. I mean, what if we'd been black people?

"Yo?"

We rushed the stall on Sev's second *yo*. It smelled like a port-o-let, like ancient turds and urine and vomit, a medicinal touch of something—Jäger, tequila—besides, like whoever'd barfed hadn't digested the liquid he'd yakked up. The door gave against our weight and we tumbled into the tiny stall. Williams was on the floor, down among the muck and the slime and the brown mire, those viscous strands that caked the base of the toilet.

"Shit." I knelt next to him, Severin crowding in behind me. What did it matter where we put our hands? "What is this?"

I grabbed him. His body's pure inertia made it look like he was sleeping, though when I knelt and touched him he was perfectly still, and the back of his head was wet. He'd been lying in this place for a while.

"Jesus!" I lifted him up. He was breathing. The front of his shirt was wet too, and I realized people had come in here and pissed on him, just let him stay crumpled where he was when they hosed him down.

"Oh!" I lifted him. Not till I got him out of the stall did I realize the liquid on the back of his head was blood. "Oh fuck, Sev, look!"

There was a blue bandanna, Crip-colored, knotted above his elbow.

"What is this?"

Sev just grunted. We were dragging him toward the sink when it hit me. If we'd searched the floor we'd have found matches, spoon, baggie, syringe. How much evidence did I need?

"Severin, what the fuck?" I turned the spigot uselessly. What were you supposed to do? When someone OD'd weren't you supposed to put him in the bath, use cold water, ice cubes, something like that? *I* didn't know. "How long has Williams been using heroin?"

We ran water on his face for a second. A pathetic trickle.

"Not long," Sev said. "And not often."

"Have you been using it too?"

Severin just looked at me ambiguously. "Let's get him out of here."

We lugged him by the hair and I draped one of his arms over my shoulders, Severin taking the other. He was breathing. Alive, but perhaps barely, and for how long?

"Christ, Sev!" It was amazing how fast you could travel when you needed to, how fast and slow you could go at once. "What exactly is going on here?"

My face and his in the mirror, my own a sick parody of its schoolboy self—with my longish hair plastered to my forehead, I looked ten again, supercilious and vacant and beautiful—while Sev's was wise and sharp-chinned. Not for the first time, that vast gulf yawned between who we were and what we knew, of ourselves and of one another. We lunged through the door, dragging our half-living friend. Outside we'd look for a cab, an ambulance, what?

"You're not going to answer me?"

We made it to the street. I hadn't seen the band return, but now that we were outside, the building started to vibrate again with muffled, cavernous sound. The night was empty, whatever time it was, that morally uncertain hour when the cars came far apart and all drove slow.

Split-second decision time. We went for Sev's car. We had to go now! Williams wasn't dead, he wasn't even bluish, quite, though his skin had a fishy pallor. He moaned as we dragged him across Sunset.

"Let's get him to the hospital," Sev said. We'd pushed him into the passenger seat and now I was scrambling into the back. "Let's fucking go."

"Fine." I was in and he was starting up the car and the radio blared the elephantine screeching of some treated art–rock guitar. "Hit it!"

"We're going to Cedars of Lebanon."

"What? Severin, there is no Cedars of Lebanon!" His car tracked out onto Sunset, racing across both lanes under a violet sky, the night that was already beginning to pale. "You're going in the wrong direction!"

True. The hospital was called Cedars-Sinai now and it was just down the hill in West Hollywood. Cedars of Lebanon had shut down when we were kids. In its place now was the Scientology Centre.

"Where are you going?" I yelled. "Sev, the hospital's the other way!"

The stereo yipped inanely. We passed Spago, the old one where Beau had taken us both to celebrate our high school graduation. We'd sat next to Prince and Morris Day of the Time, the two men dining out to plot their dominance of the future. It was 1985.

"Turn around! Severin, turn around!"

But he didn't. And Spago was closed now too, not just for the night but forever, windows sheeted with ply and the once-elegant yellow building grown fissured and decrepit, the façade splintered with spidery lines. *There is no hospital.* We raced down the Strip and I just threw my head back. Williams and my brother had been into something they shouldn't have. And what did I know, since the two of them had betrayed me this completely? Anyone could've been into anything, our father could've been the goddamn pope, Mahatma Gandhi, a pedophile. I closed my eyes and breathed, the wind whipping and fluttering through the poorly sealed joints of the car. The radio wailed. Where in God's name were we going?

II

DRUGS ENTERED OUR lives in 1977. Williams and Severin and I had been together for a year and a half, and until then, nothing could've divided us. We hammered out our bond at St. Jerome, a year in which we were all preoccupied with comic books and baseball cards and skateboards. If we argued about anything, it was that Severin was a Mets fan. Seriously? Jerry Koosman? Williams and I were Angelenos, and aside from the detestation of the Yankees seemingly shared by all reasonable people, Severin's city was a pure abstraction. It was TV, it was cop shows, it was mentioned on the news. Severin's mom had gone missing, we knew that—after his sister died, Rachel had just abandoned him in Beau's lap—but we never discussed it. Leave that to Hal Linden and Abe Vigoda. Instead we chewed our brittle pink rectangles of Topps gum and sat on my front stoop on summer afternoons. Hung out there and very occasionally at Little Will's, in the asphalt-and-seawater swamp of the Marina, where Will's parents bird-dogged us a little more closely than mine. The mood there was louche, dangerous. I don't suppose I wondered why a youngish agent and his wife would choose to live so far from Bel Air: we were too busy constructing our little cosmos, staining the sidewalk with saliva bombs, and I was too enraptured, too fascinated by the Farquarsens' more bohemian scene. Teddy and my mom shunted me to public school for fourth grade and off I went, moving from St. Jerome to Roosevelt, on Montana Avenue. God knows what my mom thought when she saw me so tight with Beau's son. In my darker moments, I've wondered if she moved me to keep Severin and me apart, but that probably isn't true. As my mother began her disintegration—those first crises of her early thirties, the quiet acceleration of her drinking—I was too youthfully self-absorbed to notice. And while Will and Sev were left in the gentle garden of St. Jerome, I was loosed into the wild. Those Episcopal hippies had nothing on the haggard lifers who ran Roosevelt Elementary, those ossified schoolmarms and weary bureaucrats, nor on the insanity that took hold across the playground's concrete jungle. As my best friends went on with their youthful arts educations, I embarked upon a different kind. Clifford Contreras pinched my chin and shook it like I was a camel at a bazaar. Kids named Matzel, Leinbach, and O'Brien—Irishers and Germans, whose last names were all anyone ever needed—punished me daily, whipping my ass at basketball and aiming for the head when we played strikeout. A girl named Bunny walked the playground and changed my life, her hair swinging like a bellpull, shaking off light. I was a scrawny little gleep with horn-rims of my own, like Severin, only blonder. The others were from the complexes closer to Wilshire, the boxy sheds whose once-modern "elegance" had curdled toward lower-middle-class neglect. Santa Monica then was just the northerly extension of Venice: not quite ghetto, but hairy enough. You could get jacked in the parking lot of the A&W Restaurant; there were chicken hawks along the pier. Closer to Pico there was a gang, the I-9ers, whose legend scared me off the streets. Severin, who still had his New Yorker's instilled fearlessness, walked them without a problem; Little Will, who lived on the edges of the Marina, where the kids were born with criminal records, did the same. Yet I was the one Jamie Cullen approached one day on the playground, while I was standing over by the green wooden backboards that served mixed purposes, for handball or for strikeout, where we chucked tennis balls and called our own pitches. A strike could bruise your ribs.

"Hey, brah," Jamie slurred. "C'mere."

"Hey, what?" He'd never talked to me, but even I knew there was only ever one chance to convince people you weren't a pussy. I *was* a pussy, but still. "What d'you want?"

Jamie was leonine, darker-skinned, quiet, and sinister. His mother was Hawaiian. He wore a heavy flannel shirt even when it was hot. He nodded. "Over here."

I walked over toward him, in the patch of shadow that fell behind the backboard. I was wary of getting my ass kicked, but Jamie wasn't really a bully. His brother was an I-9er, and this meant that he never had to prove anything. He opened his fist when I got near him. Three white pills lay on his palm, bigger than aspirin. RORER 714.

"You want to buy these?"

It was recess. No teachers were near. I half knew what he had. I'd heard bigger kids, fifth and sixth graders, talk about *Columbia gold* and *smoking out*. But Quaaludes were something else.

"How much?"

I wasn't going to buy them, but I wasn't going to flinch.

"Five bucks. Each."

"I don't have money," I lied. I was nine. "Sorry."

He slid the pills back into his pocket, the shirt I suddenly realized was a drug dealer's coat. Or maybe I didn't know that till later, since I didn't know what a dealer was yet either. Jamie's sleepy, serpentine demeanor was enough. He had raccoon eyes, pillowy lips like Mick Jagger's.

"Just thought I'd aaask, brah."

I brought money the next day. I didn't want to take drugs, but I wanted to own them.

"Hey, Jamie."

We were just where we were yesterday. He looked over as if he'd never seen me in his life, as if whatever happened back then—*when?*—was but a distant dream.

"Those, um." I watched Jamie. "Those . . . pills."

He leaned against the backboard and looked at me sidelong. Like I was a complete Val for daring to speak to him at all.

"You know? You offered me some shit?"

I got bold. Where it came from, I don't know. Junior high kids at Lincoln were onto this stuff already, not me. I was in the middle of something, an occult transformation. I'd given up my glasses, wore a replica USC football jersey, short-sleeved and porous. I felt athletic and limber, but suddenly sports were only a metaphor, and that muddy little baseball diamond behind us was just a place to win girls. An orange Corvette slid past along Lincoln, blaring Zeppelin's "Black Dog."

"Oh, riiight," Jamie said. "Naaate. That's your name, huh?"

Every vowel was extended, bent into that casual dudespeak that was just the way we were. Parody California all you like, but it meant something else to us, was simply an attempt, I think, to keep our sexuality under control. I reached into my pocket and took out twenty bucks I'd lifted from Teddy's billfold that morning. Jamie looked at me like I'd just whipped out my pecker. He shook his head and I tucked the money back out of view.

After school, we met in the bathroom. He stood by the towel dispenser, smoking a Marlboro. The floor in there was like a garage's, smooth and gray and stained.

"Hey." Jamie stepped forward and this time had a palm full of different things. A joint that was twisted super-tight at both ends and a couple of melted-looking yellow capsules.

"What's that?" I breathed through my mouth to avoid the smell of urine and borax.

"Kine, brah. And some yellow jackets."

"Yellow jackets." I sanded this off at the last minute so it wasn't a question. It didn't really matter what these did. "How much?"

"Ten."

I gave him twenty and split.

"Hey brah."

I whirled. My sneakers, twin-toned, powder and navy blue Vans, skeetched across the floor.

"Don't be a pussy. I'll fuck you up."

I was a pussy, like I said, so I hoped there wasn't a pure cause/effect between Jamie's two statements. But I just burst out into the shadowed halls and ran all the way home. I hadn't yet formed an intention. Possession for now was its own reward. I hid the stuff in my room, first in my five-dollar combination "safe," then in my hamster's cage, and finally—as I realized I didn't want to enable rodent suicide—in my sock drawer. Obvious, but my mother wasn't tossing my cell just yet. And so, without any danger of being found out, I forgot about them. My drugs. Six months passed, and it wasn't until August that they came up again.

"Whatchoowannado?"

"I dunno, man." Fifth grade was the year I became a man, and Williams too transformed from snickering punk to full-on dude, a boy child in excelsis. In Dogtown T and *vato* hat, he was Tony Alva at half size, cool as fuck. "What*choo*wannado?"

In our spare time, which was all of it, we took turns speaking like Steven Tyler, racing our words together the way he'd done to introduce the songs when our mothers took us to see Aerosmith at the Sports Arena. It didn't occur to us that cocaine would've been helpful in achieving the desired effect. Cocaine. That drug, thankfully, came later.

"Shee-yit." Williams's Tyler was actually pretty convincing. "Dunno."

We were up in my room, which was where we tended to hang out in those days. His house was too far away, involved taking the 3 or the 8 to the 2 and then a long skate down Main Street. It was too long, too risky, that pregentrified corridor of porn theaters and liquor outlets. It involved too many opportunities to be hassled (everything was "hassle." *Don't hassle me, brah*). We'd pick up our skateboards—I'd just switched my laminated Sims Taperkick for a ten-inch Alva—and joust with them, beating at each other's hands. We pored over comic books almost as fervently as we did Teddy's copies of *Swank* and *Oui*. Only now we were into *Conan the Barbarian*, the issues drawn by Barry Smith especially, and something about that barrel-chested, long-haired savage flashing his blue-shadowed pecs really turned us on.

"Dude," I said, slipping into a mellow patter to counteract all that Tyleresque speed jive. I remembered my drugs. "You wanna . . . get high?"

"Sure." Williams pissed me off by not even batting an eye. "I'd love to do that."

"You would? I've got some yellows, dude. I've got weed."

We were suddenly speaking this language, it had angles; we pretended to experience we hadn't had or else were inducted simply by assimilating its vocabulary.

I went into my closet and came back with the skinny, desiccated J and three pollen-colored pills. They looked like cheap vitamins. This was all the leverage I had in the world. "Check it out."

My bedroom was decorated in blue denim then, my bedspread and pillowcases, but the carpets were a burnt brown and the white ledge of my wall-built desk still held the trappings of my childhood: atlases, Narnia books, Ralph's glass cage full of shavings even after the animal had died.

"Huh." Williams came over, inspected. "Coo-el."

Outside the street was empty, almost frighteningly quiet. His father and Teddy and Beau were at work. They'd already made their big move. And just so, we were about to make ours.

We went outside, passing my mother who was talking to the housekeeper in the vestibule. The vacuum cleaner whined, the family terrier yapped. My mom didn't even give us a glance.

"I don't feel anything."

"You don't?" I said. "I'm waasted."

"Then you're a puss."

"No." Having said it, I couldn't take it back. "I'm fuckin' stoned."

The pills were worthless. Even I knew when I gobbled mine down it wasn't gonna do a damn thing. Wax, vitamins, God knows what they were, but I'd been conned. As for the joint, there was marijuana in it somewhere, some weak strain of local-hillbilly shake, probably, but also stuff from a spice jar. Rosemary and oregano, but we didn't cook either. We were in the alley, about halfway down the block toward Carlyle. I'd thought to go over and knock on Sev's door but Williams stopped me. This was for the two of us, only.

"Michelle Pearlman lets me squeeze her pussy."

"She doesn't." I looked at my friend, half credulous.

"She does."

Squeeze? See how young we were? It was late afternoon. The sun burned beyond the tops of the conifers, but we were in cool shadow, along a clean white wall in the wide alley that was almost like a street. These were suburbs; the only things back here were empty trash buckets and immaculate garages.

"You're a virgin."

"Fuck you." I gambled, knowing the word's purview but not its precision. "So are you. You're more of a virgin than I am."

"You're a puff," he said. "An impesal."

God knows. *Putz*; *imbecile*, I think. But I'll never know for sure. The leaves rustled, the afternoon cooled. Williams could talk about Michelle Pearlman all he wanted: one forbidden fruit was more or less the same as the next. Sex and marijuana were zones of equal ignorance, equal sanctity. My eyes burned, my virgin throat.

"We should go home," I said. Five minutes, or five hours, later. "My mom's probably looking."

My mom was probably drinking, too. Not that I'd yet begun to notice. Besides looking after me, she'd taken up screenwriting, written a feature, which would eventually be made by Orion Pictures. A true story, set in a Florida prison. My mother's restless intelligence never did find a home, quite.

"Haaa," Williams laughed. "Maybe I'm a little baked."

I looked up at the sky, the columnar cypresses that grew out of the neighbors' yard, watching these things the same way I watched the girls in my class, with wonderment and shyness and not a little bit of terror. Were we high? Who could tell?

"Let's go," I said. "My mom'll be waiting."

Williams and I walked home, but when we got there my mother was puttering around the kitchen instead. Sev sat in the dining room, sucking on a milkshake and nibbling grilled cheese.

"Duuuude." Williams fixed him with a heavy stare, dragging his vowels and his knuckles so Sev would know what was what. "What's happening, son?"

Severin glared. Fingers dripping with carbonized toast crumbs and semiliquid cheese. He was taller, *sharper* somehow behind those glasses, but he was the same geeky Sev. He propped his elbows on the dining table and crunched, contemptuously.

"Not much . . . son."

Beau was just out of the hospital. He had committed himself voluntarily for six weeks. Chest pains, hallucinations, night terrors. Some colleagues of his, Skobs and others, took turns watching Sev during this time. Even my mother chipped in. How could she not? On some level, she may have felt the tiniest bit responsible for this motherless, fatherless boy. Although Sev was more of a man than Williams or I were: grief completed him as a human being. He would always be ahead of us; we could never outflank him. Drenched in Visine, breath stinking of Tic Tacs, we were like stupid suitors swimming in cologne, while Severin, the real Mannish Boy, swept in behind us and cleaned out the hive.

"Where were you?" My mother refilled Severin's milkshake, leaning over with the blender pitcher. Williams grunted out the riff from Cheech and Chong's "Earache My Eye." *Get it, Sev?* My mom stood by the long table that was so seldom used, this room with its candelabras and chandelier, its old wooden sideboard. "What were you boys up to?"

"We were outside playing strikeout," I said.

"I didn't see you." Severin smirked.

"We were up the street, closer to your house. You know that garage with the rectangles on it?"

Good alibi; there was such a garage. My mother shrugged and set the pitcher down. Unconquered just yet by her own demons, her face traced with only the barest of lines. Severin mopped the brown froth from his mouth and gave an exaggerated *ahh*. My mom wiped the table with a towel. Bending her head so her blonde hair gleamed in the afternoon light. And that was the end of that.

III

OUR FATHERS WERE not in heaven. They had decided, instead, to form a company, to band together against the Waxmortons, the Smiligans, the old coots who had oppressed them all from the beginning. The idea had taken hold before Bryce Beller's Fourth of July party, and there were a few apostates—namely, Williams Farquarsen III—who'd been plotting this since 1974. American Dream Machine. The name was his, the idea, the ideology. All that time he'd been teaching me how to dribble, his eyes were on the prize. When I think back on my childhood, it was always Williams, that chamber of strangeness, that master enigma, who invented it all. Where Tinseltown was crawling with offices that had bland, recessive banners—International Creative Management, Talented Artists Group, William Morris, names that were as corporate as their manners were old-fashioned—American Dream Machine would be flagrant, defiant, loud. No more sad men in flannel suits and loafers, grumpy Jews eating tuna fish sandwiches at the Hillcrest Country Club, acting like the agency biz was a form of gentle intelligence work, Graham Greene without the violence or self-betrayal. American Dream Machine would have the arrogance of a studio, would function like one insofar as it would package the actors and directors, controlling the means of production in order to ransom the capital. The studios no longer had all the power, not the way they once did. Jack Warner and Louis B. Mayer could spin in their graves, but the business would at last be free. This was Williams's vision, and the others fell in with it soon enough. He was the head of Talented Artists legal department. It was easy enough for him to incorporate quietly, to found the new agency without saying a word. The old one had other shells and subsets, actors' dormant production companies and loan-outs to whom they paid monies owed, less commission. This made it easy to hide. American Dream Machine's existence didn't matter to anyone, the entity wasn't noticed by Sam or anybody else as Williams simply began to pay certain clients through it. Milton Schildkraut, from accounting, was in from the beginning. Bob Skoblow and Roland Mardigian signed on soon thereafter. Teddy Sanders came aboard, which left Beau. Who walked into Will's office one day at the very end of December and found these men all gathered together.

"What is this? The fucking Boston Tea Party?" TAG was in its new building over on La Cienega. "What are all of you doing here?"

Beau thought he and Williams were simply going to lunch. Instead they were all waiting for him, perched on his old friend's furniture, arrayed upon white couches and chairs and a bearskin rug, the louche, tropical-chalet trimmings of the corner office.

"Have a seat, my friend." Will stepped forward to greet his old colleague. "Great to see you."

No one had seen Beau since the notorious Fourth, and all were shocked to find him positively gaunt. He'd lost seventy-five pounds in five months and now looked like a cancer patient, like a normal-sized man who—at five eight and 190—bore the trace of having been annihilated by mortal experience. His hair had gone an almost coppery-blond, and he wore a full beard and big amber glasses. Williams had joked that he'd need a disguise to enter Sam's lair, but he didn't. He simply wasn't recognizable.

"You know why," Williams said. It was weird to see him, too, in such a big office, an echoic variant of Sam's original with the parquet floors and U-shaped desk. "You know what we're here for, Beau."

A roomful of dark hair, of Azoffian and Geffen-like beards, the way the hitters all looked back then. Will himself was clean-shaven, barefoot as was now his way, while through the window behind him spread the palmy path of La Cienega.

"You said there was business." Secretly, Beau'd thought they were going to ask him to bury the hatchet with Sam and offer him his old job. He'd have done it in an instant.

"There is. But first."

Roland Mardigian stood up. They all did.

"We're sorry for your loss, Beau."

"We are."

"Yes."

Everyone spoke. They used the murmurous, civilian voices you almost never heard from them, a sort of plainspeak in which the nicknames, the boasting were all gone. They'd all attended Kate's funeral, of course, and a couple had called him—some regularly— in the months intervening. Will himself had called every day. But this was informal, and because it wasn't dictated by any social code, because Williams decided to start with this, Beau was moved.

"How are you getting on?" Roland asked. Beau sank down on the couch next to him, spread his shoes out onto the white rug. "Are you sleeping?"

"Not really." Beau removed his sunglasses. "I'm still having a hard time."

"And the rest of it?" Bob Skoblow, cigarette burning, spoke. The last man in the room who still smoked. "How are you, my friend? How does it feel?"

The big question. *How does it feel?* Figures Bob, the hipster, the Bob Dylan aficionado, would ask.

"I don't know," Beau sighed. Even his cheeks were sunken, as he blew air. "I honestly can't say. I get up, I do business . . . "

"So you *are* working?"

Another sigh. "When I can."

It meant a lot to him, to see these people. Bryce was still his client. Davis DeLong. Rufus could've been charged with juvenile something-or-other, manslaughter probably, but he was all of ten years old. Davis had whisked the boy into treatment and immediately donated $250,000 to promote gun control. The gesture itself felt senseless, as idiotic and ill-considered as anything Davis had ever done or said with him from the beginning, but it was *felt*. His loyalty to Beau, unless it was just to his own career, touched Beau. It equalized the event, strangely. Not Davis's fault, not Beller's or Vana's, not even—on good days—his own. The A-bomb had fallen in his heart. There was a sense of cities, provinces, whole nations gone to ash. *How does it feel?* Good Lord. It felt like having your future reduced to nothing, and your past set so moltenly ablaze there would be no escape from it.

"We miss you," Teddy Sanders said. "We want you back."

Beau picked up his glasses and put them back on. It touched him, more than anything ever had really, to *be* missed, given how much of his time was spent missing someone else. He and Severin now lived together like friars, companions of some weird and unpredictable necessity.

"You want me to come back here?"

His voice, too, was weak, parched for want of civilized use.

"We want you to come with us," Bob Skoblow said. "We're building something new."

"Building something?"

For these five men to be sitting in an office in broad daylight and talking so openly—behind a closed door—was the height of boldness. The sense was, it was now or never. The moment they told him, they could never go back.

"What are you talking about?" Beau settled deeply into his seat. Even when he was skinny, he controlled the flow of gravity in a room. "What are you guys up to?"

His voice grew cagey. The instant it was business, he became an astronaut circling the world.

"We're starting an agency," Williams said. "We want you to be a part of it."

Everybody looked at Beau. They watched him, even though Williams was speaking. Who was the real president? Who owned this moment?

"An agency? Why start another agency?"

"Because." It was Williams who had the answers at least, Williams who held the truth in his pocket. "This place is rotten. There's something rotten in the state of Denmark . . . "

With Beau listening, he laid out his plan. They would leave in January. They had waited through October in order to receive their bonuses and had just spent the week before the holidays, a time when Sam was vacationing in Aspen, cozying up not just to their own clients but to his, checking in just as their roles—junior agent on Laurence Olivier's team, say—demanded. The sense was that some of these stars were available, as loose as milk teeth within Sam's feeble representation.

"This place is hopeless, Beau. Sam should be booking jugglers and trained apes. We're in the *movie* business, not vaudeville."

Most of their own clients would go with them too, or so they thought. Of course, there was no way to know until they actually left. Beau listened without saying a word. Watching his old friend, who still kept the long hair, the florid mannerisms, the Southern gentility of old. Even if the business had coarsened him up a little.

"We need to do this," Will said quietly. He brushed his red hair away from his face, adjusted the cuff links on his untucked shirt. "It's our time, Beau."

"What about Abe?" was what Beau said when he finally spoke. "I don't care about Sam, obviously. But what about Mr. Waxmorton?"

"We have his blessing."

"Is that right? How did that happen?"

"I spoke to him," Will said. "Mr. Waxmorton understands the situation."

Abe had finally retired the prior summer. Beau had taken Severin back to New York in the fall, just for a long weekend, and together they'd driven out to North Fork to visit him. Beau had found the same old elegant Abe, puttering around his house and missing his beloved Flora. The real impetus, of course, was to see what had happened to Rachel. Her apartment was empty, the phones disconnected. Only once since the tragedy had Beau and Rachel spoken, a transcontinental telephone call two days after it happened. Beau had been doped up on tranquilizers, could feel the rage even so—both his and hers—just pouring down the wires, concentrating itself in his jaw, his cheek, through a conversation that was mostly silence. *Forgive, please.* He couldn't get the words out, couldn't ask her for anything he wasn't able to offer himself. *The funeral's Friday.* He finally managed that. *Will you come?*

She hung up on him. Was it her inhumanity or his own that drove her away? Was it an accident? Was it what she called fate? She just evaporated. She didn't show up at the memorial, and then she was gone. He'd hired a detective, briefly, then asked Waxmorton—who else might know?—what had happened to his ex-wife. But Honest Abe just shrugged. *Haven't heard from her since she left the agency.*

"We have Mr. Waxmorton's blessing," Roland said. "We've all been to see him. He knows the business has to reinvent itself to survive."

Beau looked from one face to another. Great, lanky, goonish Roland, whose narrow eyes made him appear like some vengeful ghost. He seldom smiled, might have been a villain in a movie, played by an actor, himself. The one they'd cast a few years later as the albino assassin in *Foul Play*, what was his name? William Frankfather.

"I'm in. If it's all right with Abe. If he really has offered us his blessing."

"The only thing he asks is that we never compete with TAG in New York. No theater department."

No theater. He could live with that. When the company took on the occasional playwright, as they would David Mamet, say, Teddy would be on point. Skoblow would run the music department, Roland TV. But the play would never be the thing.

"So when do we start?"

Was it pity that moved them, these Frankfathers? I sometimes think it was. Although it might've been simply that Beau had a conscience, was in some sense still the most ethical man in the room. If Will was the mastermind, Beau was the soul. They needed his blessing, more than they did his clients.

"We'll get our things out of here by next weekend," Williams said. "Come the new year, we'll be launched. Sam will never know what hit him."

There certainly wasn't any grandeur in the beginning. Bob Skoblow and Roland Mardigian snuck file boxes out of the TAG offices daily, hid manila folders under their coats. The Rolodexes too were dismantled by stealth, the cards replaced by blanks, so Sam wouldn't see what was happening. The same way a spy might think to gull his would-be assassins by arranging a pillow in his bed, the agents who founded American Dream Machine erased themselves from those offices step by meticulous step. Until the final weekend, when they came in at night to finish the job with sudden violence. Then, at last, they took the things that belonged to them, the one-sheets and the wall hangings and the tchotchkes, the client gifts that practically defined them: their own very bodies.

"Hey Rosers, you want this?" Skoblow called from the hall, while my dad was looting Williams's office.

"Huh?"

Beau actually wore a ski cap and black clothes. They'd seen too many movies. This wasn't a jewel heist. The head of security, barely more than a janitor, had let them into their own building. This wasn't cloak-and-dagger shit yet; there were no confidentiality agreements. The agency business had been a gentleman's game, until now.

"This here." In the doorway, Skobs held up Sam's spittoon. "It's been polished."

"Naw." Beau smiled. The first smile, almost, since Kate was lost. "I've learned to use the urinal."

They took their Betamax tapes, their libraries. They took their furniture, their desk chairs, their candy jars and paperweights. They took hidden stashes of Hershey's bars, of tea and cocaine, took autographed pictures and liquor and stacks of unanswered fan mail, took deal memos and pleas and yellow legal pads. They took everything that wasn't nailed down, that didn't belong, as property, to Talented Artists Group. They left Sam's spittoon on top of his desk, gleaming and filled with water, like some sort of aqueous, pasteboard crown.

Drink up, drink up, the cup is full, read the note Williams Farquarsen left pinned beneath it. A garbled, gratuitous insult, because for all his cool and thoughtful caution, he had the smallest of reckless streaks, a place where rage erupted into nonsense. He was just like my dad, in this one minuscule respect. They ransacked the place and took off with as many of Sam's clients as they could. But they left him his pissoir.

"You boys got everything you need? They're fumigating your offices tomorrow, huh?" The security guard scratched his curly-haired dome. All the lights were off except in the lobby. "I hadn't heard."

"Yep, no worries, Gary." Williams lifted a hand as he headed back out to the garage. "We'll see you Monday."

Legal action was threatened. But none was ever taken. No one was ever able to prove any actual property was missing. The wall hangings and tchotchkes all belonged to the men, the files were duplicates, and those that were confidential were instantly hidden, buried in an Iron Mountain somewhere deep in the Valley. The scripts were already circulating around town, so the agents could claim they had gotten them through other means, hence what could be disputed? The clients? Was that what men like Sam believed they owned? No matter. The perpetrators, or purveyors, or proprietors—whichever they were—of American Dream Machine took out an ad in *Variety*, the January 10, 1977 issue, announcing their company's foundation. It took up a quarter page, the golden letters of the company's monogram shaped like a rocket, with the *A* atop the *D* atop the *M*, tapering from the bottom consonant's squat base toward the top letter's point.

"It looks like an ad for an escort service," Beau said. "Who'll know what it is?"

ADM, with the company's phone number and primary telex, a suggestion of offices in London, New York, Geneva, and Rome— these were just answering services—listed below the words "Creative Management and Representation." What the fuck was it?

"It's like something you take money out of," Teddy Sanders said.

"Exactly." Williams, resting his feet against the edge of a card table, a card table! Because their so-called offices were stuck back in Roland's garage, his little ranch-style house on Schumacher Drive. "It's exactly that."

"It's like an obscene sexual act." Bob Skoblow snickered. "It's like—"

"Exactly!" Williams popped up and slapped the table. "After we fuck 'em, we make 'em taste what it's like."

Such vulgarity wasn't much like Will, but I suppose even he had his moments, by then. There were six men in all, and just four tables, huddled in the low-ceilinged garage in which they'd plunked down some green carpet and hooked up a ceiling fan and some phone lines. Out here on the fringes, in Carthay Circle. What did they have, besides bravado? So many of their clients were suddenly hesitant, had opted to stay behind with Sam, while the studios were sluggish to respond to the new agency. What if doing business with American Dream Machine jeopardized their relationships with TAG? It turned out Sam had the leverage after all. And of course the moment the guys opened their shop they began to hemorrhage money. The cost of phones, of photocopying alone, of getting every script and every check all the way across town in twenty minutes was punishing. Roland's garage reeked of detergent and nontoxic mold, the sweat of five men—Milton Schildkraut worked out of his own home, for now—on the phone at the same time, from their varying "desks" in separate corners. It looked like a suburban teenager's rec room. Beau did half his business in the john, lying on his back under the sink like a plumber, just so his clients wouldn't know their agents were so impoverished they couldn't afford any better, and wouldn't overhear the other men talking.

"Where d'you want to meet, Brycie, the Palm?" Beau fiddled with his credit card in his pocket, hoping there was room enough to cover this. He'd skip the fried onions. "One o'clock, fine, we'll make the reservations. Cece!" he called out to Roland's wife, who was the only assistant any of them had. "Will you get us a table at the Palm, please, one o'clock?"

All of them went through this. Every one. It took Roland six months to close a deal, and Teddy was so strapped he ate nothing but sandwiches for a month. This was why I'd transferred over to public school, in fact, not that I knew it. Maybe, just maybe they'd make it eventually. But what a nightmare it was for a while.

"Hey, Rollie!" Beau hollered across the room. "Toss me that thing."

Roland threw him a soft, semideflated basketball. Milt, the accountant, was the real player, but the others—lanky nerds and stocky Jews, to a man—weren't athletic. Beau tried to spin it on his finger and it toppled into his lap.

"What the fuck are we doing, Rollie? What is this?"

Late spring. It was the absolute nadir. Olivier had redefected to Sam, Davis DeLong's career was in the shitter. Their clients were Sally Struthers and Timothy Carey, minor stars who weren't even commissionable for the most part, since their paperwork was still with other agencies. Waiting for old deals to expire, for Universal to recognize them at all, the agents of American Dream Machine fought on. In the windowless heat collector of Roland's garage—God knows, there wasn't any air-conditioning—they sweltered and worked the phones, having just cut back from six lines to three.

"We should be doing something else," Beau said.

Roland shrugged. His soft, high voice didn't fit with his long body. "It's what we signed up for."

"It's not what *I* signed up for," Beau said.

"We're in this together, remember? This isn't TAG. The old, every-agent-for-himself mentality doesn't fly."

"The hell," Beau said. Yet he believed this more than anything, what Will insisted was the company's spine. *All for one, one for all.* How could he deny the man who'd carried him for so many years? Beau breathed in the rubbery smell of the basketball. "Fucking Williams."

Williams was out now at a meeting. Teddy had gone to the airport to meet a writer from New York, while Cecilia was in the house doing dishes. Not like the phone rang, anyway. It was just Roland and Beau, with Bob Skoblow on the far wall plugging his free ear with his finger, leaning urgently into his call like a jockey.

"Right, Herb, I understand," Bob said. "But listen, listen—"

How hard it was to make threats when you had no one behind you. Bob was five foot seven; his Jewish afro was beginning to recede.

"You think it's bad for you?" Roland had been working all morning trying to put together a game show called *Factazoids.* "I'm bleeding out of orifices I didn't even know I had."

Beau snickered. He tossed Roland the ball.

"It's all I think about," Roland continued. "How much money did I lose today? How long before I'm sleeping in my car?"

"There are worse things to bleed out than money."

"That's true." Roland flung the ball back again. "That's certainly true."

Skoblow was listening into the receiver now, his face frozen in incredulity. Whether over what he was hearing on the line, or that he found himself in this position at all, who could say?

"Shit, Rosers, I'm sorry," Roland said. "I shouldn't complain to you."

"No worries." The truth was, Beau had begun to live again. Even the regular sufferings of fear were better than the ashen grayness of unfeeling, the numbness that had clutched his heart for months. Who knew that *no* pain was the worst pain, that ordinary agony was the way to feel alive? "I know how it is."

Beau didn't sleep either. He had developed an ulcer, stomach trouble, but what was this in the scheme of things? He hadn't had panic for months. Not since Kate died. In a sense, what was left to be afraid of? He lay there in his solitude on Georgina Avenue at night, listening to the whisper of traffic along San Vicente Boulevard, the oceanic stillness of Santa Monica. White fog drifting among the coral trees, dampening the air in the upstairs bedroom.

Bob Skoblow hung up the phone. He rubbed his face, then shook a Tareyton from his pack and went outside to smoke it.

"Gents, be glad you're in the motion picture side of things," he said. "Music is brutal, *brutal*!"

Maybe it was. Or maybe they were all equal in their discovery of the squeeze that one person could put on another, not from necessity—God knows, Columbia Pictures didn't care about an extra ten grand that was owed to Seymour Cassel—but because a person could, perhaps even had to in some reptilian sense. On Bob's desk was a coffee cup emblazoned with the words HE WHO DIES WITH THE MOST TOYS WINS, a phrase that had entered the lexicon not long enough ago yet to be a cliché. These men believed it. They felt that amassing their monuments and possessions made sense, that it would take them somewhere.

"Boys!" Williams sauntered through the garage's side door. "You look busy."

"Where ya been?" Beau tossed *him* the basketball now, and Williams flicked his hand up and palmed it. "We were just getting ready to mutiny."

"That right?"

"Yep." Beau said. "The natives were getting restless."

"Restless no more," Williams said. "Be restless no more, for we are saved."

"Saved? Isn't that a little Pentecostal, for show business?"

"I just signed Dustin Hoffman."

"No shit?"

Bob Skoblow came in. Like a truant he was sheepish, ducking, skulking. He wore a blue sweater vest, even on a sweltering day like this one.

"What's up, Will?"

"I just pried Dusty away from TAG." He dropped the ball and spread his arms, palms low, a messianic gesture indeed like a preacher's. "He's getting ready to direct a movie at Warners. I close that deal, and we're OK. It's always the first big one that's hardest."

Did they believe him? They had to. It was Williams, always Williams who insisted that whenever something good occurred it was everybody's success. Beau needed to feel this, most.

Cecilia Mardigian stuck her head in. "Did something happen?"

Williams told her. Cecilia was a silvering, curly-haired brunette. She and Roland had been high school sweethearts, and married for twenty years. Her complexion matched the Cremora'd coffee in Skoblow's cup.

"Wonderful!" She clapped. "That is wonderful news."

"It is. Let's go," Williams's lupine smile flashed in the garage's deadening, indoor light. "Let's close up early and celebrate."

"Where?"

"The Polo Lounge. Morton's. Let's have dinner at Scandia, I don't care. It's our office." He slid his hand in and out of his pocket, then jangled his keys in his palm. "Soon enough, we'll do business on our own terms."

IV

WILLIAMS AND HIS wife still lived in the Marina, just as they had since the sixties. In this, as in so many respects, they were not a typical Hollywood couple. Marnie Farquarsen had been to Cambridge, and before that to Harvard. She was not an actress but a sculptress, and in the backyard of their house on Dickson Street, a two-story Craftsman three blocks from the beach, she hammered granite into abstract and intimidating shapes. Perhaps it was for her sake she and Williams persisted in a neighborhood that was deep ghetto, or at least bohemian sinister. Everyone else lived in the Palisades, Santa Monica, Beverly Hills. Bob Skoblow still had his old place in Laurel Canyon, the fuckpad to end all fuckpads before he'd married in '72. For Williams to live in the Marina was beyond eccentricity, especially as the head of an up-and-coming agency who could suddenly afford a little more. Why was he there? It was typical of Will's strange assurance that no one—yet—questioned it.

Just as Williams had predicted, Dustin Hoffman's signing lured another big fish—Sidney Pollack. Bob Skoblow brought in Jackson Browne. The company could handle its operating costs and then some, by now. But Williams's Craftsman house was like his beat-up Peugeot and his untucked shirt, like his yard creeping with wild mint and brick dust, the seaside squalor, all things that were part of his signature. Together they told people he was trustworthy. The urbane dandy Beau had first met in New York had bent a little bit with the mood of the times, roughed himself up when he'd moved to California, but he wasn't just some Hollywood shark, he was a person of substance, with an intellectual wife and a family, and some interests outside the biz. Early Tuesday mornings and Sunday afternoons Williams taught Dustin how to surf. *This* was what made American Dream Machine what it was—not geezers in suits, phonies like Sam who flaunted their degrees yet were practically illiterate, but the fact that Williams was instead an artist, a low-voltage creator *just like us, man*: he'd sit there at brunch and discuss Tennessee Williams or *The Moviegoer* for an hour, long enough you'd forget he was urging you toward a deal, usually for something a little lower down the cultural food chain, but who cared? To me, his wife was an equal mystery. Marnie was brawny and strong in hip-huggers and hiking boots. She wasn't motherly in the slightest. Her strawberry blonde hair was blunt-cut across her forehead, like a feminized variant of a garage punk shag. She had thick hands and thicker glasses and a sarcastic, punishing laugh. *You kids*, she called us, while she pounded away at her rocks in the backyard. Like we were rude interlopers, amusements to her more than anything. Through Marnie we discovered forms of freakery that would've been otherwise unavailable—*Weasels Ripped My Flesh*, Stanislaw Lem, *Omni* magazine—while that house's black wooden floors and gloomy railroad interiors were pierced by her fearsome and pale sculptures. This was a different world.

"Hey, holmes." Outside in the street the kids swirled and scrapped on their bikes and boards. They were taller, leaner, skinnier, and darker than the ones in my neighborhood. "Hey Nate, man, check it out!"

One grabbed my skate and railed against the curb, rode it so hard—doing fakeys and leaping up on the metal banister leading up to Williams's door—he cracked it, my ten-inch Alva.

"Sorry, man." He handed it back to me.

"Yo, holmes, that sucks." The others jabbered in the background "Sorry, *ese*."

"No, it's OK, he's cool, Nate's cool."

The street was wide, but there was no traffic. The houses were tall and crooked, and the kids prowled in front of them like dogs, like the brick stoops were theirs to bark and piss on. Their hazing was mostly affectionate: they liked me, for some reason. Whereas young Williams had been raised here, I was just some Jewish white kid, a million miles in my experience from Tyrone and Luis and Cris and Esvaldo, eleven-year-olds with the full-on scars—physical and psychic—of men ten years older. Cris got his dick sucked under Santa Monica Pier. Tyrone had a three-inch incision from a knife fight. Esvaldo was so bad he flipped me once and gave me a concussion, smashing me down on the cracked concrete while we were "practicing" his judo. They wore white T-shirts and blue bandannas, Lee jeans and sneakers from Kmart or Sears. One or two of them had been to juvie for the shit they did, but for the most part they were all snap and snarl, too protective of Williams—and by extension, of me—to level any real threat. Will was their golden goose. He'd met movie stars. They called him Big Bird, honoring his pronated, goofy-footed stance. Severin really freaked them out. You'd think if anyone was born to get his ass kicked in this situation, was chum for the Del Rey sharks, it was him, but he moved with an almost magisterial freedom. He didn't skate, that was an LA thing, but he stood on Williams's front steps and held court like an auctioneer, the others jouncing around in front of him while he sold off scraps of information.

"Hey Severin, man, what's an *MU*?"

"Magic user. An MU's a magic user."

"And what's the difference between that and a Druid?"

"What about a phraint, *ese*? What the fuck is a phraint?"

Severin told them. Rattling the dice—they had twenty sides, or eight, or four—in his palm like torn teeth. It was late summer, scalding and humid. The sun was a pale disc in the oceanfront haze. These kids had never played D&D, but of course Severin was our dungeon master, the keeper of the keys.

"A saurig's like a lizard," he said. Drawing on all the arcane sources beyond Gary Gygax, Dave Hargrave's *The Arduin Grimoire*, or the *RuneQuest* handbook. "Like a human-sized lizard."

"Like one of those fucking things from *Land of the Lost*, hey?"

"Not quite."

They never did kick his ass, not once. I got mine kicked plenty of times in fun—their fun, at least—and I fucked up my ankle while I was skating the half-pipe Marnie built in the yard. That was the crux of it. We were there to suffer our beat downs, far more than to administer them.

"Yo, yo!" Williams had assimilated this bit of New York-ese to make fun of Severin. "Check it out!"

The half-pipe was the center of our world. It was nine feet tall, and Marnie had nailed it together in the dusty reaches of their backyard, beyond the blocks of granite that lay stacked along the western fence. There was no grass here—the surface of the vast, double-length yard was dirt—and under a gray eucalyptus at the back there was the half-pipe. The ramp was hazardous, littered with coarse and sticky seedpods and with three full feet of vertical at the top, but its surfaces were smooth. She'd done a good job with the wood, curing and sanding and bending the ply until the whole thing was perfect and there were no joints or angles to trip us up. Usually we just puttered closer to the bottom and pretended we were shredding, but today Williams had climbed up the ladder to the platform Marnie had put up—what could she have been thinking?—so we could drop in if we wanted. *You kids, little fuckers. Go on, kill yourselves if you want to!*

"Uh, Williams? Dude? You're gonna get hurt."

1979. Little Will stood on his skateboard's tail and considered the drop, both arms extended like a weather vane. He wasn't Stacy Peralta or Bob Biniak, Jay Adams or Tom Sims, some ghetto banger turned surf shop entrepreneur. He was the eleven-year-old son of a talent agent, privileged no matter how boho his parents were. He wore brown corduroys and checkerboard Vans, a T-shirt that read MR. ZOGS SEX WAX: THE BEST FOR YOUR STICK. A blue bandanna was knotted around his head.

"Watch this, you Valleys." He cackled. And Sev glanced up from where he sat on the edge of one of Marnie's dishwasher-sized granite blocks, reading a Vonnegut. The air smelled like quarry dust, eucalyptus. Inside the house, Marnie was listening to the Doors, and we could hear Jim Morrison grunting and slurring.

Williams dropped in, racing straight down nine feet and up the other side. If he didn't eat it, we'd be on to something. No helmets, no pads, just wind and skin.

"Yes!" I yelled. Watching his green Kryptonics flash as he peaked with a frontside 180. "Yes! Williams!"

He went down in a heap at the bottom, landing on his chin like Chuck Jones's coyote. His skate banged, nose-first, into his neck.

"Will?"

For a minute I felt everything shift. There had been the heroic dreams of sex and sports and music, there were girls and drugs and movies and waves. But right now, there was only this. Severin stared over too. The silence, the stillness were sickening.

"What're you kids doing?" Marnie barged out onto the back porch. "You little gremmies. Williams, get in here and do the dishes."

She watched us—hands on hips, glasses gleaming—while Williams coughed and rolled over, pushed up and grinned.

Fucking A, I thought. His mom was calm as a lifeguard, unwilling to intervene unless she absolutely had to. She didn't have to. We were astronauts now, we had the power. Free as we were to leave the earth, to feel its surfaces sleek beneath our wheels.

Sometimes, the elder Will came out and joined us. Behind his gaze was a pressure, a silence. I may have experienced him the way Beau did, as infinitely benign, a generous protector, but nevertheless he carried something frightening inside him.

"Dad! Come skate!"

Stepping off the porch barefoot, he'd come over and borrow his son's board, rocking back and forth on the half-pipe, taking fewer risks, but acquitting himself pretty admirably for an adult.

"Nate." He'd pop the board up with his feet, catch it, and hand it back to Little Will. "Your turn."

One of us. Almost. But I could feel something, as feral as it was caring, when he looked at me.

"How's Theodore? How's your pop?"

"Fine."

His stare was piercing. He seemed never to blink.

"How 'bout you, Sev? Your old man getting enough to eat?"

He was checking in, I suppose, through us. But I could feel his loneliness, his isolation not just from his colleagues, his troops, but from himself. In this, he resembled us—resembled *me*—more than any other adult I'd known.

"Come sit, Nate."

I'd join him on the porch. Did he know? *How's Theodore?* Yeah, I believe he saw all, everything, and his knowledge of everybody's weak spots grew wearying. Unlike Severin, I was co-optable. As we sat there with our feet planted on the edge of the dirt, sunlight warming his pale calves, I was afraid of him, but afraid not of adult authority; I was frightened by his own fear, whatever it was that seethed and roiled beneath his casual surface.

"Ha!" he whooped, at some daredevil move Little Will had just pulled. "Nice, son."

Whatever troubled him, it wasn't visible. But I knew it was there. Even then, I knew.

"Will! Honey . . . " There was something else I noticed too, heard and felt on those nights I slept over at my friend's. Marnie's throttled voice, in the next room, ballooned with distress. "Honey, I can't breathe!"

Marnie Farquarsen had lung trouble, severe respiratory problems. The smog almost killed her.

"Will!" she moaned to her husband. "Where's my inhaler? I can't breathe."

I slept in the back of the house, upstairs with my friend. His parents were in front, in the big bedroom that overlooked Dickson Street. On the smoggiest nights she had to sleep downstairs on a screened-in porch. Half the reason they were here and not Bel Air was Marnie's chronic bronchitis. It was marginally better for her by the water.

"Hold on, Mar." With her, too, Williams the elder was different. He seemed twittering, almost cowed, not at all the ruthless operator I've assumed he was in the world. From Williams's guest bed I listened. "I'm looking. Hold on."

"It feels like someone's crushing my windpipe."

"What do you need? Do you need a doctor?"

"I need to leave LA."

That wasn't possible. Not given who Williams was, the nonbeing into which he'd drift if ever he left Los Angeles. What was death, compared to the erasure of your name?

"Darling, I'll get you a shot."

I'd seen Marnie have adrenaline before. It was gnarly. But so too was Williams's servility, the sound of a man who bossed other men, who'd soon command a small army, bowing and scraping before his suffering wife.

"Will, stop it!"

Whatever he was doing. I heard just the spike of her annoyance against his irksome ministrations.

"OK, OK, sorry sorry."

"All right. I'm fine, but—oh, God, I can't breathe!"

I lay on my back, in Williams's spare twin. His skateboard was useless now, on the floor between us. Moonlight washed his prostrate form across the room. I was sure he was only feigning sleep.

Marnie coughed, emitting a bronchial racket. When she worked she wore a surgical mask and goggles, took long baths in a room with a humidifier afterward. A person was cursed with the needs of her vocation, forced to work with the things that would kill him. This was true for everyone here.

"Will you get me some water now, Will?"

True for me, and for Severin: eventually we'd be crucified with words. The sound of the father, on his way downstairs. This house had been renovated and expanded yet still had all its original cherry floors and beams. The brackish gleam of its interiors spooked me at night. I lay there in the dark, in the Spartan plainness of my friend's bedroom. I tried to apprehend a density of adult suffering that soon—soon, soon—would mushroom into something more terrible than I could imagine. I listened to the father's creaking footsteps, Marnie's coughing, beyond this a brittle quiet that echoed what I felt in my own home. Something wasn't right; some truth was being concealed. Water gushed from a tap downstairs. Out on the street, a pair of cats yowled and hissed. *I can't breathe.* I closed my eyes, barely daring to open them, lest all I see become falseness, oblivion, moonlight, and lies.

V

ROLAND MARDIGIAN BOUGHT a car, a beautiful E-Type Jag. He left his wife
for a restaurant hostess. And that's how it started, the men with
their plates, their blazoned vanity that signified also the beginning
of their rot. By the end of 1979, the company was up and running for real. They'd signed Jon Voight, on the heels of *Coming
Home*. They had Diane Keaton, and Sissy Spacek. Beau had Gene
Hackman, and after a long psychological duel that culminated in
an afternoon spent helicopter skiing in the Wasatch Mountains—
Williams jetting into Salt Lake on the same plane that would turn
around and whisk TAG operatives back to LA, believing their crown
jewel was safe—the agency signed Robert Redford as well. They
were shrewd, they were smart, pooling their clients and maintain-
ing their leader's ethos that agenting was a team sport. *You find the
open man.* Little by little they insinuated their way closer to dominance. Meryl Streep may have been Sam's client, but when you
were on the set of *Kramer vs. Kramer* every other day to visit Dustin,
you got to know her all the same. You paid compliments, sent gifts.
You asked, perhaps, if she had seen Elaine May's new script, if Sam
had gotten her a certain meeting? No?

Roland was the first to have the blue California license with yellow letters that read ADM RM, the initials of both man and company, affixed to the grill of his automobile. ADM FAR, ADM SKOB, ADM
TS, ADM BEAU. Teddy's white 450 SL convertible with the red leather
interior sat in front of our house at an angle, a rakish tilt toward the
street like a getaway car's.

"This stuff's much heavier than it seemed a couple years ago."

They were moving into their new offices, this time with most of the lifting performed by Starving Students Movers. Beau was carrying only a small cardboard box of files.

"It's not the stuff, Rosers—just put it over there," Bob Skoblow huffed, gesturing toward the corner where there was already a credenza, a gift from Don Henley. "It's us, man. We're the problem here."

"You think we're getting old already?"

"Everybody does, Beau." Skobs set his own box down. "Just some faster than others."

Bob might've been a prophet. But for now the company assumed offices on Century Park East, a sprawling, airborne suite that would've been unthinkable in the beginning. And for a while, even their blips were successes. Will represented Streisand for all of about five minutes, but when those minutes were spent commissioning her enormous fee, who cared? She could stay, go. She could come back again if she wanted, just like Davis did. If the rumors were true and ADM cut its percentage for one or two important clients, that was all right too. Five percent of Dustin was seventy percent of Ernie Borgnine. This kind of math my friends and I never learned in school. They lured a couple more agents over from TAG, young and hungry ones who represented Christopher Walken, Jeff Bridges. They made a rich deal for Michael Cimino at UA. And Roland's TV department boomed. This was where the real money remained even after the agencies began deferring half their packaging fees, waiting until shows turned a profit before they could collect. So, the men were delighted. They visited psychiatrists and ate their grilled fish and shopped at Jerry Magnin's and Dick Carroll's, at Alandales in Beverly Hills, where lackeys handed them spritzers and watched as they fiddled with Zegna ties; they trimmed their beards and schtupped their mistresses and squeezed their lemons over weird and bitter greens. They ate sushi, when it was said to be healthy, or else avoided it when the mercury in fish might—instead—kill you. They went to Charmer's Market, to Jimmy's, to Orlando Orsini's and L'Orangerie; later, to Tony Bill's place in Venice. They were fed and fat and fucked and fortunate: for a while, at least, they were happy indeed. In six months, Beau gained back half the weight he'd lost. The other half came creeping back slowly. He was dating an actress named Star Mullins. Why be skinny if you could get it anyway, if the things that were offered you came and came and came and came? Star was twenty-three, meaning she'd been all of ten when Severin was born. If you thought this caused *us* problems you'd be mistaken, although Beau had his misgivings about it. He tortured himself to Horowitz endlessly, turned once more to his partner for advice. *Beau*, Williams smiled. Even he could give in to the pleasure principle, now. *If it makes you happy, how could it be bad?* And on a Thursday afternoon that happened to be his forty-seventh birthday, Beau came back from one of these sessions to find his office thronged.

"What is this?" On his desk there was a rectangular box. So many people waited, the room felt like a phone booth. The company had a full half of the floor, and new agents had arrived from other places. Laura Nyde, Ken Sullowitz, Peter Jenks. "What are you people up to?"

With high ceilings and glass walls, these offices were bright and hygienic and bustling. They had secretaries now, real ones, and messengers; they had a human resources person, and a coverage department.

"Just open it. Look."

Milt Schildkraut, the man with the bald head and the bear-trap intelligence, leaned in the doorway, hand in his linen pants pocket. The free one twirled a watermelon lollipop, which he worked as if to make fun of a proposed resemblance to *Kojak*.

"Go on, Beau." *Slurp*. "This one's on us."

Beau removed the box's lid, unfolded a crinkly mass of tissue paper. Outside, Century City rose in mellow splendor, a midday quiet in which the sun was momentarily occluded by the ABC towers. You could almost forget these buildings held firms—Gibson, Dunn & Crutcher; Armstrong, Hendler & Hirsch—meant to prevent these men from eating one another alive.

"WO-HO!" Beau's voice tore the silence. It fell during that sleepy after-lunch moment, before people had telephones in their cars. "Look at this!"

He'd unwrapped the spittoon, again the spittoon, which in its elegant uselessness was now polished to a high gloss.

"How'd you get this?"

"It's not the same one. We boosted it from Claridge's ourselves."

There was an inscription along the sloping rims. FOR BEAU ROS-ERS, THE MAN WITH THE GOLDEN C_CK, LOVE DUSTIN.

"Did Dusty inscribe this? Or is that you, Will?"

Nervous laughter, the semihysterical jostling of men to whom everything was funny, lest it should ever be otherwise.

"Look inside." Williams now strolled into the room, parting the crowd of their colleagues to stand in front of Beau's desk. "Look."

The way it worked now was this: Williams and Beau each had a twenty-five percent stake in the agency, while the others had ten. It wasn't how they dispersed the money; bonuses were all generous and almost equal. But Beau and Will had sunk the most of their own cash in at the beginning, had taken the largest risk.

Beau pulled out the rectangular brass tray, the slide-out bottom in which he half expected to find something repulsive. Instead there was a thin envelope and a thick wad of cash. Two tickets to London, first class.

"Take your girlfriend. You need a vacation."

"I do? From what?"

But Williams just smiled. "Enjoy yourself, Beau. Just do."

The agency's ethos never faltered. They looked after one another, so devoted they were mocked with a nickname—"the Secret Shar-ers"—at other places. Beau *did* enjoy himself, more than he ever thought he could. He was point man for De Niro, he handled Sidney Lumet. With Williams, he shared Scorsese. On top of it all, the best part was that he loved not just his business, but his son. Some days he woke up grieving and clammy and haunted and ill, and there were times still he wanted to die. But he began to feel—at last—he had surfaced. The song of a man who has come through! Too seasoned to imagine success would last forever, he vowed to enjoy it while he could. With Star, he imagined starting a fam-ily. With Severin, he went to Dodger games, and facing the orange UNION 76 sign beyond the blue center-field wall, staring from the Dream Machine box behind home plate, he could feel their shared contentment. *Want another dog, Sev?* His son was undergoing a growth spurt, with the barest hint of a mustache along his lip. My brother may have been an alien to him, into things he could feel were Rachel's, but Beau had never been closer to another human being.

"Go on, Rosers!" Teddy Sanders said. "They make movies in England, too."

"I'll sign David Puttnam," Beau crowed. "We never said we wouldn't have a London office."

And so he went. With Star he stayed at the Connaught, then they went to Rome for a lost weekend. Sev crashed at my house, as they were gone almost three weeks. Everything was paid for by the company, everything. Meals were expensed, hotels were comped, even the ring—yes, there was a ring—came through the phone call Williams made to the props department at Disney, who had a deal with Harry Winston. If ever his life was like a movie, if ever things happened without any effort at all, it was now—doors opened themselves, drivers carried bags, reservations were so elastic that if they wanted to dine at eleven o'clock instead of eight the same table was waiting, with the same silverware and different flowers. All was an idyll. When Beau arrived home, he was married. To a girl from Topeka, who'd had her first drink on a date with him two years before.

"Hello, sweetheart." His secretary, Linda, looked up on Monday morning. She was older—thirty-one—and not beautiful, two things he'd sought out when hiring, in order to remain untempted.

"H-hey, he's back!" Milt Schildkraut sat on the edge of her desk. Milt had a slight stutter when he was excited. "How was it?"

"I'm reborn."

"You look tan. Who goes to London and comes back tan?" Milt said.

"We went to Ansedonia. We were in Rome, and Carlo loaned us his beach house."

"Which Carlo?"

"Pontevecchio." Beau grimaced, amused. It was the long hand of Williams again, of course. "He's one of our directors."

"I've never paid him."

"You've never paid anyone else. Linda, did I miss anything?"

"Davis, this morning. Gene. John Calley." They'd spoken four times a day while he was gone, rolled calls in his hotel room. Besides getting his trades a day late, there wasn't anything to miss. "Nothing urgent."

"Get Gene."

He and Milt turned and went into his office. Linda was thick-waisted and black-haired, with the densely waxen complexion of girls he'd known growing up, though she was from Hacienda Heights and not Astoria Boulevard. She was pretty by any regular standard, but since when did that standard pertain here?

"What's up, Milt?"

"Did you a-authorize this?" Milt handed him a mimeographed form.

Will's expenses. Beau squinted at it incuriously. The two men signed off on each other's expenses—someone had to—but all he saw here were ordinary hotel bills, restaurants. "So what?"

"Who lives in Chicago?"

"Bill Murray lives in Chicago. What are you being such a bean counter about, Milt?"

"My job."

Outside, Linda squawked, "Left word!"

"Are we in trouble?"

"No, n-nothing like that," Milt said. "Nowhere close."

"Then why worry?" He and Williams shared a number of clients. Certain nervous Nellies like Marty, who needed both hands held *and* another to yank them off under the table. Beau handled Bill Murray by himself, but so what? Murray was as loyal to Beau as Belushi was, in fact because of Belushi, who loved Beau, predictably enough, like a brother. Each looked at the other and saw himself. "I visited Larry in London too."

Larry, Sir Laurence. This was Will's client, in turn.

"All right, it isn't a worry. I just worry when there's nothing to worry about."

"Who doesn't?"

In the near interior of Beau's office there was an overstuffed white couch, a glass table with a large bowl of cinnamon jelly beans, a pitcher of ice water, and two cylindrical glasses. Today's *Daily Variety* reported on the weekend gross for *The Idolmaker*, the ratings for "No More Mr. Nice Guy," the season premiere of *Dallas*.

"Davis DeLong!"

"Call back."

Milt Schildkraut slipped the expense report, with which there was nothing wrong, back into its folder.

"You still married?"

"Yeah. You took the under?"

The two men chuckled.

"You gonna get her some work?"

"Nah." Roland Mardigian had done that, gotten his restaurant girlfriend a spot in a series. It hadn't worked out: they were separated already. "Not my style."

"So whatcha gonna do?"

Morning light fell through the window at the far end, onto Beau's desk and the leather-backed chair and the various trophies, on the spittoon and an autographed ball from Dusty Baker and Rick Rhoden and Ron Cey resting on a stand. Posters for *Midnight Express*, *Being There*. These offices could not have been more different from the old Talented Artists Group ones, being neither cloistered nor clubby; their plate-glass windows faced smog-tinged sky.

"We're going to have a baby," Beau said. "I'm going to knock her up."

VI

"BITCH! FUCKING WHORE! CUNT!"

Beau Rosenwald stood, bare-chested, in his elegant kitchen at night. He was yelling those things at his wife, who was soon to be an ex-wife. You came to a certain point in life, you just knew how these things went.

"Fuck you! Beau, don't."

Star was teary. She was sitting down. She wore one of the original American Dream Machine shirts, a white baseball T with red sleeves, the company logo on the front, on the back a vaudevillian cartoon dog talking to his agent. *What I really want to do is direct.* Whatever she was contrite for, and she was, it overwhelmed her. She sat and wept while her husband prowled the crimson-tiled room, banging its steely fixtures with his hand.

"I don't want to have a baby! I'm sorry, it's too soon."

"So you aborted one?"

"I did. I'm sorry."

"How could you do that to me?"

"To *you*?" She shook her hair out of her face. Teary, angry, her expression sharpened also into something resolute as an adult's. "How typical of you to imagine this is about yourself."

"What d'you know from typical?" He waved her off, dismissive. "What do you know about anything, you shiksa whore?"

This was late autumn of '81. They'd been married barely a year. I don't know where Sev was during this, but if I were to hazard a guess I'd say in his room with his 'phones on, either masturbating or listening to *The Wall*.

"Fuck you, Beau. My father used to beat me!"

"He should've beat some sense into you."

She glared. "How can you say that? You give money to Planned Parenthood, the Venice Family Clinic."

He stared back, flexing his fingers. He could feel the impulse to really let fly, just as Herman Rosenwald's voice roared in his ears. *Fat shit!* He was ugly, unattractive as he'd ever been with his bitch tits and his sloping belly, the top of it rolling over a pair of pale flannel trousers.

"I'd like to have another kid."

"I know! Why can't we wait a few years? We just got married!"

Why couldn't they wait? The refrigerator hummed, the radio, which was almost always on in here, sat quiet. The track lights were moody. He went over to the fridge and got himself a Perrier. He offered her one too.

"I can't wait," he said. "I'm sorry."

"How come?" Did he know something, was he ill? "I just want to *work*, Beau, I want to accomplish things, my career!" Her career. "I'm so close, Beau. I could wait a year, two years, three years, *five* and I wouldn't even be thirty! What's the hurry?"

She did love him. She didn't care that he was fat and rich, or that her stepson was a supercilious little prick who insulted her at every turn, lifting his eyebrows whenever he saw her with a massive paperback in her hand as if to ask, *You enjoying that?* The Other Side of the Mountain?

"I care. *I* care," he said. But he didn't in that moment and felt he might never again. "Oh, fuck it."

She blinked back, soupy with tears. Her sincerity bugged him, the way she actually meant everything. Hadn't Olivier told him, once, that the secret to being an actor was being *un*truthful?

"Get out of my house," he roared, while she sniffled and wept. "I'm serious. Get the fuck out!"

How stupid she was! How stupid *he* was, ever to fall for her. How stupid, all of it, the way he forced a gorgeous girl who truly loved him—the first one, ever—to leave, to pick up her purse and shuffle out of the kitchen, clutching the long strap of the Bottega Veneta bag he'd bought her. He could hear her banging around the stairwell and weeping, her voice carrying and echoing off the tiles in the hall. Such histrionics! He felt nothing.

"Dad."

Severin came in, later. Beau'd been sitting there for who knew how long, over at the table now with his forehead propped on his balled fists.

"What are you doing?"

Star was gone, the house was silent, Beau sat and willed himself toward a regret he could not feel, save for that lingering taste of failure. Was failure ever stronger, really, than when it was in remission? Did it ever actually go away?

"Your stepmother and I had a fight."

"I heard."

"You did? Sorry."

Why couldn't he be like Williams, in this respect, too? Why couldn't he control his temper, why did he need a different woman every twenty minutes?

"It's all right. Why aren't you dressed?"

Severin was high, really high for one of the first times. Antigravitationally, skin-meltingly, face-crushingly stoned.

"I dunno." Beau stood up, looked around the room without interest. He'd been sitting here forever, since midafternoon, reading scripts. Exactly as he'd been when Star dropped the bomb. "I had a shirt, somewhere."

"Are you an athathin?" Sev mimicked Brando in *Apocalypse*.

"Not quite." Beau laughed.

He loved his son. More than anything, he loved his son. The first spread of regret, the inkling he may have made a mistake, washed through him. Star was beautiful, stupid but magnificent. She was far better than he deserved.

"Hungry?"

Severin was scrambling eggs, cracking them now into the pan. One thing Sev could always do was cook, since who else was gonna do it? Beau couldn't.

"I'm fucking starving, son."

He watched Sev closely. Beau was aware of the marijuana in his son's life, but what was he supposed to say about it? *Don't*? He stood up.

"I'm going to put a shirt on."

He went upstairs and got one, a salmon-colored bespoke he'd had made on Jermyn Street. The bedroom was a mess, Star's shoes and jewelry flung everywhere and his tent-like clothes strewn across the floor. Who cared? This master suite was more like a hotel room, the gargantuan bed, the bottled water all over the place. A dildo stood upright on the nightstand. He'd lived like this always, the prisoner of his own sloth. He came back down, found Severin already sitting with a six-egg omelet.

"You want some of this? I'll make you some. Dad."

Sev's face was frozen, bent into some weird rictus of befuddlement and hilarity.

"You OK, son?"

"Nah. Yes. I mean yes." He was staring at his fork, at the scrap of egg at the end of it, like it contained some key to the cosmos. "I'm all right."

He yelped and dropped his fork with a spastic little laugh. Beau went over to the counter and poured himself an enormous glass of Mount Gay rum over ice. Time to start drinking again after months of eating like an insect, this actress with her actressy food. He sat down opposite his son, at the metal-framed breakfast table he'd owned since 1965. Practically everything else in the house was new.

"I'm sorry about your stepmother."

"It's OK."

"It's not OK." Beau spoke slowly, the way he did when he had to make a tender point. He sipped his rum beneath the sickly light of the kitchen, the sullen yellow that never felt particularly like home. Except now, when he sat with his boy and tried to explain the unexplainable. "I know you miss your mother. Your real mother. Star and I tried to—"

"I don't like her."

"Sev!"

"I don't. I think Star is fucking awful."

"Awful?"

"Yes!" Severin laughed. "I think she's a moron."

Beau searched his son again. Awful wasn't the same as stupid, actually, but the two things had some relation.

"Are you stoned?"

"Yes."

Beau looked at his son in amazement. "I don't want you to get high."

"But you're not going to punish me?"

"I can't do that. No. But I don't want you to do it, Severin, I don't want you to smoke pot."

"I will."

"I know, but I don't want you to. I don't want you to want to."

"Do you? Want to?"

Beau studied his kid. Stared at Sev's checkered Vans that were graffitied along the rims with all sorts of obscure hieroglyphs, his skinny-legged jeans and a faded Hang Ten T-shirt that was a last vestige of his younger, proto-Californian self.

"Yes."

Father and son got high, then. They smoked Severin's pipe and then Beau ran upstairs to get his bong, which was better. He hid it in the back of his closet, though there'd no longer be any need, he supposed.

"This is some fantastic shit, Sev."

"Thanks."

"Where are you buying your drugs?" For a moment, he'd play the concerned father again. "I want you to tell me where you got this."

"Can't."

It rankled him, also, that his son scored better pot than he could. By accident, whereas he was in touch with people whose contacts trucked it in from Humboldt themselves. In a minute it would all start up again—his car alarm would go off and he'd run outside to find Star beating on the hood of his turd-brown 911—but just now he looked at his kid and began roaring with laughter.

Beau never understood my brother. I think this is true. He never understood me either, but with Severin he at least had a chance. He loved him, and they resembled one another in ways that couldn't fully be explained. In their self-estrangement, he sometimes thought. Sev didn't know where he came from, either. What was it like, being someone whom everybody else—really—wondered about? *Beau Rosenwald's legitimate son and heir*, or later, *Severin Roth, the novelist*. What was it like? Late at night Beau came into that kitchen and found Severin writing in a spiral-bound notebook, just covering page after page with his agitated scrawl in black ballpoint pen.

"Whatcha writing?"

"Stuff."

The tail end of seventh grade. Severin hardly slept and neither did Beau, through that terminal and strange year. They were back to living as they once had, as an older brother and a weird, younger charge: some bizarre relationship that wasn't exactly father-and-son, though it certainly wasn't anything else either.

"What stuff? You did your algebra?"

"Yep."

"So what stuff?"

Beau drank milk, for his stomach. Sev drank juice, OJ that looked fluorescent—like Tang—in the late-night kitchen. Crickets trilled outside. The radio was turned down to a mumble.

"Just stuff. Papers."

"Papers?"

"Yep. Stuff."

He held the notebook on his knees so no one could see any closer. Beau wasn't all that curious, really. Boys wrote things, and no matter how closed Severin was—like a bivalve, an oyster before his father—he'd already admitted his worst sins. Don't think Beau hadn't searched the house for heavier drugs, and wouldn't have recognized the signs, given what he did all day, the people he worked with.

"You still writing those letters?"

"Hmm? Oh, yeah."

"Are you high?"

"No."

"You wanna be?"

"No thanks."

Severin had been writing and receiving letters, to and from someone in Oregon. In sixth grade his class had been required to do this, they'd been paired with a sister school—Episcopal hippies, again—up there. Yet Severin continued to write to a person, a girl, Beau gathered, from up north.

"She still sending you letters?"

It was like that book, the Saul Bellow one Nicholson was crazy about. *Herzog*, not that he'd read it. A guy who writes a lot of letters. Some movie that would make!

"Yep."

He'd seen hers, actually: they came to the house at regular intervals. Sometimes she sent packages, records or books. Beau never opened them, but he knew what they were from their shape.

"That's sweet, Sev. I'm glad you have a girlfriend."

"Screw off, Dad."

"Don't talk to me that way."

"Sorry. I'm sorry."

"Right. I never had one, when I was your age."

Severin looked him up and down. "You've made up for it, haven't you?"

This was their candor, Beau thought, and for this it was all worthwhile. He was a great father and a shitty one, a terrible husband and a fabulous agent and a hateful, loveable human being who seemed to inspire affection in others. He could be all these things at once, and if he was an imperfect guardian he was still better than he might've been otherwise. He could've been a bully, say, like his own dad.

"I'm going to sleep, Severin. Turn off the lights when you're done?"

"Uh-huh."

"And don't do anything stupid." This was close to hypocrisy, also. "Don't let Star in if she comes back around this time."

"Yuh."

"Seriously. Last time she hit me with her shoe while I was sleeping. She beat me in the eye with a spiked heel to wake me up."

"Ouch."

"Yes. I didn't just tell you that."

Beau stretched. He lifted his hands over his head. Severin just kept writing, writing and writing and writing and writing. We were already those people, locked into our fates, just like our dad.

"G'night, Sev."

"G'night."

And the sound of his pen continued, scratching away in the near-dark. It wasn't mightier than anything, in Beau's experience: the sword, the cock. It was the weakest gesture a human could make, insofar as it acquiesced before experience. *Whatever will be*. Severin made this sound, while Beau climbed upstairs. Not knowing that as he did, my brother had already overthrown him.

VII

"REN, REN, REN, REN—"

Beau Rosenwald wanted another child? It turned out he was going to get one. Teddy and my mother were fighting, late at night. From my room I listened. Teddy's voice was urgent and confidential, as he tried to calm my mother down.

"I'm trying to make this easy."

"Easy?" my mother yipped. There was the sound of something toppling, a bottle or shaker, in the kitchen below. It was 1:00 AM. "Tell me exactly how easy this is. Tell me how easy it is for *you*."

"Ren, be reasonable."

"I won't!" My mother's voice rose to a peak. Chair legs scraped against the floor as she shoved away from the butcher-block table. "I won't!"

I lay in headphones, with a pillow smothering my face. I couldn't drown their shouting out, though, no matter how I tried.

"Ren—"

"Shut up! You cocksucking fairy!"

"No, just calm down." This was Teddy's mode, the smooth-talking, rationalist salesman. Just as my mother was an emotional drunk. "I made a mistake."

"You—"

"I made a mistake. Just like you did, once. Remember?"

"Don't say it."

"I will. Ren." Teddy sighed. I could hear his weary resignation from upstairs. I took off my 'phones. What were they saying? The green lines of my alarm clock made a matchstick rebus in the dark. "Don't you think we should come clean about this?"

"Clean? You fuck some actress and now you wanna talk to me about 'clean'?"

"This isn't about me," Teddy said. "I'm talking about Nathaniel."

The next sound was the brittle clap of my mother's hand across his cheek. And then a silence so comprehensive it froze me in my bed. I waited and waited, but no one said anything. I could picture them down there, stunned. Just staring at one another in amazement, faces blazing and uncertain. Eventually, I heard a door open, and Teddy's footsteps go tramping into the backyard.

Teddy picked me up from school, two days later. This wasn't unusual. He sometimes did, when he had to leave work early to get ready for a premiere, say. But this time he pulled up in front of the house and just sat there. One hand on the wheel of his convertible.

"Aren't you coming in?" I said.

He kept his eyes on the street. The tape deck had a cassette in it, which played West Coast jazz, very softly. Teddy was never hip; he was a few years older than the others and had slightly antiquated tastes. He turned slowly to face me now. His rimless glasses pinned me inside their reflection.

"Your mother has something to say to you."

"Yeah?"

"We've been having . . . some difficulties."

"Yeah, I know."

"Look, Nate." He lifted his hand off the wheel. I could tell he wanted to put it on my arm, but ultimately he just set it back down. His knuckles were thick, and the backs of his hands had age spots. His blond hair was ashy in the afternoon light. The car bonnet too was a creamy, attenuated white. "I'll always think of you a certain way. I always have."

"Which way is that?"

I look back on this moment and feel mostly pity for him. I think I do, although it's difficult to know.

"You need to talk to your mother."

Teddy Sanders was forty-eight. I, then, was thirteen. What was it like to belong to your family, the way Little Will and Severin both did? My stepfather stared through the windshield a moment, as it spangled with small drops of tropic rain.

"She and I are going to take some time apart," he said.

I suppose I could've asked him why. But even if he knew, if the actress was the catalyst, there were other causes. I understood that also.

"I see."

"No, Nate." He turned to me. But what could he say? *I met your mother when she was pregnant*? It was her job to explain it to me now. "Go see your mom."

It was a dreary afternoon in November. The street was littered with palm roots, the brown pieces of trees that had snapped off and been blown through rains. The grass in front of my house glistened. Above the Pacific, clouds opened to show a shank of sun.

"Right." I got out of the car, laid my hand on the damp ragtop. "I'll see you."

Teddy gripped the wheel. The sultry crawl of a jazz standard, all pinging vibes, drifted out. Rain trickled in the gutter. "I'll see you, Nate."

I went up the front steps and across the walk. The car idled behind, like he was a teenager wanting to see his date in safely. Beneath the Greek Revival portico I rang my own doorbell and waited for my mom to let me in. I waited and waited. Did *I* live here anymore? Cold water dripped off the porch eave and ran down the nape of my neck.

Finally, my mother answered. She opened the door and looked at me. Almost like I was a stranger, some bit of detritus that had blown onto the lawn.

"Come in," she said.

Behind me, Teddy's Mercedes revved, the engine roaring as he gunned off into the afternoon.

"Why didn't you tell me?"

I had to ask. My mother and I sat in the dining room, that formal prison in which we'd eaten and maintained such energetic pretense, night after night and morning after morning. That day, it was a wreck of ashtrays, wineglasses, napkins, dregs, as if in the aftermath of a party.

"I don't know." Her eyes drooped. Their green was lusterless. I felt like I'd never looked at her, like I was seeing her, too, for the first time "It was a long time ago."

"How does that excuse anything?"

"It doesn't." Her speech was a little thick, but she was lucid. "Beau and I were never together. I was his . . . secretary." Tiny wrinkles, proto-crow's-feet, gathered at the corners of her eyes. "You have to understand what kind of person he was."

"What kind of person was he?"

Outside, it had gone gray again. My mother lit a cigarette. I couldn't really imagine her as a secretary either. I couldn't imagine her as anything but my mom.

"He didn't always have the clearest perspective on things." She blew smoke.

"Do you?"

She could've smacked me, but she didn't. "Don't be an ass, Nathaniel."

"Does Beau know?"

She nodded. "Now he does."

"You told him?"

Outside, I could hear the drone of an airplane, its low-flying complaint. Before me, a wineglass held a dark stain, a silty little thumbprint of Chianti.

"Last night."

I listened to the plane. I tried to imagine that phone call, or encounter. I couldn't do that either. Severin's dad—*our* dad—was so much a figure of fun to my friends and me. Huge, blustering, loud. Why couldn't it have been Williams? There was a moment in which I tried to salvage my dignity by imagining a father whose alienation, maybe, I could've understood. My mother seemed to read my mind.

"Teddy's your father," she said. "He's always acted as such."

Her heart wasn't in it. Or maybe it was. I'll never know. I got up and went to the kitchen and came back with a Coke.

"Severin and I are brothers."

She shrugged. As if, quite fairly, she'd never really given it a lot of thought.

"How do you know it wasn't Williams?" I said. I wanted it to be him, just then. Or maybe I just wanted it to be anyone but the big man. "How do you know it was Beau?"

"Fuck you," she said, as she had every right to do. "You're my son, but don't ever talk to me that way."

My mother had gotten skinny. Her beauty was gaunt, a little desolate, now. I could see her bones.

"I'm gonna go see him," I said. "I'm going over to Severin's."

"Suit yourself." She stubbed out her cigarette. It was a 100, barely narrower than her own finger. "You don't know, Nate. You don't know what he's like."

I didn't. And I didn't know if this was a warning, or just an observation. I got up and went to the door, waving away smoke.

"Thanks," I said. "I'll be back later."

I walked to Severin's house. He too lived in Santa Monica, only a few blocks away from me. I crossed Carlyle, angled up Ninth. I felt no urgency, no real impulse to speak. Not to Beau, and barely to Severin. Beau was still, in a way, peripheral: my stepdad was his colleague, and I was his son's best friend. This made him the Law, someone Severin and I were dedicated to avoiding. I was newly curious, and newly repulsed. I wandered over through the darkening humidity and drank my soda. What would he do?

"Hey." Severin answered the door. He just stood there, looking at me a long minute.

"Hey." In my hand was the crinkled aluminum column, the empty Coke can. "You heard?"

He nodded. In a way, it didn't make any difference; we couldn't be any closer than we were already. We couldn't be any more opaque to each other, either.

"What did your dad say?"

Severin smiled. Beneath the glasses, his face had sharpened. His eyes were deep and cagey like an adult's. "He's your dad too."

"I suppose."

We were thirteen, going on thirty, or twelve. The world was weird, but we weren't going to let that fact dominate us. He summoned me in.

"What did he say?"

I brushed past him into the vestibule. Beau's house was vast, cool and Spanish, and it was much bigger than my mom's. The downstairs was dark as we picked our way through a formal—untouched—living room larded with art books, expensive paintings, maps. An Ed Moses abstraction hung over the fireplace.

"He's going through some stuff right now," Sev murmured. "He's a little freaked out."

We clipped the tasseled edge of a byzantine rug; crossed the cool tiles of an unused second dining room. None of these things, so suggestive of culture and curiosity, felt like Beau. Then again, what did I know of Beau's life? Now that it suddenly occurred to me to wonder about it. A script lay on the table, a Montblanc pen. *Mine*, I thought.

We ducked into Severin's bedroom finally, that shadowy blue sanctum in the house's northwest corner. As far from his father's room, upstairs, as could be. His dad. My dad. Quite frankly, I couldn't imagine what it must be like to gain a son, or a sibling, in either of their positions. I felt a spike of—yes—envy, stepping into Severin's room.

"What?" Severin looked at me.

"Nothing." I brought the Coke can up, a weirdly automatic gesture. "You wanna smoke out?"

We did. Punching a hole in the Coke can, hunkering down at the base of Sev's bed, next to his turntable. It had never occurred to me to envy Severin before. How could it? But my resentment wasn't rooted in materialism—it wasn't about the size of his room, with its nooks and walk-in closet, nor all the toys scattered around it, a Fender Stratocaster he could barely play—nor was it about any closeness he could share with our father. It was simply authenticity, the very fact his life *was* what it appeared to be.

"Y'all right?"

I lay on my back now, smoke clouding into the air above me. His walls were swimming-pool blue, the carpet the color of seawater. My fingers tingled with that hot, illegal feeling where I'd singed them on the aluminum.

"Yeah." I felt like I'd been gone a long time, even though I'd probably left my mother's house barely ten minutes ago. "What did you mean . . . " I groped through a fog. "Freaked out?"

"Who?"

"My—your—dad."

I sat up. I wasn't sure whether I could ever call him "mine," but I folded my arms around my knees and hugged them, looked at Severin with a desperation so fierce I was sure he'd feel it.

"Divorce stuff," Severin mumbled. I was tearing up, but he just glowered into space in front of him. "Work."

"Did he say anything about me?"

Severin shrugged. The Coke can smoldered at his feet.

"He said, 'I barely even knew Ren had a kid.'"

"What?"

Severin shook his head. "He's going through things, Nate. Don't worry."

I took a breath. That Beau could be out to lunch on this scale, that Severin's best friend—I was—could register so little in his agitated and ego-mad brain. I'd known him now for seven years! My stepdad was his business partner. He'd fucked my mom, and of course he knew my name, greeted me by it whenever he saw me at school or around his house, which was often. *I barely even knew Ren had a kid.* I don't know why, but this restored a kind of reality to the situation. I started to laugh.

"That's funny?"

"Yeah." Severin and I were related! The more surreal things got, the more they turned out to be true. "It's hilarious, in fact."

The smoke was dense, slow, roiling between us. I turned down the volume on the turntable. Severin nodded finally, his lips twisting into a wry smile.

"I'm glad," he said. "I'm really, really glad."

That was the last we would speak of it for a long while. We were related already, in fact. We always had been.

"Let's get some munchies," I said, and stood up.

We trooped back toward the kitchen, just like we had a thousand times in the past. I don't know why I was so happy, except for Severin being glad too. We entered the kitchen and found Beau sitting alone at the far table. Just leaning there with his back against the wall and his belly slumped low in his chair.

"Nate," he said when we came in.

"Yeah."

His eyes were dull, and I suspected for a moment he was high also, but I don't think he was. I think he was just tripping on his life's strangeness, and suffering kinds of pain and regret I could not possibly have understood. He was home early for a work night. His tie was unknotted, and his cuffs were folded back twice.

"So what do you think?"

"What?" I said. Severin had disappeared into the pantry. I was alone with my father for the first time ever, and I was surprised by his casualness. "What do I think . . . ?"

Severin came out. He lobbed a bag of prawn crisps—fucking *crisps*, because the man had his junk food trucked in from England—at Beau, who caught it.

"Yeah." A faint smile crossed his face under the mustache, the beard. He tore open the package. "You know."

It was more than I could handle, and less than I wanted. My tongue went dry. "I think . . . "

It must've amused him, seeing me so puzzled. It might have delighted him, insofar as he'd *wanted* another child, and it probably tore him to pieces, for reasons I can only guess.

He stood up. He crossed the room on legs that were too quick, little trotters, and cuffed my cheek. Just that, mopping my face with a salty paw, a greasy thumb. *I don't see it*, he seemed to say. His eyes were veiny, a little cloudy.

"How's your mother?" He stared down.

"You talked to her."

He nodded. His shirt had fine gray lines, or wales, on it. I didn't know for sure. I was so weirded out to see him, I honestly didn't know what to say. Severin tore open his own bag in the corner. It gave a loud, rupturing sound. *PAF!*

"I've had some weird shit," Beau murmured, and he shook his head. But he didn't finish. I think he appreciated the strangeness, more than I did. "Make yourself at home."

I could smell his breath, reconstituted prawn dust. I didn't see it either. The greasy spot on my cheek was like a wound. I don't think I've ever felt an ordinary touch for as long as I did that one.

He went back to the table, and I went to the fridge to get a glass of milk. For a moment, the three of us ate or drank in silence. Again, I wanted to laugh. Were we a family? We couldn't have resembled one another less. We ate and drank, and by the time I guzzled my milk and set the glass down in the sink, I turned and saw Severin had gone back to his room.

God knows what Beau was thinking. *My father*. How on earth would I ever understand this, or him?

He snacked away. Oblivious to my presence, as he had always been, apparently. I stood with my back to the sink while he mowed down that bag of prawn crisps, then shook himself out of a stupor. When he did, finally, his eyes crossed mine.

"Nate . . . ?"

Either one of us might have said something then. We might have said anything at all. He knew more—much more—than he'd let on, I realized. *I barely knew Ren had a kid.* Bullshit. There was something in the sly vulnerability of his expression, its accidental quality, that let me in. He coughed. *You need something, Nate? Anything?*

Because I was young, and terrified and high, I just turned and left the room.

It changed my life. Not as much as other things would, but it did. This consciousness that I was made from the same stuff as that man, that I might contain as much appetite and energy, or as much craziness. I found myself studying Will's father too, trying to track what connected Beau to his partner. If Beau was my dad, then what about the man my father was *not*? Like matter and antimatter, I understood them to be mirrors of one another. So what moved Williams? What might he be hiding?

"Dudes!" Little Will's voice echoed across a crater. If this changed everything, it also altered nothing at all. "Yo, check this out!"

We'd found a pool, an abandoned concrete hole behind an unfinished condominium complex in the Marina. Severin's sneakers clanged into the links of a chain-wire fence while he hoisted himself over it to follow our friend.

"Check this out!" Little Will called again.

We were brothers. OK, half brothers, but if Sev and I were both Beau's, that didn't leave a lot of room for anybody else. His mother had been missing for years, and mine was radioactive. Teddy came back to her, then left again. There was late-night drinking, solitary benders in our kitchen. Once she wept so loudly the neighbors called the police. I scaled the fence behind Severin, then dropped down to land on the terrace.

"Yo." Williams's skateboard clattered against asphalt, and I heard the soft rush and whir of his wheels, the friction of his body in wind. "Whooo—"

Severin and I watched him glide up a wall of the empty pool and pop out, effortlessly, into the air. He wasn't afraid of anything, not eleven feet of gravity and concrete that would crush his skull. Nothing. This was what it took to carve ecstasy out of doubt.

Severin whistled under his breath. I was acutely aware that his blood and mine were the same, that if you cut either one of us, you'd find the same subcutaneous truth. But did it change our relation, really? Did it make Beau my dad?

Williams's hair helicoptered around his head. His knees, which were white from ceaseless battering, came up tight to his chest as he grabbed his skate and flashed back into the air. This was more eloquent than anything any one of us could say: the clop and clatter of the skateboard, as stately in its way as a horse's hooves.

Finally he fell. Severin and I stood shoulder to shoulder; we leaned into one another as Williams scrambled off his board at the bottom of the pool. He climbed out.

"You." He jabbed the skate at Severin, smacking its flat side into his chest. "You're next."

Severin barely skated, but what could he do? Translucent yellow wrappers blew across the patio, fast food scraps. He took the board from Williams and descended into the pool.

"Fuck," Will muttered. "I can't believe you dudes are related."

It seemed to amuse him. I suppose it made him, too, more special. He'd found this place, this half-built condo complex up on a hilltop not far from the airport. It took us two bus rides and a hike to reach it. Now we could see the ocean below, the pale mirror of the Pacific visible through gray haze.

Severin puttered crabwise, conservative around the bottom of the pool. He was tragic on a skateboard. Still, he attempted a drop-in from the midpoint of the shallow end. He went down hard, banging his elbow on the drain.

"Ow! Fuck!"

He writhed onto his back, not badly hurt, just stamping his tennies on the pool's concrete. *Ow ow ow ow ow*!

Severin came up the steps, finally, and handed me the skateboard. Around us was all kinds of detritus. There were overturned deck chairs, a pair of painter's gloves, old newspapers. A flier protesting Prop 13 was up in one of the windows of the empty units behind us.

I took the board and descended into the pool. The sun burned fiercely, almost white, and the wind stirred the long grasses on the hillside beneath us. My nose filled with the brackish smell of sea air. Finally I stumbled off the skate—I was nowhere near as good as Williams, but I could hold my own—and climbed back out over the coping. I'd banged my knee, aggravated my ankle.

"What are you looking at?" I limped around now to join them, where they sat astride the diving platform that hung over the deep end.

Between them was an old issue of *Daily Variety*. God knew where it had come from. Its pages were water-warped and wind-creased.

Severin shrugged, a little twitch of languid resignation. He and Williams sat hunched over it like chess players, facing one another. Sev's back was to the pool.

He handed it to me. Our fathers were on the front page, above the fold. The article was six weeks old, but it noted their agency had grossed $49 million last year, more than the other top two agencies combined.

"They're everywhere," young Williams said.

"Yep." Sev took the paper back. It drifted out of his fingers and fell to the bottom of the pool. "No escape."

Nineteen-eighty-two. That was the difference between us. My friends couldn't escape, whereas I was at a loss. Beau was in both of their lives. Even young Williams had more of his attention—the Partner's Son—than I did. That's how it felt, and in many ways this painful fact would direct the course of my adulthood.

"Hsssss." Williams reached into his pocket and pulled out a pipe, then packed it densely with weed. He lit it, and I listened to that small, ominous crackling sound. We passed it between us, gasping and coughing softly.

A plane roared overhead, its vapor trail drowning us out as it descended into the airport. We stood up and scampered for the fences. My palms were raw, and Severin was limping. Williams heaved his skate over the fence and climbed first, kicking a NO TRESPASSING sign with the toe of his Vans, snagging his OP corduroys. We tumbled down into the long grass below—Severin a half step ahead of us as we left, cattails whispering against my legs, behind us only silence, emptiness, voracity, a void.

VIII

WILLIAMS FARQUARSEN III had an idea. The senior statesman of American Dream Machine, its architect and president—my other, secret father—thought Hollywood ought to belong to its artists. It wasn't a new idea—Charlie Chaplin and Mary Pickford had once felt the same—but in the early 1970s its time seemed to have come again. Williams's earliest plans for ADM centered on how the new agency could wrest power from the studios. This was their pitch: *You think Sam Smiligan has your interests at heart? Sam's old enough to have sucked Louis Mayer's cock. He takes his vacations with Wasserman. How in God's name do you expect him to protect you from the studio when he is the studio?* It went something like that. Rub enough sand in an actor's eyes and he'll come crying. Williams knew what to do. It was easy enough in the beginning to square nurturing a client's career with servicing her creative vision. But as you grew, as a corporation and as a man, it became harder to see where you stood. Was American Dream Machine a solution, or was it a problem? Did enriching your clients, earning more money for Jack Nicholson or Alan Pakula, increase everyone's power or diminish your own soul?

"Beau!" The big man was on his way past his partner's office when Will called out. "Come in for a second."

Beau stepped in. He was just back from New York, where he'd been for a few days, visiting Belushi. Williams stood behind his desk. He never sat anymore. He was small and agile, still dressed in his faded jeans and radiant white shirts, still long-haired at the beginning of '82.

"Where ya been?" Will said. "Sit."

Beau grunted and remained standing at the foot of Williams's desk. Like everyone else in the company who wasn't Will, Beau wore a suit by then. American Dream Machine was a *corporation*, it behaved like one; on the floor beneath them a phalanx of accountants now worked day and night.

"Whaddya need?"

"How was New York? You saw Bob?"

"I saw John. And Marty."

Beau narrowed his eyes. You see, things were becoming complicated. Williams had been best man at Beau's wedding; they'd carried each other, in different ways, for years. Yet all this balancing of business, the striving to be equal, had its consequences. Once, they'd been such friends. Now they were mainly partners and sharers of information.

"How's Marty?"

Beau equivocated with his hands. *Still Italian, still needy, still brilliant (read: nuts).*

"And John?"

"Hungry. Fuck."

Williams laughed. They both did.

"Just so long as people stay hungry for *him*," Williams said. "That's all that matters."

"You don't sound convinced."

With or without intimacy, Beau still had a certain ability to read his partner's mind. He went over to the fridge along the far wall of Williams's office and twisted the cap off a Ramlösa.

"I'm not sure."

Their corner offices were identical. Will's glass dish was full of Hershey's Kisses instead. Beau slugged the fizzy water and shrugged. "We're not painting the Sistine Chapel here. Not everything should be *Raging Bull*."

Beau wore Italian loafers along with his blue suit. He ran his thumb absently along the margin of his silk tie.

"What's bugging you, Will?"

"I'm restless."

"How come?"

Didn't Beau understand? He'd spent the last Saturday night with Belushi, sucking down rails of cocaine until 4:00 AM. At which point, a trio of hookers came in and ate strawberries off their balls.

"Are you bored, Will?"

"Not quite."

"We put together crap movies back at Talented Artists. They were worse, not that anybody remembers."

"We had an excuse to make bad movies then. We were hungry enough to make anything."

"So?"

Beau sat, finally. Over the couch were signed one-sheets for *Rollover*, *Brubaker*, *Cannery Row*. He sipped his water.

"I think you should go to New York," Williams said.

"I was just in New York."

"No," Williams said. "I think you should go . . . for a while."

Behind him the Century City morning was mild. Sunlight laminated the oil derrick that sat on the edge of the Beverly Hills High campus. Wouldn't there always be enough to share? Williams fished a tangerine out of a small Chinese bowl.

"We decided when we formed this place," Beau said. "No New York office."

"I know." Williams peeled the tangerine.

"So are you pushing me out?" Beau smiled. "You know I'll screw you harder, you son of a bitch."

Williams smiled back. They weren't quite serious; there was tenderness inside the aggression.

"This morning I did a deal for Dabney Coleman," Williams said. He set the peeled tangerine on his desk, which was otherwise empty except for a Cross pen and a phone. "I was pushing his quote, just arguing away with the studio, and I thought . . . what am I doing?"

Beau grunted. Dabney Coleman! The skinless tangerine looked small, gelatinous, and vulnerable. Beau understood those moments when you were negotiating and the object suddenly became not to win but to save face with yourself.

"Then I thought, what would Beau do about this?"

"I'd close the deal and complain to Horowitz."

"What else?" Williams looked at him, almost pleading.

"I am not moving back to New York." Yet Beau cocked his head. *I'm listening.*

"Just for a year. Half your clients are there. Bob. John. Marty. I'll let you have Marty all by yourself."

Beau laughed. "Thanks for that. And what about my people here? Davis."

"Fuck Davis. Davis isn't working." This was true, Davis DeLong's last picture had been a flop. Eight million total gross for a film in which he played an alcoholic firefighter. "This is about conscience. This is about our soul."

"Our soul? Are you getting Pentecostal again?"

Now it was Williams's turn to laugh. These men had one essential thing in common: when they first met at TAG they had recognized each other as kin. Will was a gentleman, and if Beau could never quite be that, they still aspired to a shared condition. Nature had taught this particular beast to know his friends, and if Williams— still—read Keats and preached negative capability, and Beau continued to pronounce the name of the Shakespeare play Waxmorton once gave him with a weird emphasis on the last two syllables, they were bound yet by love.

"In the beginning we were artists," Will said. "There were cave paintings."

"Yep."

"I don't remember any of Dabney Coleman." He leaned forward now, his palms on his desk. "It's not for keeps. We just need a New York presence for a while."

"A presence." The fat man fixed him with a leaden stare.

"Yes." Williams paused. "I know there are reasons you might not want to go. Other reasons."

"Mmm," Beau said.

"How's that going?"

He and Will had never discussed me. In fact, I'm not sure Beau ever discussed me with anyone, except Horowitz. In Will's eyes, I was Teddy's boy. Except . . . he knew.

"OK," Beau muttered, shaking his head, brushing away the cobwebs. "All right."

Williams watched him. Was he probing his old friend for weakness, or was he trying to protect him from the same? I know it was strange for Beau to gain a kid. I'm sure it was painful, as it could not have been otherwise. But he didn't say a word to his partner, in any case.

"All right," Beau repeated. "Fine. I'll do it, I'll go."

"You will?" Williams sounded almost surprised.

"Yep." Maybe he wanted to get away. "Just for one year."

"Great. You don't have to worry, you know."

"Why would I do that?" Beau roared back. He narrowed his eyes. "What exactly would I have to worry about, Will?"

Williams waved his hand, as if to set him at ease. "We'll take care of everything here, you know. You can wait until the summer. Severin can go to any school you want."

Unspoken, perhaps, were the words I'd have wanted to hear, myself. *I'll look after Nate and his mother, in your absence and Teddy's.* I think that is what Williams meant, but I'll never know.

"I'll be back," Beau said.

"You're not even leaving. Your office, Linda: these things stay." Will turned for a moment to look out his window. "We just need to serve notice of the fact that we're not prisoners of this place. We're not just hostages of market forces."

"We *are* market forces. How can we be hostages?"

Williams sighed. This was the problem, at its root.

"You're the only guy who can do this for me, Beau. The only one here I trust."

Beau stood up and strode over to Will's desk. He set his palms there, against the black onyx slab that gleamed in the morning sun.

"Only me, huh?" He chortled. "I've heard that song before."

Will's desk was so clean you could eat off it; so clean it gave back the reflection of his tangerine whole, the orange-bright orb and its shining double, almost more tantalizing than the fruit itself. Will picked it up now and halved it, then handed a portion to his partner.

"What's this?" Beau said.

"It's a tithe."

"A tithe? It's my fucking company too."

"I know." Will smiled. He removed a section from his own and set it down on the table. "See that there? That's God's. That's half the ten percent he takes at birth."

"And those?" Beau nodded to the ones in Williams's palm.

"These? These are my own children." Williams laughed. "I always take less than I give."

A long look passed between them, one of those mutual searchings that had become more frequent, even as Will had never—not once—given his partner reason to doubt. Even as their bond seemed more complex, more inextricable than ever. Beau ate his tangerine. When Will tossed an extra quarter across the desk, he ate that too. Then he left. The elephant, exiting the room.

IX

I DON'T WANT to say I didn't miss him. What fourteen-year-old boy doesn't miss his father, even if that father is also a stranger? But I missed Severin more. Ninth grade was the year Williams and I retired our skateboards, our grubby, preadolescent customs. The two of us remained at Untaken, a funky private high school built by refugees from St. Jerome, while Sev was beamed up and abducted to another planet, became the Man Who Fell to Earth.

"Yo, dude." Williams called Sev from the wall phone in my mother's kitchen.

"Dudes!" Now it was Severin mocking *us* when we called. "What are you doing?"

"We're at Nate's house hot-knifing hash."

"Hot-knifing?"

Another Friday night. I guess Williams wanted to prove to Sev we were getting something he wasn't. But this, my mother's radical permissiveness, was the best he could come up with. Teddy had left her again, this time for good. And in the absence of any sort of authority—my mother was nodding out in the living room over her fourth vodka tonic—we crouched by the oven, warming knives on which we'd spread hash before vaporizing the substance into a funnel.

"It's our new thing," Will snickered, before I came over and wrestled the phone away from him.

"Whatcha doin', brother?"

"Oh, Nate!" How he soared above me now. Those six months older could've been six years, from the sound of it. "Nothing, watching *O Lucky Man!* Just sitting here in the hotel."

"How's pops?" I rolled the word around to make it mocking.

"*Phah*." He exhaled, as if this topic were beneath his contempt. "The same."

He cupped the receiver with his hand. I heard him say something inaudible, a girl's voice answering him. It would've been one o'clock in the morning, there.

"Who are you with?"

"Some chick."

God. He sounded like an actor himself, in his jet-lagged and exaggerated boredom. It was hard to miss someone like that, but I'd come to believe Sev was my only witness, the only one—in a sense—who could explain me to myself. And yet he barely deigned to do so, then as ever.

"Put Will back on for just a sec, I want to tell him something."

Bastard. He went to Dalton. He lived at the St. Regis with Beau, just like that girl in the children's stories. He had his own suite. Williams snorted, at whatever it was Severin told him after I handed back the phone. Fuck them both, really.

"Nate?"

"Huh?"

Good God, it was Monday morning. My high school was its own form of nightmare, this oasis of hippie progressivism down on the southernmost edge of Santa Monica, where the city bleeds into Ocean Park. A maze of dingy warehouse buildings, a cinder-block gymnasium. Richard Diebenkorn was the art teacher; the head of the film studies department locked us all—fifteen-year-olds—in a classroom one Saturday morning and made us watch Godard's *Weekend* three times in a row. Now my English teacher was glaring at me.

"Been somewhere, Nate?"

He stared out of his furred, blond and handsome face, a twenty-four-year-old Amherst grad who'd wound up teaching here. Laughter rippled around the room as I fought to recover myself. I didn't need hot-knifed hash, honey slides, and Popov vodka. Forgetting was already my métier.

"This your paper on *Catcher in the Rye*?" He pinched it by a corner.

"Ye—uh, yeah," I said.

"It might help if you put your name on it."

I shambled to the front of the class, approaching the bench in Flaubert—all the rooms at Untaken were named for writers—so I might sign my handiwork. I tossed my pen on his desk.

"Is something wrong?" he said.

"Huh?" I turned around to look at him. "With what?"

Everything was wrong. This place was too, named obliquely after a Frost poem: roads less traveled, paths not taken. I wore flannel, my hair was still long, even as most of my classmates had figured out you shouldn't *look* like a stoner.

"Your signature's a little shaky, here."

He held the paper up for display. I'd signed it with a big crooked X. "Something wrong with your name?"

More laughter, pinging off the concrete ceiling. The room had a blue floor, an industrial runner like the baize of a pool table. Acoustical ceilings and no windows, just eighteen desks arranged in the semicircle of my humiliation.

"Maybe," I said.

No one else knew either, no one but Williams and Sev. I was a bastard, tearing up as we read *King Lear*. I returned to the front of the room.

"Very good," Mr. Linton murmured as I signed my regular signature, amid more tittering. I shook hair out of my face and scanned the room, the long bodies propped, angled, and folded into desk chairs, the girls all a little too tall, their chests swollen.

"Verry goood, Nate," someone drawled, echoing. The room erupted. I slunk back to my desk, my face burning.

That year, I was Beau Rosenwald's son. I understood what it was to be ridiculous. But he was far away, and I was alone. I don't think he ever thought of me. Indeed, if Severin was to be believed, he had much more pressing problems of his own.

X

BEAU WAS STANDING in an airport bar when the bolt of mortality struck him. In the spring of 1982 he'd flown out to look at schools for Severin, and was waiting to catch a return flight to LAX from La-Guardia when he looked up and saw a familiar form being carted out of the Chateau Marmont on a gurney, the image captioned on a small screen. Even without words, and despite the white sheet, he would've recognized his friend's body, like the world's roliest, poliest ghost.

"Fuck!" He scrambled to a pay phone, called Linda immediately. "What the hell happened?"

"You heard?"

"I heard." He scrubbed his beard with his fist and blinked away tears. Gazing down the barren airport corridor. "Where was I?"

"You were there."

"Not what I meant."

"I know. You were *there*. John had problems, Beau."

He'd pounded the phone box with his palm. "I talked to him yesterday afternoon!"

"Come home." Linda's voice purred in his ear. "Just come home."

Imagine Beau, more affected by the loss of a friend than he'd been by the revelation of a son. But he was. He slammed the receiver down, wondering which home, besides? New York, his place of origin, felt strange to him now, while the adopted city he was soon to leave behind seemed native. First he missed Kate, then he missed John. More than anything, he missed that dopey, tousled, unshaven face. The stubbled marshmallow who was, in a sense, his own doppelgänger.

Beau sat down in the terminal. Outside, the afternoon was blustery, and men stood on the tarmac and waved their batons with extra force. His squat little presence—the sight of a heavyset fellow in a tan suit and a windowpane-checked shirt, open at the neck with the dark tie loosened as he wept—couldn't have aroused much interest in anyone. But he *was* that other person, the dead one on TV. He pressed his forehead to his knuckles. How could you be in two places at once? Living *and* dead, Los Angeles *and* New York. Two questions. But you couldn't answer one without knowing how to handle the other.

Beau was no fool. He knew that Williams had exiled him, that no matter what else had occurred on that particular day, his partner's gesture was a putsch. *Go.* Beau went, not because he was afraid to fight—since when, even dating back to childhood when the conclusions were forgone, was he ever afraid of that?—but for a whole host of reasons that began to dawn on him that day Belushi died. He wanted to go home, wanted to spend time in New York City with Severin; he wanted autonomy even if there was no way to tell it, really, from irrelevance. In Los Angeles, the earth seemed to shudder where he walked: his car gleamed at the curb in front of Morton's and women whispered in the corners of the room. A tedious illusion, but who can blame an ugly man for relying upon it, for wanting to be a symbol instead of a human being? In portions of New York, too, he was *the* Beau Rosenwald, spark-plug fixture in Rockefeller Plaza's Green Room, seen downtown eating on Carmine Street and then written up on Page Six the next day. Yet outside his comfort zone he became just a shoe salesman, a hack without a license.

"Hah!" This was what he wanted to show Sev. The perils—or were they the joys?—of failure. He slipped on an Adidas tracksuit—he was always late to these things, the last man at American Dream Machine to catch up with the fitness craze—and forced my brother to join him on a run around the Central Park reservoir. "Keep up, son."

"Keep up?" Severin was suddenly lanky enough that he barely had to accelerate his walk to match Beau's gallop. "You look totally ridiculous."

"You don't talk to me that way."

Sev had cropped his hair, wore two-tone shoes when he wasn't running. He had pegged slacks, vintage coats that might've come—in Los Angeles—from Flip, from Aardvark or NaNa. The button on his lapel read SPECIALS.

"Seriously, you look like a loser accountant who's decided to go down the disco." Severin had picked up English phrasing from import magazines. He was infinite, for the moment, in his pretensions. "Where are your rope chains?"

Beau folded over, panting. They'd gone a mile and a half and his son wasn't even breaking a sweat.

"I don't care if you don't have a mother. Severin, I can't make you respect me, but you can't *talk* in that way."

"Do you respect me? Do you respect my mother?"

This lanky little fucker had a comeback for everything. Beau was like that too, the difference was that his own father had just slugged him.

"Why should I respect your mom, Sev? She left you. She left the minute Katie died." They stood under a branch dense with greenery, on the dirt path that circled the reservoir. "You don't owe your mother any respect."

"I do."

"Fine. Then you owe me the same courtesy."

The air was unseasonably crisp, and this Beau liked. A plane traced its pale path overhead, the sky an opaque gray-blue. September. It was like discovering the world was solid again, like he'd lived all these years in a bathtub.

"I don't hear you extending a lot of courtesy anywhere, on the phone with your *fucking* this and that, your *I'm gonna tear Sid Ganis a new one*."

Beau's own father would've said, *I'll potch you*. That Yiddishism that always carried, for Beau, a certain Three Stooges tang.

"I brought you here to make you a man."

"I am a man."

"Not quite." They'd skipped a bar mitzvah, again to spite the elder Rosenwald, but here, again—again, again, again—the sins of his father were visited upon Beau. No matter how he struggled to avoid them, it seemed he would never be free. "You are not quite—"

"You smoked me out when I was twelve years old."

"Oh, Christ!" *Oh Christ, Christ, Christ.*

"Dad?"

Beau was bent over, suddenly, with his hands upon his knees. His whole body shook, his limbs and elbows buckling like they were made out of rubber. He almost collapsed, folding in on himself like a pill bug, but Sev ducked under and caught him.

"Jesus, Dad, what is it?" Somehow, he eased Beau down to the ground.

Beau's face was lacquered with sweat, even the deep green of his tracksuit—Severin was right, he really did look like a fuckin' leprechaun—patched with damp, as if his whole body had suddenly given way to the flood.

"Just lay me down. Just . . . " His chest felt like it was cracking too, yet he was lucid somehow. The air, touched with diesel fumes, woke him. "Over there. Right . . . here. God, Sev—"

"Are you having a heart attack? Dad, are you having a heart attack?"

Severin rested him down on a patch of wet grass beside a rock. *Not yet. Not now.* Maybe New York City wasn't so great if in Los Angeles, when these things happened, you were attended by ballet dancers and mineral water spritzed from the ceilings. Beau's gaze landed on the rock. He couldn't remember the last time he'd seen one of those. Traffic whished, distant and transportive.

"Dad?"

His own father was still alive. Barely. Out there in Queens, the old bastard—Beau could feel it—still breathed. The last time they spoke was four years ago. *My watch cost more than you ever made in the better part of a year*, he'd kept thinking. *My socks would've fed us all for a week.* Herman Rosenwald didn't seem impressed. *Because my son's in the motion picture business, he's too good for anything else?*

"I'm all right." Beau lay on his back. He wasn't going to let myopia and egotism, his own or his dad's, be the last note of his life. He fixed on Sev's face—that cleft chin and those horn-rims, that cropped-but-mangy hair. Those dark and soulful eyes that told

Beau his son loved him, no matter what kinds of bullshit he spouted. His nape was wet, but it was just because the grass was. His body felt cool. "I'm fine . . . "

The doctors told him what they always did. *Stress.* He went back on Librium, which was some heavy shit, but now that he'd quit everything else—the day after John died he'd cold-turkeyed every chemical in his car's glove box—he'd never felt better. He'd never felt more awake, or more sane.

"Beau, we need you to go to London to see Albert Finney."

Forty-nine years old, the one problem was mortality. That's what it was. Anyone who didn't have a problem with that—who claimed not to—was lying.

"I don't represent Albert."

"I know, but he'll listen to you. Everybody listens to you."

"Am I your errand boy now, Will?"

He spoke into a squawk box, the speakerphone on his hotel room desk. The others were all in Los Angeles, on this conference call that occurred every Wednesday morning. Beau was in his slippers and half-moon glasses. Nestled amid the gilt trimmings of the St. Regis, with the King Cole room downstairs. He looked like Scrooge at his ledgers, like Scrooge without greed.

"Of course not. For God's sake, we're all dying to go to London for some theater."

"Then do it." He sipped a glass of tap water. "Albert's Teddy's client."

"Teddy's got meningitis. He can't fly."

"Teddy's got—what?" Who had that? "My God, is he in the hospital?"

In the distance beyond Will there were other voices. Beau no longer knew everyone, the ranks who swelled in the conference room. A TV agent named Terrence Peterson, a woman named Willa Danks in the book department; there were kids under Skoblow in music, sharp little fuckers who'd give Severin a run for his money with that stuff. He'd met every one of them repeatedly, yet whenever he got them on the speakerphone, he could never remember their names. *Out of the loop.* It had always seemed a strange phrase, but now he understood it.

"What does Albert want?"

A fire crackled at the far end of his suite, and the brass spittoon, the one piece of furniture that always came with him, glowed solid beside the mantel.

"What does every actor want?" Williams said. "Albert's straight, so don't worry about the other stuff."

Laughter rippled through the conference room. Rain sizzled against the window and Beau had to remind himself where he was, that the other people to whom he was speaking wouldn't have seen precipitation for weeks.

"Albert's worried that after *Shoot the Moon* he should do something sexier." Williams launched into a litany of the actor's anxieties, which were uninteresting, those same petty grievances and concerns we all feel, in a way. "He doesn't want to be typecast. He's worried that if he does this picture with Attenborough—"

"We're all typecast."

"Excuse me?"

"Albert Finney's not a pretty boy anymore. It's not 1965. He should take what he can get."

"I've told him that, Beau. Teddy's tried to get through, but it's not working."

Was *this* working? Soon the meeting would degenerate the way it always did, with people clamoring for gossip, information about plays and restaurants ("What am I eating? Rollie, lemme tell you, I went to Il Mulino the other night . . ."), these things designed to make Beau feel important, as everybody started barking into the phone at once. Maybe they all loved him, and he was just out of his mind. Maybe, just maybe, Beau was only being paranoid.

"Albert."

"Beau."

How Beau loved the handshakes of Englishmen, the plumb way their palms lined up with his and the mellow, recessive way they met his gaze. It was as if even *hello* was a necessary embarrassment.

"Been awhile."

"Fifteen years. How's Sally?"

They sat in the afternoon darkness of the bar at the Connaught. Beau asked not after Albert's wife, but after the man's long-standing assistant. Then they settled down to discuss anxiety, which was something the two men—like all men—had in common.

"D'you know what I'm talking about here? Teddy doesn't get it."

"Of course. Teddy understands too, he's just calmer than you and me."

"Well I don't want calm," Finney sputtered. "I want an animal in my corner."

You would hardly have known Beau from the ease he displayed with his clients. This was why they loved him. By himself, in the shower or in his automobile, he was a fanatic. But in these conditions, he was the still point of the turning world. He leaned forward in his leather chair, forearms on his knees.

"We all get older, Albert. Look at me, I'm half as pretty as when we met."

They drank cowboy martinis, minty gin with muddled lime. It took him awhile to talk Teddy's client off the ledge. Being an agent was just like minding a girl: a long-form seduction in which all the players, for a time at least, kept their clothes on.

"I should go with you," Finney slurred.

"Albert, we work in teams at ADM. We don't poach one another's clients."

"I want you on mine, then."

"Fine. I'll talk to Teddy and see if we can work it out."

"Fuck Teddy."

How he loved England. Everything about it, Albert Finney—and he could remember when Albert was a true star, a client of Sam's who wouldn't give Beau the time of day—sitting opposite him in a chalk-gray suit. Albert, drunk and malleable. It was midafternoon, and the bar was empty except for two women with their belted overcoats and furled umbrellas, English roses you wanted to marry the moment you closed your eyes.

"Whatever you want, Albert." Beau picked up his glass and drained the last of his gin, which dripped off the tattered mint sprig at the bottom.

"I want to come with you."

Of course it didn't matter who your agent was. Beau could've told him that too. You were who you were, and the industry wanted you or didn't. Most of the time, the industry wanted you *and* didn't.

"All right," Beau reached for the check. The room was beginning to spin. "Whatever you want, Albert, if it'll make you happy. I'll talk to Teddy."

That was that. But my father never could have guessed how this simple, egalitarian gesture—made with the company and its brotherhood in mind—would touch off all kinds of disaster.

Severin was on that London trip too. Beau wanted to have a suit made for him, to teach his son the fruits and flavors of civilization. Sev was the first of us to set foot upon the mother ship, to cross the Atlantic and so discover the Old World. Young Will and I were still as ignorant as the days were short, unaware that his father and mine weren't getting along.

"Beau, what the hell are you doing?" The elder Williams chewed the fat man out, not three days after the latter returned to New York.

"What do you mean?"

Here they were again on the phone. Each man was trying to control the whole picture, bending the facts according to his need.

"I mean that Albert—"

"Yes, Albert. I saved him."

Just the two of them now. There was no meeting. Williams was in his car and Beau, like a petulant child, sat exiled in his hotel room.

"He won't take Teddy's calls. Says he won't speak to anyone but you."

"Oh, for God's sake." The image of Finney as some lone gunman, a maniac hostaging a roomful of innocents while negotiating with Harry Callahan, came to him. He couldn't help but smile. "Actors."

"We represent actors."

"And?"

"We represent them together. And you fucked Teddy by taking his client."

"I 'took his client'?" Beau smiled at Williams's rare profanity, too. *Uh-oh.* "Pardon me, partner, but what about the ethos of this place? He threw himself at me, anyway."

Beau stood in the middle of the room at the St. Regis, the living area of his suite, where the remains of his late breakfast—coffee, yogurt, muesli, berries—still sat on a glass table with the paper. He was putting into his fireplace at three in the afternoon. He didn't even golf! Some-body had sent him clubs for Christmas, so here he was teaching him-self to do something, out of boredom more than anything.

"Pick up the receiver, Beau. I'm going up Coldwater."

Williams would've been on the way to the Valley for lunch, en route to one of the studios. Beau crossed the room.

"What the fuck, Will? Albert was gonna jump ship. He would've gone to another agency."

"We would've survived."

"But you sent me there to *prevent that from happening*!"

"It's the principle."

"He's still our client. He still pays his commissions to us instead of ICM. Wasn't that the point of my going to England?"

"It's. The. Principle. Beau, we don't poach one another's clients. We don't do that. We're a team, here."

"Listen, you mealy little cocksucker, you tell me to do something, I do it," Beau roared. "But let's not forget where this company came from. You *needed me*!"

What set him off here, Lord knows. No one spoke to Will that way, ever. Beau had never heard his partner raise his voice, not once. Will's greatest weapon was silence.

"Let's not get hasty here, Beau."

"I'm not hasty." In his hand was still a seven iron. He was just getting used to the feel of these clubs; he needed to amuse himself here in this weird city where he rattled around like a loose tooth. "I'm not hasty, Will."

"You just cursed at me."

"I cursed because you started to lecture me on principle. Because you, who sent me to this place to *uphold* a principle—"

"I sent you?"

"Yes, Will, you sent me. The move to New York was not my idea. It was all about the soul of the company, you'll recall."

Men with short memories. The promised year was half over. Beau planned to come back the moment Severin's school ended, the very day. He'd had enough; you weren't going to understand yourself any better by returning to your roots. If anything, you were only going to grow stranger, more alienated.

"Fuck it," Will said. "You're right."

"Listen . . . how do you know all this?"

"Excuse me?" Williams's phone crackled, his voice grew tinny. Beau could imagine just where he was, the bend he'd be rounding near the canyon's peak.

"If Albert won't take anybody's calls, then how do you know all this?"

"I talked to him."

"You're nobody?"

Reception cut out for a moment. They were forced abruptly into dots and dashes, verbal Morse code.

"—*matter*, Beau, the thing is—"

"—see the percenta . . . screwing one ano—"

"—all right, it's all right, the way I fee—"

"Beau? Beau, are you there?"

The connection righted itself. Williams must've been over Mulholland by now, that candy-apple Ferrari, its silver stallion gleaming on the hood, plunging into the Valley below skies of desert blue. He didn't even keep that car in the Marina, because you couldn't. Every morning Will got up and drove his ancient Peugeot to a garage in Santa Monica. Strange behaviors and bedfellows alike, this business bred.

"I'm here. Are we clear, Will?"

"Crystal."

"Fine. I'm sorry to have upset you."

Beau hung up and went back to his clubs. He strolled over to the couch and finished breakfast, soft and easy there in his hotel robe. Spooning up blueberry yogurt and muesli.

XI

AT CHRISTMAS, BEAU came home. The offices were closed. The restaurants were empty. That last week of the year, Hollywood is a ghost town. My mother and I were away and so Beau prowled his old haunts the valets at Morton's, at least, remembered him—dining alone and with Severin, who glowered at scallops swamped in raspberry coulis. Was he losing his grip?

"Welcome home!"

When the big man waltzed into the conference room on the third of the new year, Williams stood where he always did, at the head of the oval table in his untucked white shirt. He wore black loafers, and the shirt had a red monogrammed falcon on either cuff. This was Williams's affectation, these bits of flair like a musician's—a white shirt that cost five hundred dollars—to let everyone know he wasn't a true prole.

"We want you back, Beau."

"Excuse me?"

The welcome that met him seemed Japanese, ritualized and tense. Only Will spoke. The fifty-six other agents had all offered handshakes and hugs, but now maintained a ceremonious silence.

"We want you to come home," Williams repeated. "It's not necessary to stay in New York. You've done your job."

Beau watched him. This was unexpected. He would go back tomorrow morning, had sent Severin ahead so he wouldn't miss the first day of school after vacation.

"I've done my job? Gee, thanks, Will."

He set his briefcase down, that same battered leather rectangle with the solid gold clasps he'd owned since 1967. He scanned the room. He *wanted* to come home, in his heart. But Williams Farquarsen had somehow caused that heart to secede from him.

"I'd prefer to stay through the school year. Severin loves Dalton."

Or maybe Beau simply hated being told what to do. Around the room the agents sat with their plates, filled with green cubes of honeydew, and luminous columns of water. Laura Nyde, in her tan skirt and spike-heeled boots. Wanda Pearlman—who was soon going to marry Rick Lepke, another agent, a bare-knuckled New Yorker Beau particularly liked—smiling up in her ditzy blonde innocence.

"I'll come in the spring."

"Come now. We'd prefer it."

Were these people privy to Will's perfidy? Or was there such? Perhaps Beau was making a mistake. Outside the skies were that radiant shade that follows a week's worth of rainstorms. You could see the white-tipped mountains in the distance.

"I'm sure you'd prefer it," Beau said. "But I might not."

"How come? You didn't want to go in the first place. Marty might be happier knowing you were here to kick a little ass on his behalf."

"What does it matter? My legs are longer than they look."

No one else spoke. Once upon a time, these meetings had been genteel anarchy. Beau might belly surf the conference table, be lying on his back when Will came in. *What are you, the Venus of Willendorf? You sitting for a portrait, Beau?* Running a company was once the most fun they'd ever had.

"I'll come home in June." Beau crossed the room, poured himself decaf from a silver thermos.

"Is this about what happened before Christmas, Beau? Because we're OK there, you know."

"I know. This has nothing to do with that."

"What's it about, then?"

"Freedom. It's about freedom."

"Beau—" Teddy Sanders stood up to intercede. Bob Skoblow came forward too, and might've reminded him that this was *just another word for nothing left to lose*, although I doubt that, since it isn't true.

"I—I think we should b-be cool," Milt Schildkraut said, and

everyone turned since he controlled the purse strings. "We don't need this argument."

"There's no argument," Williams said. He was calm and level, as bracing as the January light. "*All mankind is of one author and is one volume. The same poet said, Every man is a piece of the continent, a part of the main.*"

"Right."

"So if you want to stay in New York, Beau, stay. Stay and take care of Marty and Bob and we'll see you in six months. *Do what thou wilt shall be the whole of the law.*"

Here, as always, Williams had chosen irreconcilable masters. John Donne and Aleister Crowley weren't exactly the most probable bedfellows either. Yet the truth was, Beau never understood Williams even if he could—still—practically read his former best friend's mind.

"Look, asswipe, I don't need your permissions."

"Excuse me?"

This wasn't a contradiction after all. You can read your own mind, but can you understand it?

"I said, you piece of shit, you dog turd, you rat-fucking excuse—"

Beau strode forward without raising his voice, so for a moment people thought he was just being himself, the ribald fat man.

"I don't need your fucking permission." Then he lifted his voice. "I shit where I wanna shit and eat what I wanna eat and if they happen to be in the same place—"

Bob went for him. Milt too. But before they could get there, Beau lunged at Williams. The latter, who practiced tae kwon do, merely stepped aside. Beau went crashing and clattering into his chair.

"Do you need help?" Will bent down with one hand on the small of his friend's back. "Do you?"

Beau knelt, panting and embracing the black ergonomic chair. Understand, he was crazy. He had been from the beginning. Who pisses on another man's floor? But understand, too, how strong was his grip on reality. He knew Williams was gaslighting him. Wasn't he? There was never any *need* for him in New York, never any need for London or Albert Finney, nor any for him to come home. Wasn't it clear that when Will visited Chicago he was sneaking around with Beau's client? Paranoia does strange things to a man, but even Milt Schildkraut, whose reality hunger was stronger than anyone's, had seen it. Had Williams paid for John Belushi's hooker, were those *his* drugs at the Chateau? You were in deep water if you thought John Belushi was assassinated by anything other than his own lack of impulse control, but you were in deeper water still if you failed to understand the treachery, the ugliest truths to be found upon the human scene. Williams wanted everything for himself. We all do. The fact that he didn't know it, that his "generous" behavior was secretly a bid for control, might have been dark to Williams, but Beau knew exactly what he was up to. The big man understood ugliness too implicitly. Having been born, after all, with so much of it.

He pushed up off the chair. He turned to face his partner, his tormentor, his—let's call it what it is—*love*.

"We'll get you anything you need," Will pleaded. "Any kind of treatment at all, we'll pay for doctors, rehab. Anything."

Beau opened his mouth. And began to laugh. He just couldn't help it. In his beautiful salmon-colored shirt, with the sleeves rolled; a pair of John Lobb brogues he'd had made in England; his gold Rolex, which was standard-issue for the better-heeled men in this room.

"You think I need *doctors*, Will? You think this is something to fix?"

"I think you need something."

He scanned the room, the faces of the men and women all twisted with shock and horror. How backward that was, truly. Who should've appalled whom, here? There was a word for this, one that Sam or Abe or Williams, certainly, would know: *cathexis, catharsis*, one of those Aristotelian or analytic terms. But Beau just shook his head.

"I need something. But I won't find it here."

He bent down and picked up his briefcase, having come straight from the garage. And then he strolled out, whistling, with his jacket over his arm and his stride light and even.

"Personal difficulties." That was the euphemism. Beau wasn't "in rehab," nor was he on vacation: there was no tacit understanding that he'd "gone skiing" for six weeks, the way Bob Skoblow did when he needed to quit cocaine. Beau Rosenwald was away from his desk because of "personal problems," the one thing Hollywood—where the problems were always social or chemical or even mental without ever being truly private—couldn't forgive. If he'd punched a photographer, if he'd been found naked and shivering in somebody's backyard, if there had been an authentic humiliation of any kind at all, he would've been forgiven. Instead he'd attacked his business partner without provocation, inside a confidential company meeting. *The employees of American Dream Machine wish to extend our sympathies during our colleague's time of trial.* These words appeared in an advertisement in *Variety* during the third week of January. That's how big a bastard Williams actually was. Why not tar Beau with a brush, Will, and dip him in feathers? Way to further a guy's career. "Our colleague." What a fucking snake!

"More tomato juice, sir?"

I would never forgive Williams this, myself. As he had haunted me all my life, my other father, I would haunt him from beyond the grave. But Beau flew home that night. "Home" it was, for now. He needed Severin, not just since this was his life's remaining actuality, but because he knew if he told Sev what had happened, he'd be believed. Severin would get it. Who understands power struggle, the battles and the sly bullying, better than a teenage boy?

"Thank you."

The stewardess poured him his drink. He was in the first-class cabin, under a tan cashmere blanket. He had enough money in the bank to last him for years. Williams would have to buy him out, if it came to that.

"Would you like vodka?" The stewardess was touching his wrist with two fingers.

"No, thank you." He returned her smile. "Maybe some peanuts?"

Why did women like him, he wondered, watching her straighten up and deliberately turn just enough so he could enjoy a view of her ass in its blue skirt? Was it because of kindness, charm? Not quite. Money? No. It was because he was genuine, and in some sense had always been, although before he'd gained the other things it was never quite so simple. He'd stayed unlaid until he was twenty, and then of course had needed to pay for it. Now, things were different, and yet it took all that experience, so much raw humiliation, to become real.

"Sir? Sir? Club soda?"

He'd spilled tomato juice on himself. The stewardess was leaning over him with a napkin.

"Thanks."

To become real. The plane hummed, hissed, and as they soared away from twilight and into the dark, Beau wondered if this was even available to many people, if someone like Williams—privileged from the day he was born—understood that you needed to suffer? Probably not. Then, what did he know of Will's suffering? If Will had a weakness, some vulnerability—anything Beau would've recognized—it might've saved them, given the men a chance to reconcile. Blotting his shirt furiously at thirty thousand feet (*Out! Out!*) he thought of that part of his partner that was dark to him. Williams had no mistresses, no chemical dependencies, and every day of the week he ate his half grapefruit at his desk at 7:45 AM sharp. Behind that unflagging discipline lay something else, but Beau would never guess what it was.

"Ladies and gentlemen, the captain has turned on the fasten seatbelt sign . . ."

If Williams had a weakness . . .

By the time his plane landed, whatever had occurred earlier seemed unfathomably far away. Los Angeles could've been the moon, and this morning could have been the Pleistocene. He called Will from the hotel. It was 8:30 PM in LA, but his partner was still at his desk. Of course.

"Will, it's Beau. I'm deeply sorry about what happened."

"Don't mention it." Williams drew a breath. "Actually, I'd like to say don't mention it."

"Why?" Beau shifted the receiver.

Severin was in the room watching *Hill Street Blues* on the big TV. Silver room-service trays lay in front of him as he nested on the couch.

"It's going to be in Christy's column tomorrow."

"What? Who told George?"

"People talk."

"Who talks? There wasn't anyone in there except us." Beau sighed. He stared at the carpet's slate-gray patterns. He supposed expecting this to remain off the radar was ridiculous. "Never mind. Look, Will, the point is, I'll get whatever I need. Treatm—" he looked at Severin across the room—"I'll make the necessary arrangements."

"Well, that's a step in the right direction."

Severin was eating a bowl of frosted Mini-Wheats with peaches. No matter how big he got, no matter how ridiculous his hairdo, he was still a kid in some sense. Those angular elbows and knees jutted in three different directions while he spooned up bits and stared, transfixed, at the TV.

"You'll need to take an absence. If you come in here next week, they'll say we have problems. If you take time off, then *you* have problems. It's just for the good of the company."

"Of course."

"And our clients. Yours will understand. You think Marty and Bob have never wanted to hit each other before?"

Beau chuckled. "Good point."

"So don't worry about this. Don't. Worry. Take the time to get straight. Go to Hazelden, if you want to, or McLean."

"I'm from Queens, Will. Those places are a little upmarket."

"Go to Switzerland. Go to a peep show on Forty-Second, for all I care, if it helps you get straight."

"It wouldn't hurt."

Williams laughed. They were back on the same frequency. "Do what you need to do, Beau. Our door is open."

One thing you must know about Hollywood. Slow fucking is what they do best. All these men who probably cum in about eight seconds—why wait for anything, after all?—can screw each other over for years. *Revenge is a dish best served cold.* Yes. It's just more fun to brutalize someone across time, and torture isn't torture unless you really draw it out. You think I'm paranoid, that, like Beau Rosenwald, I'm misinterpreting Williams's gestures? *Our door is open. Get what you need.* This is the vocabulary of business, the tenderness with which we punish one another every day.

"Beau, it's Marty."

(*We had a great run*, says the deposed studio chief in the press release announcing his firing, *and I look forward to making movies here at Blankiversal, and to working closely with Peter and Ed.* To which the boss's boss's boss responds, *Jeremy has fantastic taste, and we expect him to be a major supplier for us these next three years.* Read this in *Variety*, over and over again, and know these are three years in which Jeremy Vana can't get Williams Farquarsen's second assistant on the phone, let alone get a movie made, from his opulent offices on the lot. If you're going to castrate someone, do it with love.)

"Marty!" His favorite director had visited him in the hospital, twice. Beau had gone through an outpatient program for alcohol—never mind that drinking was never his problem—and was now diagnosed as bipolar. Yet like many diagnoses, this was only a guess. "How are you, sweetie?"

"I'm good. Listen, Beau, I have a problem."

"You have a problem with who? The studio? Is there a problem with publicity?"

This conversation took place on the fifteenth of February. That week, Beau resumed work at the ADM offices in Century City. It was important that people see him here, know that he was back in town, out and about, negotiating. He and Williams had lunch at Jimmy's on Monday. This was important too. The two men at one table, telling jokes. Beau looked healthy and relatively slim, but this was nothing like the pallid cadaver who'd emerged into the light after his daughter died. This was him at fighting weight, fiercely lucid and ready to kick some ass.

"You want me to call Marvin Davis?" *The King of Comedy* was opening on Friday.

"Different problem. Beau," Marty sucked his teeth, "I'm leaving."

"Leaving? Where you going, Chicago?"

"I'm leaving the agency. This is difficult."

"Leaving the— Marty, where the hell you gonna go? Williams and I take care of you!"

"I'm going with Mike." You know how Marty talks, the nervous darts of his speech. "This is very difficult for me, Beau."

"I'm sure it is. Mike?" Mike! CAA! They'd seen Mike at Jimmy's that day, too. "No one likes Mike."

"Everyone likes Mike."

"They're afraid of Mike. Marty, why are you doing this?"

There in his office, Beau had the first apprehension that things were not going to go as he'd hoped. It was like coming down off anesthesia. The flowers were browning; gift ribbons had been piled in the trash. The welcome notes and compliments, too, were fading. *You look fantastic, Rosers.*

"I understand." Beau stared at the red pistils of some calla lilies in a glass. "No, Marty, I hear you. I get what you're saying, but shouldn't we have another chance?"

You know, too, how stupid a man sounds when he's pleading. Forget business. *Don't leave,* one spouse tells the other, and we've all said it—or wanted to say it, or wanted to want to say it—at some point. *Don't go, don't go! Please!*

"Marty, this breaks my heart. I knew you when you were with Roger!"

"This isn't easy for me."

Beau rubbed his fists into his eyes. *Am I dreaming?*

"What does Will say? You talked to him?"

"Not yet. I needed to talk to you first. You're my friend."

"And is this because"— Beau had no choice but to ask—"because of my difficulties?"

"We've all got difficulties. I get up in the morning and can barely shave with a steady hand."

"I've noticed."

Both men laughed, the one more ruefully than the other.

"Stay in touch, Beau. Stay in touch."

Beau was in touch. Nothing makes you more in touch than loss. But when he hung up the phone and began those breathing exercises he'd been prescribed—he was prescribed something for everything—all he felt was the ceiling starting to crumble over his head. You lost an actor, even one as talented as Albert Finney, and it was understood to be part of the game, what you paid for signing someone else and offering the new client more attention. You lost an award-winning director like this? You were halfway to being a schlepper all over again.

"Beau?" His assistant, Linda, was at the door, leaning in and fixing him with her usual tender tolerance. Maybe he should marry her and flee; she'd already seen the worst of him. Not so bad-looking, needing better hair and less makeup and fifteen fewer pounds. Easy enough. "Will, on one."

Beau sighed. As if he could escape his fate, as though the die for this, every last bit of it, hadn't been cast long ago.

"Beau"—Teddy Sanders stood in the doorway of his colleague's office, a few weeks later—"I just got a phone call."

"From who?"

"Bob."

It came down so quickly from there. Teddy leaned against the jamb. Beau was back in LA again—again! That spring of '83, he'd needed to be here constantly.

"What's Bob calling you for?" Beau rubbed his eyes.

"He wants to have lunch."

I wonder if there was pleasure in this for Teddy. Maybe there was. But he showed no particular interest in me then, either; it was all between his lawyers and my mom.

"Huh," Beau snorted. He hardly needed to ask why.

"I put him off," Teddy said. "Told him I'd get back to him."

"Don't do that," Beau said. Because you never dangled a client, no matter what. "Why don't you take him to that Japanese place?"

Teddy loitered there in the doorway. His toes barely poked onto his colleague's parquet floor. A little paunchy, he still wore that genial mustache, the face of a Midwestern uncle.

"You sure?"

Beau watched him. Who was fucking him deliberately and who was merely along for the ride, he never could tell.

"Yeah." In fact, he liked Teddy. He always had; neither my paternity nor the Finney incident had changed that. "You go ahead."

How complicit are we in our own fates? Was Beau Rosenwald just tired? Did he feel all this was like a trip to the dentist, better to have all your teeth gone in one jerk than to feel them lovingly scalloped one nerve-shearing root at a time?

"Go. Bobby could use a steady hand."

Beau knew what was happening. The American Dream Machine ideal, the notion that the agents should work seamlessly to promote their clients' welfare above even their own—that there would be no poaching of one another's clients—had crumbled some time ago. But when his own standing began to fall, he did nothing.

"What's wrong?"

Linda came in after Teddy'd left and found him sitting with his fingers laced and his forehead propped gently against his knuckles, elbows on the desk. He looked like someone at the Wailing Wall.

"Can I have a tissue?" His face was wet, cheeks streaked with a few tears. "Please?"

He didn't even like Bob. Not that he disliked Bob. He liked *being with* Bob, the way he liked being with so many actors because they resembled him more than anyone knew. Most had thin skins and limited educations and animal intelligence and an impossible degree of self-consciousness. Which part of that was Beau not going to understand?

"What happened?" Linda handed him a Kleenex and waited while he blew.

"De Niro's leaving."

"Oh. I'm sorry." She grimaced. "And good riddance."

"Nah. He's just going up the hall, to Teddy."

"Really? You could block that."

Beau nodded. "I know."

"Then why don't you? Beau."

In her searching stare was everything: *Big deal, you lost Marty, you blew a fuse, you think Abe Waxmorton hasn't got a temper, what are you doing, why don't you fight, I love you, you big baboon!* But Beau just shrugged. He set down the wadded blossom of his Kleenex. Perhaps he was tired, perhaps he was disgusted, perhaps he was just lured by the pleasure of defeat. For there is an exquisite joy in seeing a person collapse, even, sometimes, when that person is yourself.

"It's all right," he said. Linda's eyebrow curled; the sweet and crooked outcroppings of her face glowed overhead in the morning sun. "We'll live to fight another day."

What a strange year that was! In the spring of '83, Beau found himself alone. Severin was still at school in New York, or else—occasionally—in Portland, Oregon. He took mysterious trips on weekends. Beau presumed he had a girlfriend there, that pen pal he'd found in eighth grade, whose envelopes continued to arrive, unmarked but with a tellingly feminine scent. Sev was a little young still to be unsupervised, but Beau had his hands full. His clients took flight like swallows. And on April 15—tax day—he was called into Will's office. Their meeting was set for 11:30 AM, but when Beau strode in, his partner was in a meeting with an actor whose own career was beginning to show cracks.

"Hey, Beau." Will gestured to his client, who was angular and equine: the man who launched a thousand disco fingers now sat drinking coffee on Will's couch. "You know John?"

They shook hands. Nineteen-eighty-three was a shit year in the movie business, but it was a golden age compared to what was coming next. How many great films can you name from the latter half of that decade? *Blue Velvet*, sure. What else?

"You wanted to see me?"

The elder Farquarsen looked at his client, then at Beau. "Can it wait?"

Beau retreated and stood outside his partner's office. Once, he might've fumed at this snub, as Williams kept his clock with absolute precision. He never let a meeting run late. The actor's presence was a red rag, a show of dominance on Will's part. Yet somehow Beau didn't care. Nick Nolte had bailed on him, Bill Murray. He was down to two clients now: Bryce, essentially unemployable on the heels of three straight turkeys, and Davis, of whom the less said, the better. The gap between Robert Redford and Robert Wagner was narrower than anyone had supposed.

"You can go in now." Williams's assistant, Terry, motioned to Beau with his head. Inside, Williams was sipping an espresso from a lacquered demitasse cup. He stood upright behind his desk, as ever.

"Beau! Thanks for waiting."

"It's all right." Even his graciousness felt ungainly, just as Will's deliberate rudeness seemed almost like politesse. Such was the reverse-gravitational effect of power.

"You want a coffee?"

Beau shook his head. Will had had a machine, a big silver restaurant contraption, recently installed in his office. It sat on the marble counter along the room's western wall, next to the fridge.

"John's worried. Advance word on the sequel isn't great."

"Since when did the sequel require reviews to mint money?"

Williams shrugged. "Everyone worries about something."

"You don't."

The two of them were such opposites, but then that's always the case. People saw Beau as the soulful one and Will as the Cold Sensei, complementary clichés that were almost, but not entirely, accurate.

"You never worry, Will."

"You don't know me," Williams shook his head. He sipped again. "After all these years."

"I think I do."

All Beau had wanted, going in, was advice. And maybe that was all Will wanted to give him. His clients were flying and would Will, his friend and supporter for many years, whose hand was forever steady on the tiller, help him? This was Beau's gentle intent. It wouldn't be the first time he'd asked for assistance, and besides, agents were *necessarily* embattled. It was the business. Look at Sam, who soldiered on—still!—when American Dream Machine had raided his agency's stable until it was almost bare. Sam was so old he could barely keep his head off his leather blotter, probably needed his assistant to dial the phone because he couldn't see the keypad's numbers. Why quit?

"I . . . Will, I need—"

Beau opened his mouth. His partner just stood behind his desk, set his cup down on its white saucer, and watched. That great, immaculate slab of a desk, that black block of marble seemed suddenly like a tombstone! He could practically see the dates chiseled into it.

"I have to leave."

"Back to New York? You waited an hour to tell me that?"

"From the company. I have to go."

Williams's turn to stare. "Are you nuts?"

His office was cooler than Beau's. It faced northeast, and the brown towers that rose both opposite and next door blocked the midday sun. Williams swam in its reasonable light.

"Say you're kidding."

"I wish I could."

Williams walked over now and sat down on the green couch. He beckoned for Beau to do the same. For a moment they arrayed themselves almost like lovers, Williams turning to face his partner as his fingers winnowed his longish hair.

"Don't say that. It isn't possible. This company isn't itself without you."

"It isn't itself *with* me anymore, either."

Above them hung a painting by Ed Ruscha, a set of red letters arranged vertically, diminishing in size against a black background:

The word tapered to a point over Beau's head, like a dagger that might be driven into his skull.

"I need you." Williams leaned forward. "Beau, please."

A born king, was Williams. A man cut like a diamond, with all his radiant and slippery faces. But just because my father was being impulsive, this doesn't mean his decision was ill considered. He'd thought of it often, for a while he'd dreamed of it almost daily. The liberation was all in his being able, at last, to say it.

"I'm sorry, Will. I truly am."

"I am too." Will sat back and exhaled. "I am too."

Who betrayed who here? I've scrutinized this moment my entire life, searching for its small seams. I don't think I've ever understood, really, which of these men was more murderous, which truly mad.

"I could tell you why," Beau said. Calmly. "We've lost our way."

"I'll give you twenty-four hours." Stung, Williams ignored his words and pinned him with a clarifying stare. Eyes as hard as agates. "Perhaps you should reconsider."

"I don't need twenty-four hours." Beau levered up. "We can sort out the details later, what to do with my stake."

"Your stake." Will spat this word out with a vehemence that suggested, also, its alternate definition: something you'd drive into a vampire's heart. Beau just looked down at his partner and blinked. His gaze was almost pitying.

"I love you, Will. I always did. Even when I married Rachel, and you were there, I may have loved you better. You were who I wanted to become."

"Pity you didn't."

Such hatred from Will. Where he, too, had once loved Beau like a brother.

Beau strode toward the door. "You'll hear from Bert in the morning," he snapped, referring to his attorney.

"It'll be too late."

"It is already."

It had been for a while. With his heart broken so violently, as it had been before their partnership's beginning, Beau hardly needed the company to do it again. He unknotted his tie and he strode into the elevator, across the building's lobby, then into the breezeway to the garage before he dropped his briefcase and exhaled. My God, he was free! He stood there on the brick-brown tiles, panting. And then he practically skipped to his car. A seraphic blond toddler pointed as he passed, as if to say, *Look, Mommy, look. Look at the happy fat man!*

XII

BEAU CAME HOME in the fall. Severin came with him, though I hardly recognized my brother when he landed. They'd spent the summer bunkered up in New York, where Beau fought the very battle you'd expect against Will. He had a good attorney, he had a big and brazen mouth, he had a renewed sense of purpose. He hadn't felt this much like himself since the old days, the old old days at TAG. He called everybody he ever knew: Mike Nichols, Elaine May, Bob, Marty, Other Bob, Sidney. Full of beans and hopped up on hotel coffee, he made his move.

"Sweetheart? It's Beau Rosers." I can picture him now, leaning back, feet on the edge of his desk. "Listen, how would you like to play for another team? Same winning records, but different uniforms and stronger management."

You've seen the movies, you know how this goes.

"Uh-huh." A cloud crossed Beau's face. "That's true, but . . . "

Rocky punches the side of meat, Rocky runs up the Liberty Bell steps.

"But . . . "

Rocky gets his sad Guinea ass handed to him on a platter.

"I'm sorry to hear that. Really, I am."

Forget Dolph Lundgren, forget Brigitte Nielson's tits, the true and original story of man is one of defeat. If you happen to prefer your stories true and original, that is.

"We'll stay in touch. Of course, Jill." He downed a mouthful of tepid brown swill. "Call me if you change your mind."

Beau had so much going for him. All Will had were some old medical records, doctors' bills, evidence of indiscretions past. Pit *those* up against a renewed sense of purpose, and guess who wins? I tell you, it wasn't pretty.

"Dude!" Severin came up to me on the first day of school and wrapped me in a choke hold. "What's going on?"

"Yo." I writhed around so I could see him. "When did you get in?"

Beau had "resigned" in July. I'd heard that from my mother, but he and Severin had been MIA for the last few months. I really didn't know what had happened. And now I checked out Severin, emaciated and shorn. He looked hardcore.

"What the fuck is with your hair?" I said.

He shrugged. He'd shaved it all off, had nothing now but quarter-inch bristles. Young Williams came over too and gave him a hug.

"Hey."

I guessed things were all right between them, even if the fathers were at war. Even if Will the Elder had just screwed the fat man out of his portion of the company. According to my mom, Beau had cashed out with a mere ten percent. There was a lot I didn't know. All my gossip was secondhand.

"You join the army, holmes?" Williams snorted.

Once more, Severin just shrugged. "I'm learning to play guitar."

He'd ditched his glasses, wore Doc Martens too. There was something grimly studious, East Coast about him. For a moment we just stood, shuffling our feet on the royal-blue baize.

"You look fucked up," Williams muttered.

Around us, the hallway thronged with young girls in bloom, the sound of metal doors banging shut, like options, around us. People disappeared into Kafka, into Dickinson.

"I'm glad you're back," I said. But I really wasn't. I slammed my locker closed, thinking how his return complicated everything. "I'll catch you later."

Williams and I were cool, too. The fathers were at war, but that was a technicality. We knew enough then to keep our sins separate. But after all that, Severin and I just weren't quite as close as we used to be. A small crack had appeared. I still went over to his house sometimes and hung out after school, but I was conscious of a change, one more small transference of power. He'd gained an edge over me that might've lasted a lifetime.

On Thanksgiving weekend, Severin and I took LSD. Lying on the floor of his bedroom, exactly as we used to do. The room was a museum, with a baseball glove calcifying in a corner, a skateboard poking its scarred nose out from under the bed.

"Where's the old man?"

"Dunno," Severin muttered. "Upstairs, probably."

He was in seclusion. But Beau wouldn't be a big part of my life until later. When our paths crossed at Severin's, he nodded or tapped me on the shoulder and grunted. *Heya, kid.* I think I embarrassed him.

"Doing what?"

"The fuck should I know?" Severin's eyes were narrow; mine were wide. "Dad shit."

"Dad shit?" I snickered. "What would that be, exactly?"

We were tripping our brains out. Severin's face was glowing bone, candescent under UV light.

"I have no idea, man."

The air scissored with hallucination. The stereo played something grinding, abusive, a pulsating synth-drone and hiccuping vocals.

"What the fuck happened in New York?"

Sev shook his head.

"Did Dad lose it, or what?"

My brother didn't have the answers. He was just witness to something I would come to believe was a crime. He never thought so.

"Is Will's dad fucking insane?" I said.

Severin just started laughing again.

"What is it?"

But I knew. The air felt wet. Our own father was scarier, funnier, more radically absurd when we were on acid than he was when we were off of it. Which was saying something.

"Fuck!" I shouted, while my hand drew fleshy trails in the air. I lay it across my face like a starfish, like *Alien.* "Our dad!"

"Yeah," Severin chuckled. "He's into some heavy, heavy Beau shit."

Later, oh later, I would find out what this meant. Beau had ECT that year, for cataleptic depression. My mother told me this, though not till I was an adult. But I understood that leaving ADM really tore him up. *Beau shit. Heavy dad stuff.* His own father finally died that year, and it affected him less. Most people thought Beau had hung himself with his own rope, that his long-simmering craziness had simply caught up with him. But I had my own ideas.

"Do you think Williams pushed him out?" I asked my mother. "What do *you* think?"

My mom was not the most reliable witness at that time, either. Her drinking had accelerated to the point she'd pour us both vodka tonics when I came home from school. She treated me more like a bar-stool companion than like a child.

"Oh, Nate." Her voice dripped contempt. "Why do you care?"

"I care because . . . "

"You think there's something in it for you? You think if you could get to the bottom of what happened at American Dream Machine it'd make a difference?"

"No." That was exactly what I thought, though. And I couldn't help but think of Will as my own father too. I thought of his sanity and fate as being no less relevant than Beau's.

"Your father doesn't give a shit about you. He doesn't about anybody but himself."

My mother's scorn was ill timed. Who knew how much had to do with Beau and how much was meant for Teddy, or herself? We were in the dining room, that former shrine to our domestic life, which was littered with tonic bottles.

"You knew Will," I said. "You were at TAG when he came."

She blew smoke. Liquor had carved deep furrows into the corners of her face, around her eyes and lips. It looked as if she was melting a little. Just forty-two, she was blowsy and haggard, with the derelict beauty you saw in certain actresses. The late Faye Dunaway.

"I was."

"And?"

She jangled her foot against the edge of the table. Tennis-shoe clad, she was like a truant teenager herself. Drunk, but not stupid, she turned over the possibilities for a moment.

"I think Beau did it to himself," she said finally. "Williams is a nice man."

"Nice?"

"Decent," she said. "Fair."

I sipped my drink. Mine was not the most conventional upbringing, but I studied my mother very carefully in that moment, seeing
her teeter between one potentiality and the next. To assess Beau as
crazy would've excused her own decision to keep me in the dark for
so long, and perhaps would've perjured something she once felt. I
suspect she didn't want to be that easy on herself.

"Decent isn't the same thing as nice," I said.

My mom looked at me then and smiled. Her face crinkled with
pride. I had her intelligence.

"Your father . . . "

But she didn't finish the thought. I saw that she loved him, too,
or had, that whatever she saw in me she'd seen in him too, once.
Outside, the afternoon was glassy, with the flat light of primitive
spring. My mother stubbed out her cigarette.

"Go on," she said. Reassuming the role she seldom took anymore:
that of parent, protector. "Go upstairs and do your homework. Let
your fathers worry about their end of the business."

XIII

PERHAPS MY MOM was right. Maybe Williams Farquarsen had nothing to hide and Beau's mania was all there was to it. I never saw anything directly that said otherwise. Williams Farquarsen the elder was what he proposed to be: a family man who kept his cards close to the vest, at least when it came to the industry. Polite to me as he was to everyone, dedicated to his son the way he was to the business, he traveled around Hollywood by himself, and when he squired Jessica Lange to the 1983 Academy Awards, everyone knew she and Sam Shepard were together, and Williams never laid a finger on her. True. I knew from young Will his parents' marriage was solid, and from Marnie herself that she just hated going to these events. *Why should I buy a new dress, Will? I'll just wait and see it in the theater*. Of course he was going to travel stag. And after my father was ousted from American Dream Machine, Marnie and the elder Williams treated me the same, just as they did Severin. *You little runts*. We were extended family, and Williams the father gave no indication of holding Beau's apostasy against either one of us. He smiled down with an Olympic courtesy.

"Are you staying for dinner, Nathaniel?"

"Sure." I no longer even studied him for clues. I'd internalized him. His habits were ingrained in me, the rhythms of the only household I knew that had anything like a regular dad, who came home many nights by 7:15, a stack of scripts and deal memos under his arm. "If that's all right."

"Of course it's all right." I watched him stroll across the living room, still furnished with a Spartan plainness, with Marnie's LPs and only a few paintings and expensive sculptures to let anyone know the place belonged to a king. "You don't have to ask."

If he was under strain, as of course he must've been—it wasn't just Beau who'd had to hold up under legal fire—it didn't show. He tossed his papers on the couch and called upstairs.

"Hey, Little Will!"

I was slumped in an armchair with a Huxley paperback, as integrated as the family cat, a hypoallergenic Javanese who twisted around my legs.

"Come on down!"

My friend's footsteps thundered on the narrow stairs. By 8:30, Williams would be in his study, reading and reading and reading, while his son and I did dishes. This was what nights were for, not fighting with your wife or going apeshit in a hotel suite.

"You ever think about becoming an agent, Nate?"

He asked me that once, on one of those nights when I was still in high school and probably had no other place to go, Beau's house being radioactive and my mom's almost equally so.

"You're a smart kid. You'd be good at it."

I didn't know what he wanted from me. Once more I had that sense that I was being monitored with something beyond ordinary care, but maybe this was just what a father's love felt like.

"Maybe. I like books more than I like movies."

He nodded. In the dimly lit living room his pale delicacy seemed a little worn, what once was a fishy whiteness tuned down to regular pallor. He pushed his hair back, those reddish strands glistening in the lamplight; he removed his reading glasses and tucked them into his shirt pocket.

"Like I said. You're a smart kid."

But I don't think Williams ever regretted his profession. He wasn't like my father, who in some primordial part of himself still harbored—I think—a belief that if he'd been a doctor or a lawyer, he might've pleased his own dad. No, Williams was an agent, he was the industry itself: born outside, he nevertheless shaped it to his own needs, until he was no more divisible from it than marine life is from the sea. My suspicions had no basis. Even the way he handled Beau's departure—placing Beau's share of the company in a complicated trust, eventually to revert to the original partners, and also, in small part, to Severin—was seen by everyone as fair. I believe he would still be dominant in the industry if he were alive today.

If. For in 1984, the man who seemed to make no mistakes finally made a doozy. A miscalculation we would feel for the rest of our lives.

That spring, Severin turned sixteen. The Age of Mechanical Consent. Beau bought him a car for his birthday, a black Porsche 911 that was certainly in conflict with my brother's punk rock ethos, although the way he drove it wasn't. Sev banged it into palm trees, parked it with one wheel up on the curb, left the keys inside and the doors wide open. I'd look outside and see it nosing onto my lawn like an importunate dog. It's a wonder he didn't drive it straight into my living room. Once that car entered our lives, the three of us were friends again. After all, Williams and I needed transportation too. It was our chariot, our shared fate, ferrying us over to Rae's diner on Pico where we sat in clouds of cigarette smoke and broke the school's record for truancy. But that summer, Marnie Farquarsen decided to put an end to it. *You kids.*

"Will!" She spoke to her son now, not her husband. "What the hell is this?"

She held his report card, or rather what was called an "academic advisory" at Untaken, a yellow form that mapped your attendance and progress for every course. From the foot of the stairs she shook it at him.

"Do you even go to that school we pay seven grand a year for?"

Williams shrugged. "I went to drama."

"Drama, my ass. You skipped chemistry seventeen times last month." Marnie strode up the bottom two steps toward Will, who froze on the landing. "I'm taking you kids away."

"Away how?"

The floor under Marnie's feet and the newel in her hand were original walnut. She'd refinished them herself.

"I'm taking you to Saguaro National Park. All three of you rats."

"What makes you think Beau would let Severin go anywhere with you?"

"Beau's problem isn't with me, it's with your father." Marnie stood with her hand on her denim-clad hip. "I've already discussed it with Beau, anyway."

"You have?"

Marnie nodded. "Already discussed it" sounded like *already disgusted*, but she had. It was difficult to imagine Beau and Marnie talking, but no matter how opposite they seemed, the two of them had always liked each other.

"What are we gonna do at Saguaro, Mom?"

"We're going to climb Wasson Peak. And then we're gonna camp a few days at Juniper Basin."

"Mom!"

"You might want to quit smoking before trying it with fifty pounds on your back. And Severin's car won't make it. The trail's a little narrow."

Sometimes I think there were few people in my childhood more worth loving, if you imagine love has anything to do with merit, than Marnie Farquarsen. Standing at the base of the stairs with her hands on her hips and that same long-backed sixties bowl cut she'd worn since time immemorial, that spark–plug body and no-nonsense manner, she was the one who said *enough*.

"You kids will like it, I think. I really do."

The Arizona desert would be good for her—the dry air helped her breathing—but the idea, surprisingly, appealed to Sev too. His style was quasi-military in that moment, and the idea of a fifteen-mile hike in 110 degree heat seemed about right. I'm sure he wanted to get away, also. Having a parent, anyone's parent, say, *I'll take you somewhere and make you toe the line* must have been welcome. Young Will was less enchanted, but even he was impatient on the morning we took off. A Saturday in early June.

"Williams?" His father leaned in the car door. "Are your socks thick enough? D'you have mosquito repellent?"

"*Relax!* Dad." Outside the office, Williams Farquarsen III really did become a different, much softer, man. My friend sat rigid, squirming with embarrassment in the backseat of the boxy beige Peugeot wagon. "Don't be so uptight."

"It isn't uptight." The elder licked his lips, peering in from the driver's side with one hand on the roof. His wife was behind the wheel, while Sev rode shotgun. "I just worry that you're not prepared."

"We're prepared."

"OK, then." He leaned in and kissed his wife, then tapped our packs, which were lashed to the roof. "Have a good time. I'll miss you, Mar."

Williams watched us, the adolescents in the backseat. He was still a young man, himself. Forty-nine, maybe, but he looked young, *felt* young, practiced his tae kwon do and was a strict vegetarian. In an industry riven with its taste for flesh, he ought to have lasted forever.

"Bye, Dad."

"Bye, son." He leaned in and kissed his wife again, right by her eye. "Be safe."

His face was inches from mine. Close enough that I could read the little crow's-feet in his tallowy skin, watch the sun spark off the copper-wire brightness of his hair. His eyes were depthless, a bleached green.

"See you, Nate."

Did he wink? I've pictured that look a thousand times.

The car shuddered, its little tan body trembling like a geriatric's as a carbon monoxide smell filled the interior. Williams straightened and lifted a peaceable palm, like a cigar store Indian's. My friend stared dead ahead. Then Marnie put the car in gear, and we moved off into the bright and muggy morning

Everything that happened next is colored by what I now know. Everything. If I tell you we had a wonderful time, if I dig up the postcards I wrote, but never sent, to my mom, I can see that we did. These were ten days of heaven, the last of a childhood that died hard in stages. They were beautiful. So how can something so true turn out to be such a pack of shit?

We detoured through Vegas and then headed dead south, as if this glitzy machine city were a cliff you could fall right off. We rocketed into the desert, not far from where Beau had filmed *The Dog's Tail*. All of us felt close to something—God, visions, origin, the sky—we recognized but couldn't name. I saw it in Severin's face, which softened as he removed his glasses and looked out the window. I saw it in Williams, who grew supple and laughed with his mom, sounding for one final time like a boy. All of us were young again. The front window was cracked open, admitting heat and wind.

"Tie that up, now." That first night in the park, Marnie directed us. I had a rope slung over a pinyon pine's branch, the long end tied to my backpack. "Right, hoist it higher. Now tie it off."

"Are there really bears?"

She looked at me. The campground was uncrowded at twilight, with just a few other pilgrims moving around their tents. "Is that difficult to believe? You're a lot weirder than a bear."

"Am I? I don't go into bears' lairs and mess with their stuff."

"Nope, Nate, you've got worse problems. But you still should know what to do with a backpack when you're camping."

Could I have loved her any better? She encouraged self-sufficiency without just ignoring us, without simply saying *Go off and do it yourself.* Beau had bought Severin a wide array of Valley-ish things: a plastic pith helmet, a sonic mosquito repeller, an electronic gizmo that was supposed to purify water. We snapped off the helmet's crown and then used the brim as a Frisbee. We drank from long-handled tin cups and cooked over Marnie's tiny black hibachi. It was as far from our Hollywood upbringing as we'd ever been, however that indicts our youth. Driving among Conoco stations, drinking Nehi soda. The earth, imperishable earth, was closer than we had supposed. And the American desert, where it all began. We hiked the Hugh Norris Trail all the way to the top, where we were dwarfed by cristate cacti. We unlaced our boots and picnicked at the saddle, then reencased our scorched feet and walked back to the bottom and collapsed, panting, in the rare shade of a palo verde tree. We cracked ourselves up imagining Beau Rosenwald camping. *Sev, is it a little hot down here? Why don't we go back to the hotel for a massage?* I felt closer to my brother than I ever had, closer to some feeling of family that I lacked. And then the last night, we were hunkered around a fire when Marnie stood up.

"I have to call Will," she said.

We were at a KOA not far from Kingman, a scrubby little corridor of motels and coffee shops, a town whose stillness was inseparable from stasis.

"I'm going to the pay phones over by the offices," she said. "You kids do these dishes."

We did, rinsing our tin plates with bottled water and then scouring them with bandannas. We'd been taking our time driving home, exploring the desert, but now Marnie hadn't spoken to her husband for five days. The setting sun was infernal, the horizon line a carnelian seam.

"He's not picking up." Marnie returned, finally. It was nine o'clock on a Sunday, a night Will ought to have been home.

"No?" Williams looked at his mom without worry. "Where do you think he is?"

"I have no idea."

We sat back down by the firelight. Shadows played across her face. Her arms were propped upon her knees and her brow was clouded; her face looked like a bronze mask, inscrutable and permanent.

"You guys wanna go to Joshua Tree still?"

I watched her face furrow, its blunt uncertainty, as she stared straight ahead. We all felt it. Something was wrong.

"I don't think so, Mom. I think we should just go home."

All of us were barely sixteen. But we understood Marnie's needs, I think. Our planned stopover in Joshua Tree suddenly seemed a bad idea. I hardly remember the rest of that night. Severin played a little more guitar and eventually we crawled into our tents and sleeping bags, then lay down on the hard ground and tried to sleep. I found myself imagining the scorpion tucked inside my hiking boot, the embers catching a dry twig, the subtle advance of a snake. That campground, with its high pines and dusty air of abandonment alongside a comfortable RV park, became a charmed circle. It was the last place our childhood would ever be seen alive. We drove home the next morning, and if that had been an era of PDAs and cell phones, we would've had our information long before we reached Los Angeles. Marnie's phone would've rung off the hook, and if we had been in Williams's other, more Italian, automobile— the one that had such a device in it—we'd have found out too. But the old Peugeot had only a broken cigarette lighter and a Blaupunkt, which didn't give us anything until we were well within LA County.

—KABC news time 7:48. Talent agent Williams Farquarsen is still missing after a two-day search.

"Wait, what?" All of us were jumbled around now in the car. Severin drove, Williams was in the passenger seat, and Marnie was in back with me, her head cushioned with a wadded flannel shirt as she slept. "WHAT?"

Severin reached over to turn the volume up. Williams, astonishingly, stopped him.

—last seen Thursday afternoon in Burbank. Farquarsen's absence has been reported by—

"What are you doing?"

—colleagues—

Williams IV snapped the radio off.

"What the fuck, man?" Sev glared.

Will looked at Severin. And said nothing. My head spun—Williams was "missing"? What the hell could that mean?—but those two understood one another. Marnie slept on. I think in that moment they grasped what I never would, a certain kind of loss that was beyond even me. Where was Sev's mom, say? Whatever happened to her? In that brief moment, conditioned as we'd all been, I think Williams didn't need to hear any more. He knew exactly what was happening.

"What the fuck?" Severin repeated, without intensity. But Williams only stared straight ahead.

"Just drive."

We'd dropped down via I-15 through Riverside and San Bernardino, recently transited places like Rancho Cucamonga and Ontario, those godforsaken fringes of the Inland Empire. *Temecula*. Red-tipped radio towers and billboards. Indian casinos and wind.

"Hey, Severin." Marnie woke up now, stretching. "You want me to drive?"

Bellflower, Carson, West Covina. Williams could've been hiding in any of these places. *Missing*. I doubt he was recognizable outside LA metro. Within the city limits, he was the Story.

"Dad's missing," Williams said.

"What?" Marnie shot up toward the front seat.

"The radio says—"

Marnie lunged for the radio to turn it on, but Severin obliged her quicker.

"What's wrong with you?" she snapped at Williams. "Really, I wonder."

"Mom," he said. Like there was still the possibility "missing" could mean something benign.

"Will, he's your father," she said softly. "You know as well as I do he doesn't go on furlough."

I'd never seen an adult cry, not in anything other than an alcoholic frenzy, and so I stared at Marnie while she sat with her hands in her lap and wept, a mucusy storm like a child's. I handed her my bandanna and she blew her nose. Severin searched the dial through all kinds of irrelevance, the plodding tonalities of FM rock, before he found another news station that might tell us.

—*Hollywood agent Williams Farquarsen is still missing. Police say he disappeared Thursday afternoon following a meeting with Warner Communications Vice Chairman Ted Ashley—*

The radio didn't provide much, just reiterated that he was gone. Four days wasn't long for anyone else, but Williams's movements were so predictable. Even the cops knew this wasn't normal.

—*is no suspicion of criminal activity, and Farquarsen is not believed to have fled the country—*

Marnie spotted a gas station. "Pull over."

We'd just gotten off the 10 and were a few miles north of their house on Lincoln Boulevard. Marnie raced to the pay phones, and the three of us kids sat in stilted silence under the filling island's strips of yellow neon. There was the oily reek of gasoline. The radio repeated the facts. Will the elder was a no-show for work on Friday and had missed a number of important meetings over the weekend. It was now Monday night.

"I'm sorry," I said to my friend. What else should I have said? But when Little Will turned and met my gaze, I realized I shouldn't have said anything at all.

"C'mon," he said to Sev. "Let's go get some cigs."

"Grab me some gum," I said, but he ignored me.

The two of them walked off to the mini-mart and left me sitting in the car. Was something wrong with young Will's response? It seems to me now a healthy effort toward denial. I watched Marnie pump quarters into the phone, calling and re-calling Will's friends until she could find someone who might give her a straight answer. Where was I supposed to go? I lay in the backseat with both doors open and sucked air, sick exhaust, the diesel fumes from the freeway. The night was cool, and the traffic on the 10 made a frantic, serpentine hiss. But there wasn't any place to run from it, nowhere I could imagine where bad news wouldn't eventually find us.

XIV

WILLIAMS THE ELDER never came home. He just didn't surface. Weeks passed, and there were no developments.

"Anything, Mom?" My friend stood in his bathing suit, at my house, dripping after a swim. Every day he called home and each time received the same answer, Marnie's sharp voice spiking from the receiver.

"Nothing, kid. They're still looking."

My own lungs seemed to pump with dread. Just as Beau had revealed himself to me a few years ago as my true father, to my ecstasy and despair, Williams's vanishing filled me with a primary terror. The events felt related. Could dads just come and go? The cops interviewed Severin; they interviewed Beau. They interviewed everyone remotely close to the situation, including me. Everything was cloudy: the way Will's Ferrari was still garaged in the Marina, for example, or the way his monogrammed shirts still hung undisturbed in his closet, every last one accounted for. The situation fascinated Hollywood. *Where had Williams gone?* Teddy became the agency's acting president. People speculated like crazy—yes, even Beau came under some suspicion—but soon enough, they grew tired of it. Williams's life left so few toeholds: there were no drug problems, no mistresses, no gambling debts or mob ties. By mid-July the case had been pushed back into the deeper reaches of the Metro section, the City pages of the *Herald Examiner*. Williams Farquarsen was missing. Well, yes, but there were still the Olympic Games and Miss America's resignation and the first female space walker to think about. Hollywood wasn't everything, after all. Young Williams and I hunkered down that summer at my house. It was just too chilly, too vacant at his. Marnie and my mom, who'd recently begun dating a smooth New York producer type named Peter Klane—he would appear suddenly in his battered maroon Mercedes, take unexplained flights to Copenhagen or Rio—formed a loose federation based on grief. My friends and I stuck together, and young Williams stayed at my place for an entire month while our mothers went out to dinner and commiserated over Soave Bolla and steamed clams. Then one afternoon the phone rang. My mom picked it up downstairs. I knew immediately. Her voice was somber, serious in a way that had become unusual.

"Will?" she called up. "It's Marnie."

He and I were in my room. It made little difference whether we were high, now. The paranoia was with us all the time. I lay on my bed reading *The Dharma Bums* and Williams sat by the window, smoking. Anyone looking would've seen not stoners but students, two short-haired boys in khakis with coffee mugs. In a few weeks, we'd enter eleventh grade. I stood up and turned down the stereo on Brian Eno's *Another Green World*. Williams picked up the tan phone on my nightstand.

"Mom?"

What had I done with that phone, besides talk with people to whom I had nothing to say, call 976 lines and jerk off to the recorded voices of women? Had it ever relayed anything of importance to me? Williams listened in silence, and I went into the hall. Whatever Marnie was telling him was for his ears alone.

"Nate?" My mother stood at the bottom of the stairs. "Williams's dad is dead."

She stared up at me. She could still do a convincing impersonation of a rational human being when she needed to. Her big square sunglasses were propped on her head and her hair was pulled back, her gaunt, alcoholic face a rictus of concern.

"I'm sorry, Nate."

"I am, too."

That summer, my mother was writing a movie about Princess Grace. Her office, that little shed out by our swimming pool, was a hothouse ruin of gin bottles, index cards, and ashtrays, typed sheets cysted with Liquid Paper. Her skin was crisscrossed with capillaries.

"What happened?" I said.

"He was mugged."

"Seriously?"

Would I have believed her even if she were telling the truth?

"On the street, downtown. It happened while you were away, but the body wasn't identified at the morgue."

I watched my mother. I'd be able to identify her no matter what, so something would've had to mangle Williams Farquarsen's body quite a bit before no one could name it.

"How could they not have identified him?"

She shrugged. "He wasn't carrying an ID. They had the body as a John Doe. Apparently it was an accident. They think he got hurt during a struggle and bled to death."

The pieces all fit, but I wasn't sure I believed them. *Fiction in any form has always intended to be realistic.* So said the Raymond Chandler essay my English teacher had assigned me, and this was certainly realistic enough. But at sixteen you're suspicious of everyone and everything, so who knew? Maybe it was true, maybe the elder Williams had gone to an event—of what kind I didn't know, since downtown was mostly the province of painters and punks, not Hollywood *machers*—then been jumped and beaten up and left to bleed out on the street. Maybe he'd been scooped off the muck-brown pavement and locked in a metal drawer alongside the drunks and the transients no one ever wondered about anyway. Some lazy beat cop could've written him off as such. But nothing to identify him at all? And Williams was a martial artist, so any mugger would've had to be swift.

"I see," I said. Staring down at my mother's narrow, semiderelict face.

Most of her life was intolerable. If I could reel her back into its earlier years, if I could find its little seams of hope or happiness, I would. Just because a life is awful doesn't mean it's not worth having.

"Poor Williams," she said, meaning my friend. "Poor kid."

"Yeah."

"Be good to him, Nate. Look after him."

She knew something I didn't. For all the brute and horrible and careless acts she herself would commit, she knew I wasn't a good enough friend: I was already too selfish. Williams came out of my room a moment later. He looked so adult, in that way actual adults don't often, calm and responsible behind his tortoiseshell glasses. He flicked a strand of hair off his forehead.

"My dad died."

"I know," I said. "I'm sorry, dude."

"He was jumped on the street."

My mother turned away. I can imagine what this looked like to her—two boys discussing this as if it were anything speakable, sensical.

"Dude," I said. *De profundis*. What matter if I sounded like a future beer commercial? "I'm so sorry."

Williams nodded. Whatever his mother had told him, it wasn't exactly identical but it was close. A mugging. What an end for a Hollywood ruler, a man who'd governed everything but the tides.

"Thanks." His face was stark in its privacy. "I appreciate that."

Williams, my friend, was the first of us to grow up all the way. Unless, in fact, he was the last. Downstairs, my mother wept in the kitchen, her sobs competing with the clatter of dishes as she put them away. Our dog, a psychotic terrier, was chasing something out in the yard, the sound of his voice reduced to a rude gargle. I could hear his nails scrabbling on concrete, my mother's yips and wails. I opened my mouth but found nothing more articulate to offer, myself.

PART FOUR: **RECURRING**

I

"WILLIAMS! WAKE UP, MAN! Wake the fuck up!"

He lolled in the front seat. A cold, predawn wind fluttered in my ears, whistled along the car's rubberized window seams. And because I couldn't do anything, because Severin was still zooming toward a hospital that didn't exist, I took it upon myself to pull Will's damp hair and shake him.

"Wake up, buddy! Come on!"

He was our friend. He may have been an idiot, too, but were we supposed to feel any less for him?

"Sev, what the fuck?" I yelled. We were crossing La Cienega, effectively killing our chances of reaching a proper hospital in time. You went east into deep Hollywood and you were left with Kaiser Permanente, the sorts of places that would reject our shitty insurance plans instead of remembering who our fathers were. "This isn't the moment to get nostalgic!"

My brother banked sharply down La Cienega, pulling his Gremlin at a ninety-degree angle across what would've been a wall of traffic were it not 4:00 AM. Down a steep hill, past the strange ruin of the Circus Maximus. Its cracked clown faces yawned, cattails breaking through its whorehouse decay.

"What are you doing, Sev? Playing Steve fucking McQueen?"

He cackled. *Just messing with you.*

"Are you high? Did you shoot up earlier, too?"

"Nope."

The little Gremlin shot down the hill. *First gear . . . second gear . . .* I couldn't help it either; the Beach Boys rang inside my head. Day was just beginning to turn across the flats, and we sped through the flashing yellow light at Fountain, then caught the green at Santa Monica. This was the fastest way to the hospital, the reconstructed Cedars-Sinai over by the Beverly Center. My brother knew what he was doing all along.

"Why did you say Cedars of Lebanon, buddy? How come?"

He shrugged. To him the distinctions were practically moot: the past was the present, the present was the future. Severin knew just how to live. We raced along La Cienega, the moon expensive overhead, the sky's rich purple now beginning to lighten. A strip club called the Seventh Veil, a wig shop flashed past. Was there anything on this earth that did not involve the donning or removal of our disguises? We turned right on Beverly and then left on George Burns Road, pulling up in front of the ER.

"Are you using, Sev?" I jumped out of the backseat and Sev from the front, and we ran around to pull Williams out of the passenger side. "Have you been?"

"A little." The doors gasped open, their respiratory sound reassuring as we lugged Will into the lobby. "Occasionally."

"*Occasionally*, what"—Will sagged, and we buckled along with him—"what does that mean, Severin, *occasionally*? You don't do this drug *occasionally*. It fucks you up, as you can see."

I dropped my half, let Severin ballast Williams—screw them both, really, again—as I ran to the nurses' station and started jabbering at the woman behind the counter.

"Our friend . . . messed up, OD'd, heroin . . . help."

"What? What's the problem, heah?"

The woman was in her forties, possibly Jamaican. She was café con leche–colored, with freckles and a big, round face. She seemed to know her part.

"My friend overdosed." I spoke to the Plexiglas. "An hour, maybe two hours ago. I think he might die."

Other people concentrate our energies. They make our selves possible, force us to be more than just a shrieking puddle of id. This woman's calm directed me. She leaned back from her desk, turning her wide face—it was almost as big as Beau's, but it was more tender in its froggy unhappiness—to an orderly. *Helpdisboy*, I think she said. The orderly, who was big and strapping and dreadlocked himself, came round.

"What happened?"

I told him. My brother was still standing near the door with Williams hanging off him, like King Kong slewing from the side of his skyscraper. There was something funny about stolid Sev waiting there with Will, who lolled and drooled like the world's worst (or best, I suppose, depending) prom date. But then there is something funny about everything.

"Thanks," Sev grunted, as the orderly took the burden off his hands.

The orderly carried Will over to a gurney with ease. "When did this happen?"

"An hour or two ago," Severin said. "We found him like this."

Over in the ER's waiting area was a corkscrew-curled Hispanic woman with her fever-red baby, an older couple, and a pair of kids—younger than us—who sat on either side of a guy who was obviously having a hard time of his own, a bad drug experience that had him blinking, dazed, palpitating. The orderly lay Williams down on the gurney and was joined by another.

"Wake up," this new one said, an orange-haired white guy with a vinegar mustache, a little line of fur just like the stoner kids used to grow. "C'mon, Sleeping Beauty. Wake up, wake up!"

"That's what you're supposed to do?" I said. The two orderlies shook him and slapped him, cuffing his face as they lifted under his neck to keep him from gagging on his tongue. "We could've done that."

"Shh." Severin dragged me aside. "Let them do their jobs."

"Aren't you supposed to give him an adrenaline shot?" I shouted. "Something?"

They wheeled him through some double doors, taking him away from us. It was the theft of our responsibility, but what could we do? The waiting room was a warm, chalky blue, filled with ficus plants and an encouraging Freon glow. There were televisions in every corner. This place was a friendly and beautiful machine, where it seemed even the scrawny kid who sat blinking in his chair—I could practically feel his seizured pulse from here—was part of the plan.

"How high are you?" I asked Sev. Imagine, that I was still young enough to believe what the hospital signaled, to be lulled by its intimations of safety. "What are you on?"

"Nothing, now."

"Then why? Severin, why are you doing that shit, ever?"

"I like it."

We were such children, and so you might forgive the lunkhead-edness of this response. Still, such raging, idiotic self-centeredness made me seethe.

"You fucking like it? Who's the asshole romantic now, Sev? You're always on me about my Chandler thing, but who's *your* model? Thomas De Quincey?"

"I'm not shooting it."

The older couple nearby watched us. Perhaps they were just look-ing for an out, a distraction from their own trauma. They clung to each other as if for dear life, their bodies blending in a mass of tan clothes, walnut skin, dirty sneakers, and gray hair. I hope to die just so some day, in some smashed-up, transhuman calamity.

"I'm only smoking it. And not very often, Nate. Once a month, if that."

"That's a relief."

"Williams and I have done it a few times, that's all. I didn't know he was shooting it."

"Oh, excuse you."

"No, really. I mean it." We sat down in a pair of black-pleather seats beside a plastic table with magazines, sports pages, newspa-pers abandoned by last night's sufferers. "There's a difference be-tween experimenting and being strung out."

"Really? Why don't you explain that difference, huh? When ex-actly does an interest become a need?"

I wondered, not for the first time, what was really going on in my brother's head. What Will had done wasn't *truly* a surprise. It was in character. He'd been a mad dog since early childhood, and for him to slip off in the afternoon to cop on Bonnie Brae—now I could guess where he'd been—was just another dunderheaded act of self-destruc-tion in a lifelong series of the same. But what about Severin? Wher-ever he went he presented the face of mastery, a mellow intellectual calm. He'd done this since we were teenagers. But that didn't mean he wasn't troubled. Far from it. Right now he just shook his head.

"He always needed to be first," he murmured. "Will has always wanted to be first with everything."

"He might be the first one to die."

He stood up and went out to move his car. I watched him go, still wondering a bit what made him tick. He certainly had the trauma to back up all sorts of emotional disturbance, a history no less ruinous than Will's. But I'd never seen him act on it. He loped down the emergency room drive and vanished, for a moment, into the day. The air had lightened, shifted from rich dark to anxious gray. We'd gone from nighttime emergency to near daylight, to a place where our disasters were suddenly unromantic. There was no grand design here, no idea that our Will was either a hero or a victim. He was just a statistic, if that.

"What d'you think happens when we die?" I said when Severin came back, after he'd nestled down in one of the plastic chairs with the paper.

"You wanna get metaphysical?" Severin lowered the sports section, which was two days old but which—unsurprisingly, given his bent—seemed to interest him as much as tomorrow's. More. "Is this really the time?"

"When is it *not* the time?"

Severin watched me. He looked wry, amused, the way you were supposed to look when you'd been up all night after going to a rock concert and were now enjoying the paper with a friend.

"Does Williams have a soul?" I said.

"Williams? No."

Severin was leaning back in his chair, his hair once more grown out and classically mussed, his jaw stubbled and his eyes alert behind his horn-rims. He looked like himself, like the self that would multiply over the years—in the newspapers, on YouTube—until he achieved whatever degree of celebrity was attainable for an American writer in the twenty-first century. Just then he was still my brother the bullshit screenwriter and failing novelist, whose future successes were as unimaginable as his current despairs.

"Williams is going to make it," he said.

"How do you know?"

"Because you don't die when you're not ready. Because Williams is too much of a doofus to go out like this. He hasn't learned enough."

"We have?"

Severin flapped his newspaper. This world-as-vale-of-soul-making stuff was probably sophistical also—the idea that Williams mightn't die because he was insufficiently wise—but in truth, I didn't think our friend was going to die either. There was no neo-Keatsian idea behind that; I just didn't think so.

"We're a little better off than he is," Sev said.

I doubted it. But then, I was ready to doubt so many things. We'd been young and born to such privilege there had never been a reason for any of us to suspect we weren't going to prosper. Until now. I got up and went to the window to deal with paperwork, offering up a patchwork of credit cards and Williams's basic information until all this got straightened out. No one said, *The son of the agent?* No one said anything.

"Are you family?" At last, the dreadlocked orderly came back.

"Close enough," I said. "We've known each other since we were kids."

"I'm only supposed to release information to family." This guy had an impressive baritone. His hair massed, snakelike, around his collarbone.

"They're not here," Severin said. "His dad is dead, and his mom lives out in the desert somewhere, up north."

We hadn't called Marnie yet. We'd put her name on the forms, and I roughly remembered her municipality—she lived up in Madera County somewhere, a rural isolation that suited her rugged temperament—so they could track her down, but I wasn't going to call her at five in the morning. Not for this.

"All right," the orderly said after a moment. "Shouldn't do this, but come with me."

"Is he alive?" I said. "Is he conscious?"

The orderly nodded. But was there a difference? I felt there was. *I think, therefore I am.* It takes more than thought to ratify being. Or less, much less. We passed through security doors and Severin folded his hands across his Peckinpah T to hide its gory scene. The orderly just swung his arms by his sides, kept the easy rolling gait of a sailor on shore leave.

"This way," he said. "He's awake."

Will was in bed, adrift in a sea of medicinal greens and blues. The back was cranked up so he reclined at forty-five degrees. His eyes

were open, but he wore a dull, stunned expression, his lips bent in
an empty kiss.

"Will," Severin said. "Hey, man."

His head swiveled toward us without recognition.

"Will?"

It was like *Invasion of the Body Snatchers*. The strict nullity of his
gaze, the sheer vacancy with which he watched us.

"What did you do to him?" I looked at the dreadlocked orderly.
He shook his head.

"We just woke him up."

A doctor came into the room now, a woman in cat's-eye glasses. A
brunette, with her hair pulled up in a bun. She would've been sexy
if she weren't so efficient. The room was sultry, dark except for the
flickering tubes behind Williams's bed.

"We gave him a very mild stimulant," the doctor said. "He should
sleep."

Will was breathing. I suppose I ought to have been grateful he
was able to sit upright, that his eyes were open and he was not,
instead, heaving and choking upon throatfuls of vomit.

"He needs to recover. We don't know yet what that'll look like."

"How so?"

She approached. Up close she was Jewish and freckled and less
conventionally pretty than I wanted her to be, than the movies,
at least, would've made her. Her eyes were brown and her nose
was narrow, her hair was ratty and pinned up carelessly, with little
wisps straying down along her cheeks. I wanted to fuck her desper-
ately.

"He might have memory problems," she said. "That sometimes
happens when the brain's been deprived of oxygen."

"His brain's been deprived?"

"He shot a tremendous amount of heroin. It's amazing he's alive."

"Alive?" I thought. "Amazing?" He'd never looked so stupid, and
quite frankly, Williams had been looking pretty stupid to me for
some time. His hair dangled, limp and cruddy around that blunt
and supercilious face.

"What kind of memory problems?" Sev stepped forward.

"Short-term," she said. *Remember, Sev? Remember?* "Sometimes
long-term, sometimes not at all. Sometimes people have trouble

moving things from short-term memory to long-term for a while, so they experience a kind of recurring loop. I've seen that too, but it varies. Your friend needs to recover."

A kind of recurring loop. I'd seen that myself. I'd lived it. Still, I yearned for her in a way that was disproportionate: the presence of death made sex come first, gave urgency to my most idle dreaming. I went down the hall and washed my hands. The doctor was gone when I came back in, and Sev was sitting on the edge of the bed.

"Williams just said something."

"Yeah? What?"

Little Will followed Sev's gaze to where I stood. Some dumb flicker of recognition seemed to wash through him.

"Duuude."

His voice sounded strange. This wasn't our friend, not any version of him that I knew.

"Will, man, are you all right? Are you here?"

He just smiled weirdly. Not his usual smug, bullying smile, but something strange, twisted. The various smells of urine, trace vomit, and sterilizing alcohol clutched me and seemed to make pretense impossible. Cautiously, I approached the bed. I thought I might vomit, myself.

"Will."

"Nate," he said. Still smiling. "Naaate."

But then he lay back, slowly, and shut his eyes like someone performing a ritual.

"What the hell, man! Stay with us! Stay up!"

Only the faint and lingering smile let us know he was *not* dead, just sleeping. The doctor returned. She looked at Severin and then at me, blankly. She took off her glasses.

"Your friend needs to rest," she said. "Why don't you let him?"

II

THE SUMMER SEVERIN and I graduated from high school, Beau bought a
ranch in Calabasas. My father and I were on better terms then—I'd
come out and spend a day with them, sometimes an entire weekend
under his chubby wing—but we still weren't what you'd call close.
From time to time he'd let a big knuckle fall on my shoulder as we
roamed around in the dust, as he pointed out with pride an abandoned apiary, the stables he planned to repopulate; with my mom
and Teddy, he'd agreed to pay for a part of my college education. He
may have paid for all of it, in fact. I don't know. She was never a reliable witness, and Beau never told me what their arrangements were.

After Williams's death, things had become deeply strange for Beau.
The police had questioned him three times. Some people actually
believed he was guilty, and by the time Will's disappearance was explained, he'd had enough. He moved as far away from town as he was
ever going to get. And though I never thought he had anything to
do with his partner's demise, he treated me with the same bemused
detachment he seemed to direct at the rest of the world, the same
wounded opacity. That ranch had acreage, and all together we'd ram-
ble its desert distances for hours with his dogs—he'd requisitioned
a pair of Jack Russell terriers, to complete the image—but Beau Rosenwald wouldn't say much. The three of us would have dinner, and
sometimes he'd look at Severin and me, a little ironically I thought,
and sigh. *My boys.* Maybe we were the only two people left in the
world he could trust, or who trusted him completely. But of course I
didn't have the same rapport with him that Sev did, didn't have any

way through his ample defenses. I went off to Amherst College, and Sev went to Yale. Young Will went to Vassar but eventually came back to Santa Cruz, where he finished with a degree in communications. The three of us stayed close, but we were busy, each trying to carve out some semblance of private identity, something beyond a relation to our renowned fathers, and to one another. While I was away, and after her divorce from Teddy became final, my mother moved to Washington State. Her sister lived there, and she'd had enough of the movie business and the men who ran it. She planned to write a novel, although things never turned out that way. But this meant, for a few years, I was rarely in Los Angeles. My friends and I saw each other over certain holidays, or on long weekends in New York, but for a brief while it was almost as if our special closeness barely existed. And then, incredibly, while Severin and I were gone, Beau rose from hibernation. It happened during our sophomore year. A messenger mistook his driveway for that of an actor who lived next door. The actor, strangely enough, was represented by my stepfather. Teddy was the one who'd originated the package. So Beau signed for it and then, seeing who it had come from, immediately picked up the phone.

"Ted? It's Beau Rosenwald!"

"Beau?" None of his ex-colleagues had spoken to him in the last few years. But I don't think Teddy ever thought Beau had anything to do with Williams's disappearance, either: the police had questioned everyone. It was simply a matter of association. "To what do I owe the occasion?"

"To the fact you just sent me an offer. I'm afraid I can't accept. I don't do TV, and the schedule looks rough."

Teddy laughed. "What are you talking about?"

"I just got a script for Peter Strauss. I'd walk it over to him myself, but it's so damn hot out here!"

Like everyone, my stepfather just couldn't resist him. No matter how cloudy the circumstances of Beau's departure, or how complex the history between them, there was a time these men had been friends. Together they had built something that remained a colossal presence on the Hollywood scene: the agency as a whole was more powerful than ever.

"I forgot you were living out by Peter," Teddy said, disingenuously. He'd represented Strauss since the seventies, from that brief shining moment the actor was supposed to be a huge star, though of course it hadn't turned out that way. "I'd like to find Peter a job."

"He can be my pool boy," Beau said. Who knows what moved him to pick up and dial? Maybe he was just tired of being alone. He was out there on his porch, with the fat gray cordless. "I'll hire him for that."

Beau hadn't changed much, after all. He still had the brashness, the flair. Teddy said, "So how *are* things out in Calabasas?"

"Same as they are everywhere you can't get a decent corned beef sandwich. Hot, dusty. A little quiet."

Teddy laughed. "You looking for a way back in, Beau?"

Or maybe, just maybe, he wanted the thing that all Hollywood seems to want: a second chance, or in his case—why stop at two?—a third. *In everything that can be called art there is a quality of redemption*, said Raymond Chandler. All this time he'd been living the life of a retired gentleman landowner, like Noah Cross in *Chinatown*, eating grilled pheasant on the terrace of his desert estate, swanning around in duck pants and a Jeep. He had enough money; he wasn't going to have to worry about that for the rest of his life. It was crazy what you could make in this business, the killings you could accumulate in a very short time. He'd moved to the deep Valley because it suited some curious idea he had of himself, because the notion of a post-convalescent life of self-sufficiency—albeit one in which he could still zip into town to hit Spago, grab a little soup at Nate 'n Al—appealed to him. His sons were grown, his daughter was buried, and the business could go screw itself on a hilltop. It wasn't like he hadn't left it before. His life might've been a folktale, he himself like one of those clever merchants or fishermen who get tempted repeatedly by excess. This time, he ought to have been strong enough to say no. Then again, what was he doing all day? Reading wasn't his style, he played no sports, his favorite pastime—making persuasive phone calls—was against the law if applied in a slightly different context. So I suppose he did nothing, but to Teddy, sitting in his own gleaming and refurbished office in the company's new Frank Gehry–designed building, Beau sounded surprisingly hale and hearty.

"Maybe," Beau said. "Maybe I am indeed looking for a way in."

Teddy cut off this line of thinking, for now. "It's great to hear from you."

"Thanks. I'll get this package over to Peter this afternoon."

Teddy jumped off the call before Beau could say more.

The Valley was such a peculiar place. It wasn't just an "exile" Beau found himself in, it was an alternative universe. One in which he was just a big guy with a lot of dough and no identity. Out here, the light was brighter, and there was no wind, except for those occasions when the Santa Anas blew and fanned embers into wildfires, scorching blazes that ate up the Santa Monica Mountains and swatches of the surrounding land so that, twice, he'd had to be evacuated from his home. The fires had never touched him, though, and the truth was he adored them. He loved living so close to destruction you could wait for it; you expected it, even. Really, his life in Calabasas was provisional and was never supposed to be otherwise, but ruin never came. How could Beau be frightened, besides? He'd been annihilated twice already.

"Teddy?" He rang a few weeks later, this time with more deliberate intent. "I'm going to be in Beverly Hills on Tuesday for an appointment. Wanna have lunch?"

Teddy coughed. I suppose it was pity that moved him, or else his slight hesitation meant he couldn't think of an excuse fast enough. "Sure." I mean after all this time, why not? Half the pups who shared his office now barely remembered Beau Rosenwald. Some of them didn't even know there was one. "Let's do it."

Maybe Teddy agreed to meet him for me, too. Maybe Beau's regeneration is in part my own fault. I admit, I've worried about that myself over the years. Did Teddy think he owed Beau something? Whatever the case, the following Tuesday afternoon, just after the fat man's standard 11:45 with his psychiatrist, the two of them met at Hymie's Fish Market. This was a low-ceilinged room like a cross between a chophouse and an old sawdust saloon.

"Beau." The man who approached Teddy was still powerful. Big—around 225, which was more or less where he would stay for the rest of his life—and also swaggering, strong. "It's good to see ya."

"Ted." Beau clasped my stepfather's hand, softly. A gaggle of younger executives around the room noticed, but didn't recognize him. "Thanks for agreeing to meet."

The person Teddy had last seen was humiliated. This one was humble, which is such a rare property in Hollywood. Beau may have been strong—he looked like he'd been working out—but his manners were gentle. His handshake, his voice, even the amount of space he consumed around him: he seemed to exude more air than he took up, for once.

"You look terrific," Teddy said, the pleasantry with which every exchange in this place starts, whether or not it's stated. "You seem younger."

"I am younger. Stop racing around to scoop up Marty's turds and look what happens!"

He turned his palms upward. Beau always did have nice teeth: gleaming, white. No one is all ugly. But it wasn't just that he was thinner, or that his hair was well-trimmed and his beard was neat and they were both still a rich, coppery brown. It was who he became, away from the business. He wore a blue blazer and a white shirt and bucks.

"You don't have to tell me," Teddy said, although this is a lesson he never learned himself. "Maybe someday I'll retire."

"I'm not retired."

"Oh no?"

The two men looked at leather-backed menus, although this was a bluff. Who needed to be told what to eat?

"I'm resting."

"Resting? Beau, no one in this town rests. There's an old Chinese proverb, I'm sure, to tell you why not."

"Oh? What's going to happen now, Ted? Someone will steal my clients?"

Teddy laughed. He wasn't an especially petty man, but the sight of a person without anxiety can whip anyone into a frenzy.

"So." Teddy crunched an oyster cracker. "You're taking it easy."

"Yep."

"They reserve a plot for you yet at Forest Lawn?"

They ordered. Fans turned overhead. They sat in one of the long booths against the eastern wall, technically a table for four. Around them were the raw wood floors, the brassy fixtures, the white-aproned waiters scuttling to describe what was fresh. If Teddy wanted to hold his advantage they ought to have gone someplace less Jewish, more nouveau, less East Coast–feeling than this.

"So what brings you to town," Teddy said, after their food arrived. "You still seeing Horowitz?"

"Yep."

In a sense, these two men were deeply estranged; in another, still intimately connected. They'd shared a child, as well as a psychiatrist, so it wasn't any big whoop to ask. Most guys in this town shared doctors the way soldiers shared whores—come to think of it, they shared those too.

"How's that going?"

Beau equivocated with his hands. *Mezzo mezzo.* A piece of arctic char lay half-eaten on his plate, glistening and white. "I think my therapist is crazier than I am."

"How so?"

"He says . . . " Beau lowered his voice and leaned over to speak between the salt and pepper shakers. "He says he's treating Jim Morrison."

Teddy just stared at him. Was he being serious? There was that spinning instant in which Teddy wondered what was worse, if Beau was insane or if his own former psychiatrist was, before they both burst into laughter.

"Good Lord!" Teddy wiped his eyes, finally. "That's the most *fakakta* thing I've ever heard. How can you go in there and talk to the man every week?"

"How can I stop? He gives me updates on Jim's Little League team."

"What?"

"Jim coaches, apparently. A group of kids who play at Mar Vista park."

They howled again.

"It's like the world's worst sitcom," my father said, signaling the waiter for dessert. "It's like that pilot Rollie once sold where the Beatles were all still together in Chicago, learning to play the blues."

"Jesus God!"

"John Ritter as John Lennon. Remember that one?"

They had coffee, a pair of espressos, as their late partner's pretension by now—it was early 1988—had spread across town, even to the kosher belt. Beau swabbed the lip of his cup with lemon peel and dropped it inside. Teddy took his neat. He wore a lavender shirt, a black Italian suit. These two had always been the best-dressed men at ADM, and in the violent pastel clamor of that decade's latter half, their elegance marked them apart.

"The thing is," Beau nibbled a cookie, "I think it's a lousy sitcom. But it's a good movie."

"A good movie?"

"Yes! It's not episodic, even if Dr. Horror-wit decides to feed it to me that way. It's funny."

"It *is* funny."

"It's a comedy. For Dusty, say."

"Dustin's gonna play Jim Morrison?" Teddy drained his espresso, nested his elbows among crumbs.

"The older Jim Morrison. Or someone who *thinks* he's Jim Morrison. Look at it like this, there's this Little League coach—"

And Beau lowered his voice now, for you never knew who might be listening, and began to describe it. It was a funny idea, or not funny, cute—who knows, they weren't writers—but the fact remained, it had a hook. There were actors who could do it. There were actors who *would* do it, given the way those old hippies idolized one another, and who might make of it just about anything: tragedy, comedy, Jacobean revenge drama, Robin Williams or Ernest goddamn Borgnine as Jim Morrison, why not? The business was just what it had always been: an idea was "good" or "bad" depending on who had it. You were entitled to anything you could lift.

"So what d'you want to do?" Teddy said finally. After all these years, hadn't Beau earned a little mercy, a fresh round of assistance? "How can I help you out?"

"I'm not sure. It's just something that occurred to me."

"You wanna come back to ADM?" Teddy hesitated, moved a little gingerly around the subject. "For various reasons, I don't think that would wash."

"I wasn't thinking of that."

"No? What were you thinking?"

Beau exhaled. Ever since the day Teddy's package had been misdelivered, he'd been under a kind of spell, and ridiculous as this idea was, it created a certain pressure. Why should *his* psychiatrist have been the one who was crazy enough to suggest it? It seemed like fate, almost. Beau scanned the room, now like his old self, like the man who knew exactly where everybody was at all times.

"I think I should produce it." He chewed a toothpick.

"You wanna produce?" Teddy was a little startled. Surely Beau's strength was all in making deals. "With Horowitz?"

"Hell, no. The man's out of his mind." Both laughed, again. "Just me." Beau studied the dregs of his cup. "Remember I did a movie before, long time ago."

"That's right. Oh Lord, you did, didn't you? Listen, you won't be able to do it alone, but I could hook you up with Larry Gordon or Art—"

"Just me." He set the cup down. "I'm through with partners, Teddy. I'm going forward on my own."

Teddy nodded. To this day I don't know whether to thank or curse him for what came next. Though he was neither as pragmatic as Williams nor as passionate as Beau, what Teddy had was quick wits and immaculate timing. Across the room he spotted a young executive named Sandy Albin, a kid whose tastes ran to broad comedy. He and Teddy had just done a deal, in fact, for an actor Teddy represented named Ian Butterworth, now long forgotten. Tall, Byronic, just a little bit paunchy around the middle. The man was perfect, in fact, for Jim Morrison at forty-five. It took Teddy but an instant to lift his hand and summon the good-natured, baby-faced exec.

"Hey, Sandy! Sandy, I don't know if you remember, but this here is a former colleague of mine, Beau Rosenwald . . . "

There were plenty of reasons later to believe Teddy had done the wrong thing. Plenty of them, too, to think the mistake was all Beau's. But just then the fat man's problems were solved, and the truth was, he hadn't even known there *were* any before that afternoon. Arms swinging, he got into his Jag and hammered the wheel with his fists.

"Jonas?" He was on the phone, yelling at his broker, punching the car's accelerator as he drove. "I want to sell the house. Today. Now!"

He had nothing but a pitch meeting, set for next Tuesday. Then again, what more did Beau ever need? Wind tore at his hair, the stereo blared as he roared north on the Ventura Freeway. He hung up so he could scream along with the radio, whatever this tape was that Severin had left inside it.

"It's mooorree thaaan amusement now!"

This was his life. He couldn't wait to get back in the game.

III

SEVERIN AND I, well, we weren't exactly delighted by *Balls and Strikes*. Reluctantly, we attended the premiere at the Cinerama Dome, munching on peppered ahi as we circulated through the lobby. It had always been embarrassing to be Beau Rosenwald's son. But never more than now.

"Come here, boys." Beau beckoned us over. "I want you to meet Mickey Schulhof. Mickey, these are my kids."

"Hi, fellas." Another grinning gangster stuck out his paw. "You must be really, really proud."

Perhaps we should've been. That movie would make a fucking fortune, having morphed in the end into a toothless family comedy that had nothing to do with Jim Morrison at all, that was now just a story about a rock 'n' roll coach who moves to the inner city. Life rights were expensive, and music rights too. Why—here came Michael Keaton now!

"Hi, Beau." Flashbulbs popped. "These your kids?"

"If he ever makes another movie this lame let's move to Wisconsin," I whispered, digging Sev in the ribs. "At least the cheese there is *sharp*."

But here was Beau Rosenwald, unpartnered, alone. And here we were, two snotty little college students, our heads fully stuffed with nonsense grokked from our film studies classes: what did my brother or I know of what this meant to the man? We stood there with our arms folded, while Beau strode boldly into the Schwarzeneggerian Era.

"Wonderful, Beau!" Was that Frank Price, coming over to give him a hug? "Why don't you come see me one of these days?"

In the spring of 1988, our father was off to the races, his failure absolved. Whatever had happened in the past belonged there: all of a sudden, no one gave the late Williams Farquarsen a thought. No longer a crazy has-been who'd holed up out in the country, Beau was now a wily veteran with relationships—Bill, Dan, Marty, Bob—that stood him in good stead. Who cared about what had happened in the ADM conference room? Yet Severin and I skulked around the Cinerama Dome's margins, outside the range of starlets and photographers. My brother understood. It wasn't just because he had a head stuffed full of Godard. Beau's success was much harder to take than any of his prior disgrace.

Around this time, Severin dropped out of Yale and moved to the Bay Area. He worked as an usher at the UC Theater for a while, then at Amoeba Music in Berkeley. It was the beginning of his legend, the long hours spent clerking and curating the shelves in his head. Just like me, he was trying to crawl out from under our father's shadow, the uneducated man's aspirations. He wrote a novel, a primitive psychedelic noir, and then trashed it. I pecked out my own first script—even then, I knew I shouldn't compete with him—and threw it away as well. Nothing was urgent. We were just charting out the terrain of our half-related dreams. And though we were bound by blood, we were scarcely in touch for a few years. Williams, too: when he transferred to Santa Cruz, he moved outside my orbit. It wasn't until the early nineties that we all got back together. Williams broke up with his girlfriend and came home. Severin decided he'd take a tilt at the movie business himself, since it was probably easier to write a script than to work eleven hours on a retail floor. And having spent a period of East Coast Exile—I finished Amherst and went to Boston, of all places—I came back to Los Angeles too. What was the point of staying away? Did I think I could escape all this, that the problem of my bastardry could be solved simply by hiding?

IV

"YO!"

Two days after young Will's overdose, Sev and I sauntered into his hospital room. They'd moved him to a private one, upstairs. Sev was jocular, bellowing as we entered. As if by now this could be written off as just another of Will's bunglings, the way he did everything—drink, smoke, skateboard, OD—at full tilt.

"Hi," I said. But pulled up short as I spotted Marnie sitting on the edge of his bed. "Oh. Marnie! What's happening?"

"*What's happening?*" she snapped. "Why don't you tell me, Nate?"

"Dudes!" Will just swiveled his head toward the door with a big dopey grin, more like his ordinary self. "So happy to see you!"

"We're happy to see you too, boy," I said. "Never been happier."

"I seem to have had an accident."

"You do seem to have had an accident. What happened?"

I wanted to check his memory, of course. He just blinked. Marnie stared bloody murder at me, and at Sev.

"Hi, Marnie." Severin was so much better at this than I was, such a mellow parent seducer. "I'm sorry about all this."

"You goddamn should be." She stood up off the end of the bed, picked up her purse and paperback. "I'll leave you kids alone. You probably can't do much damage here."

She went outside. How different she looked now! She'd never remarried, lived alone now with her memories and her sculpture. Her blonde hair was shot through now with gray, long and silvery like a crone's. Time and loss had hammered her face. She cleared her throat with inordinate force as she moved into the hall.

"Whoa. Your mom's *pissed*," Severin said. I know it's incredible we spoke this way, but together, at least, we were still kids.

"I don't blame her," I said. "Williams, what happened? Can you tell me?"

"I don't remember."

"Really?"

He was upright in bed again, the room clean and white. From its picture windows we could see Third Street, cars crawling along in the shadow of the Beverly Center below. He wore a fresh T-shirt, and his hair was washed. On his table was a Walkman, a vase with some cut alstroemeria, a copy of Raymond Carver's *Fires*.

"Yeah. It's all a big blur to me, y'know? I just woke up here."

"Oh, fuck," I said, but then Williams broke into a big mocking smile.

"Haaaa! Just messing with you! I know what happened. I OD'd."

"Shit, man." I exhaled. "Don't *do* that!"

"I know, I know. We were at a show, I remember. We saw Guns N' Roses at Gazzarri's."

"God*damn* it, Will. Don't *do* that," I said. "You scared me."

"I'm sorry," he said.

"You should be fucking sorry. You think your death is only for yourself?"

It's hard to love someone stupid. But is it really any harder than to love someone smart? Sev pulled me outside for a minute.

"Don't do this to him," he said.

"Don't do what?" I said. We leaned away from an unhurried traffic of nurses and orderlies, people for whom emergency was so ordinary there might never be a need to rush. "What am I doing?"

"Don't blame him."

"Don't blame him? I'll tell you what, Sev, I'll blame *you* instead."

"Me?"

"Yes, you," I said. "You fucking enabled him. You did drugs with him—"

"I never said that."

"It doesn't matter," I said. "Don't you think he's been through enough? We had to add heroin?"

Whatever it was, this nonsense my brother and I were talking, this was the beginning of our adult schism. We might never get along in quite the same careless way, with that feeling we'd once had of carrying a shared burden—however unequally—between us. I couldn't help envying Little Will, almost. It was a weird feeling that came over me in the hallway: mightn't it be better to have your memory wiped?

"Fuck you, Nate. I didn't do this." Severin took off his glasses, and I was amazed to see there were tears, as he blotted his eyes with thumb and forefinger. "You don't know the half of it."

I didn't. It amazes me to look back, over the course of our troubled, ridiculous lives, and think Severin might have, already—that he knew certain key things I wouldn't learn for many years still. No wonder he and Will were in cahoots. His sister, Will's dad—my two friends understood loss in ways I couldn't yet. The disappearance of his mom, for that matter. What would it take to opiate successfully against so much pain? I ought to have been thankful Severin, too, was still with us.

I tapped Sev on the shoulder. I wasn't a total idiot. A cart trundled between us, trailing a smell of rosemary chicken and polenta, royal hospital food. But he just turned and stalked back into Will's room, leaving me to feel helpless and stupid outside.

What did he *know* then? I still have no idea. And at the same time, joyriding notwithstanding—*he* didn't have a drug problem, not like Little Will—Severin was beginning to pull his life together, I could feel it. Whereas I was still spinning around in dim circles, brooding over high school sins and the death of a man half of Hollywood barely bothered to remember. Why couldn't I be more like Sev, in my essence? Or like his girlfriend, Emily White? She was lovely, beautiful, smart, unhaunted by the industry's past as she worked for our father. It wasn't her fault Beau was making animal movies, had just scored a big fat hit with *Pete*, a basketball comedy starring an animatronic chimp.

"Yo, Nate!" Severin called. "Stop being maudlin and come back in here."

I followed him back into Will's room. How beautiful this place was. The carpets were emerald green and the windows faced the Los Angeles sky, that great beneficence of another day, those clay-colored buildings that, seen from the air, seemed like little more than reticules on a relief map. The room smelled of freesia and rubbing alcohol.

"Dudes!" Williams turned away from the sunstruck window and flashed us a dumb smile as we reentered. "So happy to see you."

"We're happy to see you too, Will. Again."

"It's nice of you to come visit. I seem to have had an accident."

Severin and I looked at one another.

"We just discussed this, Will." Severin spoke, this time. "What happened?"

"I don't remember."

Williams looked at us both, exactly the way he had five minutes ago, while my brother and I just stared.

"Don't you?" I said. But I knew what was coming.

"Ahh, just fucking with you. I know, I overdosed. We were at a Guns N' Roses show!"

Life is full of wormholes. So the doctor had warned us, too. *He might have problems with his memory. He might experience a kind of recurring loop.* So did I. Did you ever have that feeling that your life is running in place? That whatever you do leads you right back to where you started? Williams wasn't being redundant: he actually didn't remember that Sev and I had just been here. So it was, in Hollywood. Out there, Harold Ramis's hit comedy starring Bill Murray as Punxsutawney Phil Connors had beaten our father's chimp pic at the box office, but not by much. By little more than a nose, groundhogs ruled!

"Hey, guys," Williams looked up again, blinking. His eyes shone out of his shallow and handsome face. "Hey, d'you wanna know what happened to me?"

V

SAY WHAT YOU will about Beau's taste, he certainly knew what it meant to make progress. You put the past behind you and moved on. Was that so difficult? Some people—his ex-therapist—thought so, but Beau never had a lot of patience for those folks. Severin had once tried to pick an argument with him about this. *Dad, just think about what Faulkner said. "The past isn't dead. It isn't even past."* To which Beau had responded, *William Faulkner? Just look at what this town did to him!*

American Dream Machine was thriving. The company lumbered on under the supervision of Teddy and Milt and its young Turks, a group of ex-assistants who'd risen through the ranks while Beau and Will had been almost too busy warring to notice. These kids took his phone calls now, cocksure and obnoxious in ways his colleagues would never have dreamed; they sold their clients with a passionless efficiency he found almost disconcerting. Whatever happened to building a friendship along with a career? Deep down, I suppose, Beau didn't care. It just wasn't the same. Then again, it didn't have to be. That was what made life, and this country, great: not only were there second acts in American lives, there were thirds, fourths, fifths.

"Get the fuck outta here!" Beau was on the phone. "No, no—" he snapped his fingers. "Hang on a second, Amy."

He snapped his fingers again, twice, a brisk signaling there in his posh office on the Sony lot, where he sat with his sneakered feet tucked up on his desk.

"What the fuck are you doing?"

A girl, twenty-three years old, moved around the coffee table at the room's far end. The place was a playpen, a long, rectangular cell strewn with toys, stacks of scripts, boxes of energy bars, and bottled water. With its vases full of Violina roses and its gray suede couch, its six-foot stuffed giraffe that lay toppled in a corner, it looked like a child's bedroom that had been hijacked by a decorator.

"Are you fucking deaf?"

The girl, whose name was Emily White, couldn't move. She'd worked here for three months, at Beau Rosenwald's Red Sled Productions, and never once had he spoken to or acknowledged her in any way. Until now.

"I was just looking for—"

"For what?" Beau sneered, when she couldn't finish the sentence. "A chance to get your ass reamed?"

For my coverage. She'd come in here looking for a script report she'd written, and now Emily White was in trouble. She scrambled in advance of Beau's tantrum, her body a blonde blur—white shirt, yellow hair, and the palest skin imaginable—as he whisked out from around his desk, grabbed a basketball that was on the floor, and hurled it at her.

"Get. The. Fuck. OUT!" Beau yowled. He stood in khakis, aviator shades, a baseball cap, an untucked shirt. "Getthefuckout!"

The ball bounced against the wall, slapping off a framed poster for a remake of *Bringing Up Baby*, which had earned this studio $97 million last year. Emily bolted for the door. She left behind the reader's report she'd been looking for as she ran out into the hall, hoping to make it to the bathroom before she blew it even worse.

Inside the stall, Emily burst into tears. Even as she'd left the office she could hear Beau Rosenwald—my God, the guy was every bit as big a dick as people said—switching gears into the wet sycophancy for which he was equally famous, murmuring into the phone, *Sorry, snookums, my intern.* "Snookums?" Jesus fucking Christ. Was the studio executive fooled, did she think Beau was a nice person? Or did she not care? When you made as much money as Beau had—last year, Columbia's domestic take topped two hundred million, and Beau's output accounted for more than half of that—she supposed it didn't matter.

She crouched in her yellow stall and sobbed, sobbed and sobbed.

She'd wanted to work for someone else. Two summers ago, while she was still at UC Irvine, she'd interned in the mailroom at ADM and had hoped to go to work for Sydney Pollack or Art Linson. Instead she'd gotten a call from someone at Red Sled. Dill Gibson was the smartest guy she'd known in school, one of her oldest and dearest friends. His father had written some ghastly road movie Beau had produced in the seventies, one of those boring period pieces that would never rate a revival. Now he was Beau's assistant, calling to see if she'd be interested in working for him. *It's not ideal*, he'd admitted, speaking of the schlock the producer was churning out today, and of his chimp-starring basketball movie in particular. *Pete's not exactly the sort of movie we had in mind while we were taking Border Cinema and the Queer Idyll. But you could learn. Beau's a total pig, but still better than Joel Silver.* So she came in and met with Beau's VP, an anxious and unpleasant redhead named Darcy Klein, then was "introduced" to Beau, which consisted of being paraded into his office for fifteen seconds while he was on the phone, before she was hired on the spot. For no money, for nothing but the privilege of working for someone who at least made movies, whose company was not just another one of the dim satellites that cluttered every lot in town: actresses with vanity deals, some corporatocrat's nephew who had ambitions, the action star who probably never read the scripts of even the movies he was in.

Emily had to remind herself of this while she sat in the bathroom and cried. She had to remember that there were "producers" and there were Producers. Beau was among the latter, of whom there were few. After *Bringing Up Baby*, his third consecutive hit, the studio had offered Beau his deal, which was nonexclusive—first look—and included a generous discretionary fund. They gave him a lavish office in the Capra Building, where he now perched, rather pretentiously, behind an architect's drafting table. He had aspirations, apparently. It wasn't that he *wanted* to make *Balls and Strikes 2: Out of the Zone*, but there were responsibilities—Emily'd heard the spiel from the VP and knew it came down from the top—to the studio, to the audience, and to those people who loved family films. The company had real movies in development, Darcy explained: a contemporized version of *David Copperfield*, a biopic of Madame Curie, a radical reworking of *The Beast in the Jungle* that was supposed to be written by a hot young playwright from New York. Darcy hired Emily because Emily was smart, because she "got it" and had taste, and Emily decided not to mind the VP's cuntiness because she, too, had taste and was smart. Emily wouldn't want to be that way, herself, a shrill bully who abused her creative executive for being five minutes late in bringing her an energy bar, but she admired Darcy for being successful in what was still, no matter who ran the studio, a boys' club and a men's game.

Would she have to become like Darcy? This is what Emily wondered, as she finished weeping in the bathroom behind the copier. Was that what it took? Did you have to be so feral, a mean little animal in a Prada suit? She came out of the stall and ran cold water, splashed her face and stared herself back to normalcy. You could succeed in this business and be nice, couldn't you? By the time she emerged back into the drudgery of her day—she could hear Beau thundering to his assistant, *Get me my son on the telephone . . . NOW!* —Emily was calm as she ever was, running over to the commissary to get people's coffees, photocopying, photocopying, photocopying. The incident was already forgotten.

"Emily!" That night her phone rang. She picked up on a man's voice she didn't recognize. It was gruff and raspy, panting almost like a dog's.

"Yes?" She hated answering the phone at home. All day long she had to answer with the company's name (and who did this guy think he was? Rosers/Rosebud/Red Sled . . . the allusion was obvious, but Beau Rosenwald was no Orson Welles), so she struggled not to do the same on her own time.

"Beau."

"Who?"

"Your employer."

"Oh!" She sat up. What in God's name was he calling her at home for? She was there in that miserable apartment she had in Beachwood Canyon, with its dust bunnies and warped cherry floors. She lived in the same twenty-three-year-old's deep Hollywood squalor my friends and I did, then. She went to the same clubs, same parties. The walls were the color of weak tea, grimy with human contact.

"I'm calling to apologize. I did something bad today."

"You did?"

"I threw a basketball at you. You were there."

"Um, yeah."

"I'm not so far beyond the pale I think that's acceptable. I'm really sorry."

"OK."

"Did you write this coverage of *Mr. Bones*?"

"I did."

"It's excellent. That's why I'm calling, really. You're a great reader."

She sat on her couch, watching her starved gray cat, Henry—she couldn't afford to feed him either—arch his back on the sill; the dingy lintels and listing floors covered with unpaid parking tickets and note-scarred scripts and empty video boxes. *Thanks*, she was about to say.

"Have breakfast with me," he blurted.

Was he hitting on her? Probably. She was pretty enough, or almost pretty enough. She had a kind of puffy, blonde, innocent sweetness, more like that of an actress from the thirties than the stringy collagen birds of today.

"Tomorrow, at the Peninsula," he added. "Meet me there at seven thirty."

"I—"

She couldn't say no, partly because he'd started this off with an apology, but also because she wasn't sure if he was coming on to her. She winnowed a hand through her thick (dyed) blonde hair, a cornsilk yellow that was the only unnatural thing about her.

"Sure."

She was a little thick around the middle, big-chested but not "perky." She was more deliberate than the other women in his office, the vice president and the creative exec. She started to say something else, just to prove she wasn't afraid of him. Abruptly, however, he hung up. *Click.*

Emily sat for a minute in stunned silence. The thought made her flesh crawl: what if this big, hideous man was actually hitting on her? She'd been to his house once, the big Mediterranean place in

Santa Monica—she went to deliver a script when he wasn't home—
and so could picture him, alone in his kitchen, masturbating into
a cup. Why a cup? She had no idea, but this is what she pictured.
  She shivered. Then she laughed out loud.

VI

"WHERE ARE YOU FROM?"

The question took her by surprise. Any question would've taken her by surprise, she supposed because she'd never—it hit her in that moment—heard Beau ask one. *What the fuck are you doing in here?* didn't exactly count, and *Did you write this coverage?* wasn't a question so much as a request for confirmation.

"Hermosa Beach." She fumbled her way into her chair. She couldn't believe he was already there, waiting for her at 7:28 AM.

"And where'd you go to school?" He folded his *Wall Street Journal*, rested his well-kept hands on the edge of the table.

"Irvine. Film studies."

"Film studies?"

"I was an English minor," she admitted. "But yes."

"So you like books!" He cackled, like this was an important discovery.

Ah, Emily White. Would it have made a difference, I sometimes wonder, if she had fallen for me instead of for Sev? If I could've diverted her even a little? I have to wonder, given all she would eventually do for old Beau. But for Emily White, the surprise was how easy it was to sit and have breakfast with the man. Much easier than she'd supposed. The room was palmy and bright and welcoming, filled with that terror-kissed languor of LA hotels.

"So how did you end up here, at Red Sled?" He angled his wrist in a way that seemed to show off his watch. Was *he* nervous? My God!

"Dill brought me in."

"Dill?" Beau laughed. "My assistant?"

"I've known him forever," she said. "He's really smart."

"Smart enough to know when someone else is."

Emily blushed. Something about him encouraged candor. He was nervous, she realized, but not hitting on her at all. "I just wanted an internship with an active producer."

"No matter if he makes shitty movies." Beau smiled, knowing exactly what she meant. "Don't worry, I won't tell. You can say what you want about my lousy comedies and I'll pretend I never heard."

"I . . . "

She liked him! Inconceivable. Of all possible eventualities, this was the one for which she was least prepared. The man had such a reputation! They ordered milk-steamed oatmeal, and his manners were impeccable. The bananas fanned out across the top, the blood-bright strawberries too. He removed these things delicately with his jagged-tipped spoon.

"*Mr. Bones* isn't really my sort of thing. It's Darcy's."

"Right."

"But you're able to explain it to me better than Darcy can. You're brighter than she is."

"No." She was bright enough not to fall into that trap, certainly. "Darcy has incredible taste. I learn from her."

"It's good to do that," he said. Impressed by this also, the way her ambition was tempered by common sense. "Learn from your bosses, learn from your colleagues. I always did."

He smiled. Incredible how his former antagonists and foils, Williams or Sam, could suddenly be filed under the rubric of wisdom. Beau was almost sixty, now. After plastic surgery, his face had the sun beaten plainness of a middle-aged actor's, red and reticulated and swollen. His beard was down to a light scruff and his hair was the dull metallic color of unpolished steel.

"What was it like in Hermosa Beach?" He stirred NutraSweet into his coffee. "I've lived here thirty years and have never been."

"It's incredibly boring." She could see him seeing her too. Emily White. Pale, five eight, with wavy hair that fell to her shoulders, coral lips, and green eyes. She had a mole above her lip just like Cindy Crawford's, but somehow, it didn't quite add up to all-out combustible beauty. *Too sweet.* "I hated it, growing up."

"So you fled all the way to Irvine. The mean streets of the big city."

She laughed. How could she not? She thought of a proverb she'd heard growing up: *El hombre es como un oso, el mas feo, el mas hermoso.* A man is like a bear, the more ugly, the more beautiful.

"How do you afford all this?" he asked. It was eight thirty, and he showed no hurry to get back to bossing her around. The check was here ten minutes ago. "What do your parents do?"

"I don't afford any of it," she said. "Am I buying *you* breakfast?"

"Of course not." He dragged the check over now. "No way."

"Well, then. My mother was a schoolteacher. Dead, now. My father worked for Lockheed Martin, but he's in a wheelchair. He was in a car accident a few years ago, so he's on SSI."

"Oh." He rubbed his hands together. "My mother died young too. My dad had a shoe shop. In Queens."

From outside came the sound of people splashing in a swimming pool. Sugar sparkled on the tabletop, like diamond dust; at such an hour, the room's green and plant-scattered stillness seemed a form of perversion.

"Do you want a job?" Beau said, as the waiter came over and whisked the check from his hand. Emily White, I think, reminded him of what it was to be genuine. "A real one?"

VII

WHAT WAS THE bee in Beau's bonnet? When had the man become such a pain? Those little fits like the one he had back when Emily first came into his office were typical these days, and if he could still turn around and act like a pussycat . . . he really *had* become an ass. What had changed? Was it that he no longer had a partner who cooled him out, offered a more rational model of human behavior? Did he need another psychiatrist?

In 1991, he'd gotten married and was now divorcing again—blink and you missed her, that third Mrs. Ro—and lately his kids had gotten into some sort of a jam with Little Will. Oh sure, he knew all about it, the overdose and the memory loss and the whole foolish shebang. Heroin? Who did that shit? Only *schvartzes* and gangsters did when he was younger, hardcore Italians and weirdo beatniks. He'd met one of those once, in New York. Herbert Huncke. Now he was so shaken he visited Little Will in the hospital. Can you believe it? Digging deep to look after his old vanquisher's son, who seemed to be just as tough as his dad: there'd been some scare about his memory, but evidently the kid was progressing just fine. It really upset Beau, though, and the first thing he did upon finding out what had happened was drag Severin by the ear and throw him into rehab. Me he wasn't worried about—I told him I was clean and he believed me—but Sev? He hustled my brother out to Malibu for one of those thirty-thousand-dollar drug-free "vacations." *I don't want to hear about it, Severin. You're my son, and smack isn't marijuana.*

The funny thing was, it wasn't necessary. All by himself Sev kicked everything except pot and began working like a maniac to revise his second novel. Even as I kept struggling, he began taking meetings around town on his own. And you want to know what I think? I think this pissed Beau off: the fact that his son was writing, and in fact, writing well. Isn't that nuts? His son was talented, and this bugged the shit out of him.

He'd never admit it, but I know it bothered him. Even when he was finalizing his divorce that summer—the third Mrs. Ro was his dog walker, a twenty-four-year-old UCLA grad who vacillated between wanting to become a hygienist and wanting to run an animal shelter; she talked about these two things alone, so incessantly he finally had no choice but to divorce her—even that didn't wig Beau out as much as this did.

"God." He was talking to himself, now. "Why would anyone do such a thing?"

"What? " Emily was on the couch in his office. "Do what?"

"Write."

They'd just wrapped up a meeting. Six months had passed since that breakfast at the Peninsula, and Emily was now his creative executive. She and Severin had been dating for a little while, and though Beau wasn't aware of their involvement, this he would've been proud of if he'd known. Severin showing good judgment for once.

"Would it be so bad?" Emily laughed. She bent and picked up the notes she'd taken on a yellow pad, during the pitch that had just ended. "We meet with writers all day."

"Exactly." Beau nodded at the door, toward the kid they'd just dismissed. "That poor schmuck is going to do this nine times in the next forty-eight hours. And it's just gonna leave him with a lot of hard work festering in a drawer."

"OK," Emily said. Perhaps unconsciously, she took Severin's side. "But he can come up with another idea after this. He controls the future. We just sit here and wait for people to bring us the gold."

"Or the shit." Beau yawned. The girl had a lot to learn. "Not that there's necessarily a difference."

Ten thirty AM. The meeting had ended on the dot. The coffees weren't cold, the phone had interrupted them three times. Emily was the one who could handle the writers. That was why my father trusted her. She might've been full of airy-fairy ideas, but this was why he liked her. There was an openness to her, a seeming simplicity and sweetness he'd all but forgotten was possible. She smelled of distant Malibu afternoons. Is it too much to suggest she might've reminded him of someone from long, long ago?

"How come you never bring Dill into these meetings?" Emily said. "He's great at story."

Someone closer to him than anyone, maybe. More beloved than anyone had ever been.

"He's too much like his pops. His father was the most undisciplined writer I've ever met. He was so busy being a genius, he never buckled down to work. Dill doesn't ask the right questions. Someone comes in here and wants to remake *Vivre sa Vie*, he doesn't say, Who's going to *see* that fucking movie, since nobody saw it the first time? He says, *Ooh*, Shoot the Piano Player, *fucking Bresson*. He doesn't understand the—"

"We should remake that."

Emily White looked the same just then as she had in the beginning. She was perhaps a little better dressed. Gray pinstripe jacket, sunglasses propped up on her head, bottled water tucked under her arm. She'd figured out a few things, and Darcy was on vacation, so she was in Beau's office alone.

"We should remake—" Beau hiccupped. Muffin crumbs dusted his beard. "We should remake *Shoot the Piano Player*?"

"Not the Truffaut movie, we can't improve upon that." How cool Emily was, how level. She was fantastic in a room, writers loved her precisely because she wasn't just a naked cauldron of seething ambition. It was her innocence everyone loved, along with her intelligence. "But the David Goodis novel it's based on. *Down There*."

She sat on the couch now, under that idiotic poster for his Michael Keaton movie Beau was suddenly tempted to take down. A Louisville slugger, a pair of baseballs. Its tastelessness indicted him.

"Where did you come up with that?" Beau asked.

She shrugged again. So blithe. Beau wondered at times whether she actually loved movies, whether she wasn't also a creature of simple expediency. She was nothing like the young hustlers he'd come up with once. She was more about math than passion.

"I read it recently. It's good."

"*Down There*." Beau snorted. "OK. I'll check it out."

"You will?"

My father stood, windmilled his arms. He probably hadn't finished a book in twenty years. Scripts, sure, but that wasn't reading. Now this girl was actually giving him something to do. She smiled up at him from the couch. Perhaps it wasn't innocence she had, exactly, but she was clean and tender. She lacked the Hollywood taint.

"Sure." Beau nodded. "I'll read it over the weekend, and we'll talk."

"Goddamn it, Severin!" Late at night, Emily pounded on the door of my brother's apartment. "Let me *in*!"

Was Severin ever her boyfriend? I suppose it's a matter of opinion, since he was never that attached to her. But he viewed her with a certain clarity his father never managed. It was January '94, and they'd been dating off and on for some months.

"Let me in, *please*."

She was drunk. It was 1:00 AM, and she'd done half a hit of Ecstasy earlier that night, at Jabberjaw. Even when she was out of control, she was surprisingly calm. Her modest upsets had a quality of subtle performance. In the sickly yellow light of his hallway, the old Spanish-style complex that might someday have a plaque to tell the world who'd lived in it, she beat the door gently with her palms.

"Sev—"

My brother opened the door, finally. "What is it, Em?"

"Why don't you return my calls?"

Severin snorted. Ever since rehab, he'd become the littlest bit of a prick, himself. He'd grown colder, more remote. "You work in the movie business. You must be used to unreturned calls by now."

"I just came to get my clothes."

He waved her in. She stepped into his crappy, dingy studio. It smelled of burnt noodles, and Emily could feel the clammy residue of the door's old paint on her palms. *Nashville* flickered on a small TV in the corner with the sound low, and a heavy Selectric typewriter, the same one Severin had owned since college, sat on the dining room table with a glass of water beside it.

"Why are you blowing me off?"

It wasn't her: he was blowing everybody off. Me included. I bare-ly saw him in those days. I was living a little deeper in Hollywood anyway, at Franklin and Kenmore. Little Will had left town for a while, gone to New York to visit his college girlfriend. She'd come out to nurse him while he was undergoing cognitive therapy.

"I don't know, Em. I've been busy."

Busy writing, busy brooding, busy beating up on himself. Who knew what he'd been doing, really, on his own time? I didn't. She went into the bedroom and retrieved a shirt, a pair of pants, a sweater. The things she'd left there, in that brief window they'd been together. She came back out holding them clumsily over her arm, while Severin stood and waited by the plaid couch where he and I and Williams had launched our share of nights with a bong hit, shoving off into our shiftless carousing. Not now. He was in seclusion. A plate of takeout from Zankou Chicken sat cold on the coffee table, along with a dish of pinkish, pickled Armenian beets.

"How's my dad?"

She shook her head. Emily didn't want to talk about Beau, whom she loved, with his asshole son. They faced each other.

"You want to know why, Em?"

She nodded. My brother's sudden bluntness, his decision to tell her the truth meant she didn't want to know, maybe. She stood there, pale under the bare ceiling bulb above. Severin was taller, leaner. His hair glistened, Valentino black.

"You're too much like him," he said.

Emily laughed out loud.

"You don't see it," he said. "You're like the business. You *are* the business. Not the way it used to be, but the way it is now."

She gave him a weird green stare. Her eyes were cloudy in the room's feeble light.

"What does that even mean, Sev? Are you calling me ambitious?"

Severin just shrugged. Emily told me once that she worried about him, that the stresses of being Beau's legitimate son and surviving heir must've really worn on him. I see that now. At the time it seemed like he was being a dick, but he just saw what the rest of us weren't ready to. In the corner, the letterboxed *Nashville* flickered on—you could just hear Haven Hamilton singing his stately, waltz-time ballad about how America was doing something right, to last two hundred years.

"What am I like?" Emily said, sarcastically now. Traffic hissed, serpentine, along Franklin. "Why don't you tell me?"

My brother took off his glasses and rubbed them on his shirt. He gazed vaguely into the air above her. She could hear the hum of his typewriter. Outside his window, the moon rose above Italian cypresses, illuminating the grayish, humid sky.

"You're someone who doesn't have a clue what she's like."

VIII

WHAT DID SEVERIN KNOW? That's what Emily White thought, and in this she was perfectly on point. What the fuck did Severin Roth know, this kid who was brought up by—let's face it—a man with issues. She loved Beau, but his quirks were obvious. And so were his son's.

Ambitious, Severin had called her. Careerist was what he'd meant, but really, was that so damning? I would've given everything I had to be so practical, to make a simple business decision instead of drifting and waiting for the "inspiration" it seemed to take for me just to bend down and tie my shoes. Beau loved *Down There*, loved it, and in fact when she finally told him where she first came across it (*You know who gave me that book? Your son! I met him one night at the Kibitz Room and we started talking*), the producer didn't seem surprised. *You've met Severin? Small world.* Well it was, and it was a smaller town. The studio loved *Down There* too. So did Ethan Hawke. And Emily began to gain a reputation around town for being bright, being approachable, being funny. For knowing what to say, at just the right moment.

"What if he doesn't die?"

"Excuse me?"

For example, when she leaned forward in a meeting with Richard LaGravenese—it was not long after Darcy had left the company—and proposed something for that difficult script, *Mr. Bones*.

"What if he doesn't die," she said calmly, while LaGravenese stroked his goatee, fiddled with his glasses. "What if it's like a *Harold and Maude* thing, where he keeps trying to off himself and it never takes?"

Just like that, she fixed it, a movie that had been on my father's slate for three years. It was Darcy's pet project originally, loosely based on a real person—Beau could never remember his name, some poet who'd leapt off a bridge in Minnesota—but with a casual flash of inspiration, Emily solved it. It was thanks to her he could even be in business with someone like LaGravenese, a writer's writer whose credits included *The Fisher King*. Emily's brain allowed the producer newfound respectability.

"You're too much!" he roared after the meeting, after Richard had left and she'd managed to reframe this ponderous arty biopic as an absurdist comedy. Which choice would be the difference between a line on a memo and eighty million bucks. "Where do you come up with these things?"

"I learn from the best."

"No you don't," Beau said. "You're much smarter than I am."

No disingenuousness, here. He meant it, and so did she.

"Not smarter." She sucked in her cheeks a moment, face flexing hollow. "I've just read a few books."

He promoted her. *Down There* was a modest hit. *Mr. Bones* was a big one. Beau gave her an associate producer credit on the latter, and while it wasn't entirely her doing—Jack Lemmon and Sandra Bullock were both fantastic—he chalked the picture's success up to her. ("Deep down, you don't belong here," he told her. "You're too good for this business." *Deep down*. It was a phrase that resonated with her, with its intimations of depth, plenitude: such things as this city was always said to lack.)

"Come with me," he said one afternoon. "I want to show you something."

In May of 1995, they were celebrating the triumph of *Mr. Bones*. The studio had just re-upped his deal for two years, and Beau was beaming ear to ear as he materialized in the door of her office, jangling his keys in his hand.

"I have a lunch with Costigan," she said, referring to their executive at the studio.

"Cancel it." He shook his head. "This is more important."

What could be more important? By now Emily had Darcy's old office, like Beau's but smaller and with fewer toys. It had the same slate-colored carpets and mint green walls; there were piles of scripts everywhere, stacks of promo CDs atop expensive Sony components. Everything except evidence of a private life.

"Where are we going?" She followed him down the hall.

"You'll see." Beau was radiantly tan, just back from the Hôtel du Cap. "It's a surprise."

I don't think I recall my father ever being as happy as he was then. He wore success lightly, now. He treated Severin and me both with a sweetness. I credit Emily for that.

"Beau." She smiled as they stepped out into sunlight, that corridor of gorgeously mocked-up businesses—a "florist," a "bowling alley"—that made up the lot's main artery. A fountain shot towers of spray into the air. It looked like an outdoor mall. "What *are* you up to?"

"You'll see."

Jolly old Beau. She followed him out to the parking lot, past all these radiant fakes that created a backdrop for daily terror. She didn't mind. She actually *liked* the fear that dominated the lot. This place reminded her of home, for it shared with Hermosa a towny unreality, only the aggression, the venom that drove the people marked it apart.

"I told you to take time off," he said.

"I can't. I'm too afraid you'll make another animal movie if I turn my back."

"One more animal movie won't kill anybody."

They laughed. The fountain shot its diamond droplets into the air behind them, and she could feel them on the breeze, cooling her skin. By now she reported only to Beau, had inherited Darcy's old job. Beau sometimes maintained a fiction that he was going to bring in somebody more senior than Emily, but they both knew it was a lie.

"You should do something besides read and see movies," Beau said, as they ducked into his black Lamborghini. A midlife crisis car. Or whatever it was—too late for midlife, yet too soon for anything else—when you were making money hand over fist and just couldn't spend it fast enough. "You can't only work."

"You should talk."

They drove off the lot. Wind fluttered through the windows. "Don't you have a boyfriend?"

Emily shook her head. It had been a long time now since Severin. She didn't miss him, she didn't even really think about him anymore, not even as his second novel appeared in the world and garnered some small notice, or when the first one, *Kangaroo Music*, was optioned by Gus Van Sant. She'd dated people—writers, directors, agents—since then, but nothing really stuck.

"Don't you have a girlfriend?" she shot back.

Nothing stuck. Emily's conscience, her reputation, her spirit—to what extent she credited the existence of such a thing—were clean.

"I had dinner last night with Sharon Stone," Beau said, while they idled at a light.

"Did you? What was that like?"

Emily shifted on the hot leather, accepted a stick of cinnamon gum. Severin's words might've traced their distant echo. *Someone who doesn't know what she's like.*

"Her teeth are incredible," Beau sighed. "Though I suppose you really are in trouble when that's the first thing you notice."

Say what you will about Beau Rosenwald, he always did retain a little perspective, too. A date was a date, whether with Sharon Stone or some Jewish acupuncturist from the Valley. His friends were always trying to set him up, the ones who'd been married forever: Jon and Barbara Avnet, Joe and Donna Roth. It never took for him either. Maybe he and Emily *were* alike, or maybe it was just the tiresome courtliness, the ritualization that made dating in later life so boring. First call, first meal, first screening, first fuck. Usually, it was the last fuck too. What did you call this sort of thing? Rearranged marriage? *De*ranged marriage?

"Whatcha thinking?"

Beau shook his head. Emily could ask him these things even when he couldn't answer. Sharon Stone was pretty good, for a fat kid from Queens, but he couldn't live off that. He needed more reality. He hung a left on La Cienega, roared beneath the freeway overpass.

"Wanna hear a joke?" he said. "What are the five stages of an actor's career?"

They pulled up, shortly, in front of a one-story brick building with an iron grate pulled over its face.

"We're not going to lunch?"

There was nothing here, just empty lots and warehouses, yards charted with razor wire. There were auto detailers and rug steamers,

signs in Chinese and Korean. Across the street was a derelict gas
station, its signs still marked at $1.06 for unleaded.

"Nope." My father took off his *Mr. Bones* baseball cap and mopped
his face. For a second, he looked sad: this sixty-two-year-old man
with ruddy, craggy, sunburned skin, in khakis, untucked white shirt,
and unlaced Nikes, his car stereo blasting hip-hop. "Not today."

He shut the engine off. "Come on."

Under his breath he hummed the Eric B. & Rakim song that had just
been playing on the radio, or at least he hummed the one it sampled.
Yersosmoothandtheworldssorough. She'd asked him once if he really
liked this stuff, the Fu-Schnickens and A Tribe Called Quest tapes that
were left in his car courtesy of Severin. *People like it,* he'd said. *And I'm
people.* She followed him now to a door, where he pressed a buzzer.
The entrance was so discreet you almost didn't see it: it was just a
handle-less iron square in the middle of the graffiti-scabbed brick.

"Beau!" A man opened it finally, just as Emily spotted a tiny security camera peering down from the edge of the roof. "Who's this?"

"This is Emily." Beau ushered her toward the man, who was Afri-
can American, very dark, and effortlessly good-looking.

"Emily!" He wore expensive buttercream-colored clothes, the
uniform of a country gentleman. He turned an athletic, electrified
smile upon her. "I'm Lance."

He was six foot six, all muscle, bald, his clean-shaven face split
by the wattage of his teeth. *So* handsome. The room beyond was a
showroom, a waxen gallery of automobiles. There were only three
cars, spread like felines around a room much bigger than the building's exterior suggested. The ceilings were twenty feet, the floors a
worn, matte rubber.

"So, Beau, is this a girlfriend?"

"She works for me."

"Oh you *work* for him." He grinned as they slid past him, inside.
"Nice."

What was this place? It wasn't a dealership, there was nobody
here. The room was frigid, artificially cool. And even before Emily
examined the cars, she knew they weren't for sale. These were animals kept in captivity. They were too rare for the street.

"What exactly do you do for my man, Emily?"

"I'm his—"

She was about to say "vice president" but faltered over the pretend grandeur of the term, here where real money—real power, of a sort—presided. The room was like a wine cellar or a humidor: both light and climate were held at a perfect pitch.

"Conscience," my father broke in. "She's the brains of my operation."

"Conscience? Brains?" Lance laughed. "I didn't know you had those things, Beau."

Emily's shadow glossed the bonnet of a DeLorean as she crossed the room to approach a low, long-hooded car the same color as Lance's clothes, a yellow that was as close to white as possible, like a lightbulb's candescence made solid.

"Like that?" Lance boomed. "It's one of the first five hundred."

She bent to examine the car's particulars. A 1961 E-Type Jag. It looked as if it had never been driven; in fact, as if it *could* never be.

"Still has the flat floor and the bonnet latches." Lance came over and stood behind her. Her nipples stiffened. It was so cold.

"Can I sit in it?"

"Sure."

She didn't care about cars, drove the same black 3 Series Beamer half the town did, linty interior strewn with water bottles and script-fasteners, dropped In-n-Out Burger fries staling under the seats. But the cold-cream smell of this one, the feel of its leather as she slid inside it: these things were hardly resistible.

"Right?" Lance said. He saw it on her face. "It's cherry."

"How can its odometer read *zero*?" She tested the gas pedal hesitantly with her heel. It was stiff.

"Guy who sent it to us owned the factory, in England. It's never been driven."

Mysteries proliferated: What did Lance do, exactly? These were prop cars. Besides the silver DeLorean, the third was something Emily didn't recognize, like a European Mustang crossed with a tank.

"Pretty nice, huh?"

"I don't even like cars."

"These aren't cars. They're dreams."

Emily stepped out of the car at last. Goose bumps lifted along her arms and shoulders.

"So why are we here, Beau?" Still, she couldn't keep the teasing out of her voice. "What exactly did you have to show me?"

Beau held his hands behind his back, like a visitor at a museum. This *was* a museum of sorts. Emily couldn't imagine what the sticker was on the car she'd just sat in. A million dollars? Zero?

"Pick one of these cars."

"What?"

"You heard." He drew his hands out front again; he was holding, it turned out, a checkbook. "Pick one."

Poor Beau! How lonely he seemed, too. You get to that place where people are setting you up with Sharon Stone, you're less a man than an institution, with barely a claim to a private life of your own.

"You like the Jag, take the Jag."

A radio in the next room, Lance's office, played an oldies station. You could just hear it over the hum of the room's climate-control system, the great poet's eternal question: *How did it feel?*

The curator broke in. "Brother, these aren't for sale, you know that."

"Nothing isn't for sale," Beau snapped. "Nothing on this earth."

Such a weird mulch of emotions clouded his face at that moment. Emily couldn't see his eyes behind his sunglasses, but his lips were pursed and his skin was so red. He seemed enraged.

"Beau." All her life, Emily had been the voice of reason—of something, at any rate, that wasn't unchecked passion. She wasn't about to stop now. "I can't do this."

"Why not?"

"Because if I helped you make a movie that's not about chimpanzees, you can thank me in some other way. You can buy me a rare book. You can give me a raise."

They stared each other down, in the showroom. Beyond the radio, Emily was aware of that secondary hum, a mechanical drone like a refrigerator's.

"Beau." Emily exhaled. "This is embarrassing."

"This isn't embarrassing," he said. "Embarrassment is pitching zoo movies to kids half your age. You saved me from embarrassment, which I didn't even know I was feeling."

He took a step toward her. Beau was utterly sincere. But this whole I-am-just-a-humble-schmuck-with-no-taste-but-yours thing was, also, an act. She could feel it.

"Pick one." He expanded his arms. Beamed at her. "Whichever you'd like."

It was for just this that she loved him. For being so authentic in his theatricality and vice versa. It taught her something about life she might never master, herself, and it absolved her of the responsibility to say no.

"All right." Finally, she spoke, breathing in that heady Freon and carnauba smell. "All right, I will."

IX

"HE BOUGHT YOU a fucking DeLorean?"

"He did."

Emily stood at the base of a woman's desk, in another office on the same lot. She was five hundred feet and an entire world away from her employer. It was two years later.

"That story's true?" The woman's name was Lucinda Vogel, and she threw her head back and laughed. "My God, who the fuck does he think he is? Christopher Lloyd? What an asshole." She drummed her black-tipped fingernails against the desk's gleaming glass surface. "What did you do with it?"

"It's in a garage." Emily had told this story so many times—though never to an executive VP at the studio, the person who now oversaw Beau's deal—she was tired of it, right down to the bitter end. "Not like I could drive it."

"Why not?" Lucinda snorted. "It might take you right back to the eighties, when Beau Rosenfuck was relevant."

Poor Emily. There were so many things she couldn't possibly explain, not least how her boss had slipped just a little from favor, how he was no longer quite the studio's golden goose.

"How is it you've put up with him for so long?" Lucinda said. She was whippet-thin, dark-haired and narrow-eyed and lesbian and expensive. "The guy's so cheesy he probably sends fruit baskets to everybody for Christmas."

This room was cold too, and empty. In the upper reaches of the Thalberg Building, there were no toys or tchotchkes as in Beau's office. No mini-fridge holding three kinds of popsicle. This was pure abstraction. Decisions got made *here*.

"He's not that bad," Emily protested.

"He isn't? He bought you a DeLorean, which is kind of the same as buying you an eight ball and demanding that you blow him. You should sue."

"It was supposed to be a Jaguar."

"What?"

This was the part of the story Emily usually didn't tell, because she couldn't explain it even to herself. Maybe it was her way of protecting him, how she'd turned this lavish gesture into a joke by choosing a car that *no one* could drive. It cost her money to garage it.

"There was a beautiful old E-Type," Emily said. "He offered that to me first."

Like choosing a costume stone over a Tiffany diamond. Lucinda burst out laughing. Beau thought it was funny too. But Lucinda, whose ugliness was more than skin-deep, corrected herself into a sneer. "That's disgusting. I heard he once took a shit on some guy's floor."

"Not true."

"Why are you defending him?"

This was the face of the studio today: it was freckled and efficient and sharp. Lucinda had invited her to lunch, but thus far all Emily had done was drink water in the senior woman's office. Other than a narrow gold watch there wasn't an ounce of decoration on the executive, who was the scourge of Beau Rosenwald's life.

"He's been good to me."

"Good to you, hell," Lucinda said. She was Beau's own personal roadblock, seemingly devoted to stalling all his projects. The studio was having a spectacular year, with one-and-a-quarter billion domestic, three of the four top-grossing summer movies. Not one of these happened to be Beau's, "You're too special to be sweeping up his cage."

Nineteen-ninety-seven was a year without a movie for the fat man at all, in fact. Ninety-six hadn't been so hot either. While his children were rising (and we were—it wasn't just Severin who was carving out a path for himself; in 1995 I'd written a script based on Chandler's *The Lady in the Lake* that got optioned), Beau was struggling to find his place. Emily's mission, in part, was to ensure he did. She hoped to bring Lucinda around to understanding he was a good guy. She hadn't told Beau she was having lunch with his enemy, and had some trepidation that he might freak out or feel betrayed. She'd felt some fear about the meeting herself, since Lucinda's reputation was even worse than Beau's had ever been, but the moment she walked into the senior executive's office she found herself at home. It was, strangely, as if she were dreaming: she had this feeling of déjà vu, like she had been here, like everything that happened the moment she set foot in Thalberg had already occurred, long ago. Like it was written. She and Lucinda walked over to the commissary. The day's blazing heat restored her, somewhat. It made the world seem real again.

"You're shaking!" Lucinda's fork never went near her chicken salad.

"What? No." Goddamn it, Emily was. "I'm not—"

"You are." Lucinda leaned forward and touched Emily's shoulder. A dry touch, nonsexual. "Are you afraid of me?"

Yes. No. It was hot in here too, but the goose bumps on Em's shoulder gave her away. "Yes."

"Don't be. I'm only mean to people I dislike."

This wasn't true. Lucinda was brutal to everyone, screaming and snarling when she didn't get her way. Her meanness wasn't like Beau's—situational, and prone to vanish as soon as you got to know him—but indiscriminate. Executives, valet parkers, assistants all suffered equally. Everyone had a Lucinda story.

"Oh, I have a reputation." The one about her telling a young ADM agent that his client, a writer, would have to *pry her fee from my dripping cunt flaps*? True. "But you really have to be on my bad side to see it."

Beau Rosenwald was on her bad side. Beau Rosenwald *was* her bad side, all that swinging dick stuff Lucinda loathed, "honey" this and "baby" that. What a fucking dinosaur.

"I'm here to rescue you," Lucinda continued, so gently Emily could almost believe it. Once more she had that feeling she was dreaming. "I want you to bring me things."

"I do."

"No. Don't go through Beau." A thin, dry, tight smile. With her glittering dark eyes and faint freckles, she looked like an unhappy doll. "Just you. I want your passion."

Emily smiled back. She'd lived this long in the business to know a trap when she saw one. She wasn't going to sell her boss quite so easily.

"Sure thing."

Was Beau right? Did Emily simply lack passion? She walked back to the office after lunch, feeling happy, loyal, poised. She could do great things if she kept her wits about her. Sweeping her teeth with her tongue to dislodge a fragment of mandarin orange, she watched Lucinda vanish down the avenue toward the Thalberg Building. Sunstruck grass and the translucent pink cups of Iceland poppies waved in the breeze. *Poppies.* As if Lucinda were some sort of wicked witch, who could be neutralized with something as mild as mineral water. *I'm mellltinng!* Beau Rosenwald had nothing to be afraid of.

"I think it's a terrific relationship," Beau said.

"Do you? You're not mad?"

He looked up. He studied his apt little pupil in the doorway, where she stood. "I'm not mad."

So much was in motion around this time. Severin had published his third book, *Cruising the Flat Surface*—this was an enigmatic science fiction story about a shy janitor who builds a supercollider in his basement—and was just getting into his fourth, the one that would really make his career. I'd moved to New York, where I'd taken a development job myself. I'd finally gotten tired of waiting for my Chandler script to go while I envied my brother's industriousness. I went to work for a rival studio, 20th Century Fox, where I climbed through the ranks fairly quickly, discovering an economy in myself I'd never previously dreamed existed. Emily White had nothing on me. Little Will got married to his college girlfriend, then went to work as a fact-checker at *Vanity Fair*. Funny job for someone whose neuroplasticity had been endangered. Will still had his lapses, moments where recent experience would abandon him, but for the most part, he seemed no more forgetful than he'd always been. Severin, too, moved to Brooklyn. Where else was a young novelist supposed to be? Within the next couple of years, all three of us would be married, and all living in one of the five boroughs. It was a lot of change for Beau Rosenwald to process. Emily might have been all he had left. But to even his own surprise, he didn't mind her dining with Lucinda at all.

"It'll be good for us," he grunted, rooting with his spoon at the bottom of his yogurt cup. "It'll help us push things through."

"You think? Lucinda really hates you."

"I know!" He chuckled, set the spoon down. "Now that I'm not married, it's almost fun having a woman hate me that much."

"I think she's sniffing me out for a job."

Beau shrugged. He was almost sixty-five now. Once upon a time, that was considered "retirement age." Shall I tell you he'd mellowed? It isn't true.

"Let her sniff. It's her own shit that stinks."

"What are you doing?" Emily spotted something—was that a protractor?—next to the cup on his desk.

Beau looked to be sketching something, in this four o' clock lull. He covered a sheet of paper with his hand, this man who sometimes didn't even bother to close the door to his private bathroom when he took a leak in mixed company.

"Nothing." He flipped the paper over. "Glad you had a good lunch."

What *was* he doing? She leaned over the desk, squinting at the paper that, whatever else, seemed to have nothing to do with the movie business.

"Beau . . . Are you happy?"

"What the hell kind of question is that?"

"An honest one." Emily wasn't rattled anymore by his snapping fits, or by anything he said. "I was just wondering."

He shook his head, made a sound that was like a dog sneezing. *Tchhh!* He looked more than ever like a dog, now, having contracted a conjunctivitis that bothered his left eye. He led with the other when he stared at you, which made his face seem deep, interrogative, screwy.

"Go wonder somewhere else."

Was he happy? He was alone. And I think he was in a kind of pain that was difficult to imagine, with his kids gone, his former partners dead now or retiring. Rollie Mardigian flew planes in the south of France. He had a vineyard. When Beau thought of Will, and he did, often, it was to wonder what his long-ago friend would've made of the business as it was today, or of the slick tomb that now housed the company they'd built. ADM's Frank Gehry offices were half a block down from what once was Jimmy's, where he and his partner used to have lunch all the time. Together. That's what he always came back to: they'd built it together, and no matter how Will fucked him later, he never forgot. Never. The business seemed to rest now on forgetting. You were no longer as good as your last hit. You were only as good as your next one. What had happened to an industry that used to rely upon memory, that was founded, however tenuously, on some feeling for the elegance, the inextinguishable glamour, of the past?

It wasn't so very long before something else happened to remind him.

"Oh!" Beau set down his newspaper. He was at home eating breakfast on a Wednesday morning, digging calmly into his grapefruit when he saw. "Jesus."

He bowed his head as if in prayer. He pressed his elbows so hard against his wooden breakfast table that they hurt. Amazing the way some deaths really affected him and others didn't, so that a close friend could die—Jeremy Vana or Ned Bondie from the old office, or even his first wife, whom he presumed was dead after all these years—and it might seem to mean very little, where other times it came roaring at him with the force of a tornado.

"Christ."

He rubbed his forehead with his fingernails. Closed his eyes against the room's oppressively white surfaces. The quartered section of the *LA Times* told the story. It wasn't front-page news, but it was in the Calendar section, below the fold. *Former Talent Agent Dies after Long Illness. Represented Marlon Brando* . . .

Sam Smiligan. He hadn't even known Sam was sick, although . . . *complications from pneumonia* . . . Figured. Yes. *No children. Survived by his partner* . . .

All these years, Beau had rarely thought of his old enemy. It was hard to hate a man who'd quietly exited the business, or else just been whelmed by its tides. Sam was a dinosaur in '72, so imagine what it must've been like by the time it was all CGI, robot cops melting in and out of walls. You never heard about him anymore. Occasionally you skimmed a program at the Geffen Playhouse, looked at the board of directors for a Holocaust museum: he was there. But Beau hadn't seen Sam in fifteen years. Once, maybe. Sitting in a lilac pullover, eating dinner with Liza Minnelli at the Polo Lounge, hand quivering a little as he lifted his fork. He'd nodded to Beau, without warmth or hostility. Perhaps he no longer even remembered.

So why was Beau Rosenwald sobbing now?

"Gah—"

He picked up his plate and flung it, stupidly, across the room. His half ruby grapefruit landed facedown on the floor. The plate shattered at the foot of the sink. Beau sniffled and mopped his tears with his palms.

"Fuck," he murmured. "Fuck."

What does it mean when there's no one left in front of you? When the only possible cannon fodder is yourself? He looked around the kitchen and blinked, dazedly. It was weird to act emotional, too, when there wasn't anyone around to witness it, when it wasn't for anyone else to see.

"C'mere." He spoke to the dog, a fat black lab who didn't listen. "Daisy, c'mon."

Finally, she did. The dainty, heavy clicking of her nails on the terra-cotta floor. *Survived by his partner*. Beau felt a wash of happiness, or relief, to know Sam had finally come out of the closet. Everyone should come to accept himself in the end.

Had *he*? As he scratched his dog's forehead, kicked the floor with short legs as energetic as a toddler's, the answer in Beau's case was plain: not nearly. I believe he was as restless within as he had ever been. But that didn't mean he didn't dream of such peace for others. And perhaps that was the difference, too, between himself and Sam and Williams. He was a mammal, deep down, no matter how much flesh he ate. Whereas Sam was a vampire and Will an enigma, even in death: the two men were the only truly private people he'd ever encountered in the movie business, albeit to such wildly different ends.

"Ralph?" He was on the phone now with his business manager, squinting at the final lines of the obit. It didn't matter whether you were survived by a family or a foundation, or if the company you'd built had morphed into something utterly strange: you deserved to be remembered. You did. "Ralph, I'd like to make a donation . . . "

"What do you think, I'm made out of money?"

Of course, at work it continued. Emily would ask for a raise and a promotion and what was he going to say? No?

"Are you?" she teased.

"I might be," he grumbled. But there were worse things to be made of than money. He knew that. Emily's bright and fearless face was what kept him alive. It wasn't that she made him feel young. It was that she made him feel at all.

"You want anything else? A second assistant?"

Emily wouldn't wreck it by laughing. Her affection for him was almost bottomless by now: he was such a good boss! He stared back at her over the top of his gold-rimmed reading glasses, clean-shaven these days, his hair a mess.

"Nope."

He gave her what she needed. She too was like a character in a fairy tale. *Make me a queen. Now make me an empress.* Not knowing that something close to desperation had crept in, that if he didn't originate a movie soon, the studio wouldn't renew his deal. But I think she imagined him the way the young almost always do the aging: incompletely, as if his successes protected him. As if the money and the material goods indemnified against fear.

"I'll just go find us another movie." She smiled, before she turned back down the hall. The phone on his desk gave a little burp, a muted purr. "That should make it a little easier for you to afford me."

"Dark."

That's what he said, though, when she finally did bring him that movie, in the form of an article from *Texas Monthly*. She brought him exactly what he needed, and he didn't get it at all.

"We can't make this." He shook the photocopied sheets at her and burped. "It's too depressing."

"It isn't." She was ready to go toe-to-toe with him, leaning against his desk. "It's hopeful."

"The studio will never make it."

"You don't know that." Indeed, what she didn't, couldn't say was that *she* knew the studio by now a little better than he did. She had Lucinda. He was spinning his wheels, no kidding, trying to get the animatronic gang back together for a sequel to *Pete*. But chimpanzees were no longer a slam dunk. The stuffed animals were all gone now, his office's once vibrant chaos pared back to austerity. "I want to take it in."

He eyed her. This was new; she'd never tried to go around him. But y'know what, if she wanted to, why not? Why shouldn't he let her go all the way?

"They won't bite. It's not a movie."

"Wanna bet? I've got a nice car I could wager."

He laughed. But if he'd taken her up on it, he might've won a DeLorean. For once, Lucinda agreed with Beau.

"I don't know." Emily took it to her personally, walked it into her cold, slate gray office instead of faxing or e-mailing. But Lucinda squinted up like Emily's face might contain more of interest than the article. She didn't get it either. "I thought you people made comedies."

"I thought you wanted my passion."

"I did. I do. Just . . . coal miners? That's older school than Rosenfrog. You wanna bring Sissy Spacek out of retirement?"

"It's younger than that. It's complex. The characters are interesting."

Lucinda snorted. What were you supposed to do with "interesting" characters? The article was about miners caught in a collapsed shaft. Difficult material, blue collar, and a television movie in the wrong hands. By 1998, studios didn't make things like this. They did Shakespeare, if you set it in high school; they made spectacles in which the world was destroyed by fire. They did not make stories set in fucking caves, unless those caves happened to contain treasure and elves.

"Tough stuff, Em."

"Tough," Emily said, "but I want it. I gave it to David Peoples, and he loves it. He thinks the CEO is a great character."

"He is a great character, and David's a great writer, but audiences don't want to spend that much time in a hole. This is a Searchlight movie."

"Audiences do when they're spending the time with Tom Hanks." Emily flicked her finger at the executive, like she was dismissing an insect. "I want it."

"You want it."

Lucinda squinted at her, and Emily again had that feeling she was fulfilling a prophecy. When they'd met, Lucinda had asked her for her passion. This was it. Except Emily didn't feel anything; her urgency was predicated upon something else, a cool dissociation. When she was a little girl, her father had taken her to see *Bambi*. It was the first movie she ever saw, and of course, when the fawn's mother died she was completely inconsolable. Her father had carried her out of the theater and told her what parents always did: *It's only a movie, Em, it isn't real, it's just make-believe.*

It's just make-believe.

This was her life. Why couldn't she feel it?

"I do want it," she said. "I do."

Lucinda smiled. And whether it was the prospect of defeating her old enemy, or the idea of satisfying her protégée's wish, it's hard to say, but she had the capacity to make this particular dream come true.

"Rosenfrog's not into it, huh?"

Emily shook her head. "He hates it."

Lucinda nodded. Emily didn't understand that either. She didn't "hate" anything, didn't have the energy or the drive or the meanness. How much easier her life would've been, maybe, if she had.

"Yes," Lucinda said. Tiger stripes of light fell on her desk, through slatted blinds to her right. "I'll buy it for you. Not Beau. You'll produce it."

Emily should've whooped. But it turned out getting what you wanted wasn't any better. It didn't clarify things in the slightest.

"Is there anyone else into it?" Lucinda asked. "Other buyers?"

"Scott Rudin. Karen Kehela." Emily turned now, aware that piling on the names of competitors, the various entities around town who were after the same thing, was gratuitous. But it never hurt to know. Having something only really counted when you were taking it away from someone else. "I think Universal's going to make a play for it for Ron Howard."

"All right," Lucinda said. "I'll call Markhamson, and we'll make it happen."

X

"WHO?"

"Beau Rosenwald." Emily's assistant's voice crackled through the squawk box at the bottom of Em's desk in her new office in Thalberg.

"Oh." Is it so terrible that her first impulse was to say, *I'll call back*? "Put him through."

"Honey!" Beau's voice greeted her, pouring heavily into her ear. "How are you, sweetheart?"

The one thing she could never get used to: her former boss's obsequiousness, now that he could no longer just trample into her office at will to chew the fat, now that he was the needy one and she the possessor of power.

"The same, Beau." She exhaled, adjusted her headset. Sleepless, sore-nippled, but otherwise she felt the same. "I'm OK."

The possessor of everything: husband, studio checkbook, child. She didn't quite have greenlight power, that was Lucinda's, but it was close. And even so, it hadn't changed much. The new job was just like the old job. There was more of it, and having a six-month-old to look after at home certainly complicated things, but at times like this? She only wondered why it wasn't more satisfying.

"I can't believe," Beau wheezed, "you used to be my intern. You did coverage for me!"

"I did." Dear Lord, the coverage on the script Beau was flogging to her now was terrible, both as regarded the quality of the script—it was awful, a straight pass—and of the reader's report itself. Whoever wrote it deserved a basketball to the head. "A long time ago."

Her title now was executive vice president, at a branch of the studio that had been recently created to make movies oriented toward adult women. Lucinda Vogel had been tapped to run the specialty division, and Emily, to no one's surprise, had come over with her.

"So." Emily leaned back, twirled a pencil between her fingers and cocked her head, listening through her earpiece. "About this script."

Late fall, 2000. How easily she took to a job that was all about the balance sheet, where she might not in a million years have greenlit the very movie that had gotten it for her. Coal miners? Not a chance. Some idiotic comedy about a displaced mob boss who becomes an urban schoolteacher, which would've been retrograde in 1989? Less chance even than that. Severin and I may have had our hands full that summer—I was in the beginning stages of a divorce, and Sev's wife, Lexy, had miscarried in the spring—but Beau's own hands were to remain empty, even as his ex-employee was on top of the world. Through her window in the Thalberg Building, Emily could see a field of orange poppies, a blazing carpet of them. In 1939, the year they made *The Wizard of Oz*, this lot had been MGM. So much had changed since then, but so much had changed too since what Emily couldn't help thinking of as the Rosenwaldian Era. Like the Mesozoic, the Paleozoic.

"Joe Pesci wants to do it."

Joe Pesci? In her secret heart, Emily smiled. Why not Jerry Lewis? Beau just bulled along, pitching stupid comedies to anyone who'd listen. And to those who wouldn't. God bless him.

"Beau. Sweetheart." She was pretty sure he couldn't even hear her teasing him, mocking his own style. "This isn't for us. Sorry."

"What do you mean? This is for everybody. Listen . . . "

Even as she allowed him a minute to make his lamebrained case, she wondered: What *was* for "us"? Certainly not *27 Heads in a Duffel Bag*, or whatever the hell he was blabbing about exactly, but Columbia Vita had been incubated in the mid-1990s, at a time when it was somehow believed that the adult female audience was the key to the future. This notion was already in dispute by the time they were off the ground—obviously, the key demographic was adolescent males—but David Markhamson, the English muck-a-muck who oversaw all three divisions of the studio, refused to pull the plug. He was loyal to his original idea and, it was said, to Lucinda, whom he loved.

"Listen, Beau, I'm sorry," Emily said, after an interval in which she allowed him to make an idiot of himself and so feel he'd tried. "It's out of the question. Better for MGM." *Or some half-witted European financier who doesn't understand Joe Pesci's been dead since '96, who probably doesn't know Joe Pesci from Joe Piscopo.* "This movie's not for us."

"All right, Em." She could hear how crestfallen he was, too, how easily he gave up compared to how he used to be. "We'll keep trying."

Markhamson believed it was unwise to make movies for more than ten million dollars but less than eighty: you could make expensive spectacles or inexpensive indies, but the budgetary range in between was suicide. "The mushy middle," he called it. And Beau Rosenwald was, alas, of mushier middle than most. His deal was up soon, and there was no way Sony would renew it.

"That we will."

She hung up. Feeling a little twinge of sadness when Beau didn't call right back, when her phone just sat there, silent.

That fall, Emily White was thirty-one years old. She seldom even saw Beau anymore. Sometimes she'd spot him shambling around the lot, gray slacks and deranged hair, white shirt with the sleeves rolled, gold watch. He looked like a mental patient who'd escaped and mugged a Beverly Hills tailor.

"Em—"

"Huh?" She whirled. Lucinda was standing in the doorway, leaning into her office from the frame. Arms stretched behind her back.

"You going to the Markhamson thing?"

Emily nodded. "Seven thirty, yeah?"

Lucinda, too, was pregnant. The proud father was her girlfriend of three years. Prospective motherhood wasn't mellowing her in the slightest: it just gave her killer instincts new places to go. Already she was flinging money at schools, donating to the Center for Early Education on behalf of a child who wasn't even born yet. She stood in the doorway with eight months of Versace-sheathed belly thrust into Emily's office. The "Markhamson Thing" was a fund-raiser, spearheaded by the boss's wife, to fight breast cancer.

"Pick me up," Lucinda said. "Maryse is sick and can't go."

Just so, Emily wouldn't subject her husband, an entertainment lawyer, to this sort of long-form boredom either. "OK."

Things *had* changed. The two women faced off, each one the other's minor mirror in pregnancy and style. If Emily couldn't match Lucinda for sheer meanness and drive, she could still do it for expediency. Who knew if she loved her husband, or her job, or the movies? Sometimes she felt the only adult thing she'd ever loved was Beau.

"What's eating you?" Lucinda said. And Emily shook her head, so as not to admit her sadness. She stood and walked to her window, where she gazed out at the hazy gray distances beyond the studio walls. She could see the Santa Monica Mountains, barely: they were white whispers, chalk marks on a scrim. Now and then with this view, Emily got caught up in that theatrical feeling she'd had the day she first met Lucinda, like her life was a play and yet she was the only actor in it.

"Nothing. I'm just thinking."

"You don't get paid to think," Lucinda grimaced, playfully. "You get paid to do the math."

What is the matter, my lord?

"Yep."

This maxim about the math was Markhamson all over, although Lucinda lacked the Englishman's wry politesse, the way he could say such a thing without sounding crass. Pregnancy only seemed to enhance Lucinda's crassness, in fact. She was distended in the way of a boa constrictor who's swallowed a small mammal. Lipstick slashed her face in a way that was vaguely, perhaps even intentionally, crude.

"Byron Lawrence?" Emily's assistant's voice came through the box.

"I'll take it," Emily called back.

Lucinda spun and went away, her dark frame, still skinny from the back, flouncing down the hall. Emily went to her desk and picked up the phone, this time to talk to a young operator from ADM whose swift, shrewd, and incisive proposals couldn't have been less like Beau's.

"Byron?" Unconsciously, though, she mimicked her old boss's mannerisms. "How are you, my dear?"

Unconsciously, because Beau Rosenwald was almost gone from her life, but he was certainly not forgotten. Whereas Emily herself, imprisoned in the muted cocoon of her beautiful new office—it was sleek as a hotel suite, all piano blacks and elevator grays—had doubts about her own status. She leaned back, adjusted her headset, rolled up her sleeve. Her arm was pale as a calla lily.

"Hmm." She smiled. "Natalie Portman? I like that idea."

She drank from a glass of iced green tea. And wondered, even as she knew she'd arrived, where she was, and if she was ever really there.

"I HAVE TO GET BACK."

"What?" I looked at Severin. "Dude, no, let's share a cab."

"We can all share," Little Will said. "It's not a problem."

Interesting to see how far we'd come, as the three of us pushed away our plates at a restaurant called Home in the West Village. A narrow room with wooden booths jutting out of its eastern wall, a thin radiance beating down from overhead. We were scarcely three blocks from the place Beau had first come together with Severin's mom. Maybe we owed our lives to this city after all.

"I'll get it," I said, as I took a last sip of wine and reached for the check.

"No, no, let Mr. National Book Critics Circle pick it up," Will snickered.

I pushed Severin's hand away. "Rupert Murdoch'll do it," I said. "My corporation's rock beats your HP printer's paper."

Soon, I'd quit my job at Fox and be writing again. Soon, I'd finalize my divorce and move home to LA, but just then we were all together in New York, swirling around in our primitive adult fortune and dismay.

"Remember Emily White?" I said.

"Sure." Severin shrugged. "What about her?"

"She's this close to running a studio now."

"Really?"

Severin blinked, behind his glasses. I couldn't tell if he was surprised or just indifferent. Little Will murmured. *Huh.* He probably didn't remember Emily; he'd left town before her time really began.

"Yeah." I signed for the check, and together we tumbled out of our booth and into the street. Our thickening bodies roiled close to one another's. We still moved like a small pack, like the teenage wolves we'd once been.

"Look." Williams stopped to ogle some Zeppelin bootleg in the window of a basement record store, bending over a metal railing to look down. "Cool."

"You've already got that one, Will." Severin stood behind him, smiling faintly. Will's mind may have been functioning almost normally again, sure, but occasionally he was hazy around the details.

"I do?" Williams squinted, and Sev nudged me. "Fuck you, I don't."

Severin burst out laughing.

For a moment, our fuckups were something to laugh about. Severin's fourth novel, *Peckerhead*—the one about a New York orphan's search for his missing mother—had won the National Book Critics Circle Award. What could be wrong?

"I remember better than you do," Will muttered, as he spotted a cab on Avenue of the Americas and strode forward to hail it.

Our voices were dead on the empty street, caroming flatly off the faces of the brick row houses and brownstones, our steps echoing a little as we scuttled up to the cab. Will was in a hurry to get home to his wife and six-month-old son; Severin, I guess, to whatever he was writing now, or else to Lexy, his own wife, who was also a novelist. I had no particular place to go, but I ambled after them.

"You OK, Nate?" Sev grabbed my bicep after Williams ducked into the backseat.

I nodded. What was there to say? I'd gotten married, and it had lasted all of three years. The marriage was scuppered by all the things you'd expect on my side: selfishness, spaciness, and inattention. You know my flaws by now. I wasn't heartbroken so much as I was, simply, lost. I was my mother's son and first I'd been Teddy's, then Beau's. How was I supposed to know what made adults capable of living together?

"You hear from Lizzie?"

I shook my head. I'd married a Waspy girl from Connecticut, a business-school blonde. Disaster. Sev squeezed my arm, and we dodged into the cab, his lime green shirt flashing in front of me as he took the middle. My brother the famous novelist, protective of me to the end.

Or perhaps not. I flopped into the back beside him, on an unseasonably hot night in October. The cabbie shot up toward Eighth, where he'd loop around to Bowery, the direction we all needed to go. I might have envied Sev, but he was still as dark to me as he'd ever been.

He stared straight ahead. Little Will did the same. The latter didn't look like his dad, for whom I was also still searching all the time. Who knew why? The more I discovered myself in business, the more I feared I could be like him, the chilly executive; the more I felt myself and the elder Williams align.

"You talked to Beau lately?" I muttered, but Severin didn't hear. Or else he just ignored me. I thought he was on to his own apotheosis, was all: just as Beau had risen beyond his father, Severin had made it, and moved away.

The cab accelerated, plunging east and then downtown. The night was a heavy, cloud clotted gray. Will lived in Park Slope, Sev in Cobble Hill. I shook my wrist against my heavy gold Omega and watched the city flash by, thinking of the places only a few blocks away that carried, for us, a certain scent. Café Limbo, Two Boots. No matter how successful I was, I'd never match them. Both of my friends seemed more at home in the world than I was.

XII

"MY GOD, IS that Beau Rosenwald?"

It was more than two years before Emily ran into her old boss again. She and he had talked on the phone, occasionally made hopeful noises about having lunch, but it never happened. And when Beau's deal expired, and wasn't renewed, she'd simply lost track of him. Until Lucinda leaned over and tugged her sleeve. *Look.*

"Where?" Emily said. "My God, I think . . . it is!"

They were, in fact, at the "Markhamson Thing," this time in 2003. Across the dining room at the Beverly Wilshire Hotel she spotted him, in a paisley waistcoat and accompanied by a very tall, very slender blonde some twenty years his junior. Something about this woman's body language—erect, uninterested in the Hollywood honchos swirling around—made it clear she was not in the business.

"What's he wearing?" Lucinda snickered. "That waistcoat is bats."

Beau Rosenwald was seventy years old. He hadn't seen Emily yet, and a part of me will forever wish he never did. He kept his eyes on the stage, where Sheryl Crow was currently running through a mini-acoustic set of toe-tappers. The woman who sat with him was statuesque, sphinxlike, dignified in a way that made her presence at Beau's side a little puzzling. She looked, just barely, like Donatella Versace, if the latter weren't such a terrible frightwig.

Emily sat through the remainder of Crow's set, shrinking down in her seat as she did. Her first impulse was to escape. Can you blame her? She was bored, she was pregnant for the second time, and she wanted to get home, to two-and-a-half-year-old Matilda and the not altogether unpleasantly boring husband who'd already be sound asleep at 9:30 PM.

"Look, David." Natalya Markhamson pointed vaguely in my father's direction. "Isn't that the horrible man?"

David didn't look up. Natalya could've been pointing anywhere. "Yes."

"You're not watching."

"Yes, yes." David allowed himself a courtesy glance. In fact he locked in on somebody else. "I'm sure that's him."

Light sparked off Natalya's bracelet; that was what drew Beau Rosenwald's eye. In this dimly lit dining room thick with the mood of self-congratulation, and with people *this* close to going home, he spotted expensive jewelry and then Emily White. Pity.

"You're still not looking." Natalya's drawl was cartoonishly Slavic.

"Well," David said, as Emily waved back at Beau reluctantly. "They're all horrible men, aren't they?"

He was dry, punctilious, Oxonian, and close to retirement age. She was an asp-like brunette in her thirties. What drew them together, besides money, Emily couldn't imagine. She happened to know Natalya was sleeping with Lucinda and had been for some time. Not that David had a clue. With his coppery skin and gold-framed glasses, receding hair and careful manners, he looked more like an accountant than the head of all three feature divisions of the biggest entertainment entity on the planet next to Disney.

Still, Emily almost made it out. She went for the door as soon as the lights came up, mumbling something about a babysitter. David didn't mind, he liked Emily, and she'd already done her part to support the pet cause, donating an extra ten grand.

"Em!" The fat man cornered her at last, just as she was striding out of the lobby to the valet stand.

"Beau?" She turned and saw he was standing there with the tall woman. Even now, when she saw my dad she half expected him to whip a script—or Joe Pesci himself—out of his pocket and start clobbering her with it. "My God, it's been ages."

"Yeah." He beamed. "Emily, I want to introduce you to my wife."

Wife! Was he always so short, or was this fourth Mrs. Ro just excruciatingly tall? She angled her hand down at Emily and they shook.

"He talks about you," she said. "I'm Patricia."

"I'm glad," Emily said. Whatever could Beau have to say about her at this point? Mostly she was just baffled, by this woman's air of academic seriousness, by her rare—flawed, unadjusted—beauty, and by old Beau's apparent mellow contentment. He seemed positively jolly, there in his patent leather shoes.

"Me too," he said. With his arms spread apart like the star of a musical, as if he were set to burst into song. "I'm happy for all your success, Em."

That was it. The conversation collapsed around Beau's failure to accost her with a bad movie. At seventy he deserved a little peace, didn't he? He deserved his marriage to a fifty-two-year-old doctor (!), and he deserved a happy dotage. Not even a little incident Severin had stumbled into earlier this year—a father's heartaches never ended, and he would never have guessed his son was unhappy—would ruin that for him. Behind him, in the lobby, Lucinda and Natalya Markhamson stood and pretended to ignore each other. As if half the town didn't know they were fucking!

"Well," I'm mid, as her car pulled up. *Phew*. Bad enough that Beau still talked about her. "I'll see you."

She pulled off. Beau and his fourth—fifth, Emily thought, but she could be forgiven for failing to keep track—wife stood behind, there in the golden light that rained over the valet stand. People milled around in tuxedos and evening gowns, chewing gum to efface the taste of mediocre salmon. Beau watched Emily's car, a sleek and expensive green Bentley, turn left at the end of the drive. Her taillights disappeared.

"You know I bought her a DeLorean once?"

Patricia nodded. What Beau did not know was that Emily had sold the car, two years ago. Sentimentality, at last, had its limit.

Driving home, Emily's mind was on her boredom. It was not on Beau Rosenwald at all. Even as she turned left on Wilshire Boulevard, headed west toward Santa Monica—she and Beau now lived mere blocks apart, for all that they never saw each other—she was thinking of her exhaustion, of the sheer lack of inspiration you had to draw upon to work at a studio today. Everything had already happened. You couldn't make movies out of need, or even out of interest. Whereas in Beau's era the business was governed by id, this one was all superego, adjusted by some portion of the brain that hadn't been named yet: pure terror wrapped in floss.

Tiffany fluttered by, Barney's. What was once the Brown Derby, where Beau—he was only a few car lengths behind her now, pointing the landmark out to his wife as he always did—used to take Severin for lunch every Christmas Eve. Whatever reverence Emily had for the past—it wasn't much, but when she went to work for Beau she'd certainly had some feeling for what he'd accomplished, and what the industry had been—was supplanted by this feeling of being a posthumous human being. If the life of the movies was ended, what was left? Did anything exist if you no longer had hope for it? If it was no longer the object of dreams? At this hour, Wilshire Boulevard was quiet, all those low-slung, brown-and-tan buildings shuttered up behind silver grates, the mannequins glowing boldly in the windows. Emily White was as inviolable as these alarm-strung storefronts, as armored against intrusion, her eyelids drooping as she cruised through yellow lights. *I'm bored*.

Beau was only twenty-five feet behind her, yet worlds away in spirit. Driving with his wife, sipping bottled water behind the wheel of *her* BMW, he luxuriated in not caring very much, in connubial adoration, in being, finally, free. Unlike Emily White, he was *beyond* boredom, whereas Emily was boredom incarnate. Wasn't that true? Wasn't it?

"Hmm," he murmured. Feeling not even the least whisper of trouble. They were just passing Bedford Drive, the old TAG offices there on his left. His elbow jutted into the breeze. "You know what?"

"Nope." Patricia covered his hand with her own, delicate, slender, and soft. Her voice was bright and ironic. "I can't yet read your mind, sweetheart."

"I think I'm going to," my father said. He spoke as if they were having an argument, as if she were trying to talk him out of whatever intention he hadn't even yet announced. "I'm going to call Emily and ask her to lunch."

"I think that's terrific, if it's what you want to do."

Ahead he could see the old Beverly Hilton, Robinsons-May, the fountain at the corner of Wilshire and Santa Monica, which shot lavender blue spray into the air. Bryce Beller had once passed out in that fountain.

"Yep," Beau hummed. "Yep, indeed."

Just so, he did it. He made the last great mistake of his life.

XIII

EMILY WHITE WAS onto something with her first impression of her old boss then. Because Beau Rosenwald had his problems, but also, at long last, he was happy. He was—inconceivable!—in love. I'd never seen him so purely cheerful as he was in those days, and Severin, whose memory reached back a lot farther, said exactly the same thing. *He's so happy.* Like an infant, a swaddled, jolly, cooing little beast, he could not have been more so.

So why did he have to fuck it up?

The truth was, around the time Beau lost his deal, he'd been sick of just about everything. He was sick of the business, sick of kissing up to the studio and its executives, Lucinda and all the rest. He was sick of his own mind, even. And so old Rosenwald, no stranger to the more drastic forms of mental-health maintenance, took the unprecedented step, for him, of entering psychoanalysis. This wasn't about going and complaining to some unorthodox transactional hippie once a week—poor Horowitz, who'd finally come down on the side of or-not-to-be: he'd hung himself in front of Paul Revere Middle School in the late nineties—this was about discovering who he was. Beau Rosenwald must've been desperate.

"I don't believe in this shit," he barked at the woman who admitted him to her office on Fairburn Avenue, near Beverly Glen. "I don't know why I'm here."

"What's not to believe?" The woman was a willowy redhead. He hated redheads, ever since Susan Sarandon ditched him in the late days at ADM. "I haven't asked you to believe anything."

Beau looked at her, dubiously. This was in October 2001, and I suppose his confusion was the most American thing about him. It wasn't as if everyone's beliefs weren't up for question, just then.

"Sit." The doctor indicated her couch. Her hair fell across her face so he couldn't really see it that well. The hair was wavy and thick, and her hands had the brittle delicacy of tree branches. Something about the way her fingers spread, the radical articulation of her knuckles and wrists, struck him. Their parchment color. "Why do you think you're here?"

It had been so long since Beau had talked to an actual woman. I think she scared him a little, this person who was not an executive, an actress, or a trophy, who wasn't going to respond to any of his tantrums. He did not find her attractive.

"Dr. Trabulus gave me your number."

"So I gather." She smiled. "But why are *you* here?"

How do you answer a question like that, when you have no vocabulary to describe your self-state? Beau had spent his life *being* a mood; it didn't really occur to him that human beings had motives, that all that boring stuff that got talked up in story meetings actually applied.

"I don't know." He sat. "I think that's why I'm here."

He sat like a passenger on a bus, hands folded in his lap. He looked at her shelves, which were piled high with books. He stared out her window, at the open air above the intersection of Santa Monica and Beverly Glen Boulevards. There was the sound of angry honking, a rush-hour altercation.

"My last shrink was a complete lunatic," he said. Still, looking around him, craning his neck as if there might be somebody else here. "He thought he was treating Jim Morrison."

"Oh?" She folded her hands in her lap, crossed her legs, and listened.

Beau was stranded. Without a job, without a production deal or a film or a marriage—even a bad wife would've given him something to do—and yet he found himself, gradually, able to recognize this. Talking to this doctor, he admitted his despair.

"Everything happens to *me*," he said, on a subsequent visit. "It's like the old song."

"What do you mean?"

"I mean . . . " My father hesitated, over some anguished sense of victimhood he was too terrified to explain, that had never even crossed his consciousness before this. "My life—"

"Your life, what?" Her voice was golden, calm. He'd taken to lying down on the couch, not looking at her. "You have a successful son. You have a second son you worry about a little, but you think he'll be OK, once he gets it together. Yet you feel like certain things are your fault."

"I do."

Three times a week, they met. They talked about Severin (to his astonishment, she knew who his son was, owned all four of his books), about his feelings of failure, about Kate, and about me. About other things I'll never know.

"I've made a fortune. I've fucked movie stars."

"And yet you actually feel like none of it happens to you," this woman—Dr. Goldmond was her name—said, presciently. "I think you feel like it's all happening to somebody else."

Psychobabble, to him. But she went over to her shelf and pulled something down.

"Read this." It was *The Great Short Novels of Henry James*. "Read *The Beast in the Jungle*."

"I know *The Beast in the Jungle*." After all, he'd developed it unsuccessfully at Columbia. "I almost did this movie."

"You did? So you've already read it."

My father hesitated. He'd read Emily White's coverage of an adapted script. Yet now he read the novella. It was hell, of course, but he went line by painstaking line through that, and *The Ambassadors* too. Not since *Coriolanus* had he delved as deeply into a text, needed to wring as much meaning from just a set of words.

"How can that be?" This woman divined him just right. As with John Marcher, as with Lambert Strether, those Jamesian archetypes, his life seemed to have passed him right by. "I've been married three times. I've been in an asylum. I've—"

He twisted up off the couch, to amplify his aggravation, then broke off. "You changed your hair," he said.

"Three weeks ago."

It was February 2002. Through almost a dozen meetings, he simply hadn't seen it. She was blonde now.

"Why didn't I notice?" he muttered. Suddenly, he was angry. "Why did you dye your hair?"

"Why wouldn't I?" She tossed it, just so. With an unconsciously girlish defiance. "Why shouldn't I dye my hair?"

Beau Rosenwald was so Pavlovian. All she needed to do was become a fucking blonde?

"I like it," he said. Demurely, as his anger withered and he just stared.

"Thank you."

Just like that, he saw beauty. Grunting, wheezing, aging Beau. How had he missed it all before? Her eyes were green and her lips were pillowy and if she happened to be a little older than the women he usually went for—if she happened not to be twenty-five—she was authentic.

"You were saying?"

But Beau couldn't speak. This elegant, articulate woman, she looked over and saw nothing but another patient, of course. If she had seen the man, can you imagine how that would've gone? He was always yammering on about Spielberg, David Geffen, the need for a comeback, whom could he call? Patricia Goldmond had less attractive patients—Beau was funny, and his hideousness was mostly skin-deep—but this white-haired, froggy little fellow wasn't exactly her private ideal.

"I was saying . . . "

He fell hard. He couldn't help it. He knew what a cliché it was to fall in love with your therapist, but that didn't stop him from doing it. Sharon Stone herself wouldn't have stood a chance against this woman, as Beau saw her.

"This must happen all the time." He couldn't help telling her about it either. Within a week he was spilling his guts.

"No."

"Yes." He insisted; God, it was fucking humiliating. *Please uncross your legs*. "You're irresistible."

"I don't think so." She couldn't help laughing, and touching her hair, which now drove him absolutely bananas. "I think people resist me fine."

"I don't." He levered himself up off the couch and looked at her straight on. "I quit. I can't come here anymore."

"I'm sorry you feel that way."

"You're fired. Now date me."

"No."

In her gray suit, with her long curtain of blonde hair—she'd straightened it, too—she looked grave. Her face without sutures, her melancholy stare. There were lines around her mouth, creases at the corners of her eyes.

"Why not?" Who knew you could be turned on by flaws? "I date prettier women than you all the time."

"That has nothing to do with it. And it's against the ethical rules of the profession, you know that."

"I don't care."

"And I'm not attracted to you."

"That never stopped anyone before."

Old Beau was off to the races. He wanted this more than he could remember wanting anything at all. Even the movie business was secondary, tertiary: he called and left messages on her answering service, sat outside her office in his car. His hands actually shook when he considered her, just sitting there hoping to catch a glimpse. ("Stalking?" Well, that would depend on whom you asked. He wanted to see her, was that such a crime?) He felt better than he had, really, in years. There was nothing like wanting the unobtainable, and Beau had obtained enough over the years to know it. Usually, you stopped wanting at consummation, but this was different. Had his life passed him by?

"Oh . . . " He ran into her one afternoon at Bristol Farms, literally plowed his cart into hers at the end of the frozen food aisle. "Imagine running into you."

She laughed. As if it was an authentic surprise for her, where Beau had gone so far as to memorize her schedule. (It wasn't stalking, it was . . . managed coincidence.)

"You do your own shopping," she said. Gesturing toward his cart, which was full of nothing but vitamin water and a carton of power bars. "I'd have assumed you had someone to take care of you."

"Yep." He nodded toward hers, which was full. "You have a family."

"Two children," she said. "I'm divorced."

It struck them both, how little they knew. Beau, that he'd been running around in love with a ghost—it hadn't occurred to him there were actual people in her life—and she, that she'd been pity-ing this man as if he were an invalid. He still almost seemed so. But standing there in the frozen food aisle—gelato, edamame; this was the sort of market that wouldn't stoop to sell mere peas—she fell in love with him too. Crazy as it sounds, she did.

"Did you ever think"—Beau couldn't resist teasing her, much lat-er—"you'd end up with someone like me?"

"No!" Lying beside him in bed. "God, no."

"Once more," he laughed. "For emphasis."

They'd come a long way, and quickly, since that coffee in West-wood. Less than a year had passed, and they were now married. But you know Beau: why wait for anything? One second she was carrying her groceries out to her car, half regretting having just said "yes" to the relentless fat man; the next, almost the moment her younger son took off for college, she was shacked up on Fifteenth Street in Santa Monica, lying beneath his two-hundred-odd pounds of heavenly joy.

"Is it really so unlikely?" Beau said. Not quite indignant, as they lingered in bed on a Saturday morning. He would've taken *her* name, were it permissible.

"Yes," she said. "You don't read. You aren't interested in the world around you." She planked her long fingers atop his chest. "You're heavy."

He laughed. It was like she could turn these things into positives just by naming them. She stood up and began to dress. Moving with slightly exaggerated grace, a pleasure in knowing these move-ments were appreciated.

"Never thought I'd end up with you either," he said. As he watched her from the massive Duxiana mattress, propped up on one elbow. On peach-colored sheets, with the rest of the room all dark browns and expensive tans, opulent desert colors. "Never thought I'd love a girl with one tit."

Ah, yes. One more discovery for Beau, once Patricia unsheathed herself from her profession and her blouse: Mrs. Ro IV was a cancer survivor who'd had a mastectomy before they met. Her wisdom, and strength, were what allowed him to survive things now, like that episode with Severin this past spring, his son's acting upon a crushing depression. He loved how *real* she was, whether out at a fund-raiser or seminaked in their room.

She adjusted an earring, there at the foot of the bed. She was red-haired again, one more way she kept her new husband on his toes.

"Where are you going?"

"I have a patient."

"Just to make you happy," he said, "I'm going to read something while you're out."

"I've heard that before."

"I'm going to. *The Decline and Fall of the Roman Empire*, or—OK, I'll start small. A racing form, but I'll work my way up."

She laughed. And came over and kissed him, briskly, before she walked out without a word. Yellow skirt, white blouse: she wore bright colors today. Disappearing inside a self he could no longer quite imagine, the professional he'd first met. Being married to a psychiatrist was exciting. Like with a spy, or a whore: there were things you could never know.

This was where Beau was, in those days before his fateful collision with Emily. I suppose you can lay some of the blame on Patricia, as that dig about his reading would have its effect. But he stretched and sauntered downstairs, after a while, after he'd listened to her car pull away and could luxuriate—even him now, yes—in silence. This house felt lived-in today. The same massive spread he'd bought after he cashed out of the ranch in Calabasas: it had four bedrooms and five bathrooms and two kitchens and a gym, things that were stupidly extravagant through all those years he'd lived by himself. Now it was home. It smelled like olive oil and caramelized garlic and flowers and her perfume. A little corner of a rug was turned up where she'd accidentally kicked it on her way out the door.

He crossed the hall and entered the living room. All those books Patricia had piled up on his shelves were a bit intimidating. It was onerous, too, being married to someone so smart, so unknowable. Though knowing her would've been a problem also; like knowing himself. To discover that under that massive skin lay just a timid set of insecurities like anyone else's? No wonder actors do what they do.

"Hmm," he murmured, just to keep himself company. "What now?"

He took two steps up a ladder, which was set on rollers, to reach the first book that caught his eye: it was Robert Stone's *A Hall of*

Mirrors. Why that book? He liked the title, and he remembered that Teddy Sanders had something to do with packaging *Dog Soldiers*, as *Who'll Stop the Rain*, back in the old ADM days. Past that, I'll always wonder. But Beau, he took the book and went over to the couch and read it cover to cover.

"Honey?" By the time his wife came home, he was positively flattened, sprawled on the couch in his usual white shirt and tan pants, oblivious to her call. "Honey?" she repeated.

Behind him was the wall covered with photographs by Dennis Hopper; above the fireplace hung a single Jasper Johns.

"This book is great," he said finally, when she entered and broke the spell.

His bare feet were unexpectedly kempt and clean and shapely. A young man's feet, like a dancer's.

"Do I know you?" she said. Spotting the title as she bent to kiss him. "Yes, that is a fantastic book."

"It's a movie."

"Stop. It already was a movie, anyway, with Paul Newman and Joanne Woodward."

"Really?" How rare, for her to know a film and him not, unless it was Asian or Eastern European. "I don't remember that."

"*WUSA*, it was called. I saw it when I was in college. Not very good."

"It should be remade."

"No."

Patricia was right. It wasn't even a good idea. Beau couldn't help thinking like a producer, though. Nominally he still was one, and of course, bad ideas had long been his specialty.

"Are you challenging me?"

Yes, it was a civil rights drama set at a New Orleans radio station in the sixties, but the station could be Sirius, the issue could be gay marriage, or alien suffrage. There wasn't anything you couldn't drag, given enough energy, into the present. Nothing was so dead you couldn't resurrect it. He stood up, followed her back into the main kitchen. Spoiling for a fight, but she wouldn't give it to him.

"No." She circled the island in the middle of the room, laying out preparations for pasta. Her heels rang out on the terra-cotta. "I'm just saying."

"What? What are you saying?" *Matt Damon, Gwyneth Paltrow*.

She didn't need to explain, merely went to the fridge and got goat cheese. Began quartering an heirloom tomato.

"I like this book," my father said. "I like to read."

Unafraid of sounding like an idiot. Patricia just looked at him, her gaze deep and shining. *Why professionalize it?* this meant. Like her cooking. Why not just enjoy a pleasure for what it is?

"I'm glad."

How he hated it when she was like this, too. Knowing things, understanding him better than he understood himself.

"You'll see," he murmured. A little more darkly than he'd intended. "You will."

He only half meant it, though. Beau was retired. He liked being around the house when she was, liked playing with their brand-new chocolate lab puppy, who napped in a crate over by the French doors to the courtyard. He came up behind her, wrapped his arms around her waist, standing by the eight-burner stove where for so many years he'd never even made it past reheating expensive restaurant food. Never cooked so much as a can of soup.

He nuzzled her neck. Happiness, yes. Like all such, it carried the seed of its own dissipation inside it. It just wasn't made to last.

XIV

"ROBERT STONE?" Emily squinted across the table, staring at Beau's flushed face in the sun. Waiters in arctic black-and-whites swam through the shadowed patio behind him. "That's not really your style, is it?"

"You know my style," Beau said. He chuckled. "My style is everybody's style."

God love him. Even in his age, he spoke with the original force, the same old persuasion. Like whatever he had was *the* thing you needed: a script, an article, a scrap of belly button lint.

"I don't know," Emily said. Under present conditions, a scrap of lint might be more plausible than this, a drama set in a radio station. Eric Bogosian had done that, ages ago. *Play Misty for Me*—itself hardly feasible—this was not. "It's a little esoteric."

"Your mine-shaft movie was esoteric," Beau said, "and look what happened there."

"That was a long time ago."

Why didn't she just flat-out say no? Because studio heads never had to. She sat on the terrace of the Ivy on Robertson—Beau really did like to rock it old school—and ate with him, watched him eat, for pity's sake. Lime chicken, rock shrimp. Three weeks after the Markhamson event (even that sounded like what the movies had become, something calendared years in advance), the most astonishing thing had happened to her.

"So what's it like," Beau said. "Being in charge of everything?"

Emily sighed. *It's like being in charge of nothing*, she could've said, because her time, also, was too valuable to spend chitchatting with a former producer whose presence in the industry was nonexistent. The more authority you accreted, the less you could actually exercise. Or maybe the old man already knew that. He could've discovered it, long ago.

"I'm glad it happened," she said.

"Me too. I'm not big on the misfortunes of others, but Lucinda should've been canned long ago."

Em nodded. She swallowed the last of her iced tea. Lucinda had just slept with one skinny European too many. Nothing Beau was qualified to pass judgment on, surely.

"Why do you want to do this Robert Stone thing?" she said finally. "Is this a respectability trip?"

"Trip"? Even talking about Stone made her feel old. It wasn't as if Beau was Scott Rudin, bringing her *Damascus Gate*.

"It's not 1970 anymore," she said. "This isn't a good idea. Frankly, even remaking *The Dog's Tail* makes more sense than this."

To her surprise, Beau began to laugh. A rich old chuckle, substantive in its dimensions. He set his espresso cup down on its saucer and leaned back.

"What is it?"

"You want to know the worst thing, Em, about getting old?"

Emily cocked her head. *Not really*, this meant, but it didn't matter, because he was going to go ahead and tell her anyway.

"It's not that things aren't any fun anymore. It's not that you have to get up three times a night to pee, or any of the things you'd expect." He took off his sunglasses and polished them with his napkin. "It's that you know all this torture's going to end."

"Excuse me?"

He stared for a moment across Robertson, his eyes gone dead, glassy.

"When you're young, you think your misery's going to last forever. The awful part is when you find out it won't."

Maybe he saw things, in that moment. Maybe he was dreaming, as he still did all the time, of his former partner. The man with whom he'd reinvented a business, so they could leave it, apparently, to a youngster like this. Emily White was the rich, ripe age of thirty-four at the time she was boosted to run a studio. She'd scarcely been born back when Sam Smiligan had leaned over to Beau and told him, *There are worse things than being antiquated*. But she knew there were, too. And as they left she took his arm, while they walked down the granite steps to the valet stand.

"It's Paramount, you said? They own the remake rights?"

Beau had described a meeting there that was painful for Emily to imagine, pitching to an executive barely a third his age. It hurt to consider him, bumbling around that lot.

"No promises," she kissed his cheek. *One last favor this time, just one.* "But I'll see what I can do."

Why did he want it, though? Why, really? Didn't he know to leave well enough alone? *Is it a respectability trip, Beau?* A prestige thing? Well, sort of. I suppose he operated the way we all do, one part convenience to another pure coincidence. Add a dose of idiocy, or ill luck, and you get a man confronting what he believes is his unique destiny. If he'd never read *A Hall of Mirrors*, or if he hadn't run into Emily at that thing, that accursed benefit; if his wife had never teased him, or if she'd shown better judgment than to encourage Beau to call his former intern for lunch, that very week after he found the book, even if it was just to shut him up about it. If, if, if, if, if, if, if. If only something—anything—had prevented him from getting back in the game.

"Hampton Fancher."

"Excuse me?"

Indeed, Emily wished as much, herself. She did what she could, got him the rights to the book. Now he clung to her leg like a humping puppy, clogged up her phone sheet day after day after day.

"Hampton's gonna write the script." My father cackled in her ear as she whisked along Sunset, leaving a meeting at the Chateau.

"Who on earth is Hampton Fancher?"

How quickly they forget. Hampton, who cowrote *Blade Runner*, and was a friend of Severin's, was a left-field choice to be sure—farther out than that even, he was way back beyond the bleachers—but he was also, once upon a time, a genius. Maybe he was still. And here again, she decided to let Beau have his way. She called up Byron Lawrence, who had to be reminded he even represented Hampton Fancher, and hired the writer for much less than what would once have been his magisterial quote. Not only was Hampton cheap, relatively speaking, but it got Beau off her phone sheet for a bit, while they were awaiting a script. It was easy, done in the time it would've taken her to get from her appointment back to the office This was the kind of minor deal she could do without Markhamson lifting his eyebrows. Development costs. There were seventy-five projects on her division's slate alone.

"It's good." The script came in and Emily read it. She called Beau up on a Monday morning, first thing. "It's—well, intriguing."

October 2004. Beau heard this and began laughing.

"You've got the coverage right there, don't you? Hampton's script is fantastic."

"It's very good." Emily sipped green tea. "Very smart." What the reader's report actually said was that while Fancher's script had many of the same problems the novel did—it was too psychedelic, a bit fraught with religious crises and a deranged mysticism—it was also forceful and compelling. A visionary director, like David Fincher or Katheryn Bigelow—both favorites of Markhamson's, she knew—would be perfect.

"Smart!" Beau clapped his hands, on the other end of the phone. "You of all people calling my project smart."

"In the old days, you wouldn't have even thought that was a compliment."

He guffawed. Yes, yes, he was being a kiss-ass, but there was life in the old guy yet.

"Helen Mirren."

"Let's not get ahead of ourselves, Beau."

"It's not getting ahead," my father said. "She wants to do it. I saw her the other night, and I gave her the script. We'd have to make Geraldine a little older, but so what?"

Emily rocked back in her chair. David Markhamson prowled by her office at that very moment. Strange to see him wandering around on her floor. He seemed as if he were looking for something, misplaced glasses or wallet. Money, probably. Columbia Vita wasn't exactly having a great year.

"I like Helen."

Indeed, neither this division nor Sony Classics was doing what was wanted. Markhamson might love Emily's ideas, but Vita had produced no Godzillas, no Full Montys. Why did studios have specialty arms, again?

"I like her too," my father barked. "Let's go win an Oscar. Let's get a bunch of them."

Emily stared at David's back. He hunched his shoulders like the weight of the world sat upon them, a posture at odds with his dry, nimble, English manner. He dressed like a play-by-play man, blue blazer and a rep tie.

"I'll call you later," Emily said. She wasn't really in the mood for Beau's motivational speaking. "I think we might have something here, Beau, I honestly do."

"David." Unfortunately for Beau, he took Emily's optimism at face value. At a restaurant at the bottom of Santa Monica Canyon, not so very long after this, he spotted David Markhamson and his wife having dinner with another couple. He came over and placed his hand upon the magnate's shoulder. "I'm so excited about our baby."

"B—" David Markhamson had met the fat man repeatedly, but could never remember his name "Hello."

"Bhello, yourself," Beau said. He was drunk, weaving a little on his feet. Spielberg, Kidman, Q-Tip. All were there, enjoying their public privacy in the candle-studded darkness of Giorgio Baldi, a small room not fifty yards from the sand. "How are things?"

Markhamson smiled tautly. Beau winked. He just wanted to be seen seeing Markhamson, and be greeted in return. A bit of public performance that was all it would take to confirm his status, after which he could go back to his dinner in peace.

"Natalya." Beau reached over and squeezed David's wife's fingertips, briefly. She moued at him, the way she would have at any other Horrible Man. "Nice to see you, too."

This should've been the end of it. Everything good that might come of this, which wasn't much, had already been accomplished. He'd reminded David that he existed, broken the surface of the mogul's consciousness, and that was enough. The owner fluttered by and dropped off a plate of airy, sugar-dusted, Italianate cookies. Beau, in his tipsiness, reached out and took one.

"I'm so excited about this picture," he said, "I can hardly sleep at night."

"Which picture?"

"A Hall of Mirrors."

"Ah." Markhamson dabbed his lips with a napkin. He did this reflexively: Beau had white sugar mussing the corner of his mouth. "Right."

He turned back to his companions. Beau shambled over to his own table, where Patricia was waiting. He hadn't really expected Markhamson to know the script. It was almost, not quite, in preproduction yet, listed on Emily's development memos as Untitled Helen Mirren Project. Solid enough. But this was the first Markhamson had heard of any *Hall of Mirrors*.

"How'd that go?" Patricia smiled as Beau sat, turning her wineglass between her palms. He plopped down in front of his langoustines and nebbiolo and grunted.

"Great," he said. Exactly like an animal peeing on a tree: just a little reminder, so David would know the movie was out there. "Perfect, in fact."

Of course, sometimes it's much better for the other guy to forget. David called Emily White up the next morning.

"What the hell is *A Hall of Mirrors*?"

"It's Helen Mirren and Johnny Depp," Emily said. It was 9:15 AM, and she was just getting in. Since when did he call this early? "Probably Johnny Depp—"

"I mean where did it come from?"

She took a deep breath and told him. Fingers splaying along the glassy black edge of her desk.

"I'd like to read it," he said. "Send it up."

She did. The script wasn't an embarrassment—a bad movie could be, but a good script, however handicapped by its own highbrow intelligence, humiliated no one. Hampton's new draft might be a little abstruse, but with that cast? It was at the very least defensible, she told herself.

"I hate it."

"What?" She was back on the phone with Markhamson so soon she had to remember, in fact, what he was talking about. She'd just messengered it upstairs three hours ago. He'd never read anything this fast. "You hate what?"

"*A Hall of Mirrors*, Em. It's impenetrable."

"It's—"

The script might've been defensible, but it was funny how a powerful man's hatred of Beau Rosenwald could trump everything. Maybe he reminded them too much of who they were, that they could be everything except beautiful. It was funny, also, how "impenetrable" the movie business could be, Emily reckoned. You were always on the phone, always dealing in your head with people who weren't *there*, whose force was often illusory. David Markhamson was two floors, and absolute worlds, away from her. He operated according to a different system of morality and intention, answered to an alternate hierarchy of need.

"—it's complicated, sure," Emily said, "but so are, um, lots of things. *Chinatown*, or *Blade Runner*, or, uh—"

Your own reality remained doubtful also. Emily White kept that feeling, that strange chimerical feeling that deep down—*deep down*—she might not even really exist, that she might be just a figment of a larger human dream.

"We're not making fucking *Chinatown*, Em. We're not making this either."

He slammed down the phone, too analog and old to use a headset, himself. This was the only time she'd ever heard David lose his temper, all because Beau Rosenwald annoyed him more than the script itself. The project was dead. There wasn't any recourse.

It almost surprised her, to feel no regret. She slipped off her shoes and twisted slowly in her chair, rocking in her office's slash of silence.

"Call Beau," she yelled to her assistant. "If you can't get him now, just keep trying!"

XV

SO MUCH FOR a night's sleep. Espresso that late didn't agree with Beau: nothing did, at seventy-two years old, although the amazing thing was how robust he was still. He'd live to be eighty, he'd live to be *ninety*, the way he felt. His mind was crisp, and he remembered everything—everyone while his stout body remained as unexpectedly quick as it was ten years ago. The restaurant owner's face kept him up, because that man who'd brought Markhamson his cookies *was* Abe Waxmorton. He had the same convex eyes, the same prow-like nose and brownish complexion. You lived long enough and they just started coming back, all those people. Beau was older now than Waxmorton had ever been while working, older by far than Abe had been when Beau came into his office, long ago, and thought the great man was ancient. "Long ago"? It was yesterday; no time had elapsed. Everything that had happened in between made that day seem no farther away than anything else.

"Hello?" He was outside, still groggy as he took the puppy for her afternoon walk. Beau missed his mother, he missed his father. If only he'd had the sense to do that while the old bastard was alive. "Who's this?"

"Beau? It's Emily White."

"Emily! Sweet girl!" Cell phone pressed to his ear, he picked up his stride. "How's our baby?"

"Our baby's not good, Beau."

He strolled down Fifteenth Street behind the dog, watching her chocolate form frisk along new-seeded lawns that were an almost toxic green. Sunlight warmed his hands, cutting through the gray branches of the coral trees above.

"Yeah? I saw Markhamson last night and he seemed fine."

"He read the script."

"What?" The puppy squatted. Beau rolled a plastic bag onto his hand.

"He read it this morning. He asked me to messenger it to him."

"Uh-huh."

"He hates it." A faint sibilance trailed her voice, she was in her car and there were little cuts and chops as she spoke. "He hates the fucking script, Beau."

He stopped, bending down to receive the dog's large and fragrant offering, turning the bag inside out and holding his breath. "Um, OK—"

"The project's done," she said. "Even you understand that, right? It's done."

"I could take it elsewhere."

"You could. Assuming you could pay all the turnaround costs."

"So? That's not a problem for me."

Standing in the sun, clutching a bag filled with soft turds and a leash, Beau summoned himself again. What did he have, besides money and nonsense? What does anyone ever have? Time? Not much of it.

"That's not a problem," Emily said. Sun baked his face; the air smelled of fertilizer but also of sea breeze, lemon trees, and a little bit of exhaust. He loved it here. Amazing he'd ever lived anywhere else. "But David will have to let it go."

"Why wouldn't he? He hates the project."

"He hates *you*, Beau."

"Lots of people hate me. When did that ever get in the way of doing business?"

"Beau." Emily took a deep breath. "He wants your failure. Your pain makes him glad. If you want to play tug-of-war with Sony, go ahead. But I ought never to have encouraged you. I should never have bought this idiotic project in the first place."

She hung up, without an additional word. She left him standing where he'd lived now for fifteen years, on those blocks north of Montana Avenue where every other building belonged to somebody: to Steve Jobs's sister, to the head of television at Endeavor, to the lawyer at Jones Day who had just successfully defended ADM against a discrimination suit. People who—Beau felt it now—attained to a greater relevance than he did. They were more current, if not more enduring. Beau felt as if he'd just been slopped off the face of the earth.

It was quiet just now, quieter than he'd supposed. The screaming would start later, both within himself and outside. A breeze picked up. A little bit of traffic hissed along Montana, three blocks away. He watched the dog, who'd gotten tangled, wind her way clockwise around a tree until her leash came free. She padded over and looked up at him. He stared at her, stricken.

"Come," he said. *Dog.* He snapped his fingers. "C'mon!"

"Em—"

"Huh?" She was dashing past her assistant, in whatever hurry she was always in these days. The one that kept her from recognizing the inevitable, as it applied to her too.

"Your five o'clock called. The agent said he was going to be a little late."

"Fine. Did Beau call?"

The assistant, who reminded Emily of herself if she'd been red-headed and unpretty, looked up from her desk. "Didn't you just have him in the car?"

Emily shivered. She'd looked forward, all this time, to getting rid of him, and now that he was gone, did she actually miss him?

"Never mind."

Cam bent to answer the phone. This homely, freckled girl who'd been to Yale, who was so smart—they were all smart, these people behind such stupid movies—and so afraid of her, though Emily had never so much as raised her voice in Cam's direction.

Emily went inside, took off her dark jacket, and waited for her next appointment. The lot was calm now, the sudden emptiness of late afternoon. She sat in her chair, dodged a few calls, and mostly waited, waited and waited for Beau to call her back. He never did.

"Em?" Cam's voice crackled over the speaker. "Your appointment's here."

She'd forgotten who this was, some writer Byron Lawrence had been starting to sell her last week when she'd needed to leap off and take another call. *Have your office set a meeting*, she'd told him, trusting the agent's taste. She'd never even learned the writer's name, even when Byron had said, *You might know him already. He's—*

Never mind. How many writers did she have to know these days anyway, besides the ones who were A-listers? That's what your executives were for. She rocked back in her chair and then looked up, startled, when the appointment came in.

"Hello, Em," I said. For indeed, the writer was me. "Long time no see."

"Nate?" Her face went slack with astonishment, as if *I* were the figment, and not she. "My God, of all people. You're the last person on earth I would ever have expected to see!"

PART FIVE: **MARLOW/E**

I

OH, THAT I had the indictment written by my adversary! These words, from the Book of Job, popped absurdly into my head. *I would approach her like a prince.*

"Hi, Em." I smiled. "It's great to see you too."

If ever I had an enemy, or a friend or a mirror, it was Emily White. But as I approached her, in the spring of 2005, I was glowing. No longer an executive, I was on top of the world myself.

"You look fantastic." She shook her head, as if to dispel the apparition I might've been. She pushed up out of her chair.

"Thanks."

She crossed over to me, and we sat down. It was difficult to tell how much of the ritualized flattery we were engaged in was insincere. None of it, possibly.

"I talked to your father earlier." She took the power seat, while I curled up in the far corner of her couch, twisted the top off my bottled water.

"How's he?"

"He's fine." She blinked. "Irrepressible."

This might've been true, for all I knew. Just then, Beau and I didn't talk much. There were reasons for this. One was that he was still mad at me over something I'd failed to mention to him in a timely fashion. Another was my relative success. Incredible as it sounds, there was a time, however brief, when I finally eclipsed him in Hollywood, a moment when I was hot and he was old. Because I hadn't spoken to him lately I knew there was a movie that he'd been trying to get off the ground, but this was all.

"How's your brother?"

I leaned back. This was me at thirty-seven, well paid and expensive, in my Prada shoes and my black cashmere blazer. I could see my face reflected in her glass tabletop: hair thinning, but still handsome—a long, blond, Scandinavian oval. But even after all this time, I lingered a bit in Severin's shadow.

"He's . . . OK."

"OK?" Emily laughed. "Everything I read about him makes it sound a lot better than that."

"Yeah." I smiled tautly. "It does sound better than that."

Severin had won the National Book Critics Circle Award in 1999, yes. Ben Stiller had optioned *Peckerhead*, and after his last book, *Thirsty People*, my brother had received a MacArthur Fellowship. I suppose it was difficult for some people to imagine things were not so easy as they appeared. It was certainly difficult for me.

"What is it?" she said.

I'd come here to pitch at my agent's behest. I wasn't here for Beau, and I wasn't here to talk about my brother either: I had my own business to attend to. Right after I left Fox, my Chandler script had been resurrected, optioned by Malpaso. I'd done a quick adaptation of Shirley Hazzard's novel *The Bay of Noon* for Sydney Pollack and Anthony Minghella, then sold a pitch to Warner for half a million dollars. I wasn't here for my family.

"I can't talk about it."

"Why not?"

Maybe Emily White *was* my family. She was almost my father's daughter, as I was almost his son. I watched her there, as pale and cool and corporate and powerful as I was bohemian and burning. We were the inheritors of this city, and somehow, overnight, I'd managed to become an adult. But as I watched her, those subtle flaws that still clung to her body—the hollows of sleeplessness under her eyes, the ounces of baby fat that strained her blouse as she bent forward to grab her bottle of Fiji—made me believe in her. I had to confess.

II

"**WHAT THE FUCK** is wrong with him?"

"What d'you mean?" Little Will turned to me, as we crawled along the BQE. "D'you mean philosophically?"

"Philosophically, psychologically," I said. "What's *wrong*?"

Will shook his head. That same blocky, handsome, opaque face I'd known all my life, thirty years and change, only now middle-aged. You could see it in the way his features had clustered together a bit, like those of a fighter who'd been hit one too many times. There was an intimation of crow's-feet along the temples.

"I don't know, man." He swept his gaze back toward the Jackson Heights traffic and twilight. I'd just come off a plane. It was early in 2003, and everything—the branches, the buildings and birds—seemed sharp, crisp, and articulate in the cold golden sun. He drove, and I watched his profile: the hair cut short, the tortoiseshell glasses he now wore. All of us had aged, both slowly and suddenly it seemed. When exactly did *Will* become the responsible one? "You never thought about doing it yourself?"

"No." I suppose this wasn't true, but it had been awhile. "Maybe when I was a teenager."

"No?"

Behind the wheel, he relaxed, drove with his palm. The backseat was empty, but you could see the apparatus of his life back there: booster seat, juice box, a faint, diaperish whiff of something, excrement and putty.

"*You* don't think of it," I said. "You have a kid."

Williams just smiled, turned up the radio a bit. Black Sabbath's "Planet Caravan" rumbled.

(You know what I told Emily? Everything. Because I had to tell her, and because a certain level of detail was my coin, all I had. So I told her about my visit to Brooklyn, some eighteen months earlier, and I told her about Severin, the things I hadn't even been able to tell Beau.)

"Having a kid doesn't change that much," Will said. "But certain things come off the table."

"Certain things," I said. "Like suicide."

How long had I known Severin and Little Will? Long enough for us to have lived through everything, the countless emergencies that had already defined us. Will's dad's disappearance, his own overdose. How many things had to happen?

"Explain it to me again," I said. I felt like I was always asking this. "What—"

"Nate," Williams exhaled. "I don't *know*, y'know? I don't know."

I studied him. This wasn't amnesia: it was ignorance.

"He took pills," I said.

"Yes."

"How many?"

He shrugged, and exhaled again. His soft breath suggested there might even have been some sort of pleasure in it, that merely surviving long enough to turn thirty-five meant that Sev deserved pretend dying, all the love and appreciation it would bring.

"Enough."

"Enough for what?"

"Enough. Enough that he was unconscious when I got there."

It's not like I'd never wondered before about my brother, how he carried all that weight without ever seeming to show it. Like Little Will, he had his demons, and he'd had even less opportunity to master them, perhaps. It was why the two of them were so close. But at the same time, I knew. Severin's wife had left him. And so he'd swallowed just enough pills to feel appreciated. This wasn't a real attempt, I could feel it, as we chugged along the BQE on our way to get me situated before we could visit Sev at the hospital.

Unless I was wrong. For what's realer, in the mind of an aspiring suicide, than to make the effort and live?

Little Will brought me to Severin's apartment in Boerum Hill, where I would stay. I hadn't talked to Severin since he landed in the hospital. I hadn't talked to anyone. Twenty-four hours before, Little Will had called me and I'd hopped on a plane. When Sev and I spoke last, less than a week ago, he'd seemed fine. Better than fine. I was sitting in our father's study after Beau had had me to lunch. While my brother and I talked I'd found, on Beau's desk, an old business card that read *David J. Byrne, Private Investigator*, listing an 818 telephone number. Why would our father need a PI? And why would he choose one with that ridiculously familiar name? The card was ancient, torn and yellow. Severin thought it was pretty amusing too, recalling a night when Beau had given the two of us passes to see Talking Heads at the Pantages Theater, where Jonathan Demme was filming them. Only then (and it would've been right after I spoke with him, more or less, after we'd shared our laughter on the phone) he took a handful of Vicodin. That's all I knew. He was still in the hospital, and of course, since Little Will had called, I'd told no one. Sometimes I felt we were all still living through that original nightmare we'd shared at Cedars-Sinai, where Will kept repeating the same words after his OD. Did things *ever* change, or did history just run in a loop, ad infinitum?

"Did he seem distraught?"

"Distraught?" Williams turned from Sev's dresser, where he was handling one of my brother's old baseball cards, which lay out by itself, free of its polypropylene sleeve. "Not really. No."

His voice echoed, carried its own repetition within the shell of my brother's apartment. The place felt alarmingly empty, like a house that had been burgled or at which the movers never arrived. The house of a squatting intellectual. But it had always been that way. Severin was never much for "stuff."

"Not really," Will repeated. We were in the guest room, which had once been an office—either Severin's or Lexy's—but now held a rickety twin bed and a dresser and a narrow bookshelf stocked with only his own books in various translations and hers: she'd published two.

"I didn't think so either. He seemed the same."

I set my duffel bag down at the foot of the bed. And then, to calm myself, I rambled the rest of the apartment. It was two stories and big, of a size you could apparently afford to buy even in Cobble Hill when you'd won a major award and had a little help with the down payment. The rooms were cavernous and filled, when at all, mostly with books, the odd DVD. There were no tables or rugs, just filtered twilight. The bedroom had a bed in it. Severin's battered black Chuck Taylors lay toppled in a corner; a laptop sat upon the desk, its cursor still blinking on an empty document, I saw when I swiped the track pad. I stared at the blank page. Finally, I strolled back to the guest room.

"It doesn't seem like anything's wrong."

"What d'you mean?" Will was still standing next to the dresser where he'd put the baseball card down. Like a docent in a museum or a palace guard, he waited.

"I mean," I swept my arm toward the room, the shelves, the incredibly light furnishings with which my brother chose to live. "It's all the same."

"Yeah." Will might've humored me, the way he and Severin both had so often done, but instead he shrugged. "It's always the same."

He knew what I meant. I meant that whatever we did, whatever we lived through, it was the same. Severin, the success. Or Sev, suicide. They weren't any different, the signifiers clustered maybe five degrees apart, until it was almost impossible to tell ecstasy from despair. I came over to where Will was standing, next to a picture of Lexy in a polka-dot sundress. Blonde and sloe-eyed, the same image that showed on the back of her first book, *Disappearer*. I'd envied my brother so many things, not least this. I stared at her lithe and inscrutable form, and at the baseball card, some goony seventies Met with heavy eyebrows and long sideburns. Wondering just what I was missing, myself, what might have driven Severin to act out his unhappiness.

III

"HEY, FELLAS." Incredibly, Severin was chipper when he greeted me the next day. Little Will and Will's wife, Hermione, and their son and I all went to see him. Hermione and the boy, who was four, waited outside while Little Will and I went in to find my brother slippered and relaxed, dressed in street clothes. "What it is?"

"What it is?" I crossed the room to where he was standing at the window, gazing idly at the glass that was reinforced with chicken wire, but I couldn't stay mad. I put my arms around him and I kissed the top of his head. "What did you do?"

He shrugged, like it was no big deal. Perhaps it wasn't a big deal. I held him for as long as I could and then I let him go. He stayed there with his hands in his pockets. There was a narrow regulation bed behind him, and here we were at the Brooklyn Hospital Center, but there was no sense of strict confinement or emergency. Severin wore jeans and a rumpled canary yellow shirt. The old horn-rimmed glasses, his knowing and wise look. The same cool, rooster-ish manner he'd always had.

"You ever break up with a girl, Nate?"

"Sure." The question was rhetorical: I'd been through a divorce of my own, as he well knew, and yet I'd never swallowed pills to chase the experience. But neither had he, he seemed to be telling me. "Why?"

Little Will went outside, to join his wife and son and to leave us to it.

"Williams and I had a fight," he said, not answering my question.

"What does that have to do with your being here?"

I couldn't help but watch him closely, studying the sharp, almost avian lines of his face. We perched at the window, in the bleached, grayish light of the waning winter. Outside, it was in the fifties, feinting at spring.

"You don't know anything," Severin said. "Do you?"

"No." I didn't know what he was talking about, surely. "I don't."

His eyes gleamed and his pupils widened just a bit, the way they used to when we were young and high and he was about to speak and blow my mind. He opened his mouth, but then seemed to think better of it. He sighed. "Does Dad know?"

"I didn't tell him."

"That's good. I guess he'll have to find out eventually, maybe."

"Maybe." I looked him up and down. "Do they keep you?"

"No." He slipped his hands back into his pockets. "I've been here three days. I can go."

"That's it?"

Little Will and his son and wife were in the hall, which teemed with visitors, and I could hear Will say to his son, *No, Danny, don't touch that!*

"They gave me the name of a psychiatrist. But I don't need one."

"What are you talking about? We're in a hospital ward, dude."

"I already have one. Nate, it wasn't very many pills."

"Define 'not very many.'"

"Fewer than it would take to stun a rhinoceros. Or Dad."

I laughed. How could I not? Once more, I didn't have enough information. I didn't know what he was reacting to, or against: the loss of a wife or of a mother or of a sister—or if this was simply another exercise in egotism, as also seemed possible. He was, after all, our father's son. Like Beau, he had his own way of turning suffering into theater.

"Hey!" Little Will barged in, giving chase to his son, who came flailing recklessly toward Severin. "Sorry about that!"

I just didn't know. Not for the first time, I wanted to beg my brother to let me in. But Sev only looked down as Danny caromed off the bed and into his leg.

"It's OK." He bent and picked up Little Will's son, hoisted him with a gesture that looked perfectly natural, for all the world like he was born to be a dad, and this was merely another tender family outing. "Hey, buddy. Hey!"

Hermione came in. She was a redhead, freckled and big-boned and pretty but also the littlest bit mannish. Her eyes were blue, and it was only the size of her frame that made her anything but ravishing. She'd been Will's rescuer, pacing him through hour after hour of memory games, cognitive exercises. Daniel, their son, was a ringer for the elder Will even at this age: he had his grandfather's ginger coloring, his foxy features.

"I'm sorry, Severin." She had a posh English accent, thick enough that it was startling. I couldn't help thinking of the war between our fathers, Williams's and mine. Albert Finney in a hotel bar.

"It's all right." Sev braced his head against Danny's, lay his forehead against the little boy's so the two looked at each other through his glasses. He bounced Will's son almost imperceptibly in his arms. "No problem."

We waited a moment like that. Someday, maybe, I'd understand my brother's tenderness, where it came from. Finally, he put Danny down.

"I can go," he said, indicating his hospital room. "They told me today I can go if I want."

Later, Severin and I were alone.

"I'm OK," he said, as we picked through his apartment together. "Really."

"Really? You act like everything is hunky-dory, Sev. This morning you were in a psych ward."

It wasn't as simple as all that, of course. There'd been an exit interview, and then the doctors wanted to talk to *me*, as Severin's brother, to ascertain my opinion of his mental health. (As they did, I couldn't help but picture Beau. Was *he* crazy? Was I?) But they let Severin sign himself out, even so, and I would've done the same. I was haunted by the image of him holding Little Will's son.

"You never tell me anything," I said. "You're a fucking Swiss vault of secrecy."

"That's not true," he said. "You don't listen. You don't take the cues."

"What cues are those?"

We moved through the gloom of the apartment, flicking on various lights. At Severin's insistence I would leave the day after tomorrow.

"Anything, everything." He spoke with an agitation that seemed more directed at me than at anything else, as if the biggest problem were me, harrying him. "You just don't know what it's like."

"What what's like? Being divorced? I know what that's like. Being Dad's spawn? What the hell's bothering you?"

He just snorted, like a horse, like our father, as if I should understand by osmosis what the trouble was.

"What were you and Little Will fighting about?" I said.

"What?" He turned now to face me. Maybe I *did* take the cues, after all. Maybe I knew something of our shared burden, what had eluded me so far.

"You said you and Little Will were fighting. What about?"

We'd stopped in the room where I was staying, the little one down the hall that had been Lexy's office, and would've been a child's room had they managed to have one. Just another heartbreak in a life that was as full of them as any other.

"It was about something I was writing. Trying to write."

"Oh?"

We stood by the dresser, not quite touching but next to each other. For a moment I thought about all the rooms we'd been in, the different relations we'd shared inside them: friends, siblings, competitors. How through all these times we'd lived under one sign, even before we knew it. The curtains were drawn, and so we stood in an artificial darkness. I looked down at the baseball card. DUFFY DYER.

"Hey, remember Milt Schildkraut?" I scrutinized Dyer's anemic stat line.

"What?" Severin glanced down, too. "Course I do. Why?"

"The Mets card reminded me."

Right. As did many things, really. So much time had passed, you'd think American Dream Machine might've been a distant memory, not even a very interesting one, necessarily. Yet somehow it kept a nearly occult grip on all of us, an unaccountable power.

"D-Duffy Dyer." Severin imitated Milt's stutter precisely. "Number of total bases in '73? Severin!"

I laughed. That was him, the numbers guy. He used to quiz us both on such things. Severin stared, his eyes narrowing behind the glasses. There was a mirror above the dresser, and both of us were caught in it, but he was somewhere else, I could see.

"What on earth made you think of him?" Sev muttered again.

IV

I DIDN'T FIND out precisely what was haunting us for a while. Just as I didn't yet discover what Severin might've been writing before he went into the hospital. I flew back to LA, and I didn't worry about him. That sounds callous, perhaps, but I didn't have to worry. I knew Sev well enough to be sure he'd pick himself up and put it all back together. I'd seen him do it before, and like many writers, he seemed to thrive on chaos. Like me, maybe. I had my own life, a career and its tangles, to attend to. But maybe all that competition that had festered during the early years—he, the real son; I, the pretender—had spilled finally into our adult lives, and so I turned my back on him. Maybe I was tired of trying to jimmy the lock on his skull. Or maybe the experience with Little Will and his overdose had broken us, long ago. I wouldn't say I loved Severin any less since then—of course I didn't. But. But, but, but.

"Nate!" (Maybe he and I were like my father and Williams, too, blinded by a rivalrous love.) "Hey, you little fucker!"

My phone rang, a good while after I returned to Los Angeles, and there was only one person on earth who could wring so much tone from that epithet, who could fill it with such stunning portions of both affection and rage.

"Beau." I never could quite call him "Dad." "What's going on?"

This was six weeks after I came home. I'd already forgotten, or at least compartmentalized, Severin's accident. I listened for a moment to the raspy stew of our father's breathing.

"What is it?" I said.

I waited, but he just kept me listening to his accusatory silence, let me marinate in shame. I was in my home office, which was like Severin's but glitzier: it had a bigger Mac screen to stare at, bigger shelves on my walls that were stacked higher with different kinds of books. Ones on film, mostly, or novels I could adapt. Lots of Chandler arcana and Black Lizard spines. I'd found my niche. Not quite what I'd expected, but with it I'd been able to buy a house in West Adams.

"Aren't you gonna say something?"

I could feel Beau's fury on the other side, the full force of his rage. Now I knew what he was like when he wasn't on your side in business, how he could bleed concession straight out of you.

"Uh," I said. I brought my fingers to the bridge of my nose and squeezed. I blinked and stared through French doors at a sun-dappled patch of yard. "I was going to tell—"

"Bull. Shit," he said. Two words. "Bullshit, Nathaniel. D'you know who I am? Do you know *why* it would be important to me to know if my son was in trouble?"

He spoke with such venom, such purity of disgust. *I* wasn't a son to know about, in this respect.

"I do." I closed my eyes and thought of Kate. "Of course I do."

"Then why, Nate?" All of a sudden I heard his voice crack. "Why wouldn't you *tell* me?"

What a bully! He could come at me with his anger, and then manipulate me with tears. I was in a perfect place, this small Craftsman house I had purchased just south and east of the Sony lot where the last fifteen years of his life had played themselves out.

"I don't know."

I could read the spines of the David Goodis novels on my own shelves. Outside, there was a dazzling sky. I had a lawn, a hedge of purple pitcher sage. I watched a young couple walk a pit bull on a leash. Sunlight sheared across their broad, handsome faces, and only the exposure of the street, its openness and the flatness of the neighborhood around it, reminded me this place had recently been a ghetto.

"Nate," Beau murmured. "I'm not mad."

Only people who were mad ever said that. But I know why he modulated his temper now.

"It's OK." After Sev, after Kate, who was left? "I'm sorry I didn't tell you, Beau. I'm sorry."

Just me, to spare him in his infinite loneliness: I'd be all that remained to extend his line.

It got weirder. A lot weirder. Because after Beau and I made up, and after I discovered it was Little Will who'd told him what happened (Will, I think, felt obligated: in many respects our dad had looked after *him*, growing up, and even after the elder Williams's death, although the two partners were sundered, Beau kept an eye on him, went to see him in rehab and so on), Severin came out for a visit. This was almost a year later, in the spring of 2004. It wasn't specifically to see me: he was scheduled to give a reading at the Hammer Museum.

"Hey." I picked him up at LAX, reached over to unlock the passenger-side door so he could climb in. "No Beau? No limo?"

"Nope." He folded himself into my passenger seat. "He's coming to the reading."

I pulled away from the curb, drifting across four lanes of traffic. "I would've thought he'd be eager to see you."

"He is. He thinks I'm coming tomorrow."

"Ah." I gunned it, out from below the overpass into sunlight, toward the lane that would lead us out to Century Boulevard. "Why'd you fly early?"

What happened next startled me. In fact it shook me in a way few things—maybe a couple of others, maybe only one, since—ever have. We drove to his hotel. He wouldn't say why.

"I want to show you something."

"What?"

He wouldn't tell me, as we glided along the 405 to the 101 into Hollywood, into the same neighborhood we'd lived in all those years ago, with our crappy apartments and video store jobs, the sweltering depths of the city away from the beach.

"I want you to meet somebody."

"Who? You've got a new honey?"

We rode down Franklin, past his old place. My own, the old Hobart Arms, was farther east, behind us.

"Nope. It's more important than that."

God knows, I think I presumed it would be someone odd, esoteric, interesting: Philip K. Dick's widow, Hal Ashby's sister, Thomas Mann's niece. One of those people who were in touch with my brother's tastes and specialties.

"You have to promise me." He reached over and tapped my shoulder. "This is just for you, Nate. You can never tell Dad."

"What is it? Worse than a fistful of Vicodin?" My engine roared. I was driving a noisy car, a BMW M3, a real asshole machine. I suppose I was exaggerating my characteristics, being more Hollywood than Severin could ever dream, to compensate. "I won't tell him."

"You can't."

"What's he ever going to care about Fitzgerald's mistress's kid?" I said. "Dad doesn't know who any of the real people on this planet actually are."

We pulled up, at last, at the Roosevelt. It was a typical place for my brother to stay: unfashionable, august, a little decrepit, but also full of history. D. W. Griffith's ghost rode the elevators, they said. Montgomery Clift lived in one of the rooms upstairs, while he was filming *From Here to Eternity*.

I reeled after Severin, chasing him across the lobby. Whatever he was going to show me had its urgency: *It's because I love you, Nate*. He didn't even bother to check in as a guest. The moment I tossed my keys to the valet he just turned and started trotting straight up the stairs toward the bar.

"Aren't you gonna bring your bag to your room?"

He didn't say anything. Sev traveled light, the way he lived, with just a laptop and a carry-on. He remained, in those days, so purely identifiable as his younger self, but this was the last time I'd ever recognize him as the person I'd thought I'd known. A distinct trace of early silver shimmered at his temples. But otherwise? The same nerdy kid turned hipster novelist. He was the latter even when he was still just the former.

We charged across the open floor of the upstairs bar, which seemed completely empty at one o'clock in the afternoon. A tall woman occupied one of the far couches, so slender in profile I almost didn't see her. In the room's ill-lit, Gothic coolness, she was just a Brancusi bird, a long and pale mote with copper-colored hair, absorbed in her book. Only when we approached did I realize she was our target, as she looked up and recognized Severin.

"Hello, darling."

"Mom!"

It took me a minute to know what to think. It took me several, in fact, while she stood up and kissed him, on both cheeks, I noticed, and then turned to me.

"You must be Nate."

"I . . . yes, I suppose I must be. Severin." I looked at my brother. "Who is this person?"

Rachel burst out laughing. "He has his father's obtuseness," she said to Sev. "But *he* doesn't look like Beau either."

The laughter. That was part of what convinced me, part of what rendered this entire ghostly encounter persuasive. The Roosevelt, with its blood-colored tile and its doomy sconces, its crypt-light in midafternoon, only enhanced its uncanniness.

"I wanted you to know," Severin said. "I needed you to."

You needed me to know what? I almost said, because I was struck once more by how life was most real when it was least plausible, when it was more like the movies than it was like itself.

"You thought I was dead," Rachel said.

"No." That was what made it so strange. I'd thought nothing: that she was gone, but also alive. Now that she was in front of me, somehow, it was like she'd been there the whole time. "Does, uh, our father . . . "

She shook her head. Severin said, "No, Nate. That's what I meant. You can't *ever* tell him."

"OK." We sat next to each other, I in an armchair while the two of them collapsed on a leather couch. "OK."

They really did look alike, although she was pushing seventy. The bevels and angles of her face were still elegant, recognizably Severin's, and she was warmer than I had imagined: something about the S-curve of her body as she pulled up on the couch and opened her posture toward her son. Her hair was red, dyed that vivid, electrical color it had held when she was younger, which I'd seen in photographs. Only when you got up close could you see the reticulations of age, the crinkling of her fair skin. In a room like this, she did pretty well.

"You're wondering." She sat next to Severin, and I could tell they'd been in touch a long time. This wasn't anything new. "You're wanting to know where I've been."

The strangeness really wasn't in her reappearance. It was in how easily Severin accepted her absence, how comfortable he seemed when she told me. Yes, she explained, she'd disappeared from his life—and from Beau's—around the time of Kate's death. She couldn't stand our father, which I understood—she blamed him for everything—and so she unplugged completely, left her business and moved west. She'd been wanting to get out of the agency business anyway. For a while she had a bookstore in Boulder, then she worked at the Shakespeare Festival in Ashland, Oregon. Then Portland, where she was, still.

"I hated everything."

"Everything?"

It was Severin's laughter, the casual way he teased her from his place on the couch, I couldn't figure out.

"No, not everything." *Not you.* "Of course not."

Well, what did I know? I'd spent my life resenting people who were close to me (Severin, Beau) or not close enough (Beau, Severin). What did I *know*?

"Why now?" I asked Rachel, as soon as Sev had gotten up to use the bathroom, because I knew he'd never tell me. "If you guys have been in touch since he was a teenager, why would Severin introduce us now?"

Beau had never known. He probably still thought Rachel was dead, even as Severin had visited his mother right under his father's nose all the way through high school. (*You still writing those letters, Sev? Still in touch with that girl up north?*) It didn't make sense, given how secretive my brother always was with me, that he would reveal it unprompted. At the same time, I understood how important it was that Beau never discover. It would've compromised everything, had he known.

"Severin loves you."

"Really? He has a funny way of showing it, sometimes."

But maybe I shouldn't have taken it personally. Maybe I should never even have doubted. We were drinking martinis in the early afternoon. I was on my second, Rachel nursing her third. It didn't seem to faze her. Slender as she was, she could really hold her liquor.

"This is his way."

I felt light-headed. Drunk, I suppose, on the power of having my ignorance rescinded.

"I'm happy to meet you," I said. Foolishly. As if this were all my brother was trying to show me. Like he didn't have one more play up his sleeve.

The next night, Severin read at the Hammer. Afterward, he and I went out.

"Where to?"

We were trawling aimlessly toward Hollywood, not ready to go back to his hotel, basking in the intimacy we'd located that afternoon. Good times had descended between us the only way they ever seemed to in our adult lives, seemingly by accident. Beau had been at the reading, but Rachel had not.

"Dresden?" *Too far. Too ancient, again, in 2004.* We were too old to be cruising for yesterday's thrills, especially when yesterday's thrills were themselves an effort to catch up with ones that were already gone almost before we were born.

"Hamlet," Severin said. "Let's go to the Hamlet on Sunset."

That's how long it had been. The long-ago new had become nouveau-old once more. I tilted the Beamer up toward the Strip.

"Think we'll get Cloonage?"

"Wrong night," Severin said. "Wrong era."

Indeed. But I didn't want to ruin anything: this was a rare moment when I felt close to my brother, close in the way we used to be, without any drug overdoses or sibling arguments in play. He'd shown me something wholly private (Little Will didn't know about Sev's mother either), and I was touched by that. So?

We pulled over on Fountain. We smoked a little weed in the shadow of a coniferous tree, traffic whizzing past as we handed a joint back and forth in the car. It wasn't like us anymore, and I had a few misgivings about sharing dope with my brother this late in our existence, given how our most catastrophic adventures seemed to involve altered states, but so what? We were free for the moment. It wasn't even eleven o'clock.

"Yeah," I croaked, as I turned the key in the ignition finally and we banked up toward Sunset at Crescent Heights. *Why not be baked?* "It's not like today could get weirder."

But as we floated along the Strip, it did. Laugh Factory. Greenblatt's. All the old places were there, even if they'd changed identities, even if their doormen were bigger or the sandwiches they served were smaller than they had once been. The casual ballooning of perspective, too, the way some things shrivel with age, the way the palaces of childhood prove themselves to be shacks. Yet they were the same, the very rooms in which we'd wasted so many nights in our twenties, and where Beau and his rat pack had done as much for themselves.

Memories. I couldn't help it if my life was guided by them, or if I obsessed, still, over their errancy and variation. Most problems in adulthood are simply ones of relation, or scale. As we cruised down the Strip these familiar façades —the hellish neon semaphore of Sky-Bar, the soon-to-be-shuttered shell of Tower Records—blinked and winked and endured. But when we drove up in front of the Hamburger Hamlet, on that angled stretch of Doheny Road that juts up above Sunset, handed the keys to the valet, and stumbled inside, the place looked exactly the way it should've: like an old-fashioned piano bar, with that same velvety-rich palette I'd dreamed of my entire life.

"Nice," Severin said. *Welcome to 1962.*

"Yeah. Let's get something to drink."

We flailed our way to the bar, waving our arms like swimmers, like we were doing an unpopular dance step from this bygone era. The joint was jumping, which was odd given that it was Monday and most of the patrons were over sixty.

"Gin martini," I said to the bartender.

"Manhattan."

He wandered off, then brought drinks back to us, Severin's maraschino cherries gleaming like vital organs in the dark.

"Cheers." I slurped carefully off the top of my drink, felt the gin tincture my hydroponic high. It was wonderful.

"Love you." Severin hooked his arm around me.

"Holy shit!" I nodded across the bar. "Don Rickles!"

"He's lost a lot of weight." Severin, who was just as high as I was, squinted into the darkness, trying to ascertain the great man's reality.

"What is it?" We were in legend, I thought, crossing some rubicon where the present ceased to exist. This room was just as blurry in its present tense as memory itself.

"That's not Rickles." Severin coughed. "That's *Milt!*"

Fuckin' A. Bald guys, they all look alike.

"You're right," I said. Schildkraut had gotten old, had aged even more quickly than we had. "Let's go check him out."

We pushed away from the bar, as tremulous now as if we were approaching a woman. Milt wore a black jacket and a crisp white shirt, with cuff links. Even without a tie he looked appropriately Ian Fleming. His brittle elegance intimidated us, with our marijuana breath and our untied shoes, our wrinkly hipster shirts.

"Milt." I spoke first. "I'm Nate Myer."

"Severin." Sev just stuck his palm out and blurted, "Ed Kranepool played in sixty-six games in 1978."

Milt fixed him with a bovine stare. "Hit .210," he said finally. "A little better on the road."

"God, what a terrible year." Sev clapped him on the shoulder. "Are you still working?"

"I go into the office a few days a week," he said. "Just often enough to be sure I'm not dead."

At that time, Milt was seventy-six, only a few years older than Beau. His voice had that phlegmy depth old people's sometimes do, yet his frame was sinewy, robust. He picked up his ginny, cloudy drink, crystalline with ice.

"I'm glad to hear it," Severin said. "It's good to know the phone's still ringing."

"That's all you can hope for," Milt said. Checking the room, urbanely, boxing at it loosely with his glass. "That and a premenopausal woman."

As I watched him, I couldn't help thinking of other famous bald folks from the movies. *Are you an athathin? I am Oz, the great and powerful!*

"What are you doing out?" I said. "It's late."

"Speak for yourself, kid." Milt wet his crooked beak in the martini. "This place is hip again."

"It always was," I said, although this wasn't true. There would've been a time in the late eighties—the Tom Conti period, the paleo-Reynolds or the neo-Schwarzenegger—when it wasn't at all. "We've been coming here since we were teenagers."

"I've been coming here since before you were born." He looked us up and down. "The crowd used to be a little younger."

We fell into a silence. For a moment each of us was in a world of his own. Milt didn't care about us. We were the fleas to his former glory, and our father, Beau, was someone he'd probably felt had sold him out: after all, he'd stayed with Will. *He'd chosen his side.* But then, before we could mumble our excuses and go back to our side of the bar, he clapped Severin on the shoulder.

"I miss your pop," he said. "I really do."

"You should call him," I began to say, but I didn't get that far. I could see already that Milt was making a mistake.

"I was always so sorry about what happened," he murmured. "I wish I'd spent more time with him."

He wasn't talking about Beau, I realized. He thought Sev was Little Will. I could see it in his gestures, hear it in his lugubrious tone.

"It's all right."

Drunkenly, or perhaps because he just didn't care—didn't imagine anyone else would, at this point—he went on.

"I mean, we all knew. I did, at least. I suppose some people didn't. But maybe if he'd been a little more open." He shook his head. "I loved your father."

Who Milt thought *I* was, I have no idea. No one, probably. But how much more "open"' could Beau have been? He was lost in contemplating Williams, his ex-colleague.

"You turned out OK, though." To Severin, who didn't seem to have the heart to correct him.

"Yeah."

"I'm glad. I always thought that for something like that to happen . . . "

He let the thought peter out, dropping his arm off Severin's shoulder. The room hummed with chatter, an ironic bossa nova played in the background. *Knew what?* Milt's whole aging lounge lizard act was touched with a pathos, now that it was clear he could barely remember who we were. Severin shivered. A current seemed to pass through him, some extracurricular revulsion that had nothing to do with Milt, exactly.

"Nice to see you," he said.

We shuffled away, feeling dispirited and ancient: Severin and I were caught up in the collapse of Milt's memory, in the way he could mistake us even though the moment we turned away he suddenly looked sharp again, scanning the bar, eagleishly, for women. Still. How easily the whole historical record could reduce itself to mush. Even if, like Milt, you'd lived your life combing the details.

"Come on." I wasn't high anymore. We went back to our side of the bar and I had two more drinks, then a third. I couldn't seem to put a dent in my sobriety no matter how I tried. "One more."

"That's enough, Nate."

"You're telling me it's enough? Mr. Sleeping Pill? Mr. Heroin?"

"It is." He hooked his arm around my shoulder. "Take it easy."

It was amazing how alcohol could compromise my mood without doing a thing about my clarity. But he dragged me outside, eventually. I let him lug me by the elbow into the 1:00 AM coolness, where we stood, finally, in silence. The Hamlet had emptied out, and we were alone beneath the trees, the skein of laurels and cypresses that wound into the hills above Sunset. There was nothing. Just the intermittent wash of a solitary automobile along the boulevard below.

"What," I said. My tongue was thick and my mind was clear. "What was he talking about?"

Severin shook his head. "Don't."

"Schildkraut said 'like that.'" The valet arrived with my car. Severin went around to take the wheel, and I didn't argue. "He said, 'must be awful for something like that to happen.'"

"He didn't."

"He did. He wasn't talking about Dad, he was talking about Big Will."

"Yes." Severin had always been a lousy driver, and his time in New York had only made it worse: he revved the engine of my gorgeous German machine, ground the gears needlessly as we crossed Sunset, and shot down Doheny. "So?"

I suppose all he'd ever wanted to do was protect me. I know that now. Sev's relationship with Beau was complex and fraught enough. It had driven him to do and become things, both, that weren't necessarily enviable, no matter how they could seem. I believe his secrecy was also a way of taking a bullet on my behalf, of sparing me things that had exacted their toll. Why implicate me in these messes, the troubled wreck that was the life of a Hollywood son.

"So," I said. Then again, I'd been gathering my inklings of this for years. It wasn't Severin's fault I was about to put everything together. "Will died."

"Right."

"What did Milt mean, 'everybody knew'?"

Sev looked at me. He didn't share my obsession with Williams's death, of course, but it mattered to him also. He knew our fathers were linked, forever.

"He wasn't killed by a mugger, was he?" I said.

We sliced down Doheny. Alcohol, marijuana, and other things— disgust, a premonition—made my stomach jump, as we rode too fast downhill. Severin was looking at me as he drove, his face in three-quarter profile.

"You ever think much about Williams, Nate?"

The moon floated overhead, scudding through high clouds. The traffic lights flashed yellow. We bottomed out at Santa Monica, kept heading south.

"All the time. You know I do."

So did he, of course. Williams Farquarsen was our best friend's dad, and he'd shaped the course of Sev's own adolescence far more than he had mine. As we whisked past the supermarket that had once been Chasen's, home of the legendary ADM Christmas parties back in the day, I could see Williams once more, ambling tieless among the red leather banquettes, glad-handing his most treasured clients. *A visitation to whet thy almost blunted purpose.*

"What do you suppose drove him?"

"Money."

"Besides that. You know there are other things, besides that, even in Hollywood."

"Sex." I'd never thought of the older Williams as driven by anything of the kind. "Ambition, maybe. Art."

"Yeah, all of those things," Severin said. "But also secrecy."

The word rippled through the humming shell of the car. Severin wasn't driving in high enough gear, but I didn't care. *Secrecy*. This was Williams all over.

"What d'you think Williams liked?" Sev asked coaxingly.

Again, I'd never thought of him as "liking" much of anything. Conquest, maybe. I thought of him as cold and cruel, no matter how affectionate within his own family; no matter how affectionate he'd been even with me. I imagined him living on water and caffeine, his blood touched with mathematics and greed. He'd seemed to have no wants, only impulses.

"I dunno."

Doheny stretched before us, infinite, palmy. A few blocks west of this corridor, our father and Williams had forged their friendship; a few blocks east, they'd decided to form ADM. We rode this meridian between history and destiny. The monotony of the street at night was hypnotic. The Beach Boys droned at low volume, the song "Our Prayer." *Aaahhhh.*

"Williams was gay," Severin said. "He liked domination."

Did this surprise me? Not really. For a second I was just a conduit, only a shell for various harmonies: the ones on the car stereo, the thrum of the engine, and the hiss of the tires. I didn't *know* anything, just then.

"He was murdered." Severin turned his eyes, finally, back to the road, like he'd finally seen it sink in. The Beach Boys hummed. *AAAHHHHH.* "It wasn't by a mugger."

"I see," I said. "He had a boyfriend."

Severin shook his head. "He wasn't that incautious."

"A stranger?"

Severin shrugged. "That's what I don't know. Little Will might. But he's not saying."

I kept my own mouth shut a moment. "Where did you get all this?" I said at last.

"Rachel told me some. But I knew," he said. I didn't raise an eye when he mentioned his mother, called her by her first name; it just got weirder, this question of all our parenting. "My mom used to work with Williams in New York, remember, so she had some access. But."

"But what?"

We were all the way down past Washington now, as far south as my neighborhood. Sev turned left and we cruised through Culver City.

"Little Will told me one or two things. I don't know the whole story, but I know enough."

"You were going to write about it," I said.

"Yeah. Little Will asked me not to."

We rode on in silence, down the whole jumbled ruin of Jefferson Boulevard at night, past twenty-four-hour drugstores, empty coffee shops, isolated pedestrians fighting against the wind. Once more I felt the horror of my brother's life, the lonely stretches he'd suffered through with Beau, without anyone there to buffer him against the man's infinite need. How terrible it could be, really, to know things, and how curiosity terminates, only and always, in death. We whisked past the hopeless beacon of a hospital, yellow and forlorn; a big orange RTD bus sat stranded out front of it, beached like a whale.

If Williams Farquarsen was murdered, I thought. *Not mugged, but killed.*

What then?

V

"**IT DOESN'T ACTUALLY** have an ending," Emily said. She leaned forward, after I'd pitched her. After I'd told her that story about Severin and then—why not?—invented a movie on the spot, loosely based on the same facts and yet elaborated into something else: a tale of two rivalrous brothers trying to solve a family murder.

"No ending yet." I smiled tightly. "*Chinatown* didn't have one either, for a while."

"You need to have an ending. Come up with one, and I'd consider it."

Indeed. It's tough to build a noir around an invisible body, a crime that stays unsolved. I'd asked Will what happened, of course, but he didn't want to talk about it. Understandable, really.

"I'll do what I can."

She nodded. "I'm sorry to hear all that about Severin."

"It's all right. He's improved."

I stood up. Outside, it was already beginning to get dark. Street lamps were on across the lot; people trundled toward their cars. The patches of orange poppies had faded and drowned. How long had I been talking?

"That stuff with Sev was a few years ago," I added, watching Emily's strangely ageless face, with its milk-pale complexion. "A lot can change."

"Yeah." A lot could change in five seconds, after all. "It's good to see you, Nate. I'll call you, and I'll let Byron know," she said.

"Great." I gave her a hug, and right before I left, as I was turning for the door, she grabbed my arm.

"Tell Beau I'm sorry."

"For what?"

"I'd love to work with him again."

"I'll tell him," I nodded. And walked into the hall, past the poster for that movie about the trapped Texans, the one that netted Emily her first Academy Award. (*Mine*, it was called. The tagline read, *Their Story Was Everyone's Story*.) I strode out, through those gray corridors of power, out of the corporate warren where everyone seemed driven by something less personal than ambition yet more aggressive than fear. You could smell it almost, a cold, acrid smoke that bled through the air vents.

I stepped outside and crossed through the gate to my car. I drove off the lot, following Overland back to the 10. Wondering, as I passed liquor outlets and video stores that were going out of business, if, even without an ending, I hadn't found my way clear. If the real question wasn't "to be or not to be," but rather, who controls the dream? Who organizes the past in order to clarify the future?

My phone rang, over on the seat where I'd left it. Where it had been misplaced since yesterday, in fact. I was stuck in freeway traffic, bumper to bumper heading east toward downtown.

"'lo?"

"Nate, man, I've been trying you." It was Severin, calling from New York. "Why the fuck don't you pick up your phone?"

"I was in a meeting. What's up?"

The downtown skyline rose in the distance to my left. I was jockeying over to the right lane, crawling toward the Normandie exit. I could see the Staples Center, the steeples and spires of that ancient Los Angeles whose renaissance was, then, an ongoing myth.

"Have you talked to Beau?" Severin's voice crackled and faded, blurring a little bit on his end.

"No." I focused on that glimmering skyline: the library, the old Bonaventure Hotel. "How come?"

Warehouses and art galleries, the shuttered basement that had housed Al's Bar. And that skid row where Williams's body had been found, then bagged and tagged in the downtown morgue. A beetling, golden mosaic of light.

"What's up?" I repeated. Because Severin's voice had dropped out for a second, and I was lost in contemplation of that downtown:

its neglected grandeur, its strange and seedy nooks and crannies. *Forget it Jake. It's Chinatown.* "What is it?"

"Patricia called," Severin said. The lights seemed to be winking at me, saying something explicit and seductive. "Dad had some sort of a meltdown this afternoon. Get your ass over there—now!"

VI

BEAU ROSENWALD WASN'T a fool. Not even at his most foolish. As he hung up after the call from Emily White, he thought of his old pal Bryce, who had said to him once, *If you live long enough, you get to play all the parts. You get to be every person in the play.* Maybe so, Beau thought. He'd been Regan, Goneril, and Cordelia herself, but he'd never been this one. He'd never been cast so cleanly in the lead.

"C'mon," he yapped. But his beloved dog just looked at him stupidly. Leash in one hand, plastic palmful of dog shit in the other, Beau felt useless in a way that was new for him. "Come on!"

The dog didn't move. Forty-two pounds of youthful Labrador retriever weight. Once, Beau Rosenwald could move mountains. Now he couldn't budge a fucking dog.

"Come!" He yanked the leash a little too hard. And Daisy—technically, Daisy II, after her predecessor had gotten old and blind and drowned in his swimming pool—yipped and followed. "Good girl."

The fat man waddled along Fifteenth Street, where sunlight poured through a canopy of coral trees. He replayed the conversation in his head as he walked, because he knew, all along, he knew Emily spoke the truth. There never was a movie here. *WUSA* was awful—shrill and of its period, as bad a picture as Newman had ever been in—and *A Hall of Mirrors* was no more adaptable in contemporary terms than the Holy motherfucking Bible. Beau knew that. So why the hell had he chosen it?

Because—and this was the man's true beauty, that if he lacked a gift for actual self-analysis he still had a form of animal perspective, a way of seeing both inside and around himself that was almost magical—he needed *something*. Anything. He needed a goddamn movie, a third or an eighth or a fiftieth shot at that brass ring, in order to prove himself to somebody: to me, Severin, Patricia, who knows? Why not *A Hall of Mirrors*? It wouldn't have been the first time he'd touched something worthless, as he saw it, and spun it into—not "gold," exactly, but promissory notes backed by the U.S. Government. It wasn't about something "good." It was really just about what was available.

Beau's rubber-soled feet scraped along the concrete. The dog brisked across the radiant grass. There was the whisper of paws, the brittle crunch of the occasional dead leaf. A soft moan of traffic, way down along Montana Avenue.

"Daisy!" He snapped again, as the dog lifted her leg to pee. "C'mon!"

Why was this failure different from other failures? Because he knew it was his last. Dragging the dog, II, up the block—how Severin had mocked him: *Jeez, Dad, even your real animals have sequels? Doesn't the new dog get a new name?*—Beau was aware of a new superfluity. A sense that this was his final orphaning, and only senility stretched ahead.

"Honey?" Patricia called out from the kitchen as he entered the house through the garage, wiping his feet and unhooking the dog from her leash. "That you?"

"Yep." He came in through the laundry room with its black-and-white tiles and its encouraging glow, its warm aura of bleach and Tide. "Me."

"What smells?" She looked up just as he approached her across the kitchen. Vintage Picasso pottery and gleaming copper pans were everywhere. "Oh!"

He was holding the bag of dog shit, which he'd neglected to throw away. He eyed it.

"Honey?"

Beau's vision was beginning to blur. This was how it always started. A familiar silence roared in his ears. He bent down and studied the turd, still soft and warm, in his hand. *Fat tub!* He held it the way he'd once seen Bryce Beller clutch a stage-prop skull. And then he mashed it, quite calmly, into his face.

"Hon—*ugh!*"

With relish, almost, like a mime eating a peach. He carried it up to his chin like a butterfly, and gave it a voluptuary smooch.

"Oh!" Patricia shrieked. "What on earth is *wrong* with you!"

"What?" Crumbs flaked off his beard, and he shook his head. "I've done worse."

For money. Which is less than dog shit, in a way. Negative value, untouched by love.

Patricia turned. She dry-heaved over the sink. Unacquainted with my father's psychosis—he took antidepressants, but so did she, and so did half of Hollywood—she didn't know what to do. She retched, and then twisted the tap. It ran cold water.

"I've done worse!" Beau roared. "How d'you think I made my fuckin' fortune?"

He flung the bag at her. Dog shit clung to his beard. Then he turned and stomped upstairs.

Beau Rosenwald, as you know, had suffered these . . . episodes periodically, since the 1960s. His tongue felt like parchment, his heart hammered in his ears. Yet weird was the dispassion he felt, while his soon-to-be-new-ex-wife (why not? It was time for a rotation) sobbed in the kitchen and he clomped toward the bedroom, winding his way up the sun-flooded stairwell.

All his life, he had been too close to things. That was his great weakness, and his strength. He could never step away, like his two sons: he could get anywhere, everywhere, but never apart from Beau Rosenwald. This was different, today. He burned with a *cold* flame. When he'd gone after his second wife, the Kansas girl he'd never loved, his anger was genuine. But this woman, whom he loved as much as he ever could anybody, prompted only a chill disdain.

Patricia's sobs rang through the house. And as Beau stormed into the bedroom, he remembered going to the midnight showing of *Pink Flamingos* at the Nuart, with Severin and myself. It would've been right around the time he discovered I was his son, and one night the three of us got high and went to look at John Waters's disastro-kitsch masterpiece. When Divine gobbled that turd there was a collective sigh, a moan throughout the theater that was as much pleasure—this was what we'd all been waiting for—as disgust.

Old Beau licked his lips. Why not go all the way? He spat, gagged, ran water in the master bath, and then scrubbed his tongue with peppermint paste—over and over—until the memory was finally gone. It was one more thing, at least, that he'd done. In a sense, if you haven't, you've never lived. Beau washed his face, then, with soap and exfoliant. Below him, the garage door slammed. Patricia's heels clacked across the stone drive. Through the bathroom's port-hole window, he watched the proud tilt of her head, her red hair glowing in the sun. She ducked into her Lexus. Would he see her again? Who knew? The car pulled away, its license plate reading 4 DREAMS. She was an analyst to the end.

He took a hot shower. Then he shaved his beard, his mustache: everything except his eyebrows. It had been years since he'd seen his face! It was heavy, jowly, not a million miles from Hitchcock's. There was a little Brando in it as well. How age could make a stranger of you! He looked grave, humorless, intelligent, observant. *Are you an athathin?* He went on and shaved his head. Why not go all the way? Anyone watching would've thought he was mental, but if you ask me, these were among the most lucid moments he'd ever experienced. Think how much of life is vague! He was awake now, and this pure curiosity, that feeling of being alertly dreaming—the floating spark of genius that helmed the machine of the self—was new to him. What it must be like, he thought, to be an actor, or one of his own sons? That night in the theater, we had laughed and laughed and laughed, while that postdrogynous clown scarfed down a mittful of dog waste. We were all so stoned! *How does it feel?* At last, at last, at last, Beau. At long last, you knew.

VII

"ROSENWALD!"

An hour later, Beau stood in the lobby of the brand-new American Dream Machine offices. He wore a beautiful tan Brioni suit—a muted and subtle coffee color, dulce de leche—an azure shirt, a silky jet-black tie. He looked the way he did in the agency days, with his lace-up brogues and expensive socks.

"Excuse me?" The security guard in reception stopped him. He looked that way, that is, if he'd come to work each morning with scraps of toilet paper plastering the nicks and cuts on his shorn scalp, and a bug-eyed expression to go with them. "Who are you here to see?"

"Rosenwald!" Beau snapped, and then lowered his voice as if he now spoke to a toddler. "Beau. Rosenwald."

"Uh, Mr.—" The guard consulted a thick directory. The company's newest offices were once more in Century City, in a big dark building on Avenue of the Stars. They were six full stories high. "Mr. Rosenwald doesn't work here, sir."

"I *am* Mr. Rosenwald."

"Um . . . yes?"

"I built this motherfucking place."

It was late in the day. Their voices drew trails in the air, in the glass atrium that rose on four sides around them. Agents hustled along the elevated hallways, messengers, trainees, all of them with headsets and holstered Blackberries. There had to be six hundred employees at a minimum.

"Sir." The security guard stood up. He wore a blue blazer and looked like an out-of-work TV actor. Blond and ruddy and almost-handsome-enough: a Surfwad Detective. "I'm going to have to ask you to leave."

"Do you know who I am?"

"I have no idea."

"I'm Beau Rosenwald," my father repeated. "And I am one of the original founders of this company."

"Oh." The name, I suppose, rang a dim bell even to this shit-wit, because he stopped and scratched his cheek. "I'm sorry."

"You should be." Beau swung his wrist, heavy with gold Rolex, onto the marble countertop that separated them. "Williams Farquarsen wouldn't have put up with that kind of mistake."

Williams Farquarsen! The guard couldn't help but snort. American Dream Machine these days didn't have much in common with *that* place. Milt Schildkraut still came into the office—they allowed him to putter and move his little figures around, sign a few Friday checks—and Teddy Sanders, of all people, still worked here. That was it. The agency was now the province of its young Turks. It had a sports marketing department, a video-game consultancy, and now counted PepsiCo among its innumerable clients. Old codgers like this guy meant precisely zip to those sleek Ivy Leaguers, those manicured UCLA grads on a mission who gave Teddy his airtime during the Wednesday morning staff meeting and then rolled their eyes as they jogged back to their offices. Everyone else—Peter Jenks, Bob Skoblow, Laura Nyde—had succumbed to their various forms of attrition: cocaine, production deals, retirement.

"So." The guard had to restrain himself from saying *old-timer*. "What can I do for you? Sir."

"You can get up on that goddamn countertop and dance."

"Excuse me?"

Beside the guard, two blondes worked the switchboard, their fingers flying over consoles that looked as if they should've belonged to NASA. A swatch of refracted, late-day sunlight fell on the marble countertop.

"That's how it used to go down," Beau chuckled. "Before my time, it was jugglers, comedians. Acts used to come into Mr. Waxmorton's office and show their stuff."

"Who?"

"Never mind." Beau shook his head. A piece of tissue, dabbed crimson, flaked off his scalp and fluttered to the floor. "I—"

"Time to go, gramps." The guard came out from behind the counter. "Really, I better get you outta here."

The old man craned his head back. Back, back, back, staring up at the ceiling, at the halls that circled this central atrium like the tiers of a goddamn cake.

"I don't understand," he murmured. "What happened?"

What happened? To his right, the waiting area held only the most perfunctory leather couch and metal-framed table, copies of the trades left out the way you'd toss a coloring book to a bored child.

"Fuck this place," Beau snapped. As the guard grabbed his elbow roughly. "And fuck you too."

"No need to get testy, pal."

He couldn't help smiling. But to Beau, it was excruciating. Never mind the horror of their last offices—Frank Gehry's hypocritically extravagant monument to Williams's ghost, on Little Santa Monica Boulevard—this place was the pits. That the mellow splendor of Talented Artists Group should morph over time into this . . . drab, Teutonic corset? Awful.

"Where the fuck is Milt Schildkraut?" the old man yelled, bellowing up at the ceiling. "Teddy!"

Nothing. The guard hustled him into the drive. More out of reflex than anything else, Beau whirled and punched this jackass in the face. The guard lashed back with a roundhouse. He smacked the old coot in the eye.

"FUCK!" Beau yelled as he dropped to his knee. "God—OUCH!"

He slapped the ground with his palms. The guard just rubbed his jaw and stood there. He looked like MacGyver. Surferish, thick, and sleazy.

"Fuck!" Kneeling on the ground, Beau saw spots. The pain was something else. It had been a while since he'd been hit in the face. "You miserable shitlicker."

The guard just tapped him in the ribs with his shoe. It wasn't quite a kick. "Get this asshole his car." He snapped his short fingers at the hustling valet. "Pronto."

Beau knelt, pressed his fingers to his nose. It hurt, it *hurt*. More than the other, for a second: more than that pain of existence that was always at the center of his life.

Why did he hit that guard? To erase that other, greater pain. It
didn't work. He stood up, shoving himself roughly to his feet just
as the Salvadoran valet arrived with his Mercedes. It was still only
late afternoon. Across the street, the façade of the old Century Plaza
seemed to mock him. Its gray balustrades looked mangled, derelict.

You wanna know what it's like getting old? The ridiculousness, he
thought, was the worst. The ineffectuality. Saliva spread across his
tongue. A metallic whisper of swallowed blood. Above him the sky
was a luminous bronze, a color that might have been called "blaze of
glory," except that Beau had nothing in his pocket to match it. A half
chubby? A bruised kidney? How poor is man's equipment, in the end.

"Severin!" Our father's voice rasped, barked into Sev's answering
machine. "Pick up, son! Pick up, if you're there."

My brother played it for me later. The message Beau left him, just
one of a bunch from that night. Sad to say he didn't leave me any,
but he sounded sharp—typically alert and ferocious—as he flew
up the PCH toward Malibu. For a while he'd just driven around,
but now, 6:22 PM Pacific time according to the clock on his dash,
he buzzed along the coastal highway. The ocean was on his left, a
red sun plunging above the horizon. He passed Gladstones, Moon-
shadows. All those shabby landmarks, shitty fish joints, their painted boards warped and corroded by proximity to the sea. He caught
the light at Rambla Orienta and headed for Beller's. Where else?

"Bryce! Brycie?" He pounded away on the new front gate that
enclosed the old courtyard, which used to be open to the street.
"Open up, motherfucker!"

The door opened, finally. But it was Danny DeVito who stood on
the other side, blinking up at Beau. Not exactly what the old man
had expected.

"Yeah?" Small, funky DeVito was the anti-Bryce, in a way: an
impossible figure who'd miraculously become a star. "Whaddya
lookin' for?"

"Oh." Beau bounced on his heels. "Where's Bryce Beller?"

DeVito looked him up and down. The actor wore short sleeves, a
dab of zinc oxide on his cheek. He and Beau had been producers on
the Sony lot at the same time. They knew each other.

"Bryce doesn't live here anymore, buddy. He moved ten years ago." He stood with his hand on the jamb and the other on the knob of a slate-colored wooden door he'd built precisely to keep people out. "Jesus, Beau, what's the matter? You look a little agitated."

Beau just stared. Beyond the door, the courtyard was the same as it had been. Bougainvillea climbed a wooden lattice. The plant's pink blossoms were torch-like, holding the day's final glow. Those flowers had been there in Bryce's time, although the meditation shed—Beau leaned over to see—was gone.

"You wanna come in?" DeVito furrowed his brow. "Have a cup of coffee, maybe call your wife?"

Beau shook his head. He fixed the actor with a look that was mute, forlorn, doggish. Then he turned and shuffled away, hunching his back as he moved toward the black Merc that was blocking this now-private-access dirt road.

"Hey, Beau?"

Lovely man. In a minute, DeVito would go inside and call Patricia, but just then he shut the door and left Beau alone with his thoughts. Privacy was what the producer needed and deserved. The actor pocketed his half-moon glasses as he crossed the courtyard and entered the main house, which had been rebuilt: it stood white and massive and solid against the edge of the Pacific.

And Beau? Who knows what he thought then. He knelt down for a moment, just outside the garage. He was too far gone even to remember it wasn't his old friend's house anymore; was just able to grasp, in some primitive sense, that this was the site of the greatest tragedy of his life. He crouched for a minute in the center of the road. Picked up a fistful of dirt and rubbed it between his palms. *Kate. Katie.* When you'd lost that, there wasn't any way back to the family of man. You were on your own, in a sense. But then, Beau Rosenwald always was.

The thunder of the sea rose to meet him. An increasing evening coolness spread across his skin. There was a smell of jasmine, and salt water, before he got up and walked back to his car. Little spumes of dust lifted into the air behind his feet, drifted, disappeared.

"Severin? Sev?" Beau's second message sounded softer, more reasonable. I suspect our father never stopped fearing for Sev. "You there, son? It's Dad."

Severin was out. He didn't pick up this message—stamped at 10:47 PM New York time—until a little while later. Maybe he was carousing, celebrating his good fortune. On the heels of *Thirsty People*, he'd just won a Lannan Award.

"I was thinking of you, kid." Beau spoke into his Bluetooth headset. "I'm on my cell."

His voice was furred with nostalgia, as he swished back down the Pacific Coast Highway, with the city's water-drawn margin now on his right. The lights of the Santa Monica Pier twinkled in the distance.

He hung up. He switched on his headlights and swung left on Temescal to Sunset, then took Sunset east through the Palisades and Brentwood. Whispering cypresses, the dark spires and canyon greenery spread to either side of him. Beau loved his car, the heavy black machine that was built like a Panzer and ran like a Ferrari. God bless the inventor of it, author of the seat's vibration buzzing along his leg. Nothing Freudian, he thought—who needed a surrogate cock?—just $115,000 worth of German metal and intelligence. One thing, at least, those people got right.

He made a bunch of phone calls. Just random numbers, it turned out.

"Rosenwald! B-B-Beau Rosenwald! American Dream Machine! Fuck you, Williams! Fuck you, Smiligan! Fuck. You!"

Yeah, that kind of thing. Harassment, left on strangers' answering machines and voice mails. The police retrieved these later. He talked a lot about Williams, and also sang nursery rhymes. The sound of one's mad father singing "Baa, Baa Black Sheep" into a telephone is something nobody should have to hear.

"Severin!" *Finally*, he got his son on the phone. As he rolled into Beverly Hills, shortly before midnight in New York. "It's Dad."

"Dad? Where the hell have you been? Patricia was looking for you." Severin didn't carry a cell phone. He might've been worried earlier, but Beau had freaked out before. He'd decided to let it go. "What's going on out there?"

"What do you mean?"

"Dog shit? Dad?"

To my brother's surprise, Beau laughed, a rich baritone cackle that suggested—at least for a second—he was in control of the whole thing.

"They've been feedin' it to me my whole life. Seemed like a good time to know what it was *really* about."

"Um, cool, Pop. But Patricia's really worried."

Beau grunted. Under this noncommittal noise, Severin could make out Talking Heads' "The Great Curve." Years ago he'd introduced his father to this song, and now it was playing on the man's car stereo.

"What's it about?" Severin said. "Dad, what's happening out there?"

"My movie fell apart." Just then, Beau was cruising past the Beverly Hills Hotel, the Polo Lounge under towering palms to his left. *Too quiet*, he thought. "Fucking Emily White pulled the pin this afternoon."

"Dad, you've had movies fall apart before. A million times."

"I liked this one!" He kept going toward the Strip. "It was special."

Severin sighed. "I could've told you *A Hall of Mirrors* wasn't a movie. Maybe you should've tried *A Flag for Sunrise*, instead."

"Huh?"

Beverly Hills at night. Beau was practically sniffing the air, looking up at the sky-bound fronds and the gates and hedges of mansions set way back from Sunset. This strange road, with its grassy meridian.

"Maybe I should take a whack at that one," Beau said. "What's it about?"

It was never too late. Not if he was breathing.

"I dunno, Dad. That one's tough too. Costa-Gavras on acid." Severin coughed. "Will you please go check yourself in? A hospital, or a—"

"Psychiatrist?" Beau laughed, again. "I was married to one of those. Hasn't worked out."

"Dad!"

Click. Beau hung up on him. And turned his phone off, so there was nothing—nothing—Severin could've done. There were a bunch of messages from Patricia on there too, of course, but he ignored those. Beau knew what he wanted. There were times, however rare in these late years, when he needed the old thrill, became more lycanthrope than man. He wanted flesh, activity. He wanted booze, and maybe even cocaine. He wanted to feel the way he had, once, as the cocaptain of the strongest talent agency on earth. To experience the radical abasement of kings.

He roared along the Strip, dialing up the volume on his stereo until this German fortress-on-wheels shook. His shiner was darkening into complete view, and the last of the TP poultices had flaked off his head. He unknotted his tie and tossed it onto the seat next to him. There was only one place you ever went, in the old days, when you were feeling like this, when you wanted hookers and self-demolition and ecstasy. You went to the motherfucking Chateau.

Beau pulled into the hotel's drive and just left the doors open. The stereo blared as he lobbed the keys at the valet. You had a car that expensive and the big dumb gorillas who kept the door here left you alone, no matter how ugly you were.

"Uhm, Tanqueray martini." As soon as he'd settled in, Beau gave the waitress a sly smile, winking Tourettically. "Shaken, up, with olives."

What the hell was *wrong* with him? But this place had changed, too! Not in its particulars—it kept the same Spanish Gothic voodoo coolness out here on the patio, the same jungled greenery around the pool—but in its spirit. Even the help had to be beautiful these days. All the waitstaff and the actresses and the busgirls and the young men, the sharp-suited, curly-haired Italianate sorts who mobbed the lobby and nestled on its couches. These people *were* the movie business. If Beau craned his neck he could still see the bungalow where John died. But the fat man was beyond the margins, now.

"Excuse me." Some girl was approaching, tittering as she stumbled out one of the French doors onto the patio. "I think I recognize you."

"Hah?" Beau, who'd done such an interesting parody of a man with his shit together in front of the waitress, now rolled his eyes and gave this girl a bug-eyed stare. "Whashatalkinabowd?"

"Aren't you . . . Ben Kingsley?"

What, in God's name, was going through his mind? So many things had *happened* here, significant deaths and insignificant blowouts, long nights of pussy and drugs that ended with him driving home at 5:00 AM with numb teeth. Long ago, long ago. But instead he remembered quotidian things: store-bought cherry pie, heavy-lidded afternoons in his office spent scrutinizing deal memos, drab rounds of Saturday errands with his father as a boy.

These were the things that possessed him, because they *were* peak experience, it turned out. Not fucking some actress. Anyone with a bit of luck and money and some patience could do that.

"What makes you think I'm Ben Kingsley?" Beau's gruff, Queens-touched bark would've blown this notion out of the water even if everything else didn't. "I don't look a damn thing like Sir Ben."

"We thought maybe," she nodded over her shoulder at three friends, "you'd gained weight."

She teetered in her heels. Drunk. This tall, thin, brunette heron with a narrow face that drooped too far—just—to be pretty. Sitcom was her ceiling.

"A lot of weight." Beau picked up his martini and drained the dregs of it, urbanely. "He'd have to pack on a hundred pounds at least."

He set the glass down and checked out the girl. Batting his eyes.

"Are you an actress?"

"Yes."

"What have you done?"

"I just did a pilot for Lifetime."

He nodded. *Figures.* He turned away without interest, ready to let the matter go.

"So," the woman sneered. "You're not Ben Kingsley. Who are you?"

Candlelight spilled across the blood-dark tiles; lanterns glowed overhead. *Was* he crazy? He looked fevered, in this light. He looked positively malarial. But it's possible he wasn't any more crazy than anyone else.

"I'm no one."

"No one?" She swung her head haughtily. The glimmering tips of her hair swept her collarbone. "You have to be *some*body."

"Whyzzat?"

"Because there's no way"—she belched—"no way they'd let you sit here, otherwise. You're a little . . . old."

She was wasted. Her friends—two guys and another, cupcake-blonde, woman—had dared her to come over here, he realized. They stood maybe twenty feet away, laughing.

"We thought you were Ben Kingsley in a fat suit."

Beau stood up. He drew himself to whatever his full height was now exactly—five-seven on a good day. The most offensive thing

really was the suggestion that he now lived in a world where Ben
Kingsley could even be asked to wear a fat suit. Was the movie business so degraded? Had even the truly elegant stooped so low?

"No," he said. His own ugliness wasn't news, after all. "Now
get the fuck out of here, you three-inch-chinned, spastic-looking,
Down Syndrome–carrying whore. You look like Allison Janney on
the worst day of her life. Get the fuck out of here. Lifetime's too
good for you."

Astonishingly, she turned away without a word. As if all he'd
done was bid her a good evening. A dog, a miniature Doberman,
popped its head out of her purse and yipped at him as she went
back to her friends.

"Excuse me." Of course, one of the men came over right away.
"What did you just do?"

"I told your friend to take a walk." Beau was just getting ready to
leave. *There's nothing here.* He peeled a fifty out of his wallet and
placed it on the table. "That's all."

"I think it was more than that. You were very, very rude."

The old thrills, they were harder to come by than he'd remembered. These people spent more on fitness than they did on drugs.
This guy, for instance, was sickeningly big. A blond, apple-faced
Nord who was probably a personal trainer. Either that or the gover-
nor-in-waiting of the state of California.

"No," Beau said. "She insulted me first."

The other man came over now too. He was short, Jewish, Ver-
saced, with his early-graying hair cropped in a modified Caesar 'do.
An agent, the new kind. Beau could smell it on him. Both were in
their thirties.

"I think you should apologize," Nord Boy said. His skin was glossy,
his features scrunched in a steroidal knot.

"You wanna know a story," Beau looked them both over, "about
Ben Kingsley?" He trained his eyes on the agent. "Since you mistook me?"

"Sure." The agent smirked. He was from UTA or Broder Kurland—
some little *pisher* Beau'd seen around town in the past. "Sure we do."

Nobody had mistaken anybody. These guys were just fucking
with him, wondering what the old bloody-headed geezer with a
black eye was doing at the Chateau.

"I used to represent Sir Ben. Long ago, and just briefly," Beau said. Like this would impress them. "In the eighties."

"Is that right?" The agent spoke. The women were off powdering their noses, so it was just him and the other man, opposite Beau.

"One day, Dickie Attenborough calls me up, he says, *Beau, I'm making this movie about Mahatma Gandhi. And I'm interested in your client.* I said, *Which one?* And he said, *Bryce Beller . . . "*

"Bryce Beller?" The agent cocked his fists like a little prizefighter, as if just standing behind Nord Boy made him tough. "Who's Bryce Beller?"

"Actor. Tall, skinny, nervous. Used to do biker movies with Nicholson." Beau looked from one to the other. Nord Boy looked like a muscle car enthusiast. Maybe he'd remember *Ride Down the Wind*. "Do *you* remember him?"

"Nope." The trainer swung his arms. "Can't say I do."

Beau sighed. The story wouldn't be funny, the joke couldn't make sense: how Attenborough had really wanted Bryce for the Martin Sheen role, but there'd been some confusion. Beau'd gone ahead and offered the part of Gandhi to Bryce Beller. The thought of Bryce—*Bryce*! That mad-eyed, equine, eventual specialist in playing snipers, heavies, and terrorists!—cast as Mahatma Gandhi still made him laugh.

"What's the fucking point," he snapped. Wasn't that the whole agency game? If Bryce could be Gandhi, then anyone could be anyone: the doors were wide open. This was a lesson worth imparting. "If you people don't have a sense of history, I don't think I can help you gen'lmen."

"A sense of history?" The big guy squinted. "I don't think we need your 'help,' friend."

"Who's '*Gondy*'?"

The agent rubbed his chin. And Beau just stared. Anybody could be anybody, perhaps—a fat man's salvation—but was it true that everybody eventually became nobody? *Who's Mahatma Gandhi?* Jesus fucking Christ!

"Where'd you go to school, dipshit?" Beau stepped toward him. He could smell the Westside entitlement on this kid, too. "You go to Untaken? Windward?"

The bulky guy shoved him, palm to pec. He didn't like Beau's attitude. The agent said, "Beverly High."

"OK. So they didn't tell you who Gandhi was? Little bald guy. Big pacifist? Fought against colonial rule in India?"

"Naw," the guy said.

What did it say about the world, too, that Beau, not exactly an eager student, could retain at least this much, yet a boy schooled under the most privileged conditions on earth wouldn't bother? It offended Beau, it defaced Abe Waxmorton's memory, that this was what the business, and perhaps civilization itself, had come to.

"Fuck you!" Beau lunged. The trainer shoved him again. "They should teach you about Gandhi and about Bryce and me—"

The women's heels clickety-clacked across the lobby's tile floor. Which was all the impetus the trainer needed to haul off and hit him.

"Jesus, Mark!" The agent's voice skied above. Beau went down so fast it was like someone had chopped him in half. *CRACK!* "The old guy's crazy! What the hell'd you do that for?"

You could hear the splintering of bone from across the lobby. The trainer shook his fist. "He was an asshole."

"It wasn't necessary."

Maybe it was. This wasn't the halfhearted pussy tap of some cheapjack security guard in an off-the-rack blazer; this was Vanilla Thunder: a full on fist-to-the-face from a guy who bench-pressed hundreds of pounds for a living.

"Fuck it," the lunk said. "He's breathing."

Oh, he was. Like a cadaver in a horror movie, Beau swung up from the waist. It took seconds, and all of this—the hitting, his getting up—was so fast people in the lobby were only now turning to look.

"You," Beau gurgled. Blood jetted onto his shirt and he spoke with a weird nasality. The center of his face was swollen. "Motherf—"

The guy kicked him. Just once. Beau rolled onto his side and there was again that *crack*, the keening pop of a bone being broken.

Uhhrrf. He vomited. Spat a trickle of blood and bile onto the floor and lay there, still.

"Let's get out of here."

The Spanish tile, magnified. The rugs, the legs of the couches. These are the things Beau took in, because, astonishingly, he didn't hurt. He *was* hurt, but the dull ache in his kidneys, the sharp pain in his ribs—he couldn't breathe—the piss dribbling down his leg:

all this belonged to somebody else. His *face*, which was the concentration of all suffering: this, too, belonged to somebody else.

"You OK? Mister, are you OK?"

"Ahhh." Spit rolled out of Beau's mouth. His tongue didn't work. "Yath."

He pushed up. Somehow, he did it, while three or four people, including the hostess, knelt around him.

"We should call a doctor."

"No, get him out of here, man. I don't want him in the hotel."

Cloudy voices. A manager, maybe. But Beau lurched and tottered to his feet. He could breathe, if he held his left shoulder back. He could almost walk. Limping and humping his way across the lobby, he left a trail of piss and blood.

"Ohhh," he moaned. "Ohhhhhh." Was anybody going to stop him? His teeth were pink. He looked like Nosferatu.

Down the stairs he went, on autopilot, swaying and stumbling to the valet stand. He knew this place, he didn't need to see it. Because his nose was shattered, he could actually feel it pulsing, and the salty trickle of blood in his throat fascinated him.

"Jesus, buddy." Somehow he was outside, now. Another voice spoke. "What happened to you?"

Beau looked over. His eyes were practically swollen shut.

"Mala," he said. *I'm all right.* "Falaga." *Fuckyoulookinat.*

He lurched and swayed, barely conscious. But his hands were so red! He could see all that color, which came from inside him, that rich, regal liquid. Wow! He could see his hands, slick with gore, and the patches on his shirt.

"You can't drive!"

"*Falaga!*"

He snatched the keys from the valet's hand. The poor kid, just another Central American who did whatever the guests of this hotel told him, backed off. *He* wasn't going to say no.

"Hey, buddy!"

Beau shoved a bill into the valet's palm, whatever denomination he'd just grabbed—it was enough—and bolted. The other man, who was just a dark-haired blur in a tan suit, ran for him, but even now, Beau was too quick. He ducked into the driver's seat, slammed the door and hit it. A good Angeleno, in a $100,000 car, feels invulnerable. He gunned out from under the canopy, went roaring down the drive.

Piss streamed down his leg. Or blood. Whatever it was—that bastard had really done a number on him—Beau folded forward and stomped the accelerator. Gasping for shallow breath.

He hit Sunset Boulevard at about forty miles per hour. *He could see, but not see.* Beau sped into the turn, bending right toward Santa Monica. He wanted to go home.

There wasn't anything on his mind at all. There was just pain, and a desire to reach somewhere—anywhere—it would stop. A big black Lincoln Navigator, its driver a vodka-sozzled twenty-one-year-old girl from Sherman Oaks, very busy on the phone, wove right, jerking abruptly into Beau's lane. Her front grille crossed over just as he reached the boulevard.

Her car was bigger than his.

VIII

EVER BEEN TO a parent's funeral?

Strange as it may sound, I wanted to ask that question, over and over, when I attended Beau's. I wanted to ask it of everyone I saw. Beau was and was not my father, after all. Losing him was almost more a confirmation than it was a new development: it brought home more of what I'd always been missing. And yet I was there, moving among the crowd at his memorial, which was held at the house on Fifteeth Street. I shoehorned into a sun-splashed corner of the living room, listened while Severin stood up to address the guests.

"Excuse me." He cleared his throat, then did an imitation of an older person's voice: "Are you Severin Roth?"

Toastmaster Sev. Standing in front of the mantel, as suave as an actor, clutching a glass of Barolo. He wore a pigeon-colored suit, a subtle gray. The same color as Beau's old overcoat, which hung— still—on a peg upstairs.

"A woman came up to me on the plane and asked me that. I don't get recognized much, hardly ever, but when she said it, I thought of my father's favorite joke."

I hung back, to the side. The room was mobbed, actually, but I didn't recognize too many people. I didn't see Emily White, or any of Beau's Sony-era cronies. Very few were under sixty-five.

"Who's Severin Roth? Get me Severin Roth. You know, the joke about an actor's career." There was appreciative murmuring. This crowd was old—and local—enough to know it. "I said to her, *D'you know anything about me? D'you know about my dad?"*

Around the room, I saw Patricia—she was dignified, as composed as if Beau had died from a long illness instead of a reckless calamity—and Teddy Sanders. Little Will, who'd come alone, stood in the opposite corner. His wife and son were back in New York. There were a few small children scattered throughout the crowd, their faces slack, dimpled, inquisitive or bored. Through French doors I stared out at the backyard, the black-bottomed swimming pool Beau never swam in, a few dried palm fronds that had fallen during a windstorm and not yet been carted away.

"I'd never felt much like my father's son," Severin said. "Truthfully, all my life I've felt a bit more like my mother," he said. "My dad was someone I tried to get away from."

. Teddy Sanders caught my eye. Strange thing about Teddy, he still looked exactly the same. His beard and hair were a little whiter, and there were a few creases around the corners of his eyes. But he'd had that aged quality ever since I was a kid, like something mellowed in a cellar. His small nod was a way of acknowledging the history between us. Over the years we'd retained that agnostic relationship former stepparents and children sometimes do.

"But what I felt then"—and right as Severin spoke, I felt my own face get hot—"is that I am, now. I am now my father's son."

Was this something to be proud of? I shut my eyes against waves of nausea, spasms of disgust. What kind of man eats dog crap? What was *wrong* with Beau?

And how could I love someone like that so much, without hope?

"Nate." It was Teddy who came over first, as the crowd unknotted and everyone went back to circulating, snacking, kibitzing. "How's your mother?"

"OK," I said. It wasn't quite true. My mother was alive, but her drinking had taken its toll on our relationship; we saw each other every few years, if that. She'd married again, then divorced. She still lived near Seattle, and when I'd called to see if she might come down for the memorial she'd equivocated. *I don't know, Nate . . .*

She wasn't here. But I suppose the real tragedy of her life was absenteeism. At least Beau left a footprint. My mother could never decide what she wanted.

"I'm sorry for your loss," Teddy said.

"Thanks," I said. Gnawing a cracker spread with pâté. "But isn't it your loss, too?"

Maybe it wasn't. Teddy was a survivor. He'd remarried immediately after he and my mom split up, just kept right on trucking. But I wasn't being glib. I hadn't gotten up to speak before the crowd, because what would I have said? I'm *also* Beau's son? After Severin's speech, I was redundant. And I simmered with an unexpected fury. Fuck Severin, who knew what he was losing. Fuck Little Will even, who knew what he had lost. What this meant to me might take a lifetime to puzzle out.

"I suppose," Teddy said. That face! It was dense with secrecy, a born negotiator's. He fingered his nicotine yellow mustache. "I know you had a special relationship."

Did we? Or had I dreamed that too? Teddy was Beau's partner; Teddy was another one of my dads. In a way, life offered just this swirling succession of roles. The most special relationship you had was with yourself. You played one thing, but you always were another. Only Beau couldn't tell them apart. The Indivisible Man.

"Thanks," I said. Across the room I could see Severin and Little Will talking, conspiring, it looked like. I seethed. Yet Teddy went on, oblivious.

"Beau and I had some fun, in the beginning."

"I'll bet you did." Another man, with a receding silver Jew-fro and a hunched, low-hanging posture like a carrion bird's, barged over. A few flecks of spit landed on my wrist. "I'll bet you—"

"Oho we did, Bobby!" Teddy gave it up for the interloper.

My God! "Skoblow?" I clapped his bony shoulder. "How's it hangin', papa?"

He checked me out. So transformed, he was. Beady black eyes, khaki pants, and an argyle sweater-vest. He looked like a senile crow.

"Dark days." He scowled, lip quivering. "Some mornings I can't even put my pants on without pain."

"That's not just a problem of age," I said.

I gave him a wry smile and turned to join my friends, to find out what I was missing. Behind me, Teddy asked Bob how things were going in Phoenix, what was his handicap?

"About a seven," Skoblow said. "Pretty good for a kid from Arthur Avenue."

"Hey-yo!" Williams tackled me, blocked into me softly with his shoulder when I got close. "How's it going, man?"

He was pushing me backward, moving like a bulldozer while I was striving toward Severin, as if to keep me out of their conversation. Both of them had come in late last night; I'd seen them but briefly, at the cemetery this morning.

"Not great," I said. "Closed casket, y'know?"

"I do know." He grimaced. "I think I do."

I studied him. He, too, had changed very little. His hair was short and had gone the color of gunmetal. But he was still a punk. He retained the old swagger, the same pronated stride. The boxy cut of his tan suit made me feel like we might've been hanging at some kid's bar mitzvah, setting up to play Truth or Dare with the honeys.

"Something else bothering you, Nate?"

I'd asked him once what really happened to his father, and he'd just deflected the question. I never did have much tact. I don't know why I imagined that's what he and Sev were discussing just then, and that they were leaving me out of it, but I did. And I had to know, for the same reason I had always needed to know: because Little Will's dad *was* my dad, almost as much as Beau was, and because I'd been brooding over what actually happened even before Severin told me what he knew. The story of the mugging was never credible, even when we were teenagers.

"Yeah." I hesitated. "What really happened to your father?"

"Christ, man. You never quit, do you?"

"Should I?"

Here we were at Beau's funeral. Suspicion had even rested upon him, once. If not now, when would I ever know?

"Is it really any of your business?"

"Is it *not* my business?" I said. "It was my childhood too."

He just stared at me. A wary, passive, middle-aged stare. He and I had known each other now for thirty years. Once upon a time I'd scraped him out of a vomit-filled bathroom stall with a needle in his arm: you'd have thought I might ask him anything. We were the custodians of each other's catastrophes, after all.

"Just leave it," he said. "You don't really want to know."

Later, I lost my cool. I'm not proud of it, but I sucker punched Little Will. He didn't see it coming.

"What the hell?" He, Severin, and I were just on our way outside. We'd left the house through the same door Beau had used to make his final exit, passing through the laundry room and the garage. I jumped on Will the moment we stepped out into the wide stone drive. He doubled over.

"Fuck you," I snapped. Severin held me back as I lunged at Will, who was down on his knee. "Fuck you guys! You never tell me anything."

"Nate, what was that?" Severin said. He had his arms laced across my chest and over my shoulders. "What the hell are you doing?"

Will knelt, rubbing his temple. I didn't get him very hard, and he seemed more bemused, for once, than angry.

"What the fuck, dude?" He stood up. "Seriously?"

It was late. The three of us were the last to leave, and the moon floated high over the driveway. Green hedges rose to my right, grown tall for privacy. Beau's second car, the one he hadn't taken that night, still rested right in front of us. Starlight slicked its silver chassis.

"What's wrong with you people?" I said, once Severin let me go. "You never tell me anything."

"What do you imagine we're not telling you?" Sev said.

Needless to say, I wasn't at my clearest. I'd had a few glasses of wine, was fogged—as was my way—about so many things, really. Williams stood up. He came over and planted his palm against my chest, not with violence, but as a kind of steadying gesture.

"He thinks we were talking about my dad."

"Oh for God's sake," Severin muttered.

"Yeah," I said. "Maybe you were, maybe you weren't. But you guys don't talk to me."

This was an exaggeration, but what wasn't? In the end, what isn't?

"Jesus, Nate." Little Will's voice dripped disgust, or impatience. He let his hand slip off me. "It's so important to you?"

"Yes."

"Why?"

I couldn't answer. I couldn't tell him just then what it was, that in that moment knowing what had happened was everything, as he and Severin—the collective facts of our lives—were pretty much all I had left.

"I'm your friend," I said. "Isn't that reason enough?"

The three of us prowled around the driveway in circles, pacing like cats. Like the teenagers we still were, and perhaps might always be, together.

"I don't know that it is enough, Nate. A person's entitled to his privacy."

"That's true." Though as I contemplated the open, closed book that was Beau Rosenwald's life, its infinite variety and fathomless weirdness, I wasn't positive I agreed. Weren't we obligated, as friends this close, to try to understand each other, and to occupy each other's shoes? Wasn't it my own experience, too? "But we were all there."

"None of us were *there*, Nate." Little Will shook his head. "That's the problem. None of us are ever really going to know."

Sev had stepped away. He was sitting on the low iron fence that ran beneath the hedge; he was staying out of it, it seemed. Only I knew he wasn't, really. I knew my brother had as much at stake in this as I did.

"We still have a right to the facts," I said. "To what's true."

I kept my eyes on Sev. Who sat with his tie loosened, a fevered-yet-cool expression that made him look like some cerebrating hipster of the early sixties. He could've been one of the original crew at Talented Artists, all pumped up on Benzedrine and the Beatles. He took off his glasses and polished them on his shirt.

"Just tell him, Will." Finally he spoke. "Tell him what you told me."

Little Will shook his head. Maybe he was right. Who were we to ask him to sound his own suffering yet again? But Severin already knew what had happened, and given the history between our families, the pain our fathers had inflicted upon one another, and upon us, I had every right to know also. Given that none of us were islands, that we were all a part of the main.

"OK." Little Will pressed his fingers to the bridge of his nose. Obviously, it tore him up still to remember. At last, he said, "All right."

The street was silent. The wooden door to the garage was open, but there was no puppy who might escape: Patricia had given Daisy away that morning. For a moment there wasn't any sound except the wind moving through the leaves of the coral trees and the magnolias, the rustling fronds above.

IX

WILLIAMS FARQUARSEN TURNED away from the car. He'd just said goodbye, just rested his palms on the metal strip below the driver's side window and bid farewell to his wife and child.

"Bye, Will." He gave his son a pale smile. "Take care."

He watched the Peugeot go gurgling up the street and then turn right, out of view. Any one of us might've looked over our shoulders and watched him watching, seen him standing in the middle of a wide residential street on Saturday morning, barefoot and in blue jeans. Severin, Little Will, and I were there. His small frame receded, bracketed by crooked Craftsmen. He looked less like a captain of the film industry and more like an itinerant sailor, a blotch of navy and white. Only the longish red hair distinguished him, made him look—from a distance—a little like the figure on a Cracker Jack box. He turned and prowled, lithe, into the house, his feet slapping at the brick steps. His frame like a burglar's in the hazy Marina Beach afternoon.

He took a cool shower. This was his first act, once we were gone, a simple and domestic gesture most people make just once in a day, but Williams usually did twice. He washed his body, five seven, 151 pounds. He had very little hair between his head and his groin. His pale nipples were tiny. In this, too, he might've been taken for a boy only slightly younger than we were.

He washed his hair and he combed it fine. He went downstairs and he read a script and he drank an espresso. The air outside his office held that blasted beach light: almost white. He loved the

Marina for this, the way it reminded him of when Marnie and he were young and their son was an infant. Before American Dream Machine, before he was anything himself but a soldier, and this place, the Venice Boardwalk especially, was still dangerous. Asked why he never left the neighborhood—*Why don't you take a place in Malibu, Will?*—he prevaricated, but the truth was, he just preferred it. He came here when it was still feral, when there were iron bars on all the windows and the crumbling, low-slung houses belonged to hippies, junkies, and painters, squatters and fags. Looking out the window, he could feel these pressures still. Walking along the boardwalk at night, or riding his bicycle there—those things he still sometimes did—was an invitation to be killed. That hardly stopped him. Some nights he'd wheel the bike home slowly, sauntering along with his expensive watch. Nothing had ever happened.

Once, he'd stopped and sucked a man's cock. Twice. The first time had been a kind of awakening, even if he never intended it to happen again. They were in an arcade, right there on the board-walk. Neither of them had said a word. Will was on his way back from a ride he'd taken late at night, just to clear his head, and he'd spotted someone, a solitary form leaning against one of the columns holding up the portico that ran down portions of the boardwalk. Walking slowly, alongside his bike, Will wasn't afraid. He knew how to kill a person with his hands.

The man wore a uniform: blue jeans, leather jacket, T-shirt—that hypermasculine style that, in 1968, only queens wore at the beach. He was tall, muscular, and kept his eyes leveled on the horizon. Will's flesh pimpled as he approached, but it was just the cold. The air reeked of peanut oil and urine, the dereliction of the area—both the boardwalk and the Santa Monica Pier were harbors for needle traffic—felt in the stinging wind. The man just nodded. A single motion of his head as Will approached. He was clean—Williams could see the pale, masculine sheen of his skin, and even taste the hint of soap in the breeze. But the man simply reached down and began unbuttoning his fly with one hand. There was no eye con-tact. Williams, entranced, knelt down.

When he recounted this event to himself later, Williams under-stood, correctly, that it wasn't just about sex. He liked transference of power, and information: he loved to dominate a man from below. He liked the secrecy. No one in Hollywood could imagine him here, sucking a hustler's dick at 2:00 AM. The man made little moaning noises. Will spat semen onto his jeans. Then Will stood up and slapped him. Not hard, but enough to let him know that he—the rugged-looking stud who waited out here for traffic—was the loser in this transaction, the soft one. Not the small man who'd just buckled to his knees.

Williams wheeled his bicycle home, past T-shirt shops and incense stands, those same, crumbling buildings that are there today: bohemian apartments and hotels renting by the week, coffee parlors and bookshops that sold insurrectionary pamphlets. *Aspen, Dreamweapon, Fuck You: A Magazine of the Arts*. No one touched him. It wasn't that his desire was entirely a secret from Marnie. How could it be? Yet Williams kept this part of his personality locked down. It wasn't strictly a compulsion, that's what other people wouldn't have understood. It was a deliberate and rational act. You could indulge your impulses and still be in control of them. This was the biggest rush of all.

"Will, it's Teddy." His Saturday reverie was interrupted by a phone call. He looked up from a script that happened to be about a war. Blinking away cobwebs, he cradled the receiver to his ear. "Sherry Lansing just called me."

"How's our friend?" Will chuckled, looked out at the street: the day had mellowed into a hazy, lazy, June afternoon.

"She wants John."

"John's not available. Not at her price." He fingered his empty demitasse cup, studied the dregs. "He's doing *Perfect* in the fall, anyway."

"She made an offer."

Each of these men had his own style. Teddy over the phone was as encouraging as matzoh-ball soup: there was a convalescent warmth; to do business with him was to be made whole.

"Tell 'er to fuck herself." Whereas Will's style forked anger and campy affection; you were quartered until you lost. "Tell her I love her."

Teddy sighed. "Four million dollars. It's on the table till Monday noon."

"I'll talk to her Monday morning," Will drawled. All sweetness now, he studied the street. "Let her twist a little over the weekend."

Poor Beau! He was always too real, not good enough at masking his feelings. Williams loved his former partner, he did, but you could never trust a man who was that easily overwhelmed.

"John?" Williams picked up the phone and made another call. "Honey, it's Will. Listen, Sherry Lansing just called . . . "

Gossip. Rumors. These things were always there, most often around sexuality, and sometimes Will felt this was really the axis on which not just Hollywood, but all of American life, turned. You managed information, not assets. You never had to tell anyone those things that couldn't be repeated.

"So what do you think I should do?" John said.

You never even had to tell yourself.

"I think you should take a long walk, and we should talk about it Monday morning. Take the plane up, if you like. Four million dollars will buy you lots of gasoline."

For someone who always seemed to know where the pressure points were, Williams was not always aware of his own. The script he'd been reading was about a pair of generals squabbling over control of the Seventh Infantry Regiment in Saigon. For a while, he worked on in silence. But the script had planted an itch. It was always, really, about power. And the apertures left by privacy. Given time on his own, Will's restlessness expanded. Temptation went to work.

It's the dreaming itself that's dangerous, in the end.

Will's home office was narrow, as cluttered as a ship's kitchen. It wasn't opulent at all. The adjacent living area was teak-dark, sparsely furnished, its bare cots and tables like an ashram's. A Motherwell painting, one of the *Spanish Elegies*, hung on one wall.

He looked up. Outside, the street was empty, and the houses had gone gold around the edges. The phone was quiet, a minor miracle. Usually Saturdays were as bad as any other. He tossed his script aside. The glassy, twilit quiet, the gloom that crept over the yard made him think of Beau. He still did. His ex-partner would come in and disturb him, sometimes, barking and snuffling along the margins of his dreams. He missed the fat man's laugh.

The full moon had already risen. It hung over the pitched roofs opposite, a lurid circle strung in a periwinkle sky. Williams went into the living room. This house was inky, sinister: its floors and fixtures were chocolate brown, its walls a brightness-swallowing gold. As you receded within its interior—like a lot of those narrow, crushed-together Craftsmen just a few blocks from the beach, this one faced north—all you found was an ocean of shadow. At night, the effect was overpowering. The place held the phosphorized glow of an old crime-scene photograph. Again, this was the way Williams Farquarsen liked it. All day, he worked in the sky-bound openness of Century City, in one of those drab and candid towers where you looked out and found yourself floating over the horizon like a stupid pilot. Here, he felt sheltered. And he found himself alone.

He played an old country record. Set the needle down in the groove and listened to the sublime crackling. *Take the edge off things*. He closed his eyes to the sounds of Ernest Tubb, and then Webb Pierce, whose weird, hillbilly warbles were not exactly the things you'd expect the head of a Hollywood agency to listen to, but everyone has a private life. Some more private than others.

Williams got dressed. He stood before the bedroom mirror and hid himself, pulling on a threadbare gray T-shirt, ratty jeans, a baseball cap that read—this was long before the movie—CRIMSON TIDE. He looked like trailer trash, a real grease monkey. Earlier, he'd spoken to his wife and son. ("Hi, honey, where are you?" "Just outside Dolan Springs. The car overheated, we had to stop for coolant.") It gave him pleasure to stand before that mirror and be so easily veiled: from his wife, his child, himself. He loved his family, but nothing took precedence over this peacock display, this preening concealment of the self. With his hair tucked under his cap, he sucked his cheeks to look skinny, haunted, hollow-eyed, and feral. Perhaps this was drag queen stuff after all.

He took the keys to Marnie's Opel, and then he drove downtown. There were many places he could go, but like any decent actor, Williams improvised against the script. Breezing through the clammy night, he deliberated. *Left turn on Lincoln*. There were places in San Pedro, in Long Beach. He felt well hidden, in plain sight. He felt safe. He had clients who relied upon very little disguise, whose belief was that acting was largely interior. David Bowie played John Merrick onstage without makeup. Just as there were actors at the other end of the spectrum, who gained eighty pounds to be boxers, who wore silk underdrawers to become Al Capone. Williams hid his hair, changed his clothes, and the rest was intuition. Privacy was still possible in 1984. Paparazzi never staked out his house; nothing he did was ever going to show up on *Defamer*. He took the 10, heading east. Even as he passed the 405 interchange, he twitched, and there was a reptilian impulse to switch lanes and go south. But he didn't. He just kept rolling toward the light, chasing that patchy and disreputable skyline.

The car vibrated, the air hissed and fluttered. It was one of those nights when the halogen spills from the city and the wild ivy by the freeway is torn by wind and the buildings seem ready to come unmoored. To Williams's mind, everything seemed edged with meaning and yet not quite ready to fit together, like a puzzle that hasn't been cut right. Drugs give that feeling, but so does desire. The rectangular green signs, with their reflective white borders and lettering: LA CIENEGA, LA BREA, WESTERN, NORMANDIE. Each one seemed to promise whole zones of erotic distinction, through which he drove ever deeper. He needed to be farther away. The car smelled of monoxide, gas, that stale air of afternoons at the beach: of damp towels, trapped sunlight, and coconut lotion. Chewing gum wrappers sparkled in the ashtray, a crushed pack of Wrigley's Doublemint. His son's.

He got off at Alameda and followed the street north until he was near the bar he remembered. He'd been there twice before. It was a sex club, on one of the streets that held mostly artists' lofts, garment warehouses, sweatshops. There were plenty of these, and plenty of after-hours clubs too—places that were not exactly strange to young Hollywood, buzzing caverns filled with glassy-eyed teenagers and cheap MDMA—so Williams was taking a risk. But he liked risk. And there were clients of his who liked it too. He'd done it before and escaped unscathed. You could get in and out of this place without being seen. He approached an unmarked metal door and buzzed twice, then climbed a narrow set of unlit stairs. In his hand was a perfect fake California driver's license, a gift from a director who'd recently done a movie about forgery. He flashed it as he nodded at the doorman, who recognized him without recognizing him.

Inside, the room was red, that lurid, caramelized pink of strip clubs. Farther back beyond the bar there was a private section, its crimson bulbs thickening the air like a darkroom's. Will could see the bodies writhing within. There was a smell of sweat, lubricant, poppers, semen, but he stopped, instead, at the bar. Most nights, he did. He hated the indiscriminate prodding of those rooms, stupid cocks as blind as moles. He sat at the bar where there was nobody else and he ordered a Manhattan. Usually, he didn't drink, but in places like this, he had to: he had to calm his nerves. That chattering exhilaration in his upper chest and throat, a want so close to terror.

From the next room came moaning, slapping, and rustling. If you went deeper you'd find men dominating others, leather masks, ropes, punishments, sobbing sounds and groans that telegraphed much deeper forms of release. He'd done all this, once let a man put out a cigarette on his chest, but this wasn't Will's scene. Role-playing was just too overt. He liked subtlety, one-on-one: the event that pitted him against another guy, starting on the bottom but then arriving on top. In a sense, this was an exact corollary to his business. Except, there, he never bottomed anymore. So he needed to come here.

His Manhattan arrived. A fey drink, but the whiskey made it fitting for a Southern boy. There was a couple sitting at a table along the far wall, kissing. Like any other couple doing that in a bar, except the one's fly was unzipped and the other was reaching over to stroke his cock beneath the table. It was huge, Williams could see clearly from where he sat. He watched with only moderate interest. Other men getting it on did nothing for him. He lacked that mirroring response; pornography's call to echo left him unmoved. Williams *was* a voyeur, but actual voyeurism, just watching people, wasn't enough. What he really wanted was to see himself. If it wasn't impossible, for all kinds of reasons, he'd have wanted to be videotaped. As it stood, he liked to fuck in his automobile, where there were mirrors that afforded at least a tiny glimpse, and where there was privacy of a sort. He could recede to that space in his head where he watched himself, purely.

Someone came in. Will could hear the footsteps behind him. The exterior room was quiet, perhaps because it was still early, perhaps just because the bar was useless, itself. No one came here to drink. The stereo played the things you'd expect—Yaz, Frankie Goes to Hollywood, Sylvester: Hi-NRG disco classics—while behind the bar a muscle-bound skinhead poured drinks from label-less bottles. It really was a generic operation, extending its promise of anonymity even to the things you drank. Not lost on Williams was this supreme irony: his life was entirely branded, yet he came here, of all places, to find his most intimate self. Which could never be revealed. This was the problem, when you lived the way he did. You brokered the stars but were reduced to mere glimpses of your very own fugitive strangeness.

"Beer." *Burr*. The man who'd just come in was one of those cowboy types, those guys with no sense of irony. How Williams hated these! Their sameness brassed him off, just as it did the way some people typified themselves butches, queens, ladyboys, Marlboro men. Walking with a client through Earls Court in London, he'd seen acre upon acre of leather-jacketed clones. Imagine being so reducible, an actor with only one role.

"Ha." From three seats away, the man spoke. "Can I have your cherry?"

Williams just looked at him.

"What's wrong? I said—"

"I know what you said. I heard you." He turned back to the bar.

The guy had bristle-black hair, a dark mustache below a crew cut. There was a disconnect between the super-short hair and the luxuriant mustache, as furred as a caterpillar.

"Such a stupid thing to say," Will muttered. "Are you a high school boy? Is this cotillion?"

"What?"

Not too keen, this one. He had a pronounced scar, a vertical groove that cut his forehead and singed an eyebrow. Otherwise, he seemed less memorable even than most. Yet Will's voice softened, just as it sometimes did on the phone. He sounded distinctly, almost tenderly, Southern.

"I said"— *Ah sed*—"is this cotillion? Are you really that witless? I don't like cowboys."

The guy walked over. Williams already knew that they were going to have sex: "liking" didn't enter into it. The guy sat down next to him. He was ugly, with pitted skin and chapped-looking lips. Small blue eyes, cataracted with darkness.

"I'm Michael."

"Will." It might've been imprudent to use his real name, but Williams could get away with it. He still had on his CRIMSON TIDE cap, his tattered T-shirt. There was a pack of cigarettes in his back pocket. He looked like what he might've become if he'd never left Louisiana.

"You want another?" Michael leaned over and put his hand on Williams's lower back. "You OK there, handsome?"

He grunted. The last thing Will wanted from this guy—whose own name was almost certainly not Michael, he could tell—was small talk. But they had another drink and then, when Williams had drained his and set the triangular glass on the bar, the man leaned over to kiss him.

"Uh-uh." Will flinched from the gust of rank, tobacco-laced breath. "I don't do that."

He didn't. Kissing was for fairies. This man's uncleanness was especially appalling. Yet it was also, inexplicably, hot.

The guy smiled. The leer of a man who said *gringo* in the movies. But then he laughed and it was all right.

"OK." When he laughed like this he lit up, his face became more individuated and human, almost sympathetic. "Whatever floats your boat."

Williams stood up. They could've used one of the interior rooms—that's what they were there for after all—but they didn't.

"Let's go someplace a little less comfortable," Williams said, and led the man toward the door, ignoring the basket of condoms below the Department of Health's posted warnings.

He liked to fuck outside. Once more, because it was risky, but also—this was the poet in him—because it was close to nature. Even in seedy downtown LA, even in those blocks—so close to the sullen threat of the Greyhound station and the rust-covered railroad yards, that Los Angeles that had ridden on the edge of dereliction ever since the days of John Fante and the bulldozing of Chavez Ravine—even there Williams felt himself "close to nature." They passed down the narrow stairs together and walked under the street lamps. This would've been the riskiest moment. As they were close to places like Dirtbox and Radio where young Hollywood *did* go, sometimes, where you might run into an assistant or an actor and where it would've been tough for Will to explain the presence of an erectile cowboy like this one trailing so close behind him. *All clear*. They started down Factory Place, which was where Williams had parked, but then the guy turned to him.

"Let's go to my car."

"Uh-uh."

"We gonna take yours?" In the darkness he swayed. His tone was playful, just like Will's. "You got a truck we can sit in?"

Will watched him. Marnie's car was unsuitable, even smaller than his own.

"All right," Will said. "Let's go to yours."

The street was black, narrow, edged on one side by three-story lofts and on the other by a corrugated iron fence that ran almost its entire length. This marked off a scrapyard filled with industrial metals, whose value would've been puny, no matter what the sum, to Williams III. The lamplight wasn't enough to lift any of this out of obscurity. The brick, fire-escaped faces on his left; the dull, graffiti-scarred metal on his right. Between these, a heaving patch of asphalt. For a man whose life had been specificity, stars, figures, and deals, his last few breaths in open air were certainly generic. EXT. LOS ANGELES – STREET. A man leads another MAN to his CAR. A moment as vague in its way as the blueprint for a movie.

"Where are we going?" Will said. Wind carried a loud but indefinite sound, the seismic, faraway booming—terrace chants and rattling percussion—of club music. "What exactly are we doing here, honey?"

The moment they crossed Alameda, the man gripped him and pushed him back into a doorway. He clutched Williams's crotch, not hard, just cupping his cock and balls and kissing him again. This time, Williams allowed it to happen.

"Are you not into this?" The man gripped tighter, feeling Will's lack of an erection.

"Nah." Will ground back against him. The excitement always seemed to peak before, and just after. "We'll be all right."

They moved up the street. They passed a young girl who stumbled in a jaguar coat, sliding across the cracked pavement opposite. When they reached the end of the block he heard her yip at some friends, behind them.

"The fuck were you guys? I'm so pinned!"

The street grew darker. They were close to that heart of downtown, to Chinatown and the Financial District, the Biltmore and
all that, yet here the city still looked abandoned: padlocked warehouses were on either side, their awnings shading metal grates and
raised docks. No moving cars, no taxis. Only silence.

"This is yours?" They'd stopped outside a pickup truck. So casually, Williams cocked his head. "I can't fuck in a cab, sorry."

"All right." The guy smiled again. Will could see his yellowing
teeth against the street's featureless dark. "We'll use a different one."

Cars were parked all around, many of them black, most of them
littered casually at the curb, as if abandoned rather than placed.
Several of them were unlocked. Michael leaned against a sleek, German sedan. Williams raised an eyebrow.

"*This* is your car, huh?"

It was a black BMW, without an alarm. A club kid's vehicle if
ever there was, some luckless parent's misfortune. Will was being
facetious too, smiling, flirting. Michael opened the driver's side
door and they slid in, Williams crawling to the passenger's seat.
He reached below, as Will crawled over, and grabbed Will's cock,
harder this time. Will flipped around and kissed him.

The man reached down again. Will dodged, instead bending
down to unbutton the man's fly. He was ordinary-sized. Will sighed,
as he wrapped his fingers around the base. Not that he was a size
king, but topping a guy with a big dick was a greater thrill.

Will took it into his mouth. The man's cock was foul also, rancid
and unwashed. He swept the hat off Williams's head and grabbed
his hair. This was all right. Being treated like a whore—well, let's
just say that turnabout was fair play. Will always did like it when
things began a little rough. But then the man squeezed the back of
his head and pushed him down, hard, choking him with even five
inches. Will could've bitten it off but instead fought his way up.

"Just relax," he said. *Relaax.* "Just do."

Michael just grunted. They were in another person's car and the
man was careful never to touch anything with his fingers. He kept
his fists balled, which might've struck Will as a sign of excitement.
He pressed them against the upholstery as Williams blew him.
When he came, his whole body went soft. Williams spat.

"That was fast."

"Yeah." The man seemed irritated. More than men usually were after orgasm. "You're good, handsome."

"All right." Williams sat up. There ought to have been more give-and-take. First give, then take. "It's all right."

He reached into his back pocket for a cigarette. Those cigs were for show, but he reached back to take one anyway.

"Wanna smoke?"

The man's hand shot forward. Williams was smaller, but he was into Muay Thai, tae kwon do, judo, karate. If he had not been off balance, with one palm pinned under his ass-cheek, he'd have caught it easily. Instead the man drove his fist into Williams's throat, which was such a surprise Will just gagged.

"*Hkkkk*—"

He reached over and cuffed Williams's ear. And then—who would imagine a guy so big and doughy could be so fast?—he dove into his pocket and drew something out. It was the only time since they'd entered the car he unclenched his fist. His hand flashed silver. He seized a hank of Williams's hair, then yanked the knife across his throat with one clean stroke.

All of this took only seconds. I have the suspicion, though I'll never be able to prove it, that Will *let it happen*. He was still so swift and powerful, and still faster in his thinking than almost any man alive. But he'd put himself in this position. Sex with strangers was a dangerous game. And no matter what he'd once said to my friend and me, no man gambles, ever, except to lose.

The knife drew across Williams's throat. The pain, you can't imagine: the blade sawing through skin, severing tendon and touching bone. Blood spouted against the stranger's fist. Michael, whoever he was, was strong. And Williams was just conscious enough—I think—to let it really happen. He flew into it like a man.

Will buckled in his seat, his whole body slack. The man just laid his victim's head forward against the dash, pocketed his weapon, and exhaled. I can imagine that too: the audible breath, the rancid closeness of the car—expensive leather, semen, sweat, and now the smell of Will's bowels emptying themselves in the seat beside him—the heavy silence of the body, settling. The man wiped the door handles with a handkerchief briskly, slid outside, and disappeared. His footsteps quick and hollow, his body bent against the darkness as he scuttled up the street.

He left no evidence: a coating of semen in Williams's mouth, but this was before DNA testing. There wasn't anything else. In a sense, though, the man's identity doesn't matter. You want to solve a murder? Identify the victim, *really* identify him under the skin. Williams Farquarsen died in a stranger's automobile. The wasted kids who discovered him at 5:00 AM flipped out. They ditched the body on the street, then drove home and hosed out the car. Maybe they left the BMW burning on a Malibu bluff, or pushed it over the edge of Mulholland. Who knows? The vehicle too was never found. By the time Will's corpse was discovered, it really *was* a John Doe body. The cops had nothing to go on besides a fake driver's license, which turned out to reference the real social security number of someone who'd died in Modesto five years earlier. They had no illusions about the cause of death: it wasn't a "mugging," it was a sex crime fitting a familiar pattern—there'd been several in that area— but without any connection between Will and his killer, how were they supposed to catch anyone? The bouncer, the bartender, the girl in the jaguar coat: none of these people would've recognized the man, and the cops never got that far.

By the time they identified the cadaver, and Marnie was informed, it was just a matter of straightening the circumstances into a new set of facts. Why embarrass anybody? Why burden a teenager with the truth? You could call it a lie, or a small mercy. You could call it protection, the maintenance of a myth. Or else it was just storytelling, just that. What it all comes down to, always, in the end.

X

LITTLE WILL TOLD us everything he knew. And by the time he was done, I believed him completely. I might never have been a detective, but I'd committed my own share of crimes.

"Christ," I muttered. While Severin sat back at his perch on the railing, and Williams stood over by my father's uncrashed car. His voice was hard when he spoke.

"Does that do it for you?"

I nodded, slowly.

"That's what you wanted to hear, right?"

Of course it wasn't. I had the feeling again my friend was restraining violence, that he might've pounced on me now in turn. But there'd already been enough of that.

"I'm sorry," I said.

"Oh?" At the lip of experience, condolence seemed meaningless. "Are you?"

Severin stood up. He wandered over and placed a palm on each of our chests, like he was going to keep us apart. But there wasn't a need, neither one of us was ready to go at it. He dropped one arm and left his hand resting against my heart. *Nate.*

"We are sorry." He looked at me, though he spoke to Will. "We are."

He spoke to me too, maybe. He spoke against every secret he'd kept and every transgression, it felt like, every inch of our father's complicated love he'd ever absorbed. Finally he dropped his hand and cupped the back of my neck, brought my forehead forward to touch his. Williams came over and the three of us huddled like football players for a moment, letting the tension settle.

"How come this never got out?" I said finally, after we'd straightened up.

"Money shuts people up," Williams said. "When it has to."

"Some people knew," I said. "Did Beau?"

Will shook his head. There was a long silence, in which I could hear the Santa Ana again stirring through the trees. I could hear the theme music to some television show, the Mike Post score to a cop drama, drifting faintly from Patricia's window. The widow was upstairs, alone with her grief.

"He could've," Will said. "He had the opportunity to find out whatever he wanted."

"What d'you mean?"

Severin stood where he was, arms folded across his chest. He knew this part of the story, apparently.

"He hired a private investigator," Will said.

"What?"

"Of course he did," Williams continued. "It was right in the thick of it, when our dads were fighting. You know how those guys were. They thought life was the movies. You wanted to bring someone down, you hired a detective, or an ex-CIA op, or something."

Severin snorted. Maybe he thought it was funny, or maybe he thought, like I did, that our fathers had it right: life was more like the movies than anyone cared to admit. It was predicated on them, far more than vice versa.

"He hired a guy out there in the Valley. My dad did the same thing. He wanted to dig up what he could on Beau, but what was there? It wasn't like your father's problems weren't all out in the open."

"Pretty much," I said.

I pawed the pink brick of the drive with my shoe. What an odd, solid world this was, how inexplicably concrete. My father's house rose massively behind us, with its rough stucco face and its green painted door. The very weight of his possessions was boggling, their raw physical presence, and yet we still spent our time, almost all of it, among ghosts.

"I think your dad's investigator found everything," he said. "My mom told me he did."

"How did she know?" I said.

Severin stepped away from the railing and came over to me again. "She knew because Dad gave her the file."

"Why would he do that?" I shook my head. But even as I said it, I almost understood.

"He gave her the file. It was right after Big Will died. Said he didn't look at it. In the end, he didn't want to know."

He didn't want to betray the man who'd loved him. Who'd sustained him all those many years. I understood that. Severin turned away and I looked past him, to Will.

"Your dad was crazy," Williams said. "All my father really wanted to do was help him."

I nodded. I didn't agree, but my friend had a right, just like me, to his own version of the tale. And this was the best we would ever do, anyway. The meager lattice of fact wasn't more, in the end, than a springboard for all our dreams, and a scaffold for the imagination. My dad knew this, and so did his, all those years ago when he leaned against a chain-link fence and watched two boys play basketball. He was watching the future, as obsessively as I have the past.

"C'mon," Severin said after a moment. "Enough, let's go back to the hotel." He crossed over to Little Will, whose silhouette loomed, whose body seemed to rock and wobble a bit in the moonlight. "Let's go have a nightcap. You wanna, Nate?"

A nightcap for us now might've been sparkling water. Severin didn't drink much anymore, and Little Will didn't touch anything.

"Sure."

I stayed where I was a moment, though. Because I wanted to watch my brother from afar, the way it has always, also, been my privilege to know him. Perhaps only now could I at last say I knew him up close. I watched them shuffle down the drive toward my car, Sev with his arm around Little Will, the three of us forever changed and yet strangely changeless: companions, relatives, whatever we were to one another now, indivisible all the same.

"You coming, brother?"

Their voices floated back to meet me. And after a moment I pushed off the hood of my father's car and started after them. The street was otherwise empty, and walking down the sloping drive I heard the soft, surf-like stirring of the leaves, the distant whisper of traffic that sounded almost organic at night. Like the movement of the sea and the breeze, like that rough, tropic disorder that some-day will be all that remains.

XI

I WAS MINDING my own business, not long after my father's death, when someone interrupted me.

"Do I know you?"

I turned and stared at a girl I'd never seen before, who asked me this while I was at a café on Beverly Boulevard, tucked away at a patio table.

"I don't think so," I said. Blinking, while my eyes adjusted to the light. Her head was a planet eclipsing the sun beyond the awning. "Why?"

D'you want to know how quickly a life can change? Because it does, it does, more inexorably than it can in the movies, where if it happened on-screen, you'd never believe it. You'd think it was too unreal.

I'd been driving earlier through Hancock Park, just cruising along Beverly. A swatch of town that never meant that much to me, between Larchmont Avenue and June Street, a nowhere zone of Italian cypresses and golf club greenery, telephone poles and clustered pigeons. It was three o'clock in the afternoon, and something shifted. It might have been the blankness of the sky, the pale gray asphalt, the tapering conifers. This was Los Angeles at its most deglamorized and plain. I had to pull over, I was so happy. I was.

I wasn't thinking of Beau Rosenwald, or dreaming of the past— I wasn't thinking about anything, really—and yet I found myself overwhelmed. All my life I had been waiting for something, wanting an extravagant fate. It comes with the territory of growing up in this city, and of being a late-twentieth-century American. I'd wanted not fame exactly—mine is no longer a fame-seeker's profession—but visibility, an honest recognition. If I'd envied my brother, as I had my entire life, it wasn't because he was the more loved. It was just because he was the more successful. This was so small I bowed in shame, and when I lifted my head to look at the city— that place I love, as one must one's special prison—I was in tears. So stirred by its ordinariness, its complete lack of distinction.

I turned the engine over again and headed west. I felt the way I did when I was a child listening to AM radio, the Beach Boys piping out of a white plastic clock or the speaker of Teddy Sanders's long-finned convertible: so much excitement attaching itself to everything, and to nothing at all. I drove farther down Beverly, and when I reached the more populous part of West Hollywood, by the Pacific Design Center, I pulled over and wandered into a café.

"Do I know you?"

I'd just wanted to kill the afternoon, to breathe and drowse under the palms. A voice at my elbow spoke and I looked up.

"I don't think so. Why?"

"You look familiar," the woman said. "Are you an actor?"

I laughed. "God, no. I'm a writer."

She was a radiant blonde, medium height and mildly untidy. I wouldn't say she was "gorgeous" in the conventional sense, but rather her face, an oval holding long and irregular features, gleamed with a plain light. Hazel eyes, bee-stung lips. The faint freckling of a tomboy.

"That's the problem with Hollywood," I added. Inside, the image of George Clooney flickered across a TV screen mounted on a wall above the bar. "Everyone looks like somebody else."

She laughed. "I'm not in the movie business. But you do look familiar."

Who knows what principle guides a life, or what makes one human being visible to another? She might've walked right by me on any other day.

"What do you do?"

I turned my attention away from the screen and to the girl, more interesting after all than watching an actor play a part he has a thousand times.

"I'm a psychiatrist."

My turn to laugh. Even now I couldn't separate myself entirely from my father's life, its massive outline. "That figures."

Behind her, traffic slid along Beverly Boulevard. I watched its glide-and-shine; a Mediterranean-looking woman scowling at her Blackberry at one of the tables outside; the curved purple façade of a building across the street, its painted sign reading BLUEPRINT.

"Have you written anything I would know?" she said.

I smiled. "Maybe."

We talked for a while. She wore blue Keds tennis shoes and jeans, and when she left me finally—she wrote her number on a napkin and tucked it into my shirt pocket—I watched her go, watched her walk up the avenue with her golden ponytail until she was just some indistinguishable part of the landscape, a beautiful microbe in this city of millions, and I lucky to know she was.

Around me were models, waifs, girls with head shots in folders on their tables: the Casablancas Agency was just down the street. I paid my check and left them to their reckless ambition, their wish—the one that never comes true, quite—of someday being adequately seen.

Everything is everything. My brother's old maxim rang in my ears, those words he used to say when it was 4:00 AM and we, in our cloudy little heads, were trying to make some sense of this irregular world we lived in. *Was that Olivia de Havilland or Joan Fontaine in that picture? Henry Gibson or Arte Johnson?* It never mattered. We were only so lucky to be alive to disagree. I walked up the block, remembering my father also, how he and his friends had once had the same arguments. *Hey, Brycie, I think you're wrong.* The way he was when he talked, spreading his arms like he was framing the point, whichever one he was trying to make, in its most boastful physical terms, as though he were describing the apocryphal dimensions of a caught fish. *That wasn't Al Pacino, it was Elliott Gould . . .*

Everything is everything. Is that enough of a moral? It seemed so, as I strolled along in the golden twilight—that hour in which this city seems its most quixotic and fleeting, in which the palms are bronze like weathercocks and the girls along the boulevards are all twenty-three years old. My father was born a freak, and he died the same way. He grew into an ordinary American, just like me. I walked back to my car, started up my engine, and headed toward the beach. Somewhere west, the Dream Machine lumbered on under the guidance of different people, kids who grew younger and less respectful every year. (Teddy Sanders? He's dead now, or at least retired. He would've been the first to tell you this was the same thing. Milt Schildkraut? Alive! Always, alive!) The agents were yawning at their desks, eating the rag ends of their afternoon power bars, leaving word with their clients and the studios. I crossed La Cienega, like any true native, too, indivisible from my car, half man and half steel. To my right were those high, rolling hills with their platformed houses and terraced swimming pools, those epic views that went on for miles. The radio played my favorite song, the one about blossom worlds and colorful clothes. The one that always makes me Smile.

And this girl? Reader, I married her. We live by the water, and I'm sure you'll forgive me if I don't disclose any more than that, except to note that we have a life so ordinary it would bore even Beau, that monster of the common, to hear of it. This is all any of us have: myself, Severin, Williams, our dads. Even Sharon Stone spends her afternoons sighing with boredom, although no one speaks of it. We pretend our tedium extinguishes in glamour. Nothing could be further from the truth.

I said at the beginning this story would have little to do with me. Perhaps it does, and perhaps it doesn't. Perhaps this is my father's life, or yours. I don't know. Unless I am wrong, yet again, and it is *all* mine: mine, mine, mine, mine, mine. My horror and my happiness, my capital and my gains, my hope and my idiocy, my falsity and my fairness, my deformity and my energy, my revolt and my appeal, my exaggerations, my accuracy, my memory, my grief, my embarrassment, my exuberance, my despondency, my ridiculousness, my overdose, my money, my dads, my penury, my failure, my maternity, my murder, my betrayal, my funeral and my trial, my gossip, my perversion, my revenge, my forgiveness, my entrance, my finale, my authorship, my punishment, my sentences, my tragedy, my escape, my vanity, my labor and my estate, my beach and my boys, my summertime and my eternal spring, my, my, my, my (*AAAHHH*) elations!

ACKNOWLEDGEMENTS

My deepest thanks to Virginia Specktor, Fred Specktor, Nancy Heller, Jonas Heller, Jonathan Lethem, Katherine Taylor, John Hilgart, Sean Howe, Sam Feirstein, George Nolfi, Joanna Yas, Strawberry Saroyan, Gretchen Kreiger, Maryse Meijer, Jodie Burke, Morgan Macgregor, Deirdre McDermott, Catherine Park, Christian McLaughlin, Kate Zenna, King's Road Café

Tony Perez, Nanci McCloskey, Lee Montgomery and everyone at Tin House. Marc Gerald and Janelle Andrews. Kassie Evashevski and Dan Erlij. Kimberly Burns.

The *Los Angeles Review of Books*.

I am indebted to Frank Rose's excellent history of William Morris, *The Agency*.

If you have enjoyed this book, you can find out
more about Matthew Specktor
on his website

www.matthewspecktor.com

Or you can follow him on Twitter

@matthewspecktor

And keep up to date with

@LittleBrownUK
@LittleBookCafe
@TheCrimeVault

To find out more about all other
Little, Brown titles go to our website

www.littlebrown.co.uk

To order any Abacus titles p & p free in
the UK, please contact our mail order supplier on:

+ 44 (0)1832 737525

Customers not based in the UK should contact the same
number for appropriate postage and packing costs.